Jim Mosquera

The Sentinel

Rebellium

The second book in the Chandler Scott series.

Mosquera, Jaime (Jim) Jr.

Rebellium / Jim Mosquera

ISBN: 0-9832966-4-2
ISBN-13: 978-0-9832966-4-5

This work contains historical references to events and people. The story, names, and characters portrayed are fictitious. No identification with actual persons should be inferred.

No disrespect is intended towards the flag of the United States as depicted on the cover.

The text type was set in Adobe Garamond Pro

DEDICATION

To Kate and Boo.

Jim
Mosquera

The second book in the

Chandler Scott series

Part I

New Beginning

CHAPTER ONE
OPPORTUNITY

"Where the heck were you?" A sleepy-eyed Arianne, her flannel pajama pants dragging on the wood floor, shuffled out of the bedroom when she noticed Chandler tiptoe into his Manhattan apartment. The apartment sat near the corner of West Street and Battery Place, within walking distance of Battery Park, or The Battery, as the park near the southernmost tip was known to locals.

Chandler stammered, though he responded quickly. "Ahh, um, I was, was just out for a morning walk, no big deal." The morning walk included another chance encounter with the mysterious Habakk. He'd told Arianne about his previous encounters with Habakk, but now was not the time to get into that. The weighty subject just discussed in The Battery with the mysterious one, required more time for contemplation. Habakk told him he needed to work on the little things. Intellectually he knew and understood this, though how he sowed those seeds remained unclear.

They'd enjoyed a quiet dinner the night before on New Year's Eve, though without the ball drop in Times Square. With the country being very much on edge, law enforcement could not guarantee everyone's safety. It was a different country now. The 2020 presidential election produced no winner—no candidate had the required number of electoral votes. The Constitution mandated that the House of Representatives cast votes for president, with the Senate doing the same for vice president. Since those votes would be contentious, President Benjamin Jefferson froze the election results. He and others in the administration feared the country would spiral into another economic abyss during the bitter debate in the legislative bodies of government. There were already legal challenges to his freeze by the opposition parties, the Independent American Party (IAP) and the Theocracy Party (TP). Talk of impeachment swallowed the oxygen in the Capitol.

Arianne hoped her forthcoming conversation wouldn't suffocate her man.

She folded her arms behind his neck, tiptoeing to reach his lips. "We should do something today."

"And what would you have us do?" he asked with a Cheshire smile, pulling her in tight.

"Get that look off your face. I thought last night would be plenty for you," she grinned. "Honestly, I want us to sit down and do some relationship planning."

"Huh?" he furrowed his brow and walked toward the kitchen to start the morning brew. She followed.

"Yeah, Chan. We need to talk about our future. I'm not sure how long I want to stay at State, and you're ready for a career change, anyway. I just think we need to talk about this. Living apart most of the time is not easy for me. We both love each other and there's no reason we shouldn't be together."

Journalist Chandler Scott's life had always swirled around significant political or financial events. Born on October 19, 1987, Black Monday in the stock market, to a single mother, he'd spent his professional life working for an international TV news organization based out of Argentina, known as El Mundo. That would be his employer until just prior to the presidential election of 2020. Chandler had spent the better part of a year working to uncover an economic plan known as the Global Financial Union (GFU), which would have profound effects on governance in the

U.S. and abroad. The infamous hacker group, Omni, released a rogue video, unsanctioned by El Mundo, where Chandler detailed the GFU. The video's release led to his ouster from El Mundo. The United States felt the initial impact of the GFU on governance with the President's historic decision in December 2020 to freeze the presidential election results. The President's action would unleash a new instability for which the nation was unprepared.

Arianne served as legal counsel at the State Department. Unlike Chandler, she enjoyed stability and wealth during her upbringing. After a chance meeting at the White House Correspondents' Association Dinner in the spring of 2019, their relationship blossomed. She was ready to take the next step in their relationship, which her biological clock suggested lay close at hand.

On this morning, her voice expressed a frustration that had been building for several months. The previous year had strained her career primarily due to her desire to help him in his journalistic adventures. Her time for adventure had ended.

Chandler directed his personal assistant, the digitally minded Venus, to brew the morning's java. "Venus, brew coffee." The coffee machine began percolating.

"Chan?" she tried to get his attention by tugging on his shirt.

"Okay! Okay! Let me take care of this." He grabbed two coffee cups.

Emotionally, he knew she was right. Intellectually, he felt a professional void. Fired last year from his dream job, he had to figure out what to do next. The El Mundo television network had a non-compete agreement in his contract, prohibiting him from working for a national or international network. Even without the non-compete, he'd encounter difficulty finding work with the big networks. His rogue video filmed shortly before his ouster revealed the Global Financial Union (GFU) that would be the blueprint for managing the U.S. and world economy. The big networks considered him a tad radioactive at the moment. His revelation about the GFU did not have a material effect on the election's outcome, given the public's exhaustion from years of financial suffering, political corruption, and cyber mischief. While many took exception to another layer of financial controls imposed by the GFU, just as many wanted everything fixed.

When Venus finished her task, Chandler poured two cups and moved to the living room with Arianne in tow. They sat on the sofa in front of the large video screen and he commanded Venus to turn on the large video monitor. The New Year's headlines were troubling.

The FBI is reporting that they have uncovered an extensive effort by an unidentified criminal hacker organization that compromised thousands of cell phones. In the sophisticated attack, the criminal group targeted users of the popular application known as 'My Pix' that allows members to instantly share photos and videos publicly or privately. In the attack, fake personas bombarded phones with so many pictures that the receiving user had to reboot to restore operation. The reboot allowed the criminal group to be able to use the attacked phones in a botnet attack planned against the Financial Stability Board.

"A botnet? We can't get through a day without something about a hacker. Great way to start the year!" she exclaimed. She would know after she became the unwitting target of a serious attack against her and her father's company last year.

"The Financial Stability Board, I'm sure, has a bunch of

people who hate them. They're really weighing businesses down with all the regulation and paperwork," Chandler added. The Financial Stability Board, or FSB, was a cabinet level entity responsible for implementing the Global Financial Union in the United States.

She placed her legs across his lap. "Ok, so can we talk about us now? Tell your girlfriend Venus that it's my turn."

He gave the command to shut down the monitor.

They spent the rest of the day in his apartment discussing their relationship plan, she more interested in the topic than he. He periodically got distracted, contemplating six months of idleness.

Later, he achieved the ultimate distraction when the Cheshire cat indulged in his mischief. They both slept well.

***

He walked, barefoot, from the bedroom towards the kitchen, giving a quick glance towards the coffee maker.

"Venus, time and temperature."

"January 2, 2021. The time is 7:32 am. The indoor temperature is 72 degrees Fahrenheit. Outdoor temperature is 29 degrees Fahrenheit."

He was so happy she didn't give him a Celsius reading too. *Maybe I'm getting better at programming her?*

"Venus, brew coffee." The coffee machine, awakened from its overnight slumber, percolated. Venus controlled more than just the coffee maker. She had control of other appliances and climate control. Chandler could give Venus commands from anywhere in the world he had connectivity. The brave new world of the Internet of Things (IoT) sought to eliminate domestic effort. Chandler had a nagging fear that one day the machines would rise up and forbid him from consuming his favorite food or drink.

Arianne remained in the arms of Morpheus and he dared not wake her, especially after last night's indulgences.

"Venus, load news and sports feed."

He positioned himself in front of his monitor in the living room, reviewing foreign and domestic news and sports streams. There was little in the way of sports, not unexpected for the holidays. The regular news was mostly a repetition of the New Year's Day headlines. Parts of the country had not reacted well to the President's decision to freeze the election results. That said, there were many, maybe even a majority of citizens, who agreed with the President. The public had taken it on the chin for several years with economic stagnation and financial volatility.

The Fed was thoroughly discredited with their financial machinations and President Jefferson was the only one who stepped up with a solution, albeit with substantial input from outsiders like the International Relations Council (IRC) and the Global Settlement Bank (GSB). Though the economy remained ill, the bleeding proved to be under control, "control" being the operative word. The battle waged between those comfortable with government's authoritarian control and those who wanted Washington to loosen the reins.

President Jefferson and the Financial Stability Board (FSB) developed a 10-point plan over the holidays that they called the "Plan for Prosperity" or PFP. Ensconced within the PFP was the slogan "We Are the Future", meant to inspire hope. The slogan's pictorial representation depicted a man, woman, and child standing in front of the Stars & Stripes confidently looking upward and right.

As he walked back to the kitchen to pour his coffee and rustle up some grub, the distinct sound of Jimi Hendrix's Voodoo Child

14

filled the air, his cell phone's ring tone. Fortunately, Voodoo Child clocked in under 100 decibels, lest he wake the sleeping beauty. He rushed back to the living room to grab the phone from the coffee table before the third ring, then promptly executed a shallow roll onto his couch.

"Hello," he said, breathing a little quickly.

"*Chandler! Buenos días.*"

Chandler did not expect a greeting in Spanish. The voice now speaking evoked a memory. His deceased boss at El Mundo, Rafael, frequently addressed him this way given his Argentine ancestry. Rafael "Rafa" Mendoza had taken his life last year shortly before the election, and not long after the enigmatic hacker group, Omni, released Chandler's rogue video to the public. In yet another journalistic confrontation, Rafael refused to air Chandler's video where he detailed the Global Financial Union (GFU).

By that time, Chandler knew that Rafa was knee deep in a larger movement to further the GFU's goals, using the El Mundo network as a mouthpiece. An El Mundo employee passed the video file to Chandler on his last day of employment. Chandler delivered it to his mentor, Axel Schultz, who eventually gave it to Omni. As far as the public knew, Omni had hacked into El Mundo to get the video.

He pulled the phone away from his ear to look at the unfamiliar calling information.

"Hello. Chandler?" the caller asked. "You there?"

"Yes, this is Chandler Scott," he answered, thinking it best to sound professional since it could be a potential employer.

"Chandler, it's me Arty!"

"Arturo? I mean, Arty!" Chandler had partially solved the caller mystery. The caller's light Spanish accent belied his name,

"Arty", which had Celtic origins.

"Chandler, sorry to call you so early in the morning, man, and especially on a holiday weekend, but it's important."

"Yeah, sure, no problem, dude," Chandler responded. It wasn't a problem until Arianne woke up. In the early morning mental haze, pre-caffeine, he tried to draw the connection to Arturo.

A few years back, Arturo "Arty" Dutari sold a documentary film to El Mundo about the Shining Path guerillas of Peru or as they were known in South America, *Sendero Luminoso*. El Mundo always wanted to put together a film about this group, but no one relished being embedded with them in the Andean mountains. Critics lauded the documentary and showered praise on Mr. Dutari, who dedicated a few weeks of his life in the Peruvian Andes.

"Ok, listen. The reason I'm calling you is I thought that you might be interested in this project. After the work you did last year, you should like it. Here it is. With all the civilian unrest going on with Jefferson's freeze, you probably know this, but there have been rumblings about people just wanting to drop out of the system. They don't want any part of all the regulation. Some are being militant. Others just want to leave the United States and others just want to take over the government. I know you've heard of this, right?" Chandler did not expect the onslaught of information from an early morning caller.

"Ahh, yeah, I mean I heard some of this stuff last year especially with people wanting to get out from under the FSB, but honestly I was spending so much time on stuff for the election that I didn't get too deep into this other stuff," Chandler responded, overusing the word "stuff" since his vocabulary lagged.

"Ok, listen. I want to put together a documentary on all these

16

movements!" Arty stated excitedly.

"That project's gonna be as big as a Brahma bull, Arty," Chandler responded, awakening more now with the addition of his Texas slang. Being a native Texan, he reverted to the expressions he heard during his youth whenever he got emotional or excited.

"I see you haven't lost that Texas charm. Yes, it is a big project, but now's the time for it. And what else are you doing, *amigo*?"

"Well, I can't work for a national or international network for another six months and I don't want to work for any local network—not that anyone has called me, anyway. I could go work for one of those online outlets, but I don't know that they have the budget to do the things I like," Chandler explained.

"Yes sir. Forget about those El Mundo days. They're gone. What I want is for you to help me with the documentary. You're good in front of the camera and after last year, you'll add credibility to this project." Arty hoped the compliment would soften him up. "Oh, and I'll pay you installments throughout the project. I'll also give you a share of the documentary fee after I sell it."

Arturo Dutari, a journalist, could always get himself out of tight spots. Born in the mid-1970s in the Las Tablas province of Panama, he moved to the capital as a young boy growing up in the impoverished Chorillo section of the city. During the U.S. invasion of 1989 to oust General Noriega, his wooden shanty building caught fire and eventually the government resettled his family in a tall structure nearby, built after the military incursion. Living in Chorillo, he witnessed prostitution, low-level drug trades, and small gang conflicts. There were plenty of fist fights on the streets. He did just enough to get by as a student in the country's public school system, falling in and out of trouble with regularity. He seemingly had nine lives, always being able to extricate himself from one imbroglio after another. After winning two small jackpots in the country's lottery, the *Lotería Nacional de Beneficiencia*, he earned the nickname *Señor Suerte* or Mr. Luck.

In another stroke of good fortune, the U.S. government had allocated educational funding for families affected by the 1989 invasion. He received a scholarship to *Universidad de Santa María La Antigua (USMA)*, a Catholic university in the suburbs of Panama City. There, he got serious about his studies. The Panamanian government helped further his education by awarding him a scholarship to attend USC's Annenberg journalism school.

After attending USC, he worked for stations in Panama City and New York as a special investigative reporter, usually covering the War on Drugs. A few years earlier, he branched out on his own and produced independent films.

"I've got to think about this, Arty." Chandler had much to think about, especially given his relationship planning session with Arianne the day before. "There's someone else to consider now besides myself."

"That can only mean one thing, *mi amigo*. What's her name?" Arty inquired.

"Arianne."

"You mean *Ariana?*" Arty retorted. Like Chandler's father, Gustavo, Hispanic men always wanted to alter her name to their liking.

"Sure. My father calls her that too. What is it with you guys, always changing her name?" Chandler feigned dissatisfaction.

Arty laughed. "It's a Latin thing. You wouldn't understand.

Think about it for a few days and call me or I'll call you. I don't want to take you away from *Ariana* any more today. I hope to meet her soon. Have a good weekend."

"We'll stay in touch. Talk to you later, Arty."

He didn't see this coming. On the one hand, he knew he needed to find work. His severance from El Mundo was not very generous, and he had bills to pay like anyone else. Money did not drive Chandler's behavior, although his debts still needed attention. Asking Arianne for help was not an option either. Arty's offer, however, was about as close as he would get to his role at El Mundo and he would not have to travel to the far-flung corners of the globe. Covering the growing internal dissatisfaction would be important in his role as a journalist. The Presidential election of 2020 served as a catalyst for domestic events that had been brewing for some time. He knew the country found itself at a crossroads and he wanted to be part of it, covering it somehow. Arty's project would place him in the middle of it.

He remembered what Habakk had told him on New Year's Day at The Battery about doing the little things. The mysterious Habakk always seemed to appear at moments in his life when he needed guidance. The potential impact of this project surely had to count as doing the little things.

Chandler struggled with the decision. The love of his life slept nearby. Committing to someone long-term had never been part of his DNA. Being the peripatetic journalist, he could never commit out of fairness to the other party. He walled himself off emotionally from all women except his mother. Tearing down that wall and exposing himself to emotional pain would be the only path in giving Arianne the commitment she wanted.

Mostly eschewing religion, he couldn't pray about it. Perhaps his mom's exhortations about getting more spiritual were coming back to haunt him? Luckily, he didn't have to decide today.

"Chan?" Sleeping beauty emerged from Morpheus' arms. "What are you doing?"

"Hey, honey. I'm in the living room," he yelled, popping up from the couch. "The coffee should be ready by now."

The conversation with Mr. Dutari woke him up. The coffee would stimulate him further.

She walked towards the living room, the long pajama top covering to the upper part of her toned, bare thighs. "What did you want to do today?" She walked behind him and wrapped her arms around his waist, nudging her chin between his shoulder blades.

Temporarily distracted by her affection, he regained composure. "I don't know. Let's have breakfast and we can figure it out."

He thought it best to avoid discussion about Arturo's call. They departed tomorrow for D.C. and he wanted to avoid potential conflict.

CHAPTER TWO
CONGRESS BATTLES

Back on November 30, 2020 in the Oval Office, President Jefferson announced to a few Congressional leaders his intention to freeze the election results until such time the country could fully assimilate his economic plan. None of the four candidates for the office of president looked to receive the required 270 Electoral College votes. Though the Electoral College met as required in mid-December 2020, the country's leaders knew there would be no change to the final numbers, thus throwing the selection of the president to the House of Representatives. The Senate would elect the vice president.

President Jefferson urged the multi-party delegation that day to consider the division within the country and how the partisanship of electing the next President in the House would derail any economic recovery. His plan involved suspending the election results for an unspecified period. He urged them to support his decision. Jefferson's pronouncement that day met strong, yet polite opposition from IAP presidential candidate, Texas Senator Alfonso Chancellor and TP Congressman, Milton Wise of Mississippi. The Senate Majority Leader, Democrat Michael Dean, and the Speaker of the House, GOP Congresswoman Janice Rossi, were silent during this meeting.

Undeterred, the President addressed the nation on December 16th in front of reporters in the White House Briefing Room where he announced Executive Order 14666, freezing the results of the election. He cited the stability his economic policies had brought and feared that the partisan divide in Congress would wreak havoc on the nation's confidence and by extension, the economy, if they had to elect a new president.

Chancellor and IAP Senator Matt Geringer of Colorado, the father of the party, mobilized forces to proceed with an Article 2 Section 4, an impeachment proceeding. After Jefferson's address to the nation concerning his executive order, Geringer and others demanded that the new members of the House of Representatives be sworn in immediately. Geringer did not want a lame duck Congress taking part in a potential impeachment especially since there were more members of the third parties about to assume their roles in Congress.

Since the 2018 midterm elections, both the IAP and TP had seen their numbers swell in Congress and state legislatures. The reluctance to run as a third-party candidate melted away after the 2016 election when much of the population expressed a strong aversion to presidential candidates from the GOP and Democratic parties. It also became apparent that several candidates running in the GOP and Democratic primaries that year were really of a third party ilk. Those candidates had little in common with the party under which they competed for the nomination and were not welcome within them.

Given money in politics, it would have been difficult for those candidates to raise the funding required for a presidential run, not to mention the relative obscurity of running under a third party banner. The press would not have given these candidates the same attention, and joining the presidential debate stage was very unlikely. The public demanded more choices and got them. Congress had a different composition now.

Speaker Janice Rossi, easily reelected in her district, was sworn in first and then new members followed. This was a strategic move by Geringer, who wanted a greater representation of third party members for a potential impeachment proceeding.

The House Judiciary Committee had responsibility for considering an impeachment. The quickly assembled committee comprised 20 Republicans, 11 Democrats, 6 IAP members, and 2 from the TP. Congressman Javier Castro, a well-respected Mexican-American Republican from Texas, headed the committee. By December 23rd, the committee had received formal resolutions by members of the House. These resolutions were the catalysts to begin the impeachment consideration. Congressman Castro and the rest of the committee would study allegations made in the resolutions and determine whether they merited further action in the full House for consideration of a formal impeachment inquiry.

As he made his way from Room 2237 of the Rayburn House Office Building, Congressman Castro offered a few words to a crowd of reporters as he passed by the Capitol rotunda.

The rotunda served as the nexus of corridors connecting the House and Senate sides of the Capitol building. The rotunda sat under the Capitol dome, whose restoration was completed in 2017. If one were to lie face up in the center of the rotunda, the canopy of the overhanging dome would rest 180 feet above. In this canopy resided the Apotheosis of Washington, a fresco that depicted the first President of the United States becoming a god. Surrounding the rotunda were a series of eight historical paintings, oil on canvas, measuring 12 feet by 18 feet, illustrating the American Revolution and the exploration and colonization of America. A series of sculptures sat in front of the paintings representing presidents and other prominent personages of American history.

Castro lured the reporters towards the painting of the Declaration of Independence to avoid a special tour group and other Capitol foot traffic. His staff stood behind him along with two other House members.

The diminutive Castro paused for a moment to gather his thoughts. "I know y'all are wondering what we decided in committee and I wanted to let you know that we received various resolutions by the membership. Myself and the rest of the committee will review them carefully over the holidays and discuss in a closed session when Congress resumes on Tuesday, January 5, 2021. Out of respect for the holiday season, we will not meet until then. With the state of the country, we thought it more important to be home with our families. I realize some may not agree with that decision, but I personally would like to maintain a semblance of normalcy and enjoy Christmas with my wife and kids. Thank you and we'll see y'all in a couple of weeks."

He ambled away from the throng, his staff and other Congressional members in tow.

The Congressman's words made an impact with the gathered press, since none asked a follow-up question and let him depart quietly. Perhaps the reporters were ready to go home. For many, with the country in political disarray, family represented a bastion of sanity.

***

Tuesday, January 5, 2021 figured to be an eye-opening experience for the newly sworn members of Congress. The 2020 elections in the House and Senate ushered in a small wave of citizen legislators. There were teachers, law enforcement officers, businessmen, and technical managers among the ranks of the newly minted House and Senate members.

Adorning the Capitol rotunda were Plan for Prosperity (PFP) banners featuring the slogan, "We Are the Future", written underneath the image of a man, woman, and child standing in front of the flag, confidently looking upwards to the right.

Colorado IAP Senator Matt Geringer joined Congressman Castro in the rotunda for an impromptu session with the press on opening day for the legislators. The men were side by side, with the statuesque Geringer towering over the diminutive Castro. The 6'4" Geringer had a voice that could trail off into the low end of the audible range. He could have enjoyed a great career doing voice overs in Hollywood, especially those requiring the deepest of bass.

Geringer positioned himself intentionally in the center of the rotunda, making sure anyone within earshot could hear what he had to say. After waiting for the reporters to settle, Geringer stepped forward to address them.

"I want to thank my colleague Congressman Castro for the expediency with which he assembled his committee before the holidays. I also want to thank the entire committee, who I know undertook a thorough review of various resolutions during their holiday break. Americans should know they have a responsible body working for them. When I first arrived in Washington, the extent of partisanship and anger truly stunned me. That partisanship also extended to government departments and agencies. There didn't seem to be any sense of decorum or partisan deliberation. Hopefully, the American public will witness a better functioning legislative body throughout this process. President Jefferson's actions have crossed the boundary for what is acceptable executive action. Our job now is to follow the Constitution and let the process play itself out. I'd now like to turn it over to Congressman Castro." Geringer took several steps back and Castro moved forward.

"Thank you, senator. It is with great honor and conviction that I assume the role of leading the Judiciary Committee through this delicate process. This legislative body has undertaken impeachment proceedings very few times in our nation's history. That statistic reflects the fine executive leadership of the United States. We live in different times, however. The nation is suffering economically, and terrorists of all stripes are making our lives more difficult. Though he is a member of an opposition party, I have to admit that the President exercised his leadership when no solutions appeared forthcoming. Our job is to determine if he has exceeded his authority. There will be many competing opinions on the committee. Today we begin that difficult task of sorting it out. Thank you."

As soon as Castro took a step back, the cacophony of the screaming reporters made the questions directed at both men unintelligible. After the initial wave, a lone voice directed an intelligible question to Senator Geringer.

"Senator, is it true that you and a coalition of other legislators have asked or will ask the Supreme Court to test the constitutionality of the president's executive order?"

Geringer stepped forward to reply. The percussion of his voice reverberated in the Capitol rotunda. In another century, he could have doubled for Wyatt Earp with his formidable mustache. "We have engaged constitutional scholars on this matter and expect to have the Court hear the petition. I want to emphasize that this is a parallel action and will not affect the work of the Judiciary Committee. It is crucial that we attack this issue on multiple fronts. Ladies and gentlemen, the Congressman and I need to bid you farewell so we can take on the very important business of the American people. Thank you."

The throng of reporters continued to shadow the two men as they walked out of the rotunda, though by this time they had to compete for their attention with Senate staffers and other legislative support members.

Concurrent with this session in the rotunda, the President met with several newly minted members of Congress in the Oval Office along with FSB Secretary Holloway. Malcolm Holloway served as the President's chief architect of the national economic recovery plan. A former Secretary of the Treasury and high-ranking member of the Global Settlement Bank, he was usually the smartest person in the room, a highly educated policy wonk.

The meet and greet session affirmed the President's intent to impress upon the newbies the importance of the FSB's role in maintaining economic stability. He needed many allies in the upcoming impeachment fight. Unlike his predecessor in the Oval Office, Jefferson's personality allowed for this informality across party lines.

The Oval Office resided in the West Wing of the White House. The President's desk sat at one end of the oval with the U.S. and Presidential flags flanking it and the Presidential coat of arms on the carpet immediately in front. Flanking the lower edge of the coat of arms were two sofas facing each other. President Jefferson requested large, deep colored, leather sofas since it reminded him of his California home. Smaller staff members felt like children sitting in them because of their extended depth. End tables were next to the sofas with two smaller wooden leather chairs completing the horseshoe in front of the Presidential desk.

If one looked straight up, a ceiling medallion of the Seal of the United States would stare down. Portraits of former Presidents lined the walls. Jefferson also had mementos of his state of California on display, with several pictures of Yosemite National Park and scenes from the Pacific Coast Highway. Behind the large, ornate desk sat an equally ornate table with picture frames of the President's family.

The President and Holloway sat in leather chairs in front of the desk. Both men wore pins on their lapel with the PFP slogan, "We Are the Future." Three members apiece sat on the two sofas while other members stood, forming a ring around the sofas. All political parties were represented. After going around the room and asking for introductions, the president began.

"I'd like to welcome everyone today on what I'm sure will be a whirlwind for all of you. I apologize for the lack of seats. I suppose that's a good thing that so many of you graciously accepted my invitation. Just two months ago, you were elected to serve and it is a responsibility you should not take lightly. Probably at no time in our nation's history has serving the people been more important. I have to say that these are unusual times. You know, when I first took office, we were just coming off the stock market crash of 2016, then we had another in 2019. Cyber terrorists have taken advantage of our nation's economic and financial weakness and have made things worse. I'm sure everyone in this room has been affected by a cyber-terrorist hack. It has impacted even the White House. I did what any responsible leader in my position would do—I led. I realize the steps that I have taken have come under great criticism. I would ask that you be polite and listen to this criticism of my administration. But then ask those that criticize if they have another solution. My guess is they won't and therein lies the problem. I'm not going to sit in this office and twiddle my thumbs. Not gonna happen. Not on my watch. The American public expects me to lead and that's what I will do. I will now introduce Secretary Holloway, who will provide all of you with an update on what his department is doing to stabilize the economy. Mr. Secretary?"

The President articulated his case, though at no time did he mention the word "impeachment" that he knew was on everyone's mind. He wanted the newbies to think above that and place the nation's economic security foremost in their minds. Secretary Holloway provided the statistical and analytical ammunition to bombard any doubts they might have. The Secretary's knowledge and persuasiveness overwhelmed the newbies.

CHAPTER THREE
MENTOR

Chandler and Arianne traveled back to D.C. so she could resume her job at State. Chandler, with nothing else to do but spend time with his girlfriend, tagged along. On the train ride back in the nation's Acela corridor, he thought it safe to mention Arturo's offer. Arianne thought the project sounded interesting, though in conflict with what the two had discussed concerning their relationship. Chandler did not mention that Arturo would call him back soon to find out if he'd accept.

His mentor, Axel Schultz, found himself in D.C. doing research for his financial and economic newsletter that he published to a small, yet loyal international following. Subscribers paid a pretty penny for his thoughts. Axel possessed a strong Libertarian bent and advocated less government intrusion into the free market. He also had an impressive array of secret contacts that often contributed to his publication.

Axel Schultz, whose mother and father hailed from Austria, cut his teeth in the early days of technology, peddling 50 pound IBM computers. He later invested in Silicon Valley companies instrumental in the growth of computing and the Internet. He left IBM and started and sold several companies in computer and networking technology, making a small fortune. That sparked a career of financial market study and his passion of research and writing. The stocky, athletically built Axel had the mind and body of someone much younger than his sixty-something age. No doubt his nutritional regimen contributed to that.

During his brief exile in Chicago late last year, Chandler helped Axel with his letter, even becoming part of its content.

While he enjoyed the experience, it did not encompass his professional aspirations. He'd had a great career at El Mundo and missed the diversity of assignments the network afforded him. That diversity ended after the network's takeover by investors associated with the International Relations Council, whose goal it was to turn the network into a mouthpiece for the new Global Financial Union (GFU).

The GFU outsourced the monetary sovereignty of the U.S. and other countries to the powerful Global Settlement Bank (GSB), the institution responsible for the architecture of the Financial Stability Board (FSB). The FSB hoped to "save" the American economy through an Orwellian control never seen.

The student and master met at Arianne's condo in the Georgetown section of the nation's capital. While sitting in her living room, the two enjoyed their morning beverages, Chandler with coffee and Axel with tea, steaming beverages welcome on a cold winter's day. They discussed their time together in Chicago and Chandler's future.

"Chan, I know you'll be going a bit stir crazy, at least when Arianne is not around, if you don't find something to do. Why don't you come help me with the letter again? I think you enjoyed it." Axel served as a surrogate father. Chandler saw little of his biological father whom he treated like a much older brother.

"I did, but I don't think that's me. I told you that before," Chandler clarified, slurping his java, careful not to burn his tongue.

Axel worried about Chandler's idle mind. "You could help me until something comes along. I figure you have six months or maybe a little less now, before you find what you really want or more accurately stated, get offered what you really want."

"I will admit that I got energy working with you. And one

31

thing's for sure, I always learn more with you than anyone or anywhere else. It's definitely an alternate education."

Chandler carried a Master's degree from John Hopkins' School of Advanced International Studies, yet working with Axel felt like being in an intensive real world laboratory. "I mean where else would I have learned about your aversion to using cloud storage like seemingly the rest of the world does."

Axel's knowledge of the Internet and technology were exemplary, especially for someone no longer in that line of work. "Are you kidding me? If you read most of those service provider's terms of service, they pretty much say they have digital rights to everything I ever wrote. That's bullshit! And those guys are being hacked left and right. Screw that! I have way too much intelligence information that I've accumulated over the years. I can't afford to have that compromised."

The curious student needed more, placing his hot cup on the table in front of him. "So tell me again, how did you protect all that data?"

The master proved eager to oblige and did the same with his tea. "I have a distributed scheme where pieces of my encrypted data are spread in servers all over the world. So someone, or who knows the spooks in government, would have to hack into these servers, including my own, and then decrypt the data to put it all together. Good luck with that."

Tech veterans championed distributed schemes and decentralization. As the country would soon find out, there were other domestic groups also sharing this view.

"I don't have your tech knowledge, Ax, but how did you even think about doing it this way?" Chandler asked, leaning forward, his elbows resting on the top of his knees.

"Really, this is the most secure way right now. My contacts

at Omni turned me onto the idea. I could definitely see the wisdom of their ways."

Omni, the enigmatic international hacking organization, could be a friend to some and foe to others. Axel's genderless contact, Phish, proved instrumental in helping them uncover all the machinations of the International Relations Council and the Global Settlement Bank and their influence on American economic and financial policy.

The Financial Stability Board controlled American economic policy. In the minds of many, their oversight was suffocating, though the markets had at least stabilized. By no means, however, did it mean the economy was humming along. The nation's residents continued to suffer economically, though the pain exhibited a very uneven distribution. The Elite seemed to escape much of the economic pain felt by a sizable majority. Along with the FSB came greater imposition of government authority, since compliance remained an issue. This growing authority troubled the very independent, Libertarian, Axel Schultz.

"Chan, do you remember when John King talked about the Deep State during your interview?" Axel reminded him of the discussion he had with the presidential contender from the Theocracy Party.

"Heck yeah. No pun intended, but he got real deep into that topic."

"Well, much of what he said was correct. The Deep State is all around us. People just assume that it is a part of the great cosmic order. I'm sure they're editing civics courses at the grade school and high school level now, telling the next generation how much we need the Deep State. Chairman Mao said political power originated in the barrel of a gun. The Deep State doesn't need a gun. They just assume economic control. And Jefferson with that executive order is exercising a new control. I realized years ago that we basically had a Demopublican Party and a Repumocratic Party. There were no differences between the two. I say that hyperbolically since, of course, there are some differences. The lack of differences strengthens the State's power. That's why the IAP and TP were born out of the voter frustration. But even their ascendance has done little to curb the Deep State's power."

"Ax, as usual, you can do wonders for a man's spirits," Chandler said, sarcastically, leaning back on the couch.

Axel gave him a reproachful look. "This is serious, Chan." He jabbed his index finger at Chandler. "While you have people like me that abhor the Deep State, it's sensational for people in it. The State's prime directive, like the Borg of Star Trek fame, is to assimilate. The assimilation is to convince everyone that what they do is for the good of society and necessary for its well-being. In reality, they are a parasitic organization feeding off the ignorance of the masses. I'm not anti-government, as you know, but this is a leviathan that has gotten out of control."

"No doubt that's what's making all these internal groups angry. Hey, look what's happening now in Catalonia and Scotland."

Chandler paid a visit to Spain in 2019 and covered the growing secession movement in the Catalonian region. Little did he know during his visit to the Iberian peninsula that secession would be a topic for discussion in his own country two short years later. A recent vote in the Catalonian parliament gave the authority for the region to secede from the rest of Spain. Civil unrest occurred throughout the country in the vote's aftermath.

Scotland had its own unique set of circumstances. The UK's decision to leave the European Union in 2016 ignited a series of events that rekindled Scottish emotions about their union with England, Wales, and Northern Ireland. They wanted to venture out on their own, either in what remained of the European Union or as a separate entity. The Scottish Parliament debated the matter and voted to formally leave the United Kingdom in December 2020. The world awaited the UK's next move to hold their union together.

"You are correct. There is a tipping point when the authority of government or the king tilts too far in one direction and the people rebel. You saw this when you visited Catalonia in 2019. Remember how you commented about the complexity of that issue? And now with Scotland. There will probably be more of these movements, especially with the twentieth century habit of cobbling together people in one country where naturally they were separate. Rebellions are violent affairs, though I think their complexion now will be different with cyber warfare," Axel added.

Chandler leaned forward in his seat, looking contemplative. "Since we're chattin' up secession, I wanted to talk to you about an opportunity."

"An opportunity? What kind of opportunity?" Axel inquired, reaching for his tea.

Chandler detailed his conversation with Arturo Dutari and his offer to work on the documentary. Axel, unfamiliar with Arturo, wanted more information. Since Chandler grew up in a single parent household with his mom Renee, Axel could provide fatherly influence in matters like these, which Chandler welcomed.

"Arturo has his own film company, so he's the boss. I suppose that's good. Have you discussed remuneration?" Axel inquired.

"There will be progress payments and a share of the film's sale price. I'm not in this for the money."

"Ok, so my next question relates to Ari and how she'll feel about it." Relationships were not Axel's area of expertise, yet he felt obliged to ask.

"She really doesn't want me doing it. I mean, we just had this big relationship talk, and she's probably gonna leave State. She doesn't know what she wants to do next, and let's be honest, my adventure last year hurt her standing there, especially after she had to take that leave of absence. My guess is she'll want to leave DC and head back to Chicagoland. Maybe she'll go to work for her father. Anyway, she wants me to go with her and find something there. The thing is, I don't think I'm ready to do that yet, but heck, I love this woman!"

"I know about many things, though in matters of the heart, I'm no expert." Axel conveyed what Chandler already knew since he never married and seldom talked about his personal life. "So I won't comment on your relationship with Ari, but I will say you need to consider that getting into secession movements or those that might promote civil unrest will no doubt put you in harm's way. The Deep State is not just going to stand by and do nothing."

"Yeah, I've considered that, but I've been in some tight spots before and Arty's had a great deal of experience especially with all the coverage he did on the drug wars."

"Well, it's great that the drug wars have calmed down, but this is a different animal. The State doesn't like their existence threatened. That's why secession groups make them uneasy. Hell, they make everyday people uneasy. And you know that Geringer and company are putting the squeeze on the Jefferson administration with the impeachment talk. That administration is under duress from multiple angles."

"I know, Ax, but what the heck am I gonna do? I used to be

as busy as a hound in flea season, and now I've just been sitting around. I have to think about my own mental health here. And I do appreciate your offer, which would work really well for Ari since you live in Chicago."

"Well, let's do this. You probably have a few days to decide. If you work with Arturo, or Arty as you call him, why don't the three of us meet, and I can give my thoughts on how you might dig up some intelligence on some of these groups. After all, you of all people should know. My work is all about digging up information that others don't know. I can't imagine you letting any grass grow underneath your feet!"

"Axel Schultz! Where did you get that Texas slang?" Chandler did not expect his slang to boomerang back at him.

"After hearing it from you for so long, I thought I'd throw it right back to you," Axel replied, smiling.

"Very cool. Yeah, I like your idea about meeting with Arty. You guys may have some things in common, who knows. Hey, are you still good for dinner later?"

"Yes, I'm looking forward to seeing Ari. I've grown so fond of her. She's a special woman and her beauty, well enough said. I'll come by around six then. I need to get to my meeting, anyway."

Chandler walked Axel out and spent the rest of the day in contemplation. The scales were balancing his professional and personal life. There would be no discussion about the opportunity with Arturo during their dinner later. She made her feelings clear on that topic.

This reminded him of his experiences as a child when his grandmother gave him cod liver oil. He knew he had to take it eventually though he knew he wouldn't like it. The forthcoming decision about Arty elicited the same feeling. No matter what he decided, there would be some part of him that wouldn't like it.

CHAPTER FOUR
CHANDLER DECIDES

The contemplation lasted but a couple of days. His financial situation would not improve by standing on the sidelines. Axel had strongly cautioned him to protect some of his assets in the last couple of years, and he did so. While his retirement accounts did not grow much, at least they were in better shape than many of his contemporaries. By the same token, he knew that he would not touch his retirement savings until he retired. Axel always emphasized that relative wealth could be just as important as absolute wealth.

His financial reality comprised an apartment in Manhattan, a shared apartment in D.C., and a student loan from his time at the School of Advanced International Studies (SAIS) at Johns Hopkins. His D.C. roommate, a former co-worker from El Mundo, shouldered most of the shared space rent. With Arianne's departure from D.C., there would be no need to keep the shared space.

The financial aspect of the decision would be much easier than the emotional one. Emotionally connected decisions had not been part of his repertoire. Throughout his adult life, he only needed to consider himself. Things were different now. Any conversation about Arturo's project would end up in the same place—she didn't want him to do it. She made good points about not taking the project, most of which involved their relationship.

She wanted him to consider working at a local station, perhaps in Chicago. He'd never done that before, so perhaps he might like it. If he didn't, he could return to the national stage. And he also had Axel's standing offer.

He rested in bed at Arianne's place, playing a game on his phone, and decided He figured he could call Arturo while Arianne was at work and break the news to her later. After walking to the kitchen to get some water, he decided against it. Then he paced between the kitchen and living room. The certainty of the last few minutes dissipated. In his younger days, a trip to the bathroom and a magazine would help, though not today.

What other choice do you have, Chandler? You gotta do it.

After hearing his conscience, he made his way to the living room and laid down on the couch, and dialed.

"Hey, Arty, it's me, Chan."

"Yes, I saw the caller id with your number. Hopefully, you have some good news for me?" he said with anticipation.

The approving Chandler unleashed one of his Texas metaphors. "We're gonna be charging hell with a bucket of ice water, but I'm in!" The declaration brought a little grin to his face.

This moment would be reminiscent of his teenage years when he would commit an indiscretion and have fun during its commission, knowing full well what lay in store for him later. He hoped Arianne would be merciful.

"*Muy bueno.*"

"What's the next step?" the restless Chandler wasted no time.

"I want to come to D.C. immediately, like tomorrow, so we can talk about the project in more detail. No way I'm having this conversation over the phone." Arturo limited private discussions over cell phone or landlines.

Government surveillance grew more intense since the president's executive order. The Jefferson administration's national security team warned of domestic disturbances in the wake of his decision and the continuing economic malaise.

Arturo and Chandler had yet to establish a secure encrypted link for their communications. Commercially available cell phone encryption proved unreliable and there were compatibility issues between operating systems. Arianne's father's company, Maxwell Technologies, was in the final stages of commercial release of their encryption software, which would address many of the problems. The Maxwell Tech software enjoyed little support in government since it would make their surveillance effort that much more difficult. The courts would play a role in the software's ultimate disposition. The entire software project almost got derailed last year after Arianne's inadvertent introduction of the Trident virus into Maxwell Tech.

"Sounds good. We should be able to meet at Ari's condo since she'll be at work, then maybe later, the three of us can go get dinner or something," Chandler said, excitedly.

"So how did your discussion go with her when you told her of your decision?" Arturo inquired.

"Ah, I haven't, um, you know, told her yet," Chandler replied, offering a sheepish grin.

"*Coño hijo!*" Arturo bellowed. His Spanish erupted during times of emotion, much like Chandler's Texas slang.

"I know. I know. I've got some work to do."

"Ok. Listen. I'll see you tomorrow, probably by mid-morning. I'm taking the first train out."

"See you tomorrow, Arty."

Chandler ruminated on how he would break the news to Arianne. He didn't have to wait long. She unexpectedly came through the front door early in the afternoon.

"Hi, honey," she said, smiling as she took off her coat. The cold January air had turned her cheeks pink.

"Hey, what the heck are you doing here so early?" Though happy to see her, he filled with anxiety about telling her.

"Oh, no big deal. Just your everyday bomb threat at Foggy Bottom, unfortunately on a miserable, freezing day." The old-timers referred to the State Department as Foggy Bottom. "First, we had to evacuate outside and I barely had time to grab my coat."

"Well, it's a good thing you got out of there in a New York minute!"

"I know. Honestly, it wasn't that big of a deal. Everyone thinks it was a prank. Supposedly a call came in, and then there were emails sent to network administrators. Anyway, they just took the safe route and evacuated everyone. After they gave the 'all clear', I went to get my laptop and came home. I have work to do, so don't get too excited. I'm gonna change, warm up, and get myself something to eat."

She headed to the bedroom and changed into sweatpants and a sweatshirt with "Maxwell Tech" emblazoned across the front. Chandler had taken his cue and prepared something for them to eat. The conversation flowed calmly and pleasantly at the kitchen counter. It was halcyon time given what he wanted to talk about next. He cleaned up and suggested they move to the living room. They sat down on the sofa and she cozied up to him.

"I'm just going to snuggle with you for a few minutes. I gotta get back to work. " She wrapped her arms around his and laying her head on his shoulder.

He put his hand on her leg. "Hey, you know we've been talking so much about us and this offer Arty made me. This is a good offer and a good opportunity for me to get my career going again. I don't see myself working in local media and it will be awhile before I would even get hired by a big network."

He began as slowly as he could, reiterating previously

discussed points.

"Have you thought about working in communications for a large company? Maybe I could talk to my father about getting you a position in media relations or something?" she asked.

"Do you really see me issuing press releases, being interviewed on the financial channels, or making appearances at conferences and conventions?"

"It's not exactly what you want but we'd be together, in Chicago, and besides Ax lives there. Your father wouldn't be too far away and neither would your mom," she added, nuzzling up to him more.

Maxwell Tech had a home in Evanston, Illinois, while the Maxwell clan resided in Winnetka. Chandler's father taught at the university in Columbia, Missouri, and his mom, Renee, lived in Dallas.

They went back and forth on the benefits of living in Chicago, which fit the big city profile he liked. Arianne made a convincing argument, as one would expect for an attorney, for moving to Chicago, yet he needed to follow his passion. By now they created space between them, she sitting cross-legged facing him and his body rotated towards her, one leg bent on the sofa.

"Everything you say makes sense, Ari, but my heart's not into working at Maxwell or anything like it. If I don't take on these assignments like Arty's, I may not do them later and I know I'll regret it."

"So what are you saying?" Rationally, she knew the answer, though her heart could not accept it.

"Honey, I've got to go work with Arty. I'm sorry."

She moved to the other end of the sofa, faced away from him, and looked forlorn. There's was a relationship remarkably free of verbal sparring despite his adventuresome projects. Both pugilists went to their corner and the sparring began.

She spun towards him quickly. "Chandler Scott, you need to figure out what the hell you want out of life! You're gonna hop over another fence now and realize the grass isn't greener. It may well be brown and dead. Then once you get to the other side, you'll see how high that fence is when you try to jump back. You think you're getting closer to something, but that illusion just moves farther away."

He slid towards her end of the sofa and reached for her. "Honey, I'm not chasing something here. I think I know what I want and who I am."

"I have a better idea of what I want," she yelled. "I just can't understand why it's so fucking hard for us to be together. I've given you a plan. Am I not worth it?" A rush of crimson covered her face.

She completely disarmed him with that rhetorical question. The disarmament evoked strong emotions, ones he was unprepared to handle. The love of his life posed a question that only had one right answer, yet it would conflict with what he wanted professionally.

The emotion caused him to stand up in front of her while she remained seated. The veins in his neck pulsated. "I didn't grow up in the lap of luxury. My mom didn't even tell me who my dad was for several years, then it wasn't until my senior year that I even heard the whole story. I had to put myself through college. I have student debt and bills to pay and no I don't want to ask you or your dad for money or a damn job. Is that so hard to understand?" He'd never spoken to her this way.

The arguing continued for several minutes. They alternated sitting on the couch. One would get up and pace towards the kitchen, then the other would follow. He'd never seen her this angry and vice versa. The anger reached a point neither expected. While both were standing in the kitchen, she looked down at the ground for a few seconds before addressing him.

The emotional groundwork she laid over the last couple of years appeared to crumble beneath her feet. "Chan, I think you just need to leave. This is going nowhere and I need to think about things."

"Leave like for a few hours? I don't have anywhere to go and it's darn cold out there."

"No. Leave, like get your things and leave." The anger in her eyes bore a hole in him.

"Come on, Ari," he pleaded, with open palms. "You're kicking me out?"

"Seriously, Chan, get your things and leave. This is a blow to me and for us! I didn't see this coming. You knew where I stood on this and our relationship. You just did what you wanted to. I'm sorry. I don't know what else to say."

She walked away towards the living room, her hand pushed her locks of auburn hair from her forehead. She sat on the sofa and hid her face in a pillow, struggling to hold back the tears.

Chandler miscalculated her reaction. He knew she wouldn't be happy, although he did not expect to get the heave ho. He walked to the bedroom and packed. She didn't come in, waiting instead by the dining room table, looking outside at the bare trees bending in the January wind while sipping on a glass of Chardonnay. She swilled the wine in her mouth, allowing it to drain the moisture from her cheek and tongue. She swallowed and bared her teeth, drawing in the dry air of her condo. Watching him pack would deepen the pain.

When he finished, he grabbed the suitcase and hanging bag and walked up behind her. He placed his bags on the ground and wrapped his arms around her taut midriff. He loved her.

"I love you and nothing that happened here today changes that," he whispered, not knowing when he'd see her again or have her familiar scent so close to him.

"I love you too," she whispered back. She could not turn around, nor did he expect her to. The tears streamed down her cheeks.

He grabbed his bags and walked outside to wait for his ride in the unforgiving winter air. The sky was a uniform gray, empty, devoid of anything resembling sun or clouds. He emptied his heart earlier, something he'd never experienced since he never had a full heart. She filled it in so many ways. He hoped his project with Arty could fill him in other ways, though it could never replace her.

He texted Arturo and Axel with a new address for the meeting tomorrow, his shared apartment.

***

He woke up in unfamiliar surroundings, the sweet fragrance of Arianne missing. Several months back he confessed that he could find her in a crowd, blindfolded, using his nose. Her long auburn hair, often a companion as she rested on his chest, no longer tickled his chin. Despite being in the same city, the chasm in their relationship felt like the Grand Canyon. He needed to dive into this project.

It had been some time since he'd slept in this apartment. His roommate, a former El Mundo employee, worked a temporary gig on the West Coast after getting let go from the network during a major purge. The fold out queen-size sofa bed proved a far cry from the luxurious king mattress in Arianne's condo, not to mention her absence alone made the night less comfortable. He got milk and cereal, the only comestibles in the apartment. After a quick shower, he reassembled the sofa and tidied up the living area for his guests. Axel arrived first.

"Ax, hi. Let me have your coat." Chandler grabbed it to store in the closet next to the front door. "Come on in. Arty's not here yet."

"You doing OK? It had to be a rough night for you." Axel placed his hand on Chandler's shoulder, squeezing it gently, as the two walked towards the living area. Chandler had texted him about the argument.

"Yeah, for now. It stings for sure, but I've got to move forward. In time, we'll work things out. She's got some things she needs to sort out too with her professional life, you know," Chandler answered while the two stood near the sofa. "Let's sit down. Sorry I can't offer you anything to drink. I haven't been here much."

The two sat on the folded sofa bed and talked about the project. Axel didn't have the same emotional perspective, particularly when considering someone else. He lived alone and frequently ventured around the country or the world in search of material for his newsletter.

A project such as this would bring him great mental stimulation. He'd evolved into more than just a mentor, he assumed a quasi-fatherly role, wanting the best for Chandler. Plus, he liked Arianne. As a single person in their sixties, he vicariously enjoyed the young love from his old eyes.

About thirty minutes later, Arturo arrived.

Arturo Dutari, the 5'9" Panamanian, carried 170 pounds on his medium frame. His skin was dark, given his Mestizo roots. His frequent smile conveyed an infectious charm and personality. Chandler knew of his daring reputation, heck, he'd seen it on the documentary Arturo sold to El Mundo. He needed nine lives to

47

get out of some of his predicaments. Chandler always wondered if he enjoyed overwhelming luck or if he possessed inordinate skill.

After introducing Axel and Arturo, the three men sat down in the living area. Chandler and Axel placed themselves on the sofa bed while Arturo landed in the large leather chair, a chair weathered by friction and spilled beer.

"Arturo, Chan tells me that you feel confident about being able to get deep into some of these secession groups," Axel began.

"Please Axel, call me Arty," Arty smiled. "I've been following these movements for a few years now. Chandler's probably told you we met when I sold the film about the Shining Path to El Mundo. This has been brewing since at least 2008 after the financial crisis. Once we started having the domestic terror attacks where people claimed they were ISIS or Al Qaeda, it just got these domestic groups going. My guess is these groups felt government couldn't keep them safe. Add the racial strife and the country was ripe for all this. I don't want you to think I support the Theocracy Party, but when their candidate for president, King, did his attack in the debate last year, he talked about how little respect there was for the law. These groups are doing the same thing, disrespecting the law. Trust me, I've lived with domestic terrorists and even though they were from South America, you can see the same frustration."

During the contentious presidential debate from St. Louis the prior year, Theocracy Party candidate John King verbally dressed down President Jefferson on live TV. In the ensuing melee, the Secret Serviced rushed the president to Air Force One.

Axel had his own views on how the domestic groups evolved. "I agree with you, Arty, but it seems like the FBI more or less turned into an internal CIA organization trying to weed out the

Islamic terrorists. My sources told me there were so many informants out there that even the slightest mention about dissatisfaction with the government led to people snitching on their neighbor. The FBI trapped people in sting operations from the bottom rungs of society. They thought they were joining organizations that promised them an opportunity to take their country back and make their lives better. My guess is the FBI overstated the domestic Muslim threat and created another one or at least exacerbated the brewing undercurrent you mentioned."

Axel, with his legion of contacts, felt the rise of the domestic groups had many components.

"Well, that could be and who knows, maybe the FBI stings moved things along. Sort of like a be careful what you wish for, huh?" Arty chuckled.

"I'm not trying to lecture you two but nowhere in the Constitution does it say we need to have a federal police force. It wasn't until World War I that the FBI came of age when President Wilson unleashed them against people protesting the war. I think everyone thought the FBI's only role was to fight crime, though you can see they've evolved into a national security organization too, complementing Homeland Security. This is one reason I wonder if you'll be able to get close enough to these groups. If you go around and start asking questions, you may end up in a sting or hauled in for questioning." The cerebral Axel raised points about which Chandler had not thought.

"Chandler, man, your friend here is so full of worry. He's looking out for you." Arty nodded his in a deliberate rhythm.

Chandler looked at Axel and patted him gently on the shoulder. "Ax is usually on the mark. I mean, look at his newsletter. You should read it. His contacts probably rival a small country's own intelligence agency, although he'd never share his

Rolodex."

Axel dipped his head toward Chandler in concurrence. "Arty, I am of the belief that many of these so-called separatists, or secessionists, or whatever they want to call themselves will operate in a different manner now."

"You sound like you know something." Arty leaned forward, the leather chair scrunching under his pants.

Axel, normally reluctant to say much about his contacts, mentioned a Dark Net source that alerted him to an upcoming battle between the government and some of these groups. He omitted mentioning Omni and hoped that Chandler would not reveal this either.

Axel never identified Omni in his newsletter. They were an enigmatic organization that no one could identify or associate with any cause. They just seemed to appear whenever they felt they needed to shine a spotlight on a perceived injustice. Often, this meant they were fighting governments worldwide who were encroaching on individual liberties or corporations taking advantage of employees or ordinary citizens.

Some people enjoyed these cyber hacking Robin Hoods operating in the Sherwood Forest of the Internet. For the Sheriff of Nottingham, Omni proved to be an incessant pest who always mocked the government, the Elite or the corporatocracy.

"I will work on something from my sources that hopefully will give you a more precise target in your investigation. I really think if you just start poking around, you'll find yourself in trouble," Axel insisted. He didn't care for Arty's method, preferring to rely on preparation rather than fortune. He worried about Arty exposing Chandler to unnecessary danger.

"Ok. Listen. I have a group I know we can talk to and not raise too many flags. So let's check those guys out first. In the meantime, Axel can get into his rich information pool. You good with that, Chan?" Arty expected a positive answer.

"Yeah. Sure. Let's get this show on the road." Chandler slapped his leg in approval.

Arty rose from his chair to shake Chandler's hand, a broad smile stretched across his face.

Axel did not bear a smile, feeling Arty had not thought out the project thoroughly. He excused himself, leaving the two others to discuss their plan.

After Arty left later that afternoon, Chandler attempted to call Arianne several times, though it became clear she would not be answering. Each time he left her the same message, "I love you, don't give up on us."

Part II

Rebellium

CHAPTER FIVE
HONOR BRIGADE

After spending a couple of days in his D.C. apartment, Chandler headed back to New York to get ready for his trip with Arturo. The men had an early call on February 2, 2021, with a 6:00am flight out of LaGuardia for Jackson, Wyoming. Chandler met Arturo, coming in from Yonkers, at the airport. American Airlines flight 2607 took them to DFW where they had a short layover before boarding flight 2289 for Jackson. Flying into Jackson (JAC) was a new experience for both men.

The small airport, seven miles north of Jackson, at an elevation of 6,400 feet, required a prolonged approach between the peaks of the American Rockies. JAC had the distinction of being the only commercial airport in the United States within national park land, in this case, Grand Teton National Park.

After landing on the short runway 1, the men bundled up for their exit from the 737 aircraft since JAC did not use jet bridges. The Wyoming winds were unkind, staggering an elderly lady on her journey to the terminal. Arty steadied her as she regained her footing on the slippery tarmac.

The airport's main terminal reminded travelers that they were in a national park with plenty of exposed wood and fireplaces throughout. The men headed to the rental counter where they picked up a large sedan. The process took a little longer for Arty's flirtation with a beautiful, blond Eastern European customer service agent.

They headed south on Highway 191 and then west on Highway 22, later changing to 33, towards the town of Sugar

City, Idaho. During this trek, Chandler experienced the Grand Tetons from both the east and west sides. He made the observation that the Tetons reminded him of the female anatomy. Arty gave a hearty belly laugh and reminded him of the Spanish word for "breast."

A sheepish Chandler replied, "D'oh!" and slapped his forehead.

About 70 miles into the trip, an Idaho state trooper tailed them. After five miles of pursuit, the trooper turned on his cherries.

Arty, conscious of what was happening, slowed down gradually.

"What's going on, man? Why are we slowing?" Chandler had been oblivious to life, enjoying the open expanses of the West. He glanced in the passenger side mirror and noticed the trooper. "How fast were you going? Oh my gosh, I sound like my mom now. She used to tell me that if I was going any faster, I'd catch up to yesterday. But it didn't seem like we were going that fast." Chandler swiveled his head between the passenger mirror and Arty.

"Man, I have the cruise on and am doing just a little above the speed limit. This is a rental, so I have no idea what's going on," Arty replied, his eyes darting between the road and the rearview mirror.

Arty pulled over to what little shoulder existed. Chandler coaxed him to move further off the road since little snow had fallen in this otherwise flat part of the state. Arty put the vehicle in park, bringing it to rest just behind a utility pole. He left his hands high on the steering wheel where the trooper could see them. He asked Chandler to put his hands on the dash to show a non-threatening posture. The law enforcement community in most states had issued public service announcements about how to engage with their own during a traffic stop.

The trooper approached them with guarded steps from the driver side and then cut behind their sedan and came to the passenger side. He tapped on Chandler's window. Chandler carefully moved his right hand towards the power window control. The winter wind rushed into the vehicle, making the men recoil from the blast.

"Good afternoon, gentlemen. I'm Captain Matt Meier of District 6 of the Idaho State Police." The patrolman leaned in, placing his right hand near his holster.

"Hello sir," Arty replied, beaming with a curious excitement.

"Where are you headed today?" Captain Meier inquired. His ears were pink from the wind's assault.

"Sir, by law I'm only obligated to provide you my license and registration. Would you like to see them?" Arty said, still maintaining his hands within clear sight. He had particular antipathy for what he perceived to be a random stop, yet the trooper wouldn't know from the pasted smile on his face.

The captain chuckled and said, "No, no. You didn't do anything wrong. The reason I was asking where you were headed was to warn you."

"Warn us?" Chandler asked, his hands still on the dash.

"Yeah, based on where you're headed and the fact we don't get too many out-of-state vehicles through here, I wanted to let you know that once you go past this point, you will be under surveillance by the Department of Homeland Security and possibly the FBI," the captain explained, with a serious countenance.

"Ahh, I see. Thank you, sir. Are we free to go?" Arty asked.

"You're not the least bit curious why you would come under

surveillance?" Captain Meier, incredulous that after such a revelation there would not be at least the hint of curiosity, took his weathered right hand away from his holster and placed it on his hip. He did the same with the left. The deep creases in his cold hands showed signs of manual labor.

"Well, it seems like everyone is under surveillance these days," was Arty's cold and leveled response.

Captain Meier alternated his stare between the two men. "Very well then. You gentlemen drive safely, watch for wildlife, and have a nice day." The captain slightly tipped his hat and walked calmly back to his vehicle, his hands in the pockets of his jacket, his chin attached to his chest as he attempted to duck the wind.

Chandler rolled up his window and rubbed his hands together vigorously. Arty engaged the vehicle's transmission and drove as if nothing had occurred. Chandler glared at him in disbelief.

"What?" Arty asked, his attention bouncing between the road and his companion.

"You know for most people getting pulled over and being told they'd be under surveillance would be as welcome as an outhouse breeze." Any breeze at this time of the year in Idaho would be a frigid one.

"We're fine, man. He didn't have to tell me we'd be watched. I mean, look who we're meeting. You think the Feds don't know the Honor Brigade is active out here?" Arty answered.

Chandler did not expect being warned by state police about surveillance. Arty's nonchalance unnerved him.

The Honor Brigade was one of many patriot groups that emerged after 2008. Their membership mostly comprised former military, law enforcement, and firefighters, though the group's membership was not exclusive to these professions. The U.S. military prohibited active servicemen and women from joining these groups. The Brigade wanted to protect the Constitution from an increasingly tyrannical federal government. They did not hide themselves, their members, or their stated intentions.

The group had its roots in right wing talk radio who reported military exercises preparing for extreme civil unrest in cities and rural areas. After protests from the American Civil Liberties Union about excessive force during riot control following the 2016 elections, the Army developed sonic weapons to subdue crowds. The military tested these weapons on their own personnel at installations in the state of Nevada.

The Honor Brigade had many meetings and performed military-style exercises for their members. They also maintained a national web site where they sold survival gear and posted news. The web site encountered frequent Denial of Service attacks from unknown sources, though suspected to be cyber jockeys from the National Security Agency or Homeland Security. The Denial of Service attacks rendered the Honor Brigade web site unusable due to the volume of traffic directed towards it.

After driving another 20 miles past the interaction with the state trooper, the men made it to the home of Mack Crockett, regional leader of the Honor Brigade. Crockett lived outside of Sugar City, Idaho, a town wiped out when the Teton Dam breached in 1976. Crockett moved here with his family in the early 2000s after he bought a potato processing facility. He became involved in city politics and rose to president of the city council. A former member of the military, he became attracted to the Honor Brigade after what he viewed as a failure of Idaho's elected leadership in Washington. Crockett and most residents of this part of the country were no fans of the FSB and Jefferson's executive action. The recent imposition of martial law and the use of the military in cities were the last straw.

Crockett owned a sprawling ranch with great views in all directions. Arty and Chandler pulled up in his substantial circular drive. They walked gingerly over the crackling ice covering a small amount of snow in front of his home. The wind swept over the top of the frozen precipitation, buffeting the men, the cold air swirling up and slapping their faces.

"Man, it's colder than a cast iron commode out here!" Chandler yelled, bear hugging himself.

Arty smirked, less affected by the cold than his partner, and rang the doorbell.

Someone the size of an NFL offensive lineman greeted them. "You must be Arturo and Chandler. I'm Mack Crockett," he announced. The appropriately named "Mack" appeared to be the size of an eighteen wheeler. He stood six feet six inches weighing 300 pounds, clean shaven with salt and pepper hair. "Come on in guys. I know you must be cold."

The two visitors lifted their eyes at their Bunyanesque host and walked inside.

"Thank you so much for meeting with us," Arty said. Both men removed their gloves and extended their hands to greet Crockett, coming away sore from the experience.

"Let me take your coats." The two visitors obliged and Crockett placed them on a chair in the entrance foyer. "I hope you had a good trip from New York. I've got some warm tea or coffee. It's not exactly balmy weather here."

Chandler didn't think "balmy" and this part of the country could ever find companionship in the same sentence.

The men made their way to an expansive family room, finished with wood paneling where two black labs were napping in the corner on large pillows. The room could have been mistaken for a reception area in a hunting lodge. All sorts of wildlife hung from the walls. There were several deer heads, a wild boar, and birds adorning the room. A massive stone fireplace contained the embers of a roaring fire, a welcome sight for Chandler.

After dispensing the coffee from a cart, Crockett sat in an oversized leather chair while the other two made their way to a plush leather sofa replete with pillows featuring more wildlife. Chandler held his bare hand against the cup for extra warmth. Crockett kept his abode on the chillier side.

"Thanks again, Mr. Crockett, for agreeing to this interview. As I mentioned to you in our previous conversation, I'd like to make this as relaxed as possible. I'll ask you about your organization's goals, philosophy, and that sort of thing. Chandler and I will share the filming responsibilities. The goal is to have you on camera as much as possible."

After receiving Crockett's blessing, Arty set up the high definition camera.

Crockett began speaking. "First, I want to say that we're not some half-cocked right-wing extremist group. We believe in the law of the land. People hear the term Honor Brigade and assume we're some militia ready to fight the U.S. Army. That's nonsense. We conduct training exercises for our members, but it's not to fight the government. Our belief is that government won't be able to protect us from civil unrest or domestic terrorists. Let me give you an example. Remember the Mumbai attacks?"

Crockett referred to the 2008 attacks by Islamic militants in the Indian city of Mumbai over four days that killed over 160 and wounded twice as many.

Both Arty and Chandler answered in unison, "Yes."

"Think about this for a moment. Ten armed men brought that city of millions to a standstill. To make the attack even more effective, they used open-source information from traditional media, the Internet, and their cell phones to adjust their tactics mid-attack. What do you think our government could do about something like that in, say, New York City?" Crockett cocked his head defiantly, thinning his eyes.

Crockett's rhetorical question unnerved the Manhattan-based Chandler.

Arty immediately moved to a question that evoked sensitivity for both him, as an immigrant, and Crockett. "I've read that the Brigade has strong feelings about immigration."

Frustrated by the question, Crockett forced his tongue against his lower lip and frowned before answering. "Look. I have nothing against immigrants. Our southern border, we may as well not even have one. We all understand there's a huge illegal immigration problem here, and our government's done nothing to fix it. If these immigrants don't learn English, they're not going to have any sort of cultural allegiance to America. When society starts to break down, these immigrants will have a different idea about how to deal with it. It reminds me of the Goths, Vandals and the Huns in the final days of the Roman Empire."

Arty and Chandler got lost in the historical reference.

"You've shared your concerns about terrorists and immigrants destabilizing things, what concerns you about the economy?" Arty continued.

"Washington D.C. is nothing but chaos. They don't know what they're doing and with this FSB acting like Big Brother, it's just a matter of time before the economy collapses. They think they can run an economy, but I think plenty of socialist governments throughout history should tell them otherwise.

When the economy finally goes down, you'll have disorder and I don't think the National Guard or the military will be there to protect us. They'll be protecting their own families. I also have a big concern about what happens afterward and how the country gets rebuilt."

"So is this an apocalyptic vision?" Arty asked, a frightened worry gripped his face.

"Not like some big nuclear war or anything like that. That's for Hollywood. I'm just talking about a breakdown. There will be unrest which will lead to violence and the economy will be disrupted and then things get back to some level of normal. Does the new normal look like the old USA, or is there some other sort of political arrangement? That's the great unknown. Our membership is just taking steps to make sure we're ready for whatever happens."

Crockett broke to answer a text on his phone, looking perturbed for the interruption. "Excuse me." He tapped the keys. "Ok, go ahead."

"Let's say that there is some economic collapse and everything stops functioning, at least financially, how will the Honor Brigade adapt?" Chandler asked, hoping Crockett would open up the playbook.

"It's no secret we're survivalists or preppers, as some might call us. We have plans to live in self-sustaining communities for quite a long time until lawful, political organization returns," Crockett answered. "I want to stress, though, that I think our group has educated people with decent worldviews. We've thought this out and simply want to protect our families so we can have a nation to come back to."

"How long do you think it might be before things would return to normal?" Chandler inquired.

"A long time," Crockett directed his gaze towards his yard as if looking at it for the last time.

After entertaining another thirty minutes of questions, Crockett suggested they end the interview. The three agreed to meet at a VFW hall in Idaho Falls the next day, where they would be exposed to a membership meeting.

Arty and Chandler took their rental vehicle forty miles towards Idaho Falls, where they would spend the night.

***

Arty and Chandler spent most of the day in a motel on the west side of Idaho Falls discussing what they'd heard from Mack Crockett and reviewing the video. The Honor Brigade did not fit the mold of what most Americans considered a separatist organization. More accurately, they were survivalists, respectful of U.S. law, though lacking in the confidence of their government protecting them as civil unrest worsened.

Chandler called Arianne several times throughout the day to no avail. The wounds were still too fresh. As always, he remained optimistic. His "can do" Texas attitude never let him down.

Idaho Falls occupied a unique place in U.S. history when in 1951, at the National Reactor Testing Station in the desert west of the city, a nuclear reactor produced usable electricity for the first time in history. The station's name changed to the Idaho National Laboratory, where they conducted significant research on nuclear fuel. Because of work in the facility, there were military personnel stationed in the area, a fact not lost on the Honor Brigade. Though the Honor Brigade did not actively recruit military personnel, they wanted the military to be aware of their activities. They sought transparency in their actions and wanted their message exposed to military personnel.

After an early dinner at a local diner, the two made their way to the VFW hall on the opposite side of town. As they headed east on State 20, it became apparent, at least to Arty, that they were not alone. To test his hunch, he made a normal right turn heading south on Skyline Drive. The shadow remained behind him. The pursuit car's lights were too close for comfort. After making another turn into a subdivision, he confirmed the tail. Arty circled back onto State 20, this time heading west. Chandler, busy reading notes from the Crockett interview, paid little attention to the circuitous driving. He could easily stay in this state of oblivion since he owned no car and always took public transportation.

"Hang on," Arty commanded. He repositioned his hands on the steering wheel.

Chandler looked up, gaining a degree of situational awareness. "Hang on?"

Arty accelerated the vehicle and waited until it was clear on the opposite side of the road. He whipped the steering wheel to the left, quickly reorienting the vehicle in the opposite direction.

Chandler slammed against the passenger door, feeling fortunate he wore a seat belt. "What the hell are you doing?"

Arty sped up and executed a series of turns, eventually making it to a high school with activity in progress in the gymnasium. There were many cars in the school's lot. Arty nudged the rental vehicle between some of them and turned off his lights.

"Let's hang out here for a few minutes," Arty said, somewhat breathlessly. He looked in his rearview mirror and scanned his surroundings.

"Where in the cotton pickin' hell did you learn to drive like that? And what are we doing here?" Chandler yelled.

"Shh. Hold it down. I'm sure we were being followed. It's nothing, man. Really."

"Will you-" Chandler had no opportunity to finish his query.

"Stay here!" Arty demanded.

Arty pulled out something from his computer bag and exited the vehicle. He felt the cold embrace of old man winter and surveyed the lot. Chandler stayed in as directed. After a couple of minutes of doing 360 degree inspections with binoculars, Arty got back in, put them away and engaged the car's transmission.

Chandler would have no part of it and grabbed Arty's right hand with his left, preventing him from pulling the transmission handle.

"Arty, right now, I'm as confused as a goat on AstroTurf. First, you drive around this little town like James Bond, then you step outside in the cold with some binoculars. What the hell's going on?"

"We were being tailed. I just told you. And it wasn't some state trooper this time!" Arty yelled back while retracting his hand from the transmission handle, releasing Chandler's grip.

"How did you know we were being followed, and where did you learn to drive like that, and what good are those binoculars at night?" Chandler unleashed a barrage of questions.

"OK. Listen. Let's just get going. We're gonna be late." Arty reached to engage the transmission again.

Chandler attempted to grab his hand, except this time Arty caught him near the wrist and twisted back and clockwise, causing discomfort.

Chandler screamed, instinctively using his right hand to pull the left away from Arty. "Hey! That hurts. What the mothershit are you doing?"

Arty released his hand and looked down, cursing in Spanish. Chandler would be unlikely to let this subject go and they had just gotten started on the project. Arty needed to give him an explanation, though as Chandler would learn, Arty had misrepresented himself.

Arty started the car to warm the interior. The windows had significant fog on them. He needed to clear the fog off his identity. "I need to tell you something."

After being awarded the scholarship to Universidad de Santa María La Antigua (USMA) in Panama City, a condition of his continued enrollment was that he work for Panamanian intelligence post-graduation. After the Torrijos-Carter accord turning over the canal to Panamanian authorities after 1999, the government of Panama realized they would have a greater responsibility for Canal security and their nation's. U.S. authorities were also very cognizant of an emerging drug trade, particularly after the death of General Torrijos in 1981.

They sent Arty to journalism school at USC as part of his cover, thereafter receiving intelligence training in Langley, Virginia. Fully versed as an intelligence operative, he went to work for a national TV network in Panama City as a special correspondent in the War on Drugs. He always seemed to have the latest scoop by being present for several large-scale drug busts in Panama and other South American countries.

In reality, he worked for joint operations of the CIA and Panamanian intelligence. His work incorporated a significant propaganda component since they displayed busted drug runners or lords in humiliating positions during live broadcasts, often made to look like captured animals.

The CIA, who employed journalists for more than half a century, convinced the Panamanian government to use them. Recruited journalists were not "spies" in the conventional sense of the word. "Spies" were usually foreign nationals enlisted by the CIA to acquire secrets from foreign governments. The journalists instead served as conduits for information from foreign nationals, or in the case of the drug wars, informants who received compensation to rat out drug lords. The journalist might even pass along a piece of misinformation to a local who would then transmit it as truth throughout the criminal enterprise. Misinformation had value in identifying the key players in the drug trade. Journalists easily served this role, given that they were often accorded access to people and places that a mere mortal would not. The journalists were given their assignments from station chiefs. In Arty's case, he received instructions from chiefs in Panama City and Langley, Virginia.

Arty left Panama, still an intelligence operative, to work in New York City for another network, once again covering the drug wars, this time on the Mexican border. In New York, he met his wife, Ynez, where they raised two children in the Yonkers area. The work became too difficult to bear. Seeing headless bodies hung from overpasses and being away from his family for large stretches made him realize his days as an undercover intelligence operative needed to end. His wife tired of his disappearances. Arty found it difficult to craft believable stories concerning his whereabouts. She suspected another woman had encroached upon their lives.

He told his agency handlers in Panama and the U.S. that he wanted out. They weren't exactly crazy about this since he remained a source of great intelligence for them. So they came up with an alternate plan; he would become an independent film producer with a focus on domestic terrorism.

"Yeah, man. I just got disillusioned with the whole War on Drugs shit. We weren't making any progress. I'd still see the drugs everywhere, and people, innocent people, were dying. The lies I had to keep telling Ynez made my life real stressful." Arty shed a tear. Confessions of this type did not exist in the intelligence agent playbook. For Chandler, these were not crocodile tears.

"So when you sold that documentary to El Mundo about the Shining Path, you were actually working for the intelligence agencies?"

"Yeah, I mean we were following Shining Path but we were also getting leads on cocaine trafficking. I built up trust with the guerrillas in Peru and Bolivia. I even learned a little of their language, Quechua, to gain more trust with natives down there. The guerillas saw me as someone who could tell their story, objectively. And I did, yet I was feeding information to U.S. and Panamanian authorities about the coca processing mills in the jungles," Arty explained, wiping the moisture from his eyes. The windows inside the car were clear of the earlier fogging. He hoped his catharsis cleared the air.

"Holy shit!" Chandler exclaimed. "So now you work for who exactly?"

"No one. I'm out. I'm on my own now. I mean, working intelligence wrecked my marriage. That's why I started doing this indie film work. I figured I could do that like they asked me to and then get out. That's what I did. I just hope we can reconcile and be a family again. I know it's a long shot."

Chandler knew nothing about intelligence operatives. He'd never met one, and he and Axel never discussed the topic.

"They just let you go?" Chandler asked, still skeptical.

"Yeah," Arty responded, quickly.

Chandler would make a mental note to develop the topic further next time with Axel. "Wow, this explains a few things then. Who do you think was following us?"

"Somebody, obviously, who wants to keep an eye on us.

Maybe I should've paid more attention to the state patrolman," Arty said sarcastically. "To be honest, whoever it was, it wasn't a pro. Too easy to spot. Oh, and it goes without saying that what I just told you stays here in the car."

Chandler agreed to keep the secret. The confession appeared sincere, and he did not want to press him further.

"Ok. Are you gonna let me drive now?" Arty asked, grinning.

"Yeah, let's go. Crockett will wonder where the hell we are."

Their timing proved fruitful. Two men sitting in a high school parking lot at night with the lights off would no doubt attract unnecessary attention. The extracurricular activity in the gym had ended and the fans were filing out.

The men got back on State 20, also known as Broadway Street, and continued over the Snake River to a small building that housed the VFW for their meeting with Crockett and the Honor Brigade. The building looked like an oversized Quonset hut with familiar "VFW" lettering in red above the entry door. A rickety overhang afforded minimal shelter from the elements.

They entered, unsure of what they would find. The hall had laminate wood flooring, producing a hollow sound as the men walked. There were plastic, fold up tables on the sides, though not too close to the structure's curved walls. An elevated stage resided on the far end, ceiling fans overhead and American flags on its flanks. The audience comprised a few men in suits, others in slacks with button-down shirts, with others dressed in fatigues. The just ended VFW portion of the meeting discussed scholarships, trips to honor the fallen, and awards for local law enforcement officers. The hall was in a transition, with some leaving and others arriving for the Honor Brigade segment of the program.

The Bunyanesque Crockett, dressed in jeans and a button-

70

down shirt, ambled to the stage, moving behind the podium, to begin the thirty-minute program. He talked about constitutional law in layman's terms, referred to American Revolutionary War history, and discussed the Nuremberg trials, highlighting what can happen with authoritarian regimes.

Crockett's closing words contained more fervor.

"Gentlemen, we're getting closer to the day, the day our constitutional republic gets destroyed. Don't be fooled. Dictators throughout history have set aside the law during times they claimed a national emergency. It started in '08 when there were all these bailouts. They left people out in the cold and fat cat bankers got fatter. What about when federal troops confiscated some of our members' weapons after Katrina?" He banged the podium, creating microphone distortion.

The last suggestion raised loud applause.

"How many more wars are we going to fight overseas? How much money got spent? Public enemy number one for Homeland Security is no longer Islamic terrorists, it's groups like us!"

More applause followed with cheers. A few chanted Crockett's first name, "Mack."

"Men, freedom is never something we can wrap up all neat and tidy in a package. Our servicemen and women understand this with all their sacrifices. But they also understand that they shouldn't support warrantless searches or other such tyranny. And we sure as hell aren't gonna cooperate if they ever put foreign troops on U.S. soil!"

The crowd combined applause with foot stomping and slaps on the plastic tables.

"We will follow the law and set an example for America, but we must hold our leaders accountable. I want you to remember something very important.   Equity is the basis of civil disobedience. When laws are unjust, people of good conscience stand up to change them. We will wear any consequences of our actions as a badge of honor. We are the Honor Brigade!"

Crockett received a round of applause befitting a rock star. During the interview the day before, he did not have a militant edge like he did addressing this group. Perhaps he needed a certain amount of theater to fuel their passion.

At the end of his speech, he walked around the hall mingling with members. During these exchanges he disclosed that he was being interviewed for a documentary and encouraged other members to speak to Arty and Chandler, who could not film in the VFW hall.

Crockett introduced them to various members. The older members of the Brigade were calmer and more measured in their responses. They were eager to speak, but did not want their identities revealed. Younger members were not so sanguine.

One of them, a bearded man nearly the size of Crockett, asked them if they knew of government's attempt to sniff out more militant members of their group. When neither Arty nor Chandler replied in the affirmative, the bearded man explained.

Given the younger members' penchant for online games, government spies created avatars within gaming communities to spy on his group and recruit informers. Spies had infiltrated their group and taken in some members for questioning. These episodes made future admission reviews to the Honor Brigade more circumspect.

The bearded man, who still did not identify himself, suggested they meet with an organizer of a splinter group at an undisclosed location. He said he could arrange a meeting the following day. The organizer would speak to them on camera, with precautions to conceal their identity.

Arty and Chandler agreed to the meeting the next morning in a now disclosed location, a building next to the VFW hall.

***

The two men drove to the designated location the next morning. No one followed them this time. It was a blustery 20 degrees outside and both were thankful for the hot coffee the waitress gave them in to-go cups at the diner. After waiting in their running vehicle for fifteen minutes, the large bearded man they met the previous night from the VFW hall, dressed in a heavy winter coat, canvas work pants, and a nylon stocking hat opened the door to the building and motioned the men to walk in.

This building stood out for being nondescript. The windowless, two story solid brick building exhibited no identifiable sign of its purpose. In a former life, it could have served as a telephone company central office.

Arty and Chandler stepped out of their vehicle's warm confines, the whipping wind molded the pants around their legs. They followed their contact through a narrow hall and up a set of stairs to a large area on the second floor that had old cubicle walls and office furniture. The smell of residual cigarette smoke permeated the air. The man directed them to sit by a large metallic desk where they settled into worn leather office chairs, fissured from extensive use. Chandler placed the camera on the desk and awaited instructions. The contact exited through a door in front of them on the other side of the desk.

After a couple of minutes, another similarly sized man in a balaclava concealing his face, flannel shirt, and canvas work pants walked through the same door. He held an unfiltered cigarette in one hand and a metallic device the size of a wallet in the other. The man made no initial eye contact, sat opposite of them, and

73

placed the device on the desk's surface. He pulled a microphone from his shirt pocket and placed his still lit cigarette on the table, connecting the microphone to the metallic device. He greeted the two with an altered, low-pitched voice revealing the purpose of the metallic device, a voice changer.

"Good morning, gentlemen. Sorry for all the precautions. Can't be too careful these days," the man said, pulling out a Kimber 45 pistol from his pants and placing it on the table. The Kimber 45 intimidated Chandler while Arty proved immune to the arms display. The mystery man grabbed his cigarette from the table, rolling it between his index finger and thumb. His dark eyes peered out of the balaclava towards Arty. "Please set up your camera."

Arty rose from the squeaky, dilapidated chair and set up the camera on a tripod, after which time he nodded to Chandler to begin the interview.

"You're taking precautions to conceal your identity, which is understandable. Tell us why you don't see eye-to-eye with the Honor Brigade, though ostensibly you are part of that group," Chandler began.

The man hollowed out his cheeks and took a long drag before puckering his lips and exhaling towards the ceiling. "Don't get me wrong. We respect the hell out of them. I shouldn't say 'them' since I am part of the Brigade. We just think people like Crockett are being naive thinking that government is just going to let them do all this prepping. Government can't stand some group like the Brigade telling people to prepare because government can't protect them. The other thing is, our kind, we're more tech savvy than most of the Brigade members," the man replied, the gray smoke still exiting his mouth and nostrils.

"What makes your team or group more tech savvy?" Chandler

inquired.

"We've created a bazaar on the Dark Net where everyone plays out their lives entirely away from the eyes of government. No more cumbersome FSB forms or all this reporting crap. We have our own search engine and we use Rot," the man said emphatically, extinguishing his cigarette on the floor with his boot heel, exhaling another cloud towards the ceiling.

Reperio enjoyed the broadest usage of any web search engine. Civil liberty advocates claimed that search requests and results were being reported by the eponymously named company to Homeland Security. Though the company denied the allegation, organizations like this Honor Brigade splinter group were loath to use the product. Axel Schultz, for one, did not conduct online searches with Reperio and had warned Chandler about using the application for all but very basic searches. Rot, the universal anonymizer for doing Dark Net searches, attempted to conceal an individual's Internet activity. Rot was the next generation anonymizer after government computer scientists compromised Tor.

"Couldn't the government spooks just shut down your bazaar?" Chandler asked.

The man reached for another cigarette from his shirt pocket before abruptly stopping and shaking his head. "Let me put it to you this way. It's not as if there's some centralized, online store that anyone's managing. That's the beauty of what technology's done by decentralizing everything. The 'spooks', as you call them, would have to find every bazaar user and shut them down. Good luck with that." He decided against the smoke.

"Is your group organized regionally, nationally, internationally?"

"We're really not organized in the sense you may think. Some of us belong to groups like the Honor Brigade, and others are independent. We have contact with secession groups in Catalonia, Scotland, and Canada. We share a common philosophy. If things get bad enough, many of us will move to a country, don't ask me which one. Some will stay in North America and hide out, maybe in the wilderness. There's lots of land in the U.S. and Canada."

For members that did not leave the country, they sought to create smaller geographical networks for self-reliance. That smaller structure would produce whatever they needed for survival, and perhaps some amenities beyond that. These smaller, local arrangements would cut government's regulatory prowess.

Arty raised his head from behind the camera. "How are you going to keep people out of that mystery country once the cat is out of the bag?"

The man turned his attention away from Chandler towards Arty, as if annoyed by the question. "Listen, man. We hope to privatize everything. Anyone would be welcome as long as they could pay for their residence and not expect to rely on others for their welfare. You understand?"

Arty nodded in concurrence.

Chandler continued with his question stream. "So if you hide out somewhere, that will be the end of all Dark Net communication, right?"

"Yeah, we know that some of our communications can be cut off easily but we have some smart hackers that can get into satellites and other systems. Plus, we can generate power too. So you are right in what you say. We'll be temporarily disrupted but not cut off. Even if they cut us off, our self-sustaining communities will get us back to basics, if you know what I mean?"

"Any concerns about government agents just coming after

you guys and taking you into custody?" Chandler inquired.

"Let them try. For several years now, we've been buying weapons on the Dark Web." The man tapped on the Kimber laying on the table. "Our suppliers send them in separate components over many shipments with parts hidden within other things you might not expect. Then we put it all together. Many of our members have 3D printers, so we can make weapons that way. Some of our suppliers even use what they call dead drops."

"What's a dead drop?" Chandler asked, imagining someone getting "dropped" by a bullet.

"A dead drop is where we buy something from the Dark Net and then the supplier leaves part or all of it in a public area. They could disguise it as a shrub or dog crap, or even a dead animal. Sometimes we'll actually have to open up a dead animal where they've hidden something inside. Not the most fun thing to do, let me tell you, although for our hunting members, it's no big deal."

The transaction remained unclear in Chandler's mind. "So how do find the dead drop?" Arty covered his mouth, concealing his giggle.

The man rotated his left arm, revealing a large watch face below his palm. "GPS coordinates. The supplier sends us a secure message and tells us where to find stuff. Sort of like an electronic treasure hunt, if you know what I mean?"

"And all payment in DigiNote or something similar?" Chandler presumed they were using the digital currency that was a thorn in the side of the FSB.

"Yeah, mostly DigiNote. We have others too. That's all I'll say."

"I noticed you took out a gun. Do you carry that with you all the time?" Chandler asked, still leery of a weapon lying a few feet from him.

The man laughed. "Hell, yeah! That ain't all of it either. Most of us carry AR15 rifles, lots of ammo, knives, gas masks, water purification tablets, ready to eat meals, first aid kits, anything we might need for an encounter. We carry this stuff in a bug out bag, you know for when the shit hits the fan."

"An encounter? When the shit hits the fan?" Chandler inquired. The metaphor of excrement contacting whirling blades could mean different things to different people. He needed clarity.

"You know what I mean. That's just what we carry. There are safe spots where we can ride out the storm where we have enough to keep us going for a few years. Then after the dust settles, we can put together our little communities," the man said assuredly.

Not getting the desired clarity and with no facial clues in evidence because of the man's balaclava, Chandler moved on to his next question. "Won't government surveillance find these safe spots?"

"Our groups have bought MANPADs on the Dark Net and with those, we can take down spy drones or other sorts of aircraft." He referred to a man-portable air defense system.

"But you don't envision, I mean, you don't see yourself having to fight the U.S. military, do you?"

"Hey look, we're just one group looking to ride this thing out. There are others out there, trust me, that are bigger and badder than we are. But yeah, if they come after us, we'll fight. Hopefully, they'll leave us the fuck alone. At the end of this mess that government created, we'd like to make a government the way our Founding Fathers intended it to be."

"When do you think that will be?" Arty blurted.

"Who knows man, but I get the sense that this thing is coming to a head soon. I mean like real damn soon." He took no joy in making this prediction. With that statement, the man in the balaclava and disguised voice concluded the interview with a dual fist smash on the table. "We're done here. Thanks. Thanks guys."

Before he could stand, Arty had one more question. "I have to ask, if I may. Why do this interview? What purpose does it serve?"

He offered a reproachful gaze from behind his facial covering. "You know what? We want people to know what's going on out here, you know? We're tired too. If this helps spread the word and more people join our cause, we might be able to rebuild this thing later. Ok? That's it. I need to go."

He acknowledged both of them with a head nod, gathered his gun and metallic box and headed out the door. Unsure of what to do next, Arty and Chandler sat waiting for instructions.

After a few minutes, their contact from the night before who let them into the building returned, instructing them to gather their gear and wait five minutes before exiting the building. He moved with alacrity, his boots thumping on the tile stairs. Arty and Chandler followed instructions and proceeded with caution down the stairs five minutes later.

After stepping out of the building into the winter elements, Chandler posed an interesting question. "You think the guy in that balaclava is the same guy who let us in the building?"

Arty, fishing the keys from his pants, replied, "I wondered about that myself. Not sure why he would do that. This was a great start for our project though, wouldn't you say?"

"Yeah, they have some ambitious plans," Chandler replied, teeth chattering.

"They do. I'm not sure this is gonna end well for these guys if they start shooting down drones and planes."

CHAPTER SIX
DOMESTIC INTRANQUILITY

Satisfied with a successful trip to Idaho, Chandler had a little bounce in his step. The morning after his return to New York, he called Arianne incommunicado during his time away. He didn't know how long she'd stay at her job at State, though he surmised it would not be more than a few months.

Still in bed, he wasted little time after waking up. This time she answered.

"Hey!" Arianne greeted him with an enthusiasm he missed.

"Hi. Arty and I got back last night. Our trip was good too," Chandler said. He hoped the excitement in his voice could lay the foundation for a conversation.

"Good. I guess the weather system didn't affect you guys," she speculated. She did not know his trip itinerary and wondered if the February storm that hit the East Coast impacted their return.

"Yeah, we got in just ahead of it, I guess. Can we talk?" he asked, wiggling his way up the bed's headboard.

"Chan, you know we've been going around in circles. I'm not sure what else I can say."

"We still love each other, so that's the best thing we *can* say. This project won't last forever and who knows, maybe when it gets done, it will open up something new for me."

"It's the word 'maybe' that's the problem. It's not like my parents tell me what to do, but even they're questioning why you're off on another adventure. They have respect for what you do, don't get me wrong. Selfishly, they want their daughter to settle down. That means marriage, kids, a stable life, that kind of

81

thing. My dad is still chafed about our escape out of D.C. last year. I'm sure you can understand that."

"Sure I do. You and I were raised differently, though. My world was a lot smaller than yours. I have a strong need to get out and explore, see things, enrich myself. And I have a responsibility as a journalist, now more than ever," he added, becoming more animated as he finished the sentence.

"Sure, I get it, but haven't you gotten enough of that by now?"

"I guess I still feel like I have to get out of the shadow of my mom's apron," he answered, not literally though he still felt like he needed to prove himself on a professional level. Journalists always wanted to find their career-defining story.

"When you do, call me, but there's no guarantee that I'll answer. Chan, I need to get going, OK?"

"I love you!"

She delayed a couple of seconds before answering. "You too."

He felt good about their brief conversation, although they covered no new ground. In a couple of hours, Axel would come by his apartment to visit with him about his trip and to suggest other avenues for the documentary. In the meantime, he received a text from his mother, Renee, wondering if he'd returned from his latest adventure, which also did not meet her approval. The two most important women in his life were firmly against him.

Axel, punctual as always, arrived with a couple of small paper bags.

"Ax, let me grab your coat. Wait, did you bring me food?" Chandler stowed the coat in the hall closet before getting a more thorough whiff of the food, a welcome fragrance given that he'd eaten nothing for breakfast.

"I figured with you being gone, there probably wasn't

anything decent for me to eat here, so yes, we have lunch," Axel replied. He moved to the kitchen and unpacked sandwiches, chips, and green tea from the bags. "Let's sit down and you can tell me all about your trip out west."

The two sat at the kitchen counter, and devoured their spread.

Hearing about the Honor Brigade excited Axel. He wondered if he could incorporate what he'd learn in a future letter, albeit after Chandler's documentary made it on the air.

Chandler waited to tell Axel about the most disturbing part of the trip, at least for him. After they finished eating, they moved to the living area where Chandler's mood became more serious.

"I wanted to tell you about something that happened." Chandler creased his forehead in preparation.

"Sounds ominous," Axel replied, raising his eyebrows in anticipation.

"It's about Arty." Though he vowed to keep his secret, he felt troubled enough about Arty's past to share it with someone he could trust.

Chandler explained the pursuit, the vehicle maneuvers, and the confession. "What do you think?" He trusted Axel's judgment more than anyone.

Axel leaned back in the sofa, staring up and to the right, rubbing his chin with his right hand. A long pause followed. Axel always thought before he spoke. There were meetings where he would remain silent until the end, at which time he'd unleash a barrage of mental streams that took people by surprise.

"Fascinating. After you introduced me to Arturo, ah Arty, I did a little research on him. The guy did some good work while he was in Panama and then New York. His depth of reporting was amazing. Hell, he gave the impression he almost got killed a couple of times. But you know what I've told you about getting intelligence. It's a hard process that takes time. I confirmed his work with intelligence as he confessed, but I didn't find anything negative about the guy. Some people I talked to wondered how he was able to get the information he covered. It's easy to see why our intelligence agencies would be drawn to him since he checked off the important boxes, one, of course, being language proficiency."

Arty checked the most important box with the continuation of his university studies. He made a Faustian bargain with the intelligence agencies since he knew they were his only path towards an education and escaping the poverty of his upbringing.

"He told me he's out of the intelligence business now and that this documentary work is 100% legit." Chandler made this point, hoping his mentor would challenge him.

"It could very well be. I don't know honestly. I guess you can operate on a trust but verify plan. At this point, focus on getting this documentary finished so you can figure out what you'll do next. I'm sure Ari wants to know." Axel hit the nail on the head. Though no expert on love, he could see how this project affected his relationship with her.

"Tell me about it. I'm not sure what to do right now. We still love each other, yet we're headed in different directions. I doubt she'll be in D.C. much longer and then she'll open a new chapter in her life and I'm afraid I won't be part of it." Chandler had every reason to worry. The allure of the project and his journalistic responsibilities tugged at him.

"I'm not the best person, you know, to talk about relationship issues. Are you kidding? I've been a solo operator for so long that I doubt anyone would have me," Axel laughed, slapping his leg.

"And that doesn't bother you?" Chandler asked pensively,

concerned for his mentor's solitary existence.

"Yeah, sure. But once I quit publishing the letter, my life will change. Who knows, maybe I'll move to your father's country, Argentina. I could see myself living in the Mendoza region, drinking good wine every day." He cleared his throat heavily. "If things get dicey in the States, you never know." Axel had never discussed the finality of his newsletter.

As Axel finished his thought, Chandler's digital assistant, Venus, interrupted the conversation with an announcement. "Breaking news would you like an update?"

"Hmm. Must be important," Chandler whispered to himself. "Yes!"

"Derek Thomas, El Mundo anchor, taken in for questioning by Department of Homeland Security," Venus announced.

"Man, he must have dug up more snakes than he could kill." Chandler speculated, his pupils widened thinking about his former colleague's detention.

"By that, I take it you mean he got into something he shouldn't have?" Axel queried, never 100% sure of Chandler's expressions.

"Yeah, I talked to Michelle Reyes, you know the White House correspondent for El Mundo, the other day and she told me she got called by higher-ups and told not ask certain questions about the FSB during the press conferences in the Briefing Room."

"That's disturbing. This is going into a new phase now," Axel commented, shaking his head. "I think it was Orwell who said, 'The further a society drifts from the truth, the more it will hate those who speak it.' I think you're witnessing this front and center."

That statement alone gave Chandler a jolt. There could be no question what he needed to do.

Axel continued, "We've been talking and I wanted to know if you and Arty could meet me tomorrow, right here is fine, so I can tell you about a lead I got for your film?"

"Crap, I have to wait till tomorrow now, huh?" Chandler asked, despondently.

"Yeah, be patient, grasshopper."

Tomorrow it would be.

***

This time, Chandler had food for his guests. The three men arranged for a mid-morning meeting at Chandler's Manhattan apartment. Axel stayed in a hotel in Newark where he had business the previous night while Arty came from Yonkers.

Chandler proudly served his guests at the kitchen bar, a spread of fresh blueberry muffins, juice and coffee, not that he prepared any of it. A breakfast shop, a block from his apartment, served as caterer. Despite their warm, beckoning steam, Axel inspected the muffins, to Chandler's dismay, and decided he would only eat half of one since he couldn't identify all the ingredients, nor could Chandler name them. Axel had no specific allergies, yet he always needed to understand what he ate. Arty had no such problem and gladly ate two muffins plus the other half of Axel's.

After the meal, they moved to Chandler's living area where Arty and Axel sat next to each other on the sofa. They deployed their laptops on the coffee table. Chandler, who sat in an adjacent chair, felt no digital impairment with Venus nearby.

"Ok guys, let's get down to business. Ax you said that you had something of interest for Mr. Dutari and me," Chandler opened, still charged up from the detention of his former colleague, Derek Thomas of El Mundo.

"Huh, I guess you're ready this morning?" Axel remarked,

sarcastically. "I have some contacts that can arrange for a meeting with a secessionist group that wants to get their message out through a known and trusted vehicle. Chandler, they know of your work last year with the video release prior to the election and you impressed them. It seems my Orwellian quote yesterday lit a fire under you."

"You got my tail up with that one," Chandler replied.

Arty gave Chandler the RCA dog look, the dog version of "huh?"

"Inside joke, I guess." Arty shook off the need for clarification. "Your contacts, and I'm guessing you won't reveal them, aren't they concerned that Chandler's video last year came out through Omni and that he got canned by El Mundo? No offense, Chan, but you took a hit with that video in some circles."

"First of all, you are correct. I'm not revealing the contacts. Second, this group doesn't care that networks viewed him as a rogue. What Chandler covered in the video, and which got noted by presidential candidate John King during the debate, came to fruition. That suggested to them that he did some good investigatory work and wasn't throwing BS out there," Axel replied, casting his expressionless eyes towards Arty.

"OK, so who is this mysterious group?" Arty questioned.

Axel pivoted towards Arty and held up his index finger, pulsating it gently. "There is one stipulation my contact made before I reveal this group's name."

"Just one?" Arty chortled. "I thought you were going to say that I had to sign some non-disclosure agreement or something."

Axel showed no appreciation for the attempted humor. "No, you'd never see anything like that from them. The stipulation is that I travel with Chandler to meet this group."

Arty's levity quickly turned to hostility. He now thrust his very stiff index finger at Axel. "You? But you're not even part of this project. I don't want to pay you too. This is my damn project!" He turned to Chandler. "Sorry, Chandler, I should have said 'our' project. But it's my idea and it's gonna have my name and yours." Still unnerved by the stipulation, he directed his ire towards Axel again, throwing his hands in the air. "Now you're asking me to give up control? *Coño huevón.*"

Chandler did not know that Spanish expression. "I'm guessing you're none too happy with Ax. It's not his first rodeo, you know."

"Sorry, Mr. Dutari. That's the condition and from what I can see, talking to this group would be essential for developing your story. Trust me. I would even go as far to say that this would be the most important group to have in your film. The bottom line is they don't know you, so they don't trust you. They don't trust anyone. Don't take it personally. Since I have a great deal of currency with my contact, they can vouch for me and honestly, if I ever double-crossed my contact, I'd be finished with my newsletter, if that tells you something. I'm taking a risk here. Oh, and you don't have to pay me anything," Axel said, unwaveringly, the muscles in his neck tightening.

Arty looked at Chandler and shook his head. "I don't know about this man. This is weird for me. I've never had anyone else do my work before. It's strange."

"No doubt, but if Ax says something with this much conviction, I don't question him," Chandler shrugged. "Besides, we won't be able to do this without him."

"Yeah, you guys know each other. I haven't known him long. I guess he doesn't trust me," Arty said.

Axel waved his arms like a member of the ground crew bringing a 737 to the gate. "Hey guys, I'm still in the room."

"Sorry man. OK. Listen. How's this going to go down, *Señor Schultz*?" Arty asked, twisting the corner of his mouth, still annoyed at his exclusion.

"We travel to an undisclosed location in Illinois. They haven't told me yet. Then we meet someone who would take us to where we need to go. Apparently, we don't have to worry about lodging or meals."

"To where we need to go? That sounds vague," Chandler said, wrinkling his nose.

"You know that's how these things work. Remember about this time last year and the warehouse?" Axel's comments reminded Chandler about their visit to an abandoned warehouse on 141st St. in New York City. From there, they traveled with a burly man wearing a ski mask in a windowless van to a suburban location where Chandler received his introduction to Phish and Omni via a remote computer connection.

"True, you have a point there," Chandler remarked, nodding his head.

"Huh, well. I guess this can work. I suppose you're good with this Chan?" Arty asked rhetorically.

"Yeah, I'm good. Ax and I have been on an adventure or two before and besides-"

Venus interrupted their skull session, "Breaking news update, activating monitor." Chandler's TV monitor in the living area came to life with local channel NBC4.

We have just received word that the House Judiciary Committee has agreed to move forward with the impeachment vote of President Benjamin Jefferson. Sources inform us that committee chair Javier Castro, Republican from Texas, will hold a brief press conference later today at the Capitol. It is apparent that the foundation laid by IAP

Senator Matt Geringer of Colorado has solidified the committee's position on this matter. The impeachment vote is slated to occur on Thursday, February 25th. We will share more with you as it becomes available.

"That's coming up soon. I should go visit with Geringer. Arty, this could be part of the documentary somehow." Chandler hoped Arty would agree with this point of view, not to mention the fact he could sneak a visit with Arianne.

Arty wagged his finger. "*No señor.* This one's on you. If you want to include some material, fine, but it's on your nickel. I gotta watch my budget."

Axel got up and excused himself from the gathering, shaking hands with both men. "I'll confirm the trip with my contact and make arrangements. Don't get up, I'll let myself out."

As Axel walked toward the door, Arty yelled at him, "Hey! You never told us the name of the group you guys are gonna meet."

Axel looked down, pausing as if troubled to make the revelation. "The group's name is the Five Tribes." He grabbed his coat from the hall closet and walked out.

"Five Tribes? Interesting name," Chandler remarked, a curious wash painting his face.

That would be the least descriptive adjective Chandler would use when talking about this group.

CHAPTER SEVEN
IMPEACHMENT

Chandler's welcome to D.C. did not have the usual fanfare. His roommate remained in California, and he didn't have Arianne to greet him. The apartment felt hollow and so were his emotions. He shared a brief phone conversation with Arianne after his arrival, though nothing of substance came up. He called his old friend, Senator Matt Geringer of Colorado, also known as the father of the Independent American Party. They arranged for Chandler to visit him in his Hart Senate Office Building the next day, hopefully in time to coincide with the impeachment proceeding in the House.

His accommodations did not have the comforts of his New York apartment. He dreaded the queen sofa bed and the lumpiness from its aging springs underneath. The pillow, or lack thereof, yielded another challenge since he'd have to satisfy himself with sofa cushions. That night, Chandler awoke around 3:00am for no apparent reason. Though in a deep sleep, he had the sense that something in his dream unnerved him, though he could not remember what. After rustling around the covers for an hour, he grabbed his e-reader and caught up on material suggested by Axel. After thirty minutes of this, he drifted off and awoke at 8:00am, about an hour later than intended. Venus' absence made him run behind schedule.

After summoning a driver on a rideshare phone application, he arrived at the Hart Building where security pinned a badge on his shirt. Geringer's chief of staff, Molly Sanders, escorted him to the senator's office. They stopped briefly in the lobby so Chandler could admire the massive Mountains & Clouds sculpture bathed by the morning light shining in the atrium. The Mountains stood as a separate structure weighing 39 tons. The Clouds, a mobile structure, hung from the ceiling. The House of Representatives would scale their own mountain in their effort to impeach the president. Molly knocked on the senator's door, opening it slightly, and awaited Geringer's acknowledgment.

Geringer's office sported an enormous oak desk with a credenza behind it. A video monitor and family pictures rested on the credenza while above it hung a picture of the IAP logo, an aggressive looking eagle over a light blue background, wings fully deployed carrying an American flag. An outer blue ring surrounded the eagle with the words "Independent American Party" in gold lettering. Flanking the senator's desk were the flags of the United States and Colorado.

Geringer sported cowboy-rugged, chiseled looks and a considerable mustache. He could have been the Marlboro man, except he didn't smoke. An avid outdoorsman, he felt as comfortable on a horse herding cattle as he did negotiating a double black diamond in Steamboat Springs.

His arrival in Washington as senator coincided with the great financial crisis of 2008. In 2016, he mounted a run for president on the Republican ticket. By the time of the GOP convention in the city of Cleveland, no candidate had enough delegates to secure the nomination. After a contentious battle, Geringer did not receive the nomination. Influential party leaders suggested a run as an independent. Geringer sought something other than a one and done third-party candidacy. That year marked the birth of the Independent American Party, a party focused on becoming a legitimate challenger to the established GOP and Democrats in future races.

Though Geringer lost in the general election, his strong

performance solidified the party's standing and helped them win seats in the 2018 House and Senate races when more voters from the GOP and Democratic parties defected. In 2020, he put the country's needs ahead of his personal ambition when he declined his party's nomination for president. During that time he forged a bond with Chandler and Axel who helped him uncover the Global Financial Union.

Geringer raised his tall, lanky frame from behind the massive desk and greeted Chandler warmly, though a little too sternly for his hand.

"Chandler, it's so good to see you. Gosh, it's been awhile, huh? Please sit."

Chandler grabbed a chair in front of the senator's desk. "Yeah, a few months, anyway."

Geringer settled in his large leather chair. "How's Arianne?"

"Ah, um, maybe we can chat about something else?" Chandler squirmed in his chair. This was not the time or place to have that conversation.

Geringer wrinkled the corners of his mouth and shook his head. "Don't worry. We've all been there at one time in our lives. This too shall pass."

Chandler didn't know if that implied a future with or without her.

The senator directed most of his attention these days towards the impeachment of President Jefferson and the legal challenge to the election freeze. The House Judiciary Committee, under the leadership of Javier Castro, drafted two articles to take the matter to the full House for a vote.

Article One deemed that Malcolm Holloway's nomination be set aside, since the Senate never confirmed him. Article Two centered on the charge of abuse of power for Jefferson's freeze of the election results.

The impeachment would pit the third party members (IAP and TP) and some Republicans against the Democrats who would rally around their party's leader.

Geringer turned on his video monitor, which displayed the feed from the floor of the House and their historic vote.

Before the roll call began, Chandler discussed his documentary. "Matt, I wanted to get your input about that documentary I'm working on with my colleague, Arturo Dutari. I think I mentioned when we spoke earlier that the subject relates to the separatists and secessionists and their movements."

Geringer grew pensive, stroking his long mustache. "Those groups are adding to our nation's malaise. They're totally misguided. Believe me, I know that what Jefferson did was flat wrong, illegal, and a violation of the Constitution. But we have a process and that's what I've spent the last several weeks orchestrating."

Chandler respected Geringer as much as anyone he knew. He'd proven himself a principled public servant, particularly when dropping out of the 2020 campaign. Chandler hoped this documentary would not drive a wedge between them and hoped to have members of government be part of it.

"I agree with you in principle. But, I hope you can respect my role as a journalist too. What I wanted to know is if you had someone I could speak to internally that could provide the federal government's view on these separatist groups? I guess government calls them domestic terrorists these days."

"Interestingly enough, I was talking with someone at DHS the other day who complained about how government might treat these groups. This person might talk to you, but probably as an unnamed source kind of thing," Geringer suggested.

"That could work. I wonder if-"

Geringer interrupted Chandler with a halting hand. "Oh! It looks like the vote is starting."

The two men directed their attention to the monitor on the credenza showing the House of Representatives in session. The American flag hung vertically, stars in the upper left quadrant, underneath the official motto of the United States of America, "In God We Trust." The unofficial motto of the country had been *E pluribus unum*, or "out of many, one" until 1956.

The Speaker Pro Tempore stood on the upper of three stage tiers facing the House membership. Speaker Janice Rossi of the GOP served as the presiding officer of the House. The Speaker had the option of delegating the Pro Tempore title during important debates, of which an impeachment vote qualified. The Speaker delegated this responsibility via the designation of a Speaker Pro Tempore that translated from Latin as "for the time being."

For the time being, the Speaker for the impeachment debate would be GOP Representative Judd Hartman. Representative Hartman had served 12 terms in the House and had a reputation for fairness and equity. During an impeachment debate, it was imperative for Hartman to give members wishing to contribute ample time for deliberation. Representative Hartman would be the moderator of the historic vote on February 25, 2021. The vote would be one of the few ever taken against a president.

Speaker Pro Tempore: "A resolution impeaching President Benjamin Clark Jefferson for high crimes and misdemeanors. The chair will allow debate on the resolution, first recognizing the gentleman from Texas and afterwards, the gentlewoman from California."

Javier Castro: "There is considerable evidence that the president's actions were unconstitutional and he failed to execute our nation's laws. He had no authority to create an entire department, much less appoint and confirm its secretary without proper Senate approval. The president exceeded his constitutional authority in freezing the election results and not allowing the election's resolution in this body of government. Our nation must maintain the abiding principle that no person, Mr. Speaker, no person is above the law, especially not the occupant of the highest office in the land. Thank you, Mr. Speaker."

Speaker Pro Tempore: "I recognize the gentlewoman from California."

Madeleine Turner: "The actions we take today in this body are the true crimes and misdemeanors. This impeachment vote threatens to undermine the substantial work done by our president in rescuing the economy and providing security for our nation. The process set forth by members of the Republican, Independent American, and Theocracy parties is cynical and dangerous. The fact that we debate this issue takes us away from the pressing legislative matters before us. Let it be recorded in history that those bringing these charges against the president will be on the incorrect side of this issue. Thank you, Mr. Speaker."

Speaker Pro Tempore: "I would ask the members that are carrying on conversations to please direct yourselves to the cloakroom for their continuation. Also, please, any member or staff in the chamber should take their seat. Thank you."

The debate continued for several hours. As expected, the Democrats and some Republicans felt strongly that the impeachment vote reflected a disservice to the country. Aligned in opposition were the members of the Theocracy and Independent American parties and most Republicans. Chandler and Geringer enjoyed their time together, occasionally drifting away from the action in the House and discussing family matters.

Speaker Pro Tempore: "The members will now vote on Resolution 934. I will now read the text. Resolved, that Benjamin Clark Jefferson, President of the United States, is impeached for high crimes and misdemeanors, and that the following articles of impeachment be exhibited to the United States Senate: Articles of impeachment exhibited by the House of Representatives of the United States of America in the name of itself and of the people of the United States of America, against Benjamin Clark Jefferson, President of the United States of America, in maintenance and support of its impeachment against him for high crimes and misdemeanors.

"Article One: Unlawful Appointment

"Benjamin Clark Jefferson, President of the United States, at Washington, in the District of Columbia, unmindful of the high duties of his oath of office and of the requirements of the Constitution, that he should take care that the laws be faithfully executed, did unlawfully, in violation of the Constitution and laws of the United States, issued an order in writing for the creation of the Financial Stability Board and appointment and confirmation of Malcolm J. Holloway to Secretary of the

Financial Stability Board without the proper and mandated approval by the United States Senate.

"Article Two: Abuse of Power

"Using the powers of the office of President of the United States, Benjamin Clark Jefferson, in violation of his constitutional oath faithfully to execute the office of President of the United States and, to the best of his ability, preserve, protect, and defend the Constitution of the United States, and in disregard of his constitutional duty to take care that the laws be faithfully executed. This conduct includes the following:

"Wherein no candidate for the office of president in the year 2020 received the constitutionally required number of Electoral College votes and as required by the Constitution to proceed with the election of the President in the House of Representatives, Benjamin Clark Jefferson suspended the results of the presidential election and the process required to complete the election.

"Benjamin Clark Jefferson has undermined the integrity of his office, has brought disrepute on the Presidency, has betrayed his trust as president, and has acted in a manner subversive of the rule of law and justice, to the manifest injury of the people of the United States.

"Wherefore, Benjamin Clark Jefferson, by such conduct, warrants impeachment and trial, and removal from office and disqualification to hold and enjoy any office of honor, trust, or profit under the United States."

The House defeated Article One by a vote of 259-176 and passed Article Two by a vote of 274-161.

Geringer took little time to comment on the results. "Well, I'm not surprised by how this went down. I didn't think Article One would pass. There are still too many Republicans that fear letting go of the FSB now that it's in place. And frankly, Holloway intimidates the hell out of most members. I wonder, though, for the few Democrats that voted on Article Two, what will happen to their political careers for going against Jefferson. Goodbye fund raising for them." Geringer had a good idea about the vote's outcome since he'd been lobbying members very hard for weeks. Republicans, who controlled the House, would align tightly with the IAP and TP members against the Democrats.

"Jefferson got impeached, but now there is another hurdle, getting it through the Senate with the trial," Chandler commented, outlining the next step in removing a sitting president.

"That's going to be hard. Democrats control that body and there are very few third party Senators. I would also bet that a decent number of GOP members will vote against impeachment. Jefferson and the FSB propaganda machine will call them un-American. You know, it's all about 'We Are the Future' now," Geringer said, derisively. "Chandler, it's been real good visiting with you but I'm going to have to get on the phone now as you can imagine." Geringer needed to talk to Senate membership about the impending presidential trial.

"No worries, Matt. Oh, and let me know if you can get that DHS person for an interview."

"Sure. I'll have Molly walk you out," Geringer offered, reaching for his phone.

"I'm good. Thanks. I sure don't envy what you've got ahead with this trial."

Geringer rubbed his face and nodded in agreement.

Chandler left the senator's office and opened his rideshare application on his phone. There were several drivers nearby showing low fares. One would be at his location in five minutes. He waited outside on 2nd Street, tugging his coat collar higher to protect from the cold wind attempting to burrow into his neck. The driver approached in a four-door, shiny black Fiat. Chandler jumped in the back seat. The driver offered a curt greeting, which Chandler returned with a dip of his chin.

The surroundings had a sense of familiarity. The leather, the car smell and the driver made him recall something. He studied the driver further, inspecting his clothes, a dark shirt and khaki pants. A dark coat covered a stack of papers in the front passenger seat. He spied a look in the rear-view mirror, noticing the driver's cinnamon skin and curly black hair.

Then it came to him. This was the driver who rescued him, in a manner of speaking, from his pursuer in the Mall on a warm August evening the previous year. After a conversation with the elusive Habakk by the Lincoln Memorial, he got the sense someone had followed him. He never determined if his fears had any foundation. The driver arrived just in time, in Chandler's mind, to extricate him from a dangerous situation.

"You're that driver. From the Mall last year. You dropped me off at Union Station, remember?"

The driver flit his eyes to the rearview mirror. "Yes, I am. So you know that I am a friend of Habakk's?"

"That's right. Habakk who always just seems to show up and apparently you too. And you're driving for extra money now, or is this your permanent job?"

The driver ignored his question and fixed the steely glitter in his eyes on the mirror. "He has a message for you. The little things he suggested you do will bring increased danger. It doesn't mean you should stop just be situationally aware."

"Oh, so now Habakk thinks I should be as brave as the first man to eat an oyster?"

The trip to Chandler's apartment continued with more questions and no answers from the smiling driver.

When they arrived, the driver had one final comment. "The ride's on me. Have a great day and don't forget what he said."

Chandler stared at the back of his head as if waiting to be told to leave the vehicle. The driver did not respond. Chandler could only see the omnipresent smile in the rearview mirror. Shaking his head, he got out of the car and walked to the apartment, mystified by another encounter with this driver. Besides, there were more pressing matters like his trip the following week to meet the Five Tribes, a group unlike any he'd ever met.

CHAPTER EIGHT
FIVE TRIBES

Chandler took an early Southwest Airlines flight from Reagan to Midway, where a spring thaw did not greet him. Axel did greet him, providing more detail about their meeting with the Five Tribes. Axel, always cautious about revealing too much about his contacts at Omni, gave scant detail during their meeting with Arty. The Five Tribes were advocates of living separate of the established United States of America. Chandler hoped this journey to an undisclosed location would clarify how they would accomplish this feat.

They took US 55 heading south out of Chicago. The March snow, stained with dirt and cinders, formed a range along the shoulder of the interstate.

While driving, Axel activated a switch in his vehicle's dashboard, which caught Chandler's attention.

"What the heck is that?" Chandler inquired, moving his hand towards the switch.

Axel slapped his hand gently. "Don't touch it! That's my device to defeat the ALPR."

Cities used ALPR or Automatic License Plate Reader, an optical character recognition technology, to track vehicle movement. The technology had the ability to store the image of the vehicle, its license plate, or even a photograph of the driver. Law enforcement and others used the technology to create a map of a vehicle's travels. Government authorities warehoused a large database in an unknown location that had innumerable vehicle tracking records. Ostensibly used for tracking crime suspects and domestic terrorists, civil liberty advocates condemned its use as a massive invasion of privacy. Axel's device, presumably legal in some states, projected false images on his plate to confuse the reader.

After the 100 mile ride to Pontiac, they parked at Flo's, a greasy spoon and gas station favored by truck drivers, where they would await their next contact, someone who would identify himself as Blago. The men waited inside their vehicle for half an hour, observing many big rigs pull in and out of the establishment.

The cab portion of an eighteen-wheeler pulled into Flo's parking lot and out came a pudgy, middle-aged man wearing overalls covering a flannel shirt, no coat, a hat bearing an agricultural implement dealer logo with a ponytail sticking out of it, and a long beard. He appeared as if he were looking for someone, which indicated to Axel that this would be their ride. The two got out of the car and took cautious steps toward the man. Axel had been told to expect a bearded foreigner in a truck. Beards and trucks were in ample supply, so the verification would come through hearing the man's voice.

Blago would not be what they expected. His accent sounded a bit like Dracula. "You mohst be Ahxel and Chandlerr."

"Yes, that's right," Axel replied. "Your accent, is it Slavic?"

"Correct. Eee am Serrbian from Vojvodina. Eee drrive you to next location."

"Our next location? You mean you're not taking us all the way there?" Chandler asked.

"Correct. Eee hirred to drrive you only. Eee get call and they tell me they need my trruck but not the containerr. Strrange. They tell me darrken vindows in cab. Perrson pay me with DeegeeNote. Eee like that. Eee know nothing else. Boss perrson give me this scanner. Eee will check your fingerrs. Please come."

The men followed Blago towards the cab. The forward tilt in his gait and his locomotion reminded Chandler of the cartoon character, Shrek. He pulled a small fingerprint scanner from the passenger seat of the cab.

He removed Chandler's glove and placed his index finger on the scanner and then did the same with Axel. He hit another button on the device and after a few seconds it emitted two green flashes. Blago smiled and told the men they could not bring phones or anything with a GPS device. Both men retreated to Axel's car where they emptied their pockets as instructed and grabbed their clothing and the HD camera. Axel had no idea how long they'd be gone though he'd only packed for a couple of days.

Blago traveled in style. The men entered through a side door and were surprised at the area behind the driving compartment. There resided a small kitchen, a table, a couple of bench seats, and a video monitor that would keep them comfortable during their ride to the undisclosed location.

Blago had one more instruction for them, pointing to water bottles and what appeared to be capsules in a small dish. "Plees drink vater on table and take peell. Peell vill not hurrt you."

"Pill? Why?" Axel asked, arms raised at his sides.

"Plees take peell," Blago repeated, once again pointing towards the water and pills in the dish.

Axel and Chandler looked at each other. It became clear Blago would not leave until they complied. They each grabbed a water bottle and downed the pill, a white capsule the size of a large vitamin. Blago reassured them that they should have no concerns. Chandler took no comfort in that, especially after Blago identified himself only as a driver. Neither man had any idea how Blago would verify their pill-swallowing compliance.

Blago encouraged them to eat and make themselves

comfortable. First, he closed the side door serving as their entry to the rear of the cab and then the door separating them from the driving compartment. Chandler and Axel had no view of the outside world, only the satellite broadcast on the monitor. There were no clocks in the cab, though judging from the satellite programming, they traveled for about five hours before coming to a halt. A small bathroom made adult diapers unnecessary.

Blago opened the side door and asked the men to exit. They encountered a desolate road with barren fields covered with small amounts of snow and the leftover harvest. A person wearing a Guy Fawkes mask over a stocking hat waited for them in a dusty, extended cab pickup. The pickup bed had decomposing corn stalks and miscellaneous equipment. Fawkes wore jeans and a flannel shirt under a dark winter jacket. Fawkes artfully waved them over and unlocked the rear door, saying nothing. Chandler expected a blindfold or perhaps another pill, though neither came. The men stowed their gear between them in the back seat.

After a 45-minute ride over a combination of chipseal and dirt roads combined with off-road travel, they arrived via a gravel road at an abandoned grain silo complex next to a field left fallow. The three silos were 20 to 25 feet in height. Next to them were several gas generators and a solar panel array that would get little nourishment from the setting sun.

Fawkes parked by one silo and unlocked the doors. Chandler and Axel didn't move, so Fawkes exited the cab and opened the door, motioning them out with a dip of his head and a wave of the arm. The men grabbed their gear and continued behind Fawkes towards a silo door. He punched a code on the door and waved the men in. The men moved forward with trepidation, Fawkes' frozen smile offering little comfort.

Immediately that door closed behind them and they faced

another in front. Fawkes would not be with them. They were in a compartment that looked like an elevator with no internal control. A few seconds passed before they heard a repeating sequence of three beeps. After several rounds of the annoying sound, they realized they had a problem.

A synthetic voice from above clarified it. "The subject on the left, please remove your NIR lights."

"NIR? What the hell is that?" said a very confused Chandler, jabbing his finger in Axel's arm.

"That would be me," Axel replied, sheepishly.

Whenever Axel left his hometown of Chicago, he often wore clothing or accessories with Near Infrared (NIR) LED lights. The NIR lights worked by overloading light sensors on cameras. Axel wanted to hide from any facial recognition cameras that tracked his whereabouts. Most people would not notice the NIR LEDs and presume the blurry, fuzzy images produced by their cameras suggested a technical malfunction. The technology in this silo did not get fooled.

Axel removed his watch and jacket and stood still. His action produced a single, long beep.

The opened door revealed a living room, kitchen, dining area and a small powder room. The silo bore no resemblance to anything Chandler had ever seen.

The erudite Axel immediately chimed in with detail and mathematical approximation. "I've read about these designs in an architectural magazine I get and I'm guessing the radius of this place to be about 13 feet. We have roughly 530 square feet of nice living space on this level."

"Let's see, we travel all this way, most of it in the back of a truck cab driven by a guy who walks like Shrek, from Vojvodina, we can't see anything, then get driven in a pickup by someone wearing a Guy Fawkes mask and you're calculating the floor space?" Chandler said, dropping his jaw and placing his hands on his hips.

There would be more for Axel to discover. The circular staircase in the middle led to a second level that had two bedrooms and a bathroom. During this exploratory period, nary a word came from anyone other than themselves. The place remained eerily silent save for the low hum of a fan.

They returned to the first floor, where a wall-mounted monitor in the living room came to life. After displaying a blue screen, an image appeared. The men froze in their tracks initially and then approached the monitor cautiously, like humans encountering the first aliens.

The silhouette of a head sitting in an executive style chair staring in the opposite direction of the camera spoke in a voice reminiscent of Professor Stephen Hawking. Slowly more light appeared above the figure, revealing the cleanly shaved bald head of a dark-skinned male.

"Good evening, gentlemen. I would like to welcome you. Please make yourselves at home. There is food and drink in the refrigerator. The tablet on the dining table will control environmental functions, entertainment, and window darkening. The silo is locked electronically. In the event of an emergency, the door will open and you will be escorted to a safe location. Is there anything else I can get to make you comfortable?"

"What sort of emergencies would make the door open?" Chandler not only felt tired of being trapped during this trip, but now had the concern of asphyxiation.

"Please don't worry. You should feel safe here. Trust me," Hawking replied.

"To whom are we speaking?" Axel inquired.

"We will talk at length in the morning. You must be tired. I bid you good night."

They were tired although hunger prevailed as well. The food to which Hawking referred comprised MRE packets of spaghetti and meatballs. Vanilla ice cream from the freezer served as dessert. A water distiller provided ultra-fresh tasting water for making tea, coffee or other unidentified powdered drinks.

After dinner, the men explored the Dark Web via a couple of tablets. They could not access the Surface Web. These tablets had proprietary browsers and search engines that Axel had never seen. Chandler took out his HD camera and filmed inside the silo and took screen shots of the Dark Net sites, particularly those that belonged to the Five Tribes. A Five Tribes web site served as the homepage for both tablets.

Two hours passed while the men browsed the underworld. Satisfied with their web journey, they retreated to the bedrooms where their host provided pajamas and slippers for both, with tailored fits. Their host also provided a Virtual Reality (VR) headset for each. Chandler's prurient mind speculated about the programs on the headset. It had been some time since he enjoyed Arianne's company so anyone could forgive his mental drift.

When he donned the headset, the programs were all of national park adventures. He chose Yellowstone and enjoyed watching the buffalo roam the plains. Old Faithful would be the last memory from his virtual reality escape.

***

The sounds of a waterfall emanating from speakers in their room awakened the men, who had a sound night of sleep. Chandler rubbed his eyes and noticed the VR headset on the small table next to the bed. He surmised that he must have woken up some time in the night and placed it there. After a minute of wakefulness he experienced an unsettling feeling, much like he had recently with a dream he could not remember. Except this time, he remembered.

In his dream, he awakened to see the sun rise well above the horizon and then quickly fall in the eastern sky, to where it appeared as a nautical dawn, or twelve degrees below the horizon. It never rose again after falling. In the sky he observed small fireballs hurtling towards earth. The dream ended as abruptly as it started.

He struggled to understand the dream's meaning, if it even had one, never mind its astronomical impossibility. He thought that maybe he conflated the dream with VR images from the night before. That seemed unlikely, given that he spent his virtual experience in Yellowstone. The feeling, like the one from the dream he didn't recall, remained consistent. Both were unsettling. He would not tell Axel about the nocturnal experience.

He showered in a hi-tech unit with voice control that dispensed water from different angles. A body dryer made the post-shower towel routine almost superfluous. Chandler met Axel on the main level, where the latter prepared coffee and fresh scrambled eggs. Neither remembered eggs in the refrigerator the night before. They combined the eggs with a packet of freeze-dried potatoes and corn beef hash that they mixed with hot water.

An announcement on the living room monitor said they would start promptly at 9:00 am. The monitor indicated a time of 8:00 am. The windows lightened electronically, allowing them to watch the sun rise above the horizon — unlike Chandler's dream. No telling how cold it might have been outside on this early March morning, given the hermetically sealed cylinder in which they found themselves.

Chandler set up the camera on a tripod pointing towards the

monitor and sat next to Axel on the living room sofa awaiting the return of their host. Beginning at 9:00 am they would plumb the depths of the secessionist movement.

The monitor once again revealed the back of a bald, dark-skinned man's head sitting in the executive chair.

Hawking's synthesized voice came alive. "Good morning, gentlemen. I hope you slept well. Mr. Schultz, last night you asked me to identify myself. I pronounce my name 'Kween-kweh'."

The erudite Axel identified the name's origin. "Latin for the number five?" Axel's command of the English language received support from his knowledge of Latin.

"Correct. You may call me this name or just call me Five. In Latin my name is spelled Q U I N Q U E or if Spanish is your pleasure, Chandler, C I N C O."

"Interesting choice of name," Axel said.

"Don't consider this name as applicable to one person. There are several with this name, and we are the leaders of the Five Tribes."

"So there are five leaders then?" Chandler asked, sheepishly.

The host chuckled, albeit strangely with the synthesized voice. His head bobbed away from the camera, stiffly. "Not exactly. Let's use the Latin appellation for now."

"Very good, Quinque. Tell us about the Five Tribes and their beliefs." Chandler had prepared few notes for the interview, so he began with as general a question as he could, refining them as Quinque provided answers. He felt comfortable interviewing in this extemporaneous manner.

These Five Tribes espoused the belief of integrating cultures into a larger culture where everyone lived in peace and tranquility. Represented in the Five Tribes were the five major religions of the world (Hinduism, Buddhism, Islam, Christianity, Judaism), though they honored and respected all religions. They would never attack another's faith. They also used the number five to identify the 4 major races of the world (Caucasian, Mongoloid or Asian, Negroid, Australoid) plus anyone of mixed race.

It featured an inclusive society that believed in small governing units, since technology permitted governance at ever smaller levels. This view of governance proved antithetical to those espousing larger organizational units.

They believed in a panarchic government where territory could very well be non-contiguous. There could be overlapping jurisdictions where you might have two adjacent households belonging to two different panarchic governments. One could belong to the Five Tribes and the other household to another similar governmental style. It would be up to the household to decide which government to join. The Five Tribes would not influence the selection since that infringed on the household's freedom.

This structure represented the ultimate individual freedom, the freedom of political selection. According to the Five Tribes, current forms of government suffocated any semblance of freedom left on Earth.

With the camera rolling, Chandler jotted down questions elicited by Quinque's commentary. "I have to ask. Why are you allowing me to conduct this interview?"

"We don't trust the media. Look at what happened with your former employer, El Mundo. They were acquired by a group of investors with very close ties to the International Relations Council who in turn is tied to the Global Settlement Bank who is closely aligned with all governments. There is more media censorship now. How do you explain the detainment of Derek

111

Thomas by Homeland Security? When Omni released your video last year, and you were fired by El Mundo, we sensed, at least we hoped, that you were one person with integrity, someone who could tell our story objectively. We don't care if most people, or you for that matter, disagree or hate us. Our system may not work for everyone, and that is OK. It is important, however, for everyone to understand our goals. We want to be left alone." Quinque's head remained still, almost lifeless, as if an automaton.

"So how many people know about you?" Chandler asked.

"Good question. We know the Reperio search engine results are manipulated by agencies like the NSA." Quinque referred to the world's most popular search engine. "So if someone searches on Five Tribes, they will not get complete results, if they get any at all. If something does not appear on a screen, the public will think it doesn't exist."

"So you're saying that the government is controlling what we can find on the Surface Web?" Chandler struggled to believe that the public lived in such a filter bubble.

The Surface Web comprised sites with things about which most people cared. That included sports, news, weather, or shopping to name a few. The Deep Web referred to sites not accessible to the web crawlers of search engines. Experts felt that 90% of all web content resided in the Deep Web. To get to a site on the Deep Web, a user had to know a specific address.

The Dark Web or Dark Net represented sites that were also not accessible to web crawlers and only accessible through specialized browsers. Tor was a specialty browser used for Dark Web access. After the government hacked into this browser, enterprising developers released Tor's successor called Rot.

One of the most common uses of the Internet, whether that be the Surface Web or the Dark Net, involved performing a search, looking for something. If you wanted to find out about someone, you performed a web search. If you wanted to know something about a specific topic, you performed a web search. Reperio enjoyed universal acceptance as the world's number one search engine. If something existed on the Surface Web, Reperio found it. Reperio's prescience unnerved many who thought the search engine could read minds. Reperio's ubiquitous usage made it a fertile intelligence ground for governments worldwide.

Quinque stunned Chandler with his revelation about browser manipulation. "Let me give you an example. Everyone saw the presidential debates last year when John King made his allegations against President Jefferson. In fact, Mr. Scott, you discussed King's allegations at length in your video." Chandler acknowledged him with a nod of the head.

Theocracy Party candidate John King accused President Jefferson of hiding the Global Financial Union plan from the American public. The spectacle on live TV turned into a melee among the debate attendees at Washington University in St. Louis. The Secret Service quickly evacuated Jefferson.

"Do you honestly believe that this is something that Jefferson wants out there? Is there a laptop on the table in front of you?" Quinque asked.

"Yes," Chandler answered, moving the laptop closer.

"OK, that device is not like the others you used last night. It has the Reperio browser that most people use. Execute a search on the 2020 presidential debate from Washington University," Quinque commanded, as he slowly moved his head to the right.

Chandler did as suggested, expecting to see the video clip of John King's rant. "Hang on a second." Nothing appeared in the search, so Chandler tried with different terms. "This shouldn't be as hard as putting socks on a rooster. I want the viewers to note

113

that the search proved unsuccessful." Chandler moved the laptop in front of the camera, temporarily blocking Quinque's image to show the failed search.

Quinque rotated his head back towards center and offered a synthesized chortle. "You have some interesting expressions, Mr. Scott. You see my point. Since it doesn't appear in the browser, it's like it never happened. The video is still out there, of course. We know Omni has it, but my point is the average citizen cannot recall it on their computing device. Unless someone downloaded the raw video, the event got discarded in the dustbin of history. There will be other historical revisions along the way. Trust me when I say this. I predict that history texts will be rewritten very soon to inoculate the next generation."

"I never thought about it that way, but you're absolutely right," Chandler said, never having considered how electronic omission could revise history.

"We hope that our interview with you can show people what you just saw now and make them think about other forms of governance. Watching government become more authoritarian and intrusive, especially with the election freeze, was the last straw, frankly. This new level of corruption is primarily due to one reason. Care to guess?"

After thinking about it, Chandler looked at Axel as if waiting for an answer since he had none.

Axel looked down before his eureka moment. "The profusion of laws?" Axel said, raising his index finger.

"Correct again, Mr. Schultz. We argue that the biggest problem with the government is the many laws, rules, and regulations that exist—too many in our opinion. The Roman emperor Tacitus made the same observation about Rome and its corruption. Instead of simplifying, they make everything more complex and inefficient. The name Rube Goldberg comes to mind. Let's not be fooled either. People actually become dependent on complexity. How many people are afraid to start a business or expand it for fear of going afoul of some Financial Stability Board regulation? Then the people who can't find work need support from the State, and they get it. We would suggest that more freedom is the social safety net, not more complexity."

"My sense is that the Five Tribes is a peaceful organization. You said yourself that you want to be left alone, yet I also get the sense that you wouldn't mind torpedoing the government in some way," Chandler speculated.

"Frankly, Mr. Scott, we may not need to do much. Their own complexity will collapse them. Nietzsche had it right when he said, 'that which is about to fall deserves to be pushed.'" Quinque gave a reverberating belly laugh. "We have pushed them a few times."

Quinque revealed that they brought down the International Relations Council (IRC) social media page on Connections, the most popular social media site in the world. People used Connections to create an online network of friendships, file sharing, and instant messaging. With more than a billion and a half users, the site became fertile ground for advertisers who had the ability to achieve the nirvana of target marketing. It also allowed government intelligence agencies to purchase user behavior data that would become a pillar of the domestic surveillance apparatus. What people thought they were using for "free" became a treasure trove of information for marketers and intelligence agencies.

The Five Tribes discovered that the IRC created thousands of fake personas on Connections. These personas, equipped with automated bots, sent connection requests to legitimate users. The

IRC made personas look like interesting, highly attractive people. They built fake profiles that included fictitious families, pictures, interests, and occupations. These fake personas had an association with the IRC home page. These second order connections attracted more people to the IRC page, where they could spread their pro-government and pro-FSB messages. They had also created a page for the FSB's pet slogan, "We Are the Future." This deception by the IRC infuriated the Five Tribes.

The Five Tribes took special pleasure in working with Omni to commandeer several cloud service providers' computing services to crack the passwords of IRC and FSB email accounts. Such a technique allowed them to attempt half a billion password iterations in as little as 30 minutes. They hacked into IRC accounts, revealing more details about the Global Financial Union that embarrassed the Jefferson administration.

Both the IRC and FSB were antithetical to the Tribes' beliefs of decentralization and limited oversight. The Five Tribes considered themselves laissez-faire and the government as socialist.

Exploiting weaknesses in the Internet of Things, they hacked into the Federal Reserve Bank of New York and disrupted appliances, climate control devices and security cameras.

"We know these actions are mostly an annoyance for the State and their apparatus. The State has yet to feel our fury unleashed, though," Quinque boasted.

"What would unleash your fury?" Chandler inquired.

"We watch the political scene in the U.S. carefully. There is much going on now in government. We hope for a satisfactory resolution to the nation's challenges of governance." Quinque did not provide the level of detail Chandler sought.

Chandler correctly sensed that a follow-up question would

bring him no further clarity, so he moved on. "I'm getting off the subject here a bit, but why did our driver, Blago, have us swallow those pills?"

"Please turn off your camera. Please," Quinque requested and Chandler complied.

"The pill served as an RFID tattoo. Stomach acids activated the pill, which served as an authentication token. That token authenticated you when you walked through the first silo door. I wanted to ensure that the people coming into the silo were the same people picked up by your driver. I would ask that you not mention this in your documentary. You may turn on the camera again if you wish."

Chandler activated the camera and continued. "Will the outcome of the impeachment trial of the president matter to you?"

"No, it's too late. The government has made political and economic power one and the same. They gained political power through the language of taxation, conscription and violence. We want to diminish this."

Given this response by Quinque, Chandler revisited an earlier question. "You said earlier that government has not felt your wrath. Is violence in the offing?"

"Not the way you might believe. Today's battlefield is in cyberspace. Clearly we cannot wage a war in the conventional sense against government. We're not stupid. Any secession or separatist group that takes this approach is foolish. Computer code has 20 or 30 bugs per thousand lines. Most apps have 50 to 100 million lines so that creates many opportunities for exploitation, and we have and will continue to succeed."

"Ultimately, what do the Five Tribes want government to do?" Chandler asked.

Quinque paused before answering, gyrating his head slowly from side to side. "What we favor is a broader separation between private companies and government or getting rid of the corporatocracy. Our version of the military would have no global aspirations and would be organized around smaller militias covering non-contiguous territory. We would divest ourselves of government debt. I believe John King of the Theocracy Party called this unlawful debt."

John King served as the Theocracy Party's candidate for president in 2020. Chandler interviewed him prior to the election where King discussed the concept of "unlawful debt" or debt that the American public had not willingly undertaken, mostly resulting from unwanted and undeclared wars. King would later disrupt the last presidential debate after he found out about the Global Financial Union, aggressively attacking President Jefferson on live TV.

"We will introduce sound money, whether that is DigiNote or any other currency with blockchain characteristics." Quinque used the term "blockchain" to refer to a distributed database with an ever-growing list of records protected from unauthorized revision. Blockchain served as the guts of early digital currencies like Bitcoin.

"We have the technology to create electronic wallets and many forms of local currency. With blockchain technology, we can create several currencies, accept payments or manage transactions. Taking this a little further, we'll use blockchain for peer-to-peer selling, such as energy, and not have to rely on large grids. Ours would be an economy of those who can both produce and consume. Last, the number of laws we would have in our panarchic style of government would be a small fraction of what exists today. In many ways, it would return people to a more natural form of living. So you see, we do not need the government or large business enterprises as you know it."

"Simple, yet far-reaching." Axel, who'd been quiet throughout, came to life.

"Correct, sir. Humans are evolutionarily wired towards smaller communities. This incessant pursuit of bigger, whether in government or their material lives, has made people unhappy and emotionally distressed. We've asked government for more and it gives it to us. But it's not working. People are missing out on the social solidarity typical in these smaller communities."

Axel, as usual, distilled the entire interview into a concise observation. "I understand now. Your name, Tribes, provides the very foundation for this organization. At its most fundamental level, humans are meant to be arranged as tribes, which is how society was organized at one stage of our evolutionary history. That said, your tribes are not narrowly defined since they can include anyone."

"You would make a fine member of the Tribes, Mr. Schultz. I would add that we value individualism, though only as it allows us to become part of a group. This is why our groups are so inclusive. Race or religion, candidly, is immaterial to us. We look at the individual. This will allow us to remove all the hypervigilance on racial matters afflicting the country. Given our inclusiveness, we anticipate having a racially diverse community."

Chandler resumed his interview, pleased that Axel contributed. "I agree that Mr. Schultz would be an asset to the Tribes." Chandler smiled at Axel before returning his attention to the video monitor. "How can people become part of the Tribes?"

"I cannot provide a direct answer for this question. I want to leave you with one final thought. Equity is at the heart of civil disobedience. When laws are wrong or unjust and government no longer provides a vehicle for appeal, people of conscience must stand up to change the status quo. I must ask now that we conclude our interview."

Chandler wondered if Quinque wanted the interview to serve as a recruiting tool or to have people think differently about government. He explained how society could function well with overlapping jurisdictions, people living side by side with different governing entities. "Thank you for providing very candid answers to your organizational and governing beliefs. Thank you also for your hospitality."

"You are certainly welcome. Please get your things together and eat and drink something if you wish. There will be someone coming to get you in one hour. Thank you."

With that, the image of Quinque faded and the screen turned off. Axel and Chandler looked at each other with smiles of satisfaction.

***

After taking Quinque's advice and getting something to eat, they packed their gear and awaited their ride. Both continued to marvel at the exquisite interior of the cylinder that had been their home for the last day.

They heard a mechanical noise that created a small vibration, followed by the appearance of their ride, Mr. Guy Fawkes, coming through the door. He bowed and made a sweeping motion with his left arm, directing the men out of the building. The two took one last look inside the silo. In the distance, they could see the same pickup truck that transported them here. It seemed very incongruous to have Mr. Fawkes driving a pickup, although they were grateful to have such a rugged vehicle for the expected terrain.

Once they stepped out of the silo, winter's fury greeted them, wind with snow flurries, in contrast with the perfect environmental conditions in the silo. Chandler glanced back at the cylinders, wondering what or who occupied the other two units. Perhaps Quinque lived in one of them. Despite his curiosity, he would not rush towards the other silos, fearing draconian security measures.

Though they had no idea where they were, the men sensed they traveled along a different route during their return. Their journey took them through previously plowed wheat fields, making the ride considerably more rugged. Chandler and Axel bounced in the back of the truck cab in a similar manner to the mechanical bulls of Chandler's youth in Texas. Only the occasional band of trees interrupted the previously amber fields of grain. Thankfully, they made it to a gravel road where they stopped bucking.

Contrasting the first time when they encountered Mr. Fawkes on the side of a road, they stopped next to a large storage building. Unsure if this represented the end of the road for them, the situation clarified when they saw Blago's cab. Fawkes waited until Blago pulled his truck out of the building and then gave the signal, an artistic wave of the hand, to exit. The men grabbed their gear and walked toward their Serbian driver as Mr. Fawkes sped away.

"Hello. Yourr veesit vahs good?" Blago asked. Blago had the distinct look of someone who'd had a long night of booze.

"Yes, thank you. Should we get in? Do we need to take another pill?" Axel inquired, rhetorically.

"Yes. No peell. You may enterr." Blago proved more helpful this time, grabbing Axel's travel bag.

Chandler and Axel made their way to the back of the cab via

the side door. Blago entered through the driver side and closed the door to the driving compartment. As before, they had no view of the outside. Since they didn't know where they were, they didn't know if their trip back to Pontiac, Illinois, would be five hours or longer. Regardless, they filled their minds with the satisfaction of a job well-done and would have plenty to discuss on the way back. They sat facing each other on the bench seats with the fixed table in between.

"Do you think they can pull this off?" Chandler asked his traveling companion.

"What's interesting is these guys are less apocalyptic than what you told me about the splinter group from the Honor Brigade. Quinque never mentioned a societal breakdown. Either they don't care about that or are naïve. They're so technically sophisticated. So much so that I wonder if their membership and Omni's somehow overlap."

"Would Omni ever tell you if there was overlap?"

"Probably not. There have been times I've asked them certain things and they don't respond. Over the years, I've gotten to understand my limits."

Hours into the journey, the truck behaved erratically, braking suddenly, lurching side to side. While they expected that sort of ride on the terrain with Mr. Fawkes, this startled them.

Blago's voice emerged from speakers in the back compartment. "Please gentlemen, be calm. Slight prroblem."

The cab's soundproofing and lack of outdoor visibility made the jostling in their seats more disconcerting. Both started banging on the barrier separating them from their driver. Chandler felt as if blindfolded on a violent thrill ride.

Blago spoke again. "Sorrry, trruck ahcting strrange. Eee don't know how to feex."

Axel expected a microphone in the compartment and yelled, albeit in a calm voice, hoping to grab their driver's attention. "Do you have a wifi or cellular connection of some sort?"

"No. Eee have satellite."

Axel remained calm. He suspected commands were being sent to the vehicle's operating system. "Blago, see if you can turn off the satellite from your control panel."

"Yes, let me see." A few seconds passed and then he announced, "OK. Eee turn it off."

The truck kept behaving erratically. Chandler and Axel were holding on to whatever they could. They strapped their bodies to the bench seats via lap belts.

Axel had another idea. "Did you plug in any electronic media into the truck's entertainment system recently?"

"Yes, last night ah nice vooman at barr gave me moosic. Vee drrank. Had good time. Eee leesten to music today."

The truck's movements were not improving, and Axel figured it out. "Chandler, this truck's firmware has been hacked and that's why it's acting this way. Best right now to prepare for a crash." For someone facing impending doom, Axel remained exceptionally calm, though focused on what he needed to do to survive.

"Crap, I think this is going to be worse than hugging a rosebush." Chandler's Texas metaphors barely concealed his fear.

"If we get out of this, you'll want to hug a rosebush. Get into a crash position, now!" Axel commanded. His pupils widened in anticipation.

They grabbed cushions, placing them around the table in front of them. Another cushion sat on their lap. If done correctly, they'd assume the position illustrated on safety cards in airplanes.

Seconds later the truck tilted towards the driver side,

temporarily balancing before completing the tip over and sliding a considerable distance. The sickening screech hollowed their breath.

"Ahh! Shit! Axel!" Both men used their arms to squeeze the life out of their legs while remaining in their tucked position. The rasping sound of the cab skidding on the pavement sickened their stomachs. They squished their eyes anticipating a collision and maybe their death. They struck nothing before coming to stop.

Chandler didn't hear the chorus of angels, nor was he blinded by a white light. The interior of their compartment sustained minimal damage. Chandler ended face up looking at Axel who hung from above. Neither sustained head injuries, though each experienced bruising from the seat belt and flying debris.

Chandler unbuckled and helped Axel do the same. Axel got himself safely to the new floor, formerly Chandler's side of their compartment. The next challenge involved opening the door that now sat above them. Chandler exited first, using the table as a step. Axel tossed the gear and coats to Chandler, who laid on the side of the cab by the open door, catching his partner's vertical heaves. The duffel bags containing personal belongings survived, the HD camera did not. Fortunately, Axel stored Chandler's digital media in a separate compartment in his duffel bag for extra protection. Axel then climbed out with a helping hand from his partner.

The men quickly donned their winter gear. The setting sun quickly dissipated any warmth provided by its rays. They saw no other vehicles, just asphalt and desolate fields covered with a thin layer of snow.

They walked to check on Blago; the snow crunched under their steps. Axel got to him first, finding his crumpled body smashed against the windshield, blood from his head wounds pooling on the icy ground. His left arm extended out the driver side window. The big Serb did not wear a seatbelt. Axel grabbed his wrist and shook his head.

***

From the looks of the road, they were not on an interstate or even a regular state road, given the absolute lack of traffic. The truck slid well off the road and, fortunately for them, had struck nothing rigid. Blago's phone, equipped with the latest blend of metallic glass, flew 50 feet from the crash site and did not survive. They were in rural America with no phone to call for help since theirs were in Axel's car in Pontiac, Illinois. They discussed their options with the sun getting low on the horizon and winter asserting itself.

One option had them returning to the overturned cab to shelter. Though they did not smell gasoline, they were fearful of entering the vehicle. Axel planned how they would build a fire if it came to that. They walked back to the truck to acquire any resources they might use for warmth and signaling. They would not require this effort. Lady luck proved to be on their side.

A law enforcement vehicle approached from the Iowa County Sheriff's Department and came to a sudden stop on the shoulder, just ahead of their position. An average sized white male in his mid-thirties walked daintily over the ice on the road's tiny shoulder.

"Are you gentlemen OK?" The male subject sported a dark brown jacket with fur lining the neck area. His unzipped jacket revealed a 9mm holstered on his right side. A sheriff's badge clipped onto his belt.

"Yes. Yes. Just a little banged up is all. Boy, are we glad to see you!" Chandler exclaimed, thrusting his hands in the air. He looked at Axel with a sense of relief.

"What the hell happened here?" the sheriff asked, butting his fists against his hips.

"Hmm. Kind of a long story, but this truck, I believe, was the victim of a firmware hack. It started acting erratically and the driver lost control. We slid off the road and frankly, we're lucky to be alive," Axel explained, using his hands to show the path they took once they slid off the road.

"A hack? Well, it's a miracle neither of you got hurt. That driving compartment looks in bad shape," the sheriff noted, examining the wreckage.

"Sheriff, we didn't all make it." Axel shook his head and motioned for the sheriff to walk closer to the wreckage.

"Is he?" the sheriff asked.

Axel nodded, looking down in disappointment.

"I'm sorry your driver didn't make it. We don't get many rigs passing through on this road." He paused, scanning the wreckage, still trying to make sense of the vehicle's presence on this back road. "Sorry guys, my name is Rob Trotter and I'm the sheriff here in Iowa County. We're a few miles from Marengo and lucky for you guys, I was on my way back to my office. I'll have to identify both of you and the driver. Do you know the driver's name?" he said, looking at Axel.

"No, he just called himself Blago," Chandler answered instead.

"Come over to my vehicle so I can do one of those biometric scans," Sheriff Trotter commanded, curling his gloved fingers.

Trotter walked ahead of the two towards his vehicle, a white, full size SUV.

The U.S. government required all residents to have their fingerprints in a national database. This became the de facto method of identifying everyone. Axel, the staunch Libertarian, was no fan of this, but the government made it impossible to operate a normal life without it. Any interaction with government required this form of identification. They now required even private businesses to know their customers. What was formerly a standard for the financial industry became standard for all in the wake of regulations established by the FSB.

The sheriff pulled a small device out of his passenger seat. He scanned both men's index fingers.

"You guys wait here, please." Sheriff Trotter pointed at the ground beneath their feet.

The sheriff walked towards the wreckage and squatted near the front windshield where Blago lay. He donned surgical gloves and wiped Blago's left index finger with an alcohol pad, placing it on the scanner.

After returning to his vehicle, where Axel and Chandler had turned into icicles, he connected the scanner to an interface in his car. The sheriff confirmed the driver as Goran Blagoyevic, a Serbian immigrant from Vojvodina with residence in Joliet, Illinois. He also confirmed the identities of Axel and Chandler.

"I'm sorry guys, you must be freezing. Why don't you get in the back seat?" Trotter recommended, frustrated with himself for not suggesting it earlier.

"Thank you, Sheriff Trotter. Allow us to retrieve our gear from over there," Axel replied, pointing to their belongings on the far side of the wreckage.

He and Chandler jogged quickly, though cautiously over the frozen terrain, to get their gear and just as swiftly, returned to the warm confines of Sheriff Trotter's vehicle.

Sheriff Trotter called for an ambulance and a tow truck while Chandler and Axel sat in the back seat. Satisfied with the arrangements, Sheriff Trotter began the drive to Marengo. The sun had dipped below the horizon, taking the last of its warmth with it. Its position let Axel know they traveled in a northerly direction.

"I'll take your statements when we get back to the station. Based on who you gentlemen are, I'm curious what you were doing way out here in Iowa," Trotter speculated, his eyes darting between the road and the rearview mirror.

Chandler replied, "We're journalists working on a story. I can fill you in."

They drove about ten miles before arriving in the town of Marengo. Darkness enveloped the town and save for a few streetlights, they could discern little activity. They drove by a small park before pulling into City Hall, where the sheriff checked on the exterior of the building.

"These teenagers around here. I have to drive by this place sometimes to make sure they're behaving," Trotter explained. After a quick drive around the block, they headed south towards the Iowa County Sheriff's office and the adjacent county jail.

Sheriff Trotter's wife had brought him dinner, and fortunately for Chandler and Axel, she prepared enough for Trotter's 350 pound deputy, not yet on duty.

"You guys must be hungry. We can eat something and then you can tell me your story. My wife cooked enough for a family of four, which is usually what my deputy eats by himself. Lucky for you, he's not here yet," Trotter chuckled.

After eating a meal of chicken and dumplings in a small conference room, Trotter took their statements at his work desk. Their statements elicited questions about their interview location and conversation around the secession movements around the country.

"You men are absolutely positive that you had no idea where

these silos were located?" Trotter asked, throwing his head back into his chair.

"Sheriff, as I noted, the driver, Mr. Blagoyevic, insisted that we bring no communication devices or anything with a GPS. We had no view outside of his truck, and remember, we're coming from Pontiac, Illinois. I would imagine there are plenty of silos in the Midwest. The only thing that appears certain is that the silos were located in southern Minnesota, Iowa, or northern Missouri, based on the time we spent in the truck." Axel's analysis provided a target area, albeit a large one.

"I've read about the Five Tribes and the Honor Brigade. We had a fella from the FBI come by my office a few months back warning us about these separatists or whatever they call them these days. I do sympathize with people who are fed up with Washington. I really do. But I have the law to uphold so until someone tells me otherwise, I have to conduct myself as the people who voted for me expect me to." He added that his county voted for the Theocracy Party candidate, John King, last fall.

The sheriff had a difficult time wrapping his arms around the firmware attack on the truck. He'd never been witness to or read about such a thing, lamenting that this would be yet another frontier in the war on crime.

"Sheriff, I suppose there's not a hotel in this town so is it safe to assume we'll be spending the night in jail?" Chandler asked, not sure what to make of that experience.

"Oh yeah, we haven't had lodging here in probably, heck, ten years. Not as many people live in Iowa County now. Jail's empty now, as you can see."

The sheriff pulled out bed clothing from a closet and directed the men to grab a cell. He assured them the cells would remain unlocked.

"My deputy should be here soon. Hopefully, he already ate otherwise he'll be mad at you for taking his supper. He might arrest you for that!" Trotter chuckled.

"Sheriff, may I use your phone to call someone?" Chandler hoped to leave a message for Arianne.

"Certainly. Oh, there's my deputy now! I'll see you men in the morning and we can figure out how to get you to your next destination. Have a good evening." Trotter walked over to his deputy, huddling with him near the door, identifying their overnight visitors.

Chandler called his love, though his attempt went straight to voice mail. No doubt Arianne, not recognizing the Iowa number, ignored the call. At least that is what he hoped. Exhausted from the day's events, Chandler found comfort in the jail cell while Axel shared a few words with the deputy before hitting the hay himself.

***

It proved to be a restless night in Sheriff Trotter's den. Chandler woke up in the middle of it, unsettled once again by his dream, the sun rising and falling quickly with fireballs in the sky. He tried to make sense of it, though the rationale proved elusive. Never one to assign too much meaning to a dream, he questioned whether he should mention it to Axel. He knew Axel had delved into financial astrology once, however dream interpretation was not his ball of wax. Chandler's knowledge of astronomy fell into the novice category.

He experienced his only brush with an astrological phenomenon in August 2017, when he returned to his alma mater in Columbia, Missouri to observe a total solar eclipse. That sun only disappeared for a couple of minutes. The sun of his dream fell quickly, disappearing over the horizon. Dreams played tricks on people. The ancients viewed the passing of the sun through the sky as a sign of its revolution around the earth. That geocentric view of the earth later dissolved with Copernicus's model of the universe. Chandler's dream made little sense even on Pluto where the Sun rose in the western sky and settled in the east.

Chandler and Axel washed their faces and brushed their teeth using toiletries provided for prisoners.

Sheriff Trotter's wife showed up early with biscuits, sausage and coffee, a welcome treat. After breakfast they went over a few more details with Trotter, who remained surprised that a Five Tribes encampment resided not far away from his county. Trotter offered the men a ride to Iowa City, where they could rent a vehicle to make the journey back to Pontiac.

After a forty-minute ride, the sheriff bid them farewell. "You gentlemen have a safe trip home. I may need to call you if I have more questions, though I think I'm gonna refer this to the FBI. Once I receive the toxicology report, I can determine if that driver really got hacked or if he was just drunk."

Axel reasoned with the sheriff. "Sheriff, with all due respect, I don't believe our driver was drunk. He definitely looked tired, but not drunk. If he wanted to kill himself and us, why go through all the maneuvering. It would have been simpler just to crash the vehicle into something. I believe the vehicle's firmware got hacked."

"If you're right, Mr. Schultz, it's definitely going to the FBI cuz I don't have that sort of capability here."

The three shook hands, after which Axel and Chandler grabbed their gear and headed to the rental vehicle facility. The men spoke little on their ride to Pontiac. They were no doubt processing the accident, the interview with Quinque, and for Chandler, the recurring, disturbing dream. He still would not breathe a word of it to Axel.

Two hundred miles later, after arriving at Flo's truck stop, Axel inspected his vehicle around its perimeter and underneath. The incident with Blago made him hypersensitive to danger, not knowing if he and Chandler had been the intended targets.

Chandler wondered if Blago left behind family. If he did, they were spared the misfortune of seeing Blago's crumpled body.

Chandler drove the rental vehicle to a drop-off location close to Axel's condo at Great Lakes Tower, a 70 story building jutting out into Lake Michigan. Axel's 55th floor condo overlooked Navy Pier and on a clear day, you could see the states of Michigan, Wisconsin, and Indiana.

He adorned his living room walls with fine art, much of it purchased in Europe. A fine Italian sofa, two chairs and a marble top coffee table rounded out the living room. One of his two bedrooms served its traditional role, while the other served as an office.

The two men drove to Great Lakes Tower from the rental location and retreated to Axel's exquisitely modern kitchen after arriving. There they debriefed from the events of the previous day.

Axel, sipping hot tea at the granite kitchen counter, explained the accident in the sober manner befitting someone of his intellect. "You know, Chan, something that makes sense to me is that someone may have thought that Blago was connected to the Five Tribes. From all appearances, and from the comments made by Sheriff Trotter, Blago was what he claimed to be, an immigrant truck driver. He didn't fit the profile of someone the Tribes would recruit. They gave him, or someone gave him, a single task, he performed it, got paid and you see what happened. I think he was an innocent victim. There is no way he was a Tribe operative of some sort, not like Mr. Fawkes."

Chandler, sipping his own tea opposite his host, dropped the cup, rattling the dish underneath. "What exactly are you suggesting here? Who? If he was just a truck driver, why take him out?"

"You know how I have that anti-ALPR software so they can't track my car?" Axel reminded him of the precaution on the outbound trip.

"Yeah, the national database and how the authorities are tracking vehicles, yeah, sure."

"So here's a guy who probably has a defined route, maybe a few. Then one day, he drives to, what, somewhere in Iowa? If that's where we think the silo camp was, or maybe Minnesota or Missouri. Then probably stays there overnight. It's outside his normal pattern. I'm sure DHS, the FBI, and other agencies know there's probably some Five Tribes activity in that area, so they make an example out of him, sending a message to the Tribes." Axel had a sound theory, albeit a scary one.

"So what about us? You don't think we were the targets then?" Chandler asked, fearful of other exposure to danger as he continued to develop the documentary.

"Probably not. We were collateral damage. I'm no threat to anyone and even you as a journalist, you can't inflict the damage these groups can. Maybe at some point journalists become a threat to the government. It's not there yet, even after what happened to Derek Thomas."

"As usual Ax, you summarize things concisely and clearly," Chandler added, raising a single eyebrow before completing his thought. "Though disturbingly."

"Look at it this way, there's no reason to take us out in that convoluted way. They could get us anytime, right?" Axel's sardonic smile worried Chandler even more.

"Says the man who can look death in the eye."

"Hey, I've lived a good life. I don't want to sound macabre, but if I die, then I die."

"OK, Captain Doom. I need to call Arturo and set up a meeting with him and make my travel plans. I want to catch a flight out tomorrow. Maybe Ari will return my call this time."

After his brief call with Arturo, he dialed Arianne, who remained incommunicado.

CHAPTER NINE
PRESIDENT GOES ON TRIAL

The nation glued its eyes to the televised action in the nation's capital. After President Jefferson received his impeachment on a single article by the House, the Senate trial began a couple of weeks later. Through an agreement brokered by Colorado IAP Senator Matt Geringer, all participants agreed to complete the trial and render a verdict in one week. The impeachment prosecutors and the president's defense team wanted to avoid a circus.

The nation continued to struggle economically and secession fears were growing. If Jefferson was guilty, the Senate needed to determine that quickly. Likewise, if he was not guilty, expediency should prevail. With only one article to contest, it seemed a reasonable approach. The midnight oil needed burning. Washington and the nation held its collective breath.

Day 1 of the trial comprised formalities required by the Constitution, including the swearing in of all arguants and one hundred senators by the Chief Justice. Each senator walked to the front of the chamber to sign an oath book pledging to perform "impartial justice" on behalf of the American people. House Judiciary Chairman Javier Castro assumed the role of chief prosecutor supported by a team of six Republicans and a single IAP member. The president's team featured prominent D.C. and California attorneys.

The Vice President of the United States lawfully served as the President of the Senate. For this proceeding, it was customary to appoint someone to the position, usually a senior member of the majority party, in this case, the Democrats. Democratic Senator Michael Dean would serve the role of President Pro Tempore, or

President "for the time being."

The trial continued with a presentation of the charges against the president.

President Pro Tempore: "The Articles of Impeachment against Benjamin Clark Jefferson, President of the United States, will proceed. The managers of the House of Representatives are before me and ready to present their case."

Javier Castro: "With the Senate's permission, I will read the Articles of Impeachment. House Resolution 934, resolved that Benjamin Clark Jefferson, President of the United States is impeached for high crimes and misdemeanors. The following Article of Impeachment exhibited by the House of Representatives of the United States of America and the people of the United States of America. In maintenance and support of its impeachment for high crimes and misdemeanors is Article Two. In his conduct while President of the United States and of the best of his ability to preserve, protect, and defend the Constitution and in violation of his constitutional duty to care that the laws be faithfully executed has willfully corrupted and manipulated the electoral process of the United States by suspending the results of the presidential election of the Year of our Lord 2020 and not permitting its lawful resolution in the House and Senate bodies. He has betrayed his trust as president and acted in a manner subversive of the rule of law and justice to the manifest injury of the people of the United States. Wherefore Benjamin Clark Jefferson through his unlawful conduct warrants impeachment and trial and removal from office and disqualification to hold any office of honor or profit under the United States."

Later that day, the parties agreed to a resolution on rules and procedures. The casual observer might conclude that a trivial achievement, though it proved to be important for maintaining their imposed schedule.

Day 2 placed the trial in a one day recess period as both sides presented briefs. The briefs summarized each side's position on the impeachment trial. Each brief stated the facts, evidence, and legal arguments the House managers and the president's legal team would present to the Senate body. The briefs included citations of statutes, case law or rules supporting each side's position.

On Days 3 and 4, both sides presented their case with opening statements and a thorough analysis of the briefs. Partisan rancor surfaced in the Senate as the Republicans, IAP and TP members were vigorous in their support of the prosecution. They pinned their hopes on the first-ever removal of an elected president. Senators in the chamber passed numerous written queries to the Chief Justice, who read them aloud to the House prosecutors and Jefferson's lawyers. This was the manner in which the Senate body would conduct their investigation. They wanted to avoid partisan stain by using the Chief Justice as the Senate body's mouthpiece.

Javier Castro: "The president has conducted himself in a disgraceful manner through the willful, premeditated, and deliberate corruption through a gross abuse of power."

Chief Counsel: "As the president's chief counsel, I am honored to be here today on behalf of the president to address you. I have served this president for over four years and am very proud to serve our country and this president on the floor of the Senate today. I have listened to the impeachment charge against President Jefferson and the president, as the leader of this country, should be afforded latitude in times of national distress. I submit to you that our nation is under great stress. The prosecution is discounting the severity of the nation's economic and financial problems, problems that threaten the State of the Union. These circumstances require unique care. The people of the United States, already affected by the distraction of the impeachment trial, would bristle at the thought of a protracted fight in the House and Senate in electing the next president. There have been numerous legal challenges threatened. The president outlined a plan whereby the election can proceed in the House and Senate after achieving economic stability and domestic security."

After Days 3 and 4, public opinion polls reflected a popular President Jefferson. Despite his executive action, many voters, even those who voted for the GOP nominee, expressed support for his drastic measures. Most, if not all, Senate Democrats would vote to support their president.

On Day 5, House prosecutors interrogated FSB Secretary Malcolm Holloway, National Security Advisor Trent Carter, Federal Reserve Chairwoman Anna Walker, and the Attorney General behind closed doors for hours, with the questioning recorded though not immediately released to the public. Both the prosecution and the defense were in concurrence that cyber terror organizations could use the information revealed during this testimony to disrupt the country further. Freedom of Information Act requests were summarily denied.

On Day 6, each side presented closing arguments within a three-hour time slot.

Chief Counsel: "The House managers have focused on retribution, with partisan ends being most important. Americans understand that the president's actions are unprecedented, and they also know how much he has done for this country. If you believe the president behaved in an irresponsible manner and abused his privilege, then you will vote to remove him from office. But I caution all of you. Taking such an action would invariably accelerate this nation's demise. It is also hard to conceive that our citizens' liberties would be threatened by leaving him in office. To the contrary, derailing the president's plan would threaten everyone in this great nation. We ask that you explore your sensibilities and vote to acquit."

Javier Castro: "If you believe that President Jefferson abused the power of his office and simultaneously vote down the conviction, you raise the most serious question about whether he is subject to the law. A failure to convict will place no boundaries on the Executive branch and take us down the path of the restoration of the divine right of kings. Let us take our rightful place in history on the side of integrity and honor."

With closing arguments completed, the Senate used the rest of Day 6 in a closed-door session, deliberating on the single article of impeachment, with each senator limited to five minutes of speaking time. The IAP and TP members of the Senate had unsuccessfully lobbied to open this process to the public. Day 6 did not conclude until well into the morning.

Given the late night of Day 6, the Chief Justice began Day 7 a little later. On this day, he directed the Senators to gather in open session for the final roll call. A solemn mood prevailed.

Chief Justice: "I will now direct the Senate body to address the question of whether the respondent, Benjamin Clark Jefferson is

139

guilty or not guilty. Please stand when called and cast your vote orally."

Each senator stood when called and uttered "guilty" or "not guilty." When they tallied the vote on Article Two, the charge of abuse of power, 61 senators, including 6 Republicans and 55 Democrats voted not guilty.

Chief Justice: "The Senate, sitting as a court of impeachment, is adjourned."

Without the two-thirds majority, the president received his acquittal on the single charge and would serve the remainder of his term of office, which had yet to be determined. There would be another fight at the Supreme Court on the issue of the election suspension.

Hours after his acquittal, President Jefferson made brief remarks in the East Room, appearing confident yet visibly enervated by the stress of his ordeal.

"My fellow Americans. Today the Senate has fulfilled its constitutional responsibility and brought this trial to a conclusion. Our unnecessary national nightmare has come to a close and we can focus on the salient issues at hand. Tomorrow, I will return to my office, invigorated and ready to work for the American public. Remember, we are the future. Thank you for your patience and God bless the United States of America."

Despite attempts by a throng of reporters to ask questions, the president pivoted neatly on his right foot and walked away from the podium, head down.

The morning following the announcement in the Senate of his acquittal, President Jefferson received an important briefing in the Oval Office from the Office of the Director of National Intelligence (ODNI) and its leader, Gerald Burkemper. This department had a very focused mission: to integrate intelligence activity of various departments including the National Security Agency (NSA), Federal Bureau of Investigation (FBI), Treasury, the Armed Forces, and the Financial Stability Board (FSB), just to name a few. They sought to make the nation more secure through this integration. Ultimately, their office provided timely and objective intelligence to the Executive Branch, department heads, senior military commanders, and Congress.

The intelligence apparatus of the U.S. collected information from six different sources: Signals, Imagery, Measurement & Signature, Human-Source, Open-Source, and Geospatial. For combating the nation's domestic threats, intelligence utilized these sources with the majority being derived from Signals (SIGINT), Human-Source (HUMINT), and Open-Source (OSINT).

An emerging branch of intelligence gathering, Financial Intelligence (FININT), collected financial transactions in order to predict future intentions. Historically FININT centered on tax evasion, money laundering or other such criminal activity. After 9/11, world governments used FININT to track activities of terrorist organizations.

Before an interview last year with the Secretary of the FSB, Malcolm Holloway, Axel told Chandler what he knew about FININT. He noted that there had been unusually high trading activity in the stocks of two airline companies, American and United, in the period up to the 9/11 attacks. No other airlines experienced the same unusual activity.

Refinements in FININT data mining and matching techniques allowed British intelligence to foil a plot to blow up several American Airlines jets flying between the UK and the US in 2006.

The legalities of obtaining financial information were complex, which is why legislators enacted laws in the U.S. and abroad to facilitate its collection. In the absence of laws, the Financial Stability Board merely issued regulations to circumvent a lengthy legislative process in the United States.

In the early days of the development of the FININT discipline, it fell under the auspices of the Office of Terrorism and Financial Analysis. Since the creation of the FSB, they moved the function to the new department. The FSB, besides serving as the nation's financial watchdog, now played a key role as an intelligence gathering organization on equal footing with any other.

ODNI Director Burkemper had a distinguished career in the military retiring in 2000 as a general in the Air Force after 30 years in uniform serving in various intelligence roles. After his retirement, Burkemper served as a consultant to the Department of Defense and the Department of Homeland Security, focusing on matters of domestic terrorism. President Jefferson appointed him to the position in 2018.

While the mood in the White House was more ebullient on this day after the president's acquittal, he faced troubling reports of civil unrest in various cities and increasing activity by separatist movements.

Burkemper met alone with President Jefferson in the Oval Office. They sat across from each other on leather sofas in front of the president's desk. Burkemper dressed conservatively in a dark suit, his dark hair cut military style, graying at the temples. He voted Republican his entire life, although as a former member of the armed services, he respected the office of the president and took his privilege of serving the nation seriously.

After handing the briefing to the president, he allowed Jefferson a few minutes to survey the document.

Burkemper spoke after observing the president with a look of concern. "Mr. President, you will see in our briefing today some of the recent SIGINT compiled by the NSA and the communications intelligence interception. Do you have any questions on this, sir?"

"I know we've been collecting phone conversations for years now and as you know, that is something I constantly have to defend to the public and especially members of Congress from the IAP and TP."

Civil liberty advocates were relentless in their condemnation of this practice.

"Sir, let your constituencies understand that our agencies seldom listen to these conversations in real time. We'll record them and a trained linguist analyzes the data later looking for key words and phrases. As the briefing indicates, they are keying on terms like 'breakup', 'separation', and 'anarchy' to name a few. Our software identifies the conversation and then the linguist interprets it."

"Interesting. Please continue."

"Most of the danger we're seeing right now, sir, seems to be concentrated around this group known as the Five Tribes. Our Open Source Center has compiled a significant amount of OSINT on some of this group's activities. We believe they are growing in strength and have become more insidious through an apparent alliance with Omni. This is not a group to be taken lightly, sir." Burkemper's stentorian tone conveyed certainty.

"Hmm, that's very troubling, Mr. Director. What about that Honor Brigade? Anything new with them?"

"As we discussed in the last briefing, sir, the National Clandestine Service (NCS) is orchestrating an operation where there

143

are several moles within that organization. They're easier to keep track of since they're out in the open. I don't want to minimize their importance. They have their adherents and we believe a splinter group could pose a violent challenge to law enforcement. For the most part, though, since there are many ex-law enforcement and retired military in their ranks, they respect the constitutional process. They're all about taking care of their own with a lot of prepping. That said, they would be a formidable opponent if things turned sour. Sir, please draw your attention once again to the Five Tribes."

"Yes, of course. Tell me more," the president requested, leafing through that portion of the briefing.

Burkemper admitted that the ODNI struggled with learning more about this organization since they were mostly underground. They had difficulty tracking an organization which worked primarily on the Dark Net and made ample use of encryption.

"Mr. President, I could live next to a Five Tribes adherent and not even know. They don't wear anything on their sleeve. They don't advertise. There are no political rallies. The intelligence on them is very thin."

Burkemper's statements unnerved Jefferson. "Shit, Gerald, I thought with all this intelligence gathering, the INT this and that and all the integration, that we had something better than this!"

The president flipped the cover of his briefing binder, bouncing on his lap.

Burkemper did not react to the president's outburst. "Sir, believe me. Our intelligence analysts scour the Dark Net 24 hours a day. We lay traps for them. They're on top of their game. Sir, there is a lead we are pursuing that may provide us more insight. We have an agent who's doing some covert work that could help in this matter. The agent will need more time, however."

The president pivoted the conversation to something with which he had involvement. "Do you think there will be any reaction by them as a result of the acquittal? Anything we should be prepared for?"

"Probably not immediately, sir. That is not their M.O. My guess is they'll be opportunistic and wait for more economic calamity, or cyber terror, or both to make a more definitive move. Troubling for us is that they're working with Omni. Some cyberattacks, like the one at the FSB recently where the email passwords were compromised, had Five Tribes digital fingerprints on it but our analysts agree they had help, probably from Omni, though we can't be certain."

"The Supreme Court will hear oral arguments on the matter of the presidential election freeze in a couple of days. That damn Matt Geringer is a bulldog and won't let this go. These guys have not come to realize the damage they are doing to our country with the impeachment and now this."

"Yes sir. Is there anything else, sir?" Burkemper asked, with an air of deference. Politics were not his thing.

"No, thank you. I'm sorry if I lost my temper earlier. You can imagine the stress I'm under. Thanks. We'll talk again soon, I'm sure." The president stood to shake the Director's hand. On cue, Burkemper stood and reciprocated and walked out of the Oval Office, the president escorting him part of the way.

Jefferson ambled back to his desk, hoisting a picture of his family from the credenza. The picture captured his family on a vacation in Hawaii when his children were young. He replaced the picture and stared at other pictures from his home state of California. Those were simpler, happier times. He yearned for a drive down the Pacific Coast Highway in his convertible.

**

The action remained in Washington, D.C. IAP Senators Matt

Geringer and Alfonso Chancellor, the party's presidential nominee in 2020, continued their plan of thwarting President Jefferson's December 2020 election freeze. The first step of bringing the impeachment vote to the House proved successful after the membership brought the matter to trial in the Senate. The second facet of their effort failed when the Senate acquitted the president of the charge of abuse of power. They understood impeachment would be an uphill battle given the Senate's composition; the Democrats enjoyed an advantage. Few Democrats would vote against the president, thus the slim likelihood of a two-thirds majority required for conviction.

The Supreme Court presented another opportunity. The Court's majority came about through appointment by Democratic presidents, with the last appointee being made by Jefferson shortly after he arrived in office in 2017. The Supreme Court had been absent one justice since the death of conservative Antonin Scalia in February 2016. Jefferson made it a priority to replace the deceased justice immediately after being sworn into office.

The Court had the obligation to interpret the law regardless of political allegiance. Oral arguments before the Court encompassed interpretations to the Constitution or federal law. The court required a minimum of four justices to hear a case. The importance of this case gave the incentive for all nine to be present. This case would test the justices like none other.

The case of Geringer v. United States challenged the constitutionality of Executive Order 14666, where President Benjamin Jefferson froze the 2020 presidential election results when none of the candidates had garnered the required number of Electoral College votes.

President Jefferson invoked his executive privilege in the interest of national security when he felt that an election in the House of

Representatives would be too contentious. The partisanship could also derail the implementation of his financial stability plans as orchestrated by the FSB, given that Congress still had the power to provide funding for the expanding bureaucracy of that department. A House election also carried the risk of distracting the nation to such an extent that it could plunge it into further economic chaos. The ensuing chaos would be a breeding ground for increased domestic terror. There could be no economic recovery without a safe environment in which to conduct business.

The president took a calculated risk with his executive order, knowing that such action would bring an equal and opposite reaction from the other political parties. He considered the opposing reaction the lesser of two evils.

Representing Geringer would be attorney Marissa Carpenter, the older sister of IAP chairman Alex Carpenter. Representing the government would be both the Solicitor General and the Associate Attorney General. The attorneys provided legal briefs to the Court outlining plaintiff and defense positions on the salient points of law. Many constitutional scholars argued that Geringer would win this case before the Court, since there was no legal basis or precedent for the president's action. On the other hand, scholars considered the possibility that the Court feared an existential threat from economic collapse or internal terror. The Jefferson administration had done much to infuse fear in the minds of the highest court in the land. Even they were familiar with the president's Plan for Prosperity and the ever-present slogan, "We Are the Future." They wanted to be part of this future.

On a brisk St. Patrick's Day in the nation's capital, the Court sat for the arguments in this historic case. Despite the Court's agenda, the annual St. Patrick's Day parade continued as planned along Constitution Avenue near the Supreme Court Building. The parade had been a tradition since 1971 and organizers felt the event would be safe from any terror activity. Law enforcement presence would be thick prior to the noon start.

The Supreme Court Building also enjoyed unprecedented levels of security. At 9:55 am the nine justices entered the Courtroom via three entrances behind the Bench. The Chief Justice and two senior associates approached the Bench from the center while the other six split their entry through the other two entrances. The male justices dressed in their traditional black robes, with standard business attire underneath. The female justices wore lace jabots pinned at the throat. Once seated, the Chief Justice occupied the center chair with the rest sitting in order of highest seniority from left to right. The Clerk sat to the left of the Bench while the Marshal, similar in responsibility to a bailiff, sat to the right. Marissa Carpenter, the Solicitor General and the Associate Attorney General, both attired in morning dress, occupied tables facing the Bench.

On March 17, 2021, promptly at 10:00 am, the court sat for a one hour argument. The Court closed the morning argument to the public, the media, and members of the Supreme Court Bar. The Court kept the argument process punctual with warning lights on the lectern from where attorneys presented their arguments. Despite the punctuality, the justices reasoned that more discussion was necessary, thus they convened for an afternoon session as well.

The Court had no set timetable for the decision, though their summer recess began in June. Scholars suggested this decision would take some time given its political and economic implications, yet the uncertainty of the Court's decision created its own problems.

CHAPTER TEN
NEXT PHASE

Used to calling his own shots, Arty had been none too keen about introducing Axel to the documentary effort. Axel's introduction became the second major point of contention between Chandler and him, following the incident when they met the Honor Brigade and Arty revealed his past life.

After speaking with Chandler, Arty could not have been happier with the Quinque interview. While he expressed reservations about being excluded, his post-interview conversation with Chandler allayed his concerns. The near-death escape at the hands of Blago's hacked rig also softened his tone. The two filmmakers now had material from two groups, the Honor Brigade and the Five Tribes, two groups on the government's radar. During Chandler's Five Tribes excursion, Arty received contact from a whistleblower with ties to the intelligence community. The whistleblower alleged that he had information of great interest.

A mild spring thaw descended upon New York, marking the vernal equinox on March 21st. On this day where light equaled dark, Arty hoped that his partner would see eye-to-eye with him on how to approach the next stage of their documentary.

Arty would make the trek on the Hudson line train from Yonkers, mid-morning, to Chandler's Manhattan apartment. He arrived to a post rush-hour crowd at Grand Central Station. As he walked to catch the MTA subway number 7 train, he witnessed protesters clashing with New York's finest. The protester's signs contained the usual messages about election fairness and the president's executive order. By now, everyone knew what

"14666" meant.

During his walk to Chandler's apartment after deboarding the number 3 train, he saw competing protesters on opposite sides of the street. On one side, there were posters of President Jefferson with his face emblazoned on an American flag. Other supporters waved the "We Are the Future" banners. Jefferson hung in effigy on the opposite side. Some held posters decrying Executive Order 14666 with that number stamped on Jefferson's forehead.

Given what he would shortly propose to Chandler, he feared they might be on opposite sides.

As they spoke in Chandler's living room, the men argued about pursuing this lead.

Arty spoke, gesticulating as he passionately outlined the merits of his position. "OK. Listen. This person is supposedly stationed in St. Louis working for the National Geospatial Intelligence Agency."

This agency had responsibility for GEOINT or the analysis and interpretation of security-related activities on the planet. They integrated imagery, imagery intelligence and geospatial information.

Chandler narrowed his eyes in doubt. "So why would someone from that agency be tracking domestic cyber terrorists?"

"It may not be cyber terrorists they're tracking. The contact said they are working at that agency now, but who knows, they may have other information," Arty countered.

Chandler shook his head in disbelief. "I don't know man. Something seems weird here. And they just contacted you out of nowhere by sending you a letter disguised as a sales and marketing brochure?"

"Hey, I have at least *some* reputation as a documentary

150

filmmaker," Arty said, derisively.

Chandler still had reservations about Arty, especially after the incident in Idaho Falls where he revealed his former life. He continued to wonder if Arty held something back.

"Arty, I'm not convinced. How did you tell this mystery person that you would even agree to meet them?

"I was told to go to Riverdale Park, it's along the Hudson not too far from where I live, and leave a bag with unshelled peanuts next to a specific bench."

"Whaaat?" Chandler's formerly narrow eyes widened.

"Look intelligence work requires discretion. You should know this working with Axel, right?" Arty had a point that Chandler could not challenge so he had to come up with a different angle, a change of subject. The incident with Blago and Arianne's reminders about his tilting at windmills surfaced in his mind.

"I think we also have the unresolved matter about my stipend." Arty had not paid Chandler the agreed upon amounts to date. Chandler wasn't ready to go to the outhouse, though like anyone else, he had his bills.

"You're right. I'll wire something to you tomorrow. While you were gone, my ex and I had a fight about money and she threatened to take me to court claiming something about child support, so no worries. I'm on it." Arty didn't mention his personal life often, though Chandler knew the strain his former job caused his family. "OK. Listen. I can go meet this person myself. You just went off on your adventure. Now I'll do mine. Let's take a look at your video."

Arty pulled out his computer from a backpack and placed it on Chandler's coffee table. Chandler inserted the undamaged media from the Blago accident, and the two watched raw footage from the Quinque meeting.

The two discussed more details about how to present the video collected and their own dialog. Arty mentioned how important it would be to have an intelligence insider for the film. Chandler discussed his conversation with Geringer during the impeachment vote and his offer to find someone from the intelligence community to give their side of the story.

"OK, so you made a backup, right?"

"Yeah," Chandler replied, lifting the corner of his mouth.

"Let me take this home and get to work on it. I'll make preparations to check out that whistleblower. Now I just have to make sure I don't get something thrown at me by protesters when I walk back to catch my train."

"Hey, man. Just wear neutral colors from now on." Chandler had a point. The protests groups supporting the president tend to wear red, white and blue colors. "Keep me posted."

The two shook hands and Arty departed.

Chandler called Arianne. He'd only talked to her briefly since his return with a conversation best described as cordial. At least they were still communicating.

"Hey," he said, after sprawling out on the sofa.

"Hi, Chan."

"Glad you answered this time."

"Yeah, sorry. I wanted to let you know that I'll be giving my resignation real soon, maybe another three weeks 'til I give them notice. I've talked to my dad and I don't know what I'll do honestly. But I'm definitely heading back to Winnetka and staying with my parents. You know we've talked about this. Well, it's happening now."

He knew this day would come. "Oh." Chandler said, pensively. "What do you think that means for us?" His hand rubbed his forehead, fearful of the answer.

"Us? I don't know. I'm making a big career change and I'm moving with no plan. I'm in my 30s, I don't know, I saw my life headed in one direction with you and now it's not going that way. What do you want me to say?"

"You're right. I'm coming to D.C. in the next couple of weeks. Maybe we can get together?"

Arianne, on the verge of emotion, ended the call. "Maybe. I have to go. Let's talk later this week, OK?"

"OK, bye. I-"

Arianne hung up with no words of affection. It crushed him. He sensed her slipping away. It had been two years since they met at the White House Correspondents' Dinner, and until the last few weeks, it had been more fulfilling than any relationship he'd ever had.

So why had it become so complicated? He knew the answer.

He needed to get his mind off her. Recalling that it had been several weeks since he'd talked to Geringer, he paid a call to remind him of the DHS contact mentioned the day they watched the impeachment vote in the House.

He dialed, still sprawled on the couch. "Hi Matt!"

"Mr. Scott. How are you? Did you follow the impeachment events in the Senate?"

"A little recap on the news. You probably didn't expect to win there, huh, with the Democrats being able to have the votes?"

"True. That is why the Supreme Court case is so important, although we've got something else if that fails."

The revelation propelled him to sit. "Really?"

"Yes, but I'm not discussing that on the phone. What can I do for you?"

"You mentioned someone who retired from or still works for

DHS that could be a good interview?"

"Oh, yeah. Sorry I haven't gotten back to you. Too many things on my plate. That person won't talk now. They're still at DHS. We both thought it was probably not in their best interest to have that conversation now. Don't forget that the people in the security community are just centerline Americans. They're ordinary people placed in extraordinary circumstances with the expectation of heroic operation. And they have bills to pay and soccer games to attend. Talking to a journalist right now wouldn't be good for them and frankly, they'd be limited as to what they could say. Believe me, I understand their position." Geringer explained in very human terms.

"OK. I understand."

"I wanted to mention, though, that I know someone who retired late last year with whom I was conversing and I think she could be a good candidate."

"Sounds promising. Who is that?"

"Let me send that information to you separately. I really need to go now. Let's stay in touch." Geringer hung up abruptly, not clarifying how he would pass the name.

One method came to Chandler's mind.

A courier service had recently come online in some large U.S. cities. A customer hailed the company with an app that brought a messenger to the premises. The client would hand the messenger something as simple as a written note that the messenger placed in a sealed envelope in front of the client. Intracity and intercity deliveries were offered. A broken seal implied a compromised message. Old technology had its day again by circumventing electronic surveillance. Perhaps that's what the senator had in mind.

Chandler went to his bedroom and stared at the ceiling. Arty still troubled him. Axel told him in a recent conversation the difficulty of an intelligence operative disengaging from their former work. The lifestyle proved intoxicating for some. He didn't know if that was the case with Arty, given his desire to reconnect with his family. Axel advised Chandler not to be overly suspicious, for now; otherwise, it would drive him crazy.

He got restless in bed, doing nothing. His physical conditioning, a perpetual source of consternation for him, lagged, so he headed to his building's fitness center.

The elevator ferried him to a lower floor. A few cardio machines, a deflated exercise ball, and a smattering of very light dumbbells rounded out the equipment. A sign on the door indicated the room was closed for repair. He saw no one performing any repair and the place looked safe enough to at least get on a treadmill. After using his key card, he spied a janitor, dressed in a dark shirt and khaki pants, sweeping in the opposite corner.

Chandler walked towards the janitor, hoping to solve the mystery. "Excuse me, sir. Do you know when they're going to come back and start the work?"

Habakk turned around, offering a cheek-to-cheek grin.

A puzzled Chandler reverted to old expressions and shook his head. "I'm as confused as a goat on AstroTurf. How'd you get in here? You have an access card for the building?" He placed his hands on his hips.

"I saw a help-wanted sign and grabbed a broom," Habakk replied, tongue firmly implanted in cheek. "I can tell by the look on your face that the weight of the world is on your shoulders again. No offense, but you're not Atlas."

"I don't know how it is that you always seem to know what I'm feeling. And just like always, you just show up out of

155

nowhere."

Habakk leaned the broom against the wall. "It's unfortunate this room does not offer a masseuse to loosen you up."

Chandler suspected he would not get answers to his questions, so he relaxed by leaning against a treadmill. "My girlfriend is drifting away, I'm working with someone who deceived me and we're in the middle of this challenge to the presidency. I'm tired, honestly. I wonder whether the country should just go on with things and let Jefferson do what he needs to do. I mean things haven't gotten any worse with all his executive orders and new departments."

"Maybe your standards are too low, Chandler. Perhaps things are not worse. Are you confident they'll improve?"

"Who knows? In this documentary I'm doing, I've seen how some people just don't trust anything. Another group is waiting for everything to fall apart, and others who just want to drop out of society altogether. That can't be healthy."

"They are simply expressing their free will, Chandler."

"Oh, that's what you call it now, huh? And remember what you said about my love life last year? I don't think we're on this journey together." Chandler's face grew more flush as he repositioned his lean on the treadmill.

"There is a famous story about a cabinet meeting in Britain during World War II. France had just capitulated to the Nazis. Churchill outlined the situation in the starkest colors. Britain stood alone. There were many faces of despair during the silence after he spoke. Churchill, sensing some were ready to quit fighting said, 'Gentlemen, I find it rather inspiring.'" Habakk paused to let the historical event sink in. "Chandler, you're doing good things, the little things we talked about on New Year's Day." He placed his right hand on top of his heart. "Be inspired."

Habakk patted him on the shoulder and meandered in his half-moon paces out of the fitness room. He disappeared into the elevator.

Chandler shook his head. *I'm not chasing him.*

CHAPTER ELEVEN
WHISTLEBLOWER

Arty flew solo, literally and figuratively, in his quest to meet the whistleblower. Chandler thought the encounter was a fool's errand. Arty took Southwest Airlines flight 1309 from LaGuardia to Lambert in St. Louis arriving late in the evening and then drove to the western suburb of Wentzville where he checked into a motel. The early spring emissions from the Poplar trees did his sinuses no favors. A powerful dose of an antihistamine aided his sinuses and later his sleep.

The following morning he walked to the cozy Duello Diner next to his lodging. He sat himself.

A friendly, red-haired waitress greeted him, bearing her flawless teeth as she chewed her gum. "Good morning, Sugar. What can I get you?" She placed her hand on her hip and tapped her foot.

He normally had little for breakfast. "Just coffee and that pancake order, the Duello stack, the little stack," Arty replied, simultaneously eyeing the curvy waitress who accentuated her figure by thrusting her hip to the side.

"Sure thing. Hey. You don't look familiar. I know most of my customers this early in the morning," the waitress commented, looking at him askance. Her chewing sped up.

Arty moved his eyes from her nether region to her face, smiling as he answered. "Yeah, I'm a journalist in town covering a story."

She placed her hand on his shoulder. "Well, be careful, Sugar. There's violence in the city and county these days. They even the scare cops in some parts!"

"Thanks for the warning. I think I'll be OK." Arty appreciated the concern, though he lacked no confidence, especially in dealing with rough situations.

Intelligence operative training allowed him to extricate himself from many harrowing situations. During his early development as an operative, he traveled to Israel to receive instruction in Krav Maga, a self-defense system developed for the Israel Defense Forces. This training supplemented earlier instruction received in judo and karate. Though a little older now, a confrontation with Arty would be uncomfortable, especially with his ever-present tactical pen. The pen served as a writing instrument on one end and weapon on the other. The clever design had never prevented him from boarding a flight.

He wolfed his short stack, slurped his coffee and drove quickly to St. John Baptist de la Salle Catholic Church or La Salle as the locals called it. When he arrived for the 7:00 am service, he found very few worshippers in the pews. The small, old structure, built in the mid-1800s, had an understated charm, simple compared to many Catholic churches. Surrounding the interior walls were a series of fourteen pictures representing Jesus' progression from condemnation to his eventual crucifixion and burial. Only a single crucifix hung on the rear wall of the simple altar.

Arty walked to an empty middle row, genuflected, made the sign of the cross, and sat in the middle of the pew. He rotated his body so that he could see in front and behind. The situational awareness habits of a trained intelligence operative never changed. The whistleblower revealed no details about this contact other than to be present at this Mass and receive Christ's body. Presumably the whistleblower knew what Arty looked like.

The priest entered from the sacristy with the altar boy

following. During the short service, the homily featured Paul's letter to the Romans.

"May the God of hope fill you with all joy and peace in believing, so that you may abound in hope by the power of the Holy Spirit," the priest concluded. Despite the divisiveness permeating the nation, he felt it important for everyone to maintain hope.

As the priest prepared the body and blood of Christ, Arty readied himself for communion. He'd received the sacrament while living in Panama.

Arty positioned himself to be the last one to receive communion and approached the altar cautiously, giving furtive glances to others in line, though not the priest. His grandmother insisted he never disrespect God's humble servant.

He inched his way towards the priest, shuffling his feet on the worn ceramic floor.

"The body of Christ." The priest offered the host.

"Amen." Arty looked directly at the sacramental bread.

Unlike the other parishioners, Arty opened his mouth to receive communion, the traditional way he'd learned it as a boy when he went with his grandmother to the *Iglesia Del Carmen* Catholic Church in Panama City, a magnificent church featuring Gothic architecture. La Salle's grandeur paled in comparison.

He made his way back to the pew, casting an eye over the church. Though the service neared its conclusion, there had been no contact with this whistleblower. He suspected the whistleblower duped him into this meeting and considered the possibility of a trap, reasoning that it might be the government trying to use a honey pot technique. He also dreaded an "I told you so" moment with Chandler.

Before kneeling in his pew, he noticed the wafer the priest

placed in his mouth possessed unusual thickness, feeling like a cellulose wrapper. Reaching into his mouth would have made his grandmother roll in her grave. Absolution would have to come later. He reached into his mouth, tugging gently on the wafer now sticking to his tongue. The wafer proved not only thick but rigid. He extracted the strange wafer from his mouth, glanced at his surroundings, and snuck it in his jacket pocket.

When the Mass concluded, the priest reentered the sacristy and the parishioners, most of them elderly, sauntered to the parking lot. Several of them commented on their substitute priest performing the morning Mass. The parish's regular priest, a young man with blond hair, bore no resemblance to the one today sporting salt and pepper hair with cinnamon skin. According to parishioners standing near Arty, this priest didn't look like the guest priests from elsewhere in the St. Louis Archdiocese who had served them in the past.

"And why is he not walking out to talk to us?" an elderly woman asked another.

The ever suspicious Arty walked around the side of the church and saw the back of a man, it appeared to be the priest, enter the passenger side of a black SUV and drive away. He did not know what to make of the man's hasty departure.

He retreated towards his rental vehicle to further examine the communion wafer. Upon further inspection, the cellulose wrapping he felt in his mouth concealed digital media. Arty surveyed his environment once more before grabbing his travel bag and pulling out a media reader attached to a small tablet. The media revealed a series of videos and PDF files. The realization of the priest's connection to the whistleblower hit him in the face.

Given that he'd already checked out of his motel, he didn't have a suitable place to inspect the media. The empty church lot sufficed. He played videos and read PDF files. Overwhelmed by what he saw, he called Chandler and told him they needed to meet the following day in New York City.

***

After Arty and his wife divorced, he bought a foreclosed home in Yonkers, near the Glenwood train station, requiring significant rehab. With his ex-wife and kids still in Yonkers, he wanted to be close to them. After a couple of years of owner-contributed and contract labor, his home overlooking the Hudson turned into a neighborhood gem. If you asked Arty, he'd say the rehab project proved as difficult as anything he'd ever done.

He trained security cameras 360 degrees around his property. Multiple satellite dishes and Internet connections provided him robust connectivity to the rest of the world. He built a studio replete with cameras, monitors, and computers.

Chandler took the Hudson line train to Glenwood, where Arty met him for the short drive back to his home. The men gathered in the remodeled second floor studio where Arty explained the interaction at the church, the unusual communion wafer, and the substitute priest.

"But, of course, that's not the reason I had you come out. Watch this." Arty directed Chandler's attention to a large, wall-mounted monitor where he played the videos provided by the whistleblower.

The video started with a man in a black office chair with a white wall behind them. The lighting in the room appeared to be artificial. No other furniture or electronic equipment appeared in view, just the chair. The man covered his face in a crudely developed latex mask with what appeared to be fake eyes. The whistleblower used voice distortion, commonplace with many of their subjects in the documentary.

162

"I cover my face since I cannot risk that an ocular scan reveal my identity. My apologies for the distorted voice. I hope you understand. I am not creating this video under any coercion. I am a veteran of the intelligence community who is tired of the federal government's abuse of power. There is no way what I'm about to reveal would ever be shown on an American or even any foreign network. You might ask why I don't just release this information myself. Part of my reasoning is the credibility I feel you will bring. A solo operator like me would be unable to simply approach the press in this country. I have no confidence that they would do anything with it. Moreover, I would risk criminal charges if a journalist turned me in. I trust that you will release this to the public and do it justice."

Secret videos were nothing new for Chandler, and probably not for Arty either. Chandler hoped for something more substantive ahead.

"First of all, people share every thought online as if they're having private conversations. The legal system doesn't think so. Social networks in the U.S. are not private, they are considered public spaces so legally the information there is covered under the third party doctrine meaning it is not private. The public thinks the Fourth Amendment protects them from unreasonable search and seizure. Bullshit! This point is very important.

"If you don't believe me, look at the terms of service for the most popular search engine in the world, Reperio, or the most popular social media site, Connections. Most people aren't going to look. I realize that. These companies take your data and sell it to other companies. And guess what? Sometimes the buyers are the government and intelligence agencies. The intelligence agencies are profiling people

163

just by tracking their digital bread crumbs. The intel agencies can tell by looking at your Connections profile what your personality traits are, your IQ, and your emotional stability. They build a profile and identify you as a domestic terror threat or criminal. Feel good about all these free web sites now?"

Arty creased his brow. He understood the implications of these allegations. Chandler harkened back to conversations with Axel and the Quinque interview.

"Intelligence agencies, sponsored elements of the IRC, GSB, and FSB are hacking into unsecure web sites and taking data that is freely volunteered by people. They use this to gather intelligence, for sure, and for punitive reasons too. They target organized crime rings that are active on the web though the expansion of their power is far-reaching into the lives of private citizens."

Chandler spent much of the year 2020 investigating the influence of the International Relations Council (IRC) and the Global Settlement Bank (GSB) on U.S. government policy, yet never dreamed that they were coordinating with intelligence agencies. It came as no surprise that the Financial Stability Board (FSB) involved itself with intelligence gathering given all the financial surveillance they conducted on the economy. The plethora of regulations and reporting requirements suffocated many small businesses. This didn't seem to bother the FSB, which focused their attention on tax revenue and eliminating black market activities. The FSB, IRC, and GSB wanted 100% electronic money that they could track anywhere in the economy.

"Everyone's concerned about their conversations being recorded.

That should be just one of your worries. Law enforcement works with intelligence agencies to use cell phones to form associations between people. If cell phone 'A' is always around 'B', which they know by GPS tracking, then they know the owners of the two phones have an association. I've seen employees of intel agencies spy on wives, husbands and significant others. Pretty sneaky, huh?

"*Let me tell you about another technique. Some of your viewers know the popular sexual encounter application called Eros. In order to sniff out young male secessionists or separatists, the intel agencies created bogus online profiles of women seeking men who identified as Liber, Liber being a Latin adjective for 'free.' Many people thought Liber meant a particular sexual preference, yet it also meant something else in the secessionist community where it meant free of the government. Anyway, they created these profiles with verifiable life histories and digitally altered pictures to make the women look irresistible.*

"*When it came time for the hook-up, the authorities were waiting for the unsuspecting men who were detained for questioning. Depending on the answers to the questions, they were released or detained in reorientation camps. Once word started to spread, Eros users changed their descriptions, eliminating words like 'Patriot', 'Liber', and 'Tribe.'*"

Chandler looked at Arty with amazement. He realized he never understood the depth of intelligence gathering. If he were a single man, or at least more single than he found himself these days with Arianne, he might be a user of Eros. An eager male like him would fall victim to a bogus woman.

"*I mentioned reorientation camps. These camps have been under development for several years, but not because the government*

165

anticipated secession movements. The government thought they'd get a flood of refugees from Central American and Caribbean countries and from the Middle East. They needed a place to put all these people. The camps were built by contractors with design specs provided by the Corps of Engineers, plenty good enough for refugees. They also built pop-up units the size of shipping containers, self-contained with solar panels, showers, toilets. Homeland Security loves the pop-ups since they're very eco-friendly.

"When the secession movements were born, they had another plan for the camps—it had nothing to do with refugees. They bring them in and give them a full medical exam and assess them psychologically. They're assigned a psychological operations (PSYOP) officer who reviews the assessment, focusing on military training and political indoctrination. Someone who is former military gets their attention. So does someone who did any sort of political organizing.

"Compliant detainees immediately begin reeducation training using virtual reality. They get a bunch of patriotic themes and positive vibes about federalism and large government programs, basically indoctrinate them about how good of a caretaker the government is. There's more to this program. I just don't have all the details.

"Everything I've said here today is true. I know you may not believe some of it or maybe all of it. I'm fed up like everyone else. The thing is, I can't rat out the government since I still work for it. I gotta think about my pension. These market crashes and manipulations by the Fed and now the FSB have wrecked my investments. Without my government pension I have nothing, so I hope you understand. Good luck and Godspeed."

The whistleblower got up from his chair and walked toward the camera, his body consuming the shot. The screen went dark.

Arty stopped the video and turned off the monitor, waiting for a reaction. Chandler questioned the veracity of the camp allegation. The whistleblower never claimed he had firsthand evidence. Was this a third party account? Where was the tangible evidence?

Arty directed Chandler's attention to another monitor. "Oh, I wanted to show you something else too. I got an email with an attachment from an unknown address. It didn't get marked as spam. Normally, I'd just delete something like this, but I had a hunch I needed to open it. So I just took precaution by opening it up in my virtual machine."

Arty mitigated the possibility of foul play by creating a virtual machine, or an emulation of a real computer system, and shutting off its access to the Internet. This would allow him to read the file safely.

Arty worked the mouse connected to his computer. "This whistleblower sent another file. I guess he didn't have access to it when I got the first set of files." This file had more detail on the questions used by the PSYOP officer.

Arty suggested there could only be one way to verify the allegations. "We gotta go see it for ourselves, Chan." He forged a smile waiting for a reaction from his partner.

Chandler heard the echoes of his mom and Arianne yelling at him. This was the story of a lifetime, and he never backed away from a challenge. He remained torn. This verification required a great deal of thought. There would be the very significant matter of how they could locate the camp and infiltrate it. The security had to be formidable.

"We're gonna have to have more guts than you can hang on a fence to pull that off, dude," Chandler remarked. "Let me give that some thought. I got my mom and Arianne popping up in my brain right now. Before I forget, I was gonna ask you about something."

Earlier in the day, Chandler had read about an upcoming rally in D.C. called Citizens for Unity. This organization wanted to promote national unity given the tearing fabric of the nation.

"Have you heard about this Citizens for Unity group? It might be good if we covered them, don't you think?" Chandler asked, his mind temporarily off the camp investigation.

"I don't know man, we could probably just get some video from somewhere on that. I'll let you handle that." A forced smile creased Arty's face.

Chandler pushed his eyebrows tightly against his forehead. "Yeah, but don't you want to feel the event? Get in and mingle?"

"I'm good, man, really. Ok. Listen. I'm still a little tired from my trip to St. Louis yesterday. Let me get a nap and then work on editing this whistleblower video. Don't mean to kick you out. But you can think about probing this whistleblower allegation more and figuring out this camp thing."

Chandler's shoulders sagged, hoping for more conversation with his partner. "No worries, I'll let myself out."

"Let me give you a ride, man."

"It's a short walk. I'll be fine."

He didn't ask Arty for a ride back to the Glenwood station, thinking that it would be a great time to ponder the whistleblower's video and the Citizens for Unity rally. As he made it to the station, he marveled at the original Yonkers Power Station that sat next to the railroad. The station, originally built in 1907, supplied electrification for the railroad. He'd need plenty of mental energy to process what he'd heard from the whistleblower, especially the reorientation camps.

Not desiring idle conversation with strangers, he found a

solitary seat in the train's last car. Some riders recognized him, though did not approach. The progression of stops on the Hudson line train funneled passengers in and out from Yonkers, Ludlow, and then Riverdale. As the train approached Spuyten Duyvil Creek near the Inwood Hill Park, he recalled a romantic picnic with Arianne the previous year. Her velvety skin shone in the sun that day and the way the light bore into her deep blue eyes made him feel alive, a day where he was oblivious to the world around them. They were one. That day seemed like it occurred in another lifetime. He feared there'd be no more memories with her.

The sense of longing suggested that he should call her. She answered, telling him of her condo's listing and her short-term status at the State Department. He mentioned coming to D.C. for the Citizens for Unity rally and wondered if she'd join him. With initial hesitation, she agreed, knowing that it could be one of their last times together before she moved back to Winnetka. Reassuringly, she closed the conversation by telling him that the sun had not set on their relationship.

CHAPTER TWELVE
CITIZENS FOR UNITY

In Washington, D.C., throngs of residents and tourists flocked to places like the Tidal Basin, a reservoir between the Potomac River and Washington Channel, to enjoy the cherry blossoms in early April each year. Chandler had hoped to enjoy the nearly 4,000 trees around the basin in a romantic walk with Arianne. He hoped he could still do so, though it would not be at the blossom's peak that occurred a couple of weeks earlier.

Arianne's small condo in Georgetown featured one bedroom and one bathroom in a boutique building built in the 1960s. One could only detect the building's vintage on the outside. A little less than two years ago, he returned from a trip and had the most romantic of weekends with her before departing on another trip to Spain.

He walked up the brick-lined path to the building's main door. The yellow iris flowers were still in the same planter box. Not long ago, he would have just let himself in. Two years earlier, he waited for her to come out to greet him. He'd come full circle awaiting her arrival before they headed to the rally.

She dressed in fitted jeans and a long sleeve, loose fitting, nylon athletic style shirt. She dedicated more time recently to exercise, which Chandler noticed. Her body never lacked for appeal, yet watching her come through the building's main door only heightened his male senses. She greeted him with a long hug. He wasn't sure how long to hold her — she let him know by releasing first. The kiss he hoped for never came.

The streets around the Mall would be closed today for the rally, so they took a cab to the Foggy Bottom Metro stop and rode it to the Capitol South station. Inside the train, a digital board scrolled the very familiar "We Are the Future" slogan and the ten-point Plan for Prosperity (PFP). There were so many people on the train that both had to stand. Chandler held the overhead rail and placed his other arm around her waist. She leaned back affectionately into his body, her familiar scent caressing his nostrils. The train emptied at Capitol South. Apparently, everyone headed to the rally.

On a spectacularly sunny May Day of 2021, the organization called Citizens For Unity (CFU) arranged a rally around the National Mall. D.C. and Capitol police closed many streets—the event fell on Saturday. CFU promoted peaceful dialog regarding the challenges facing the nation. They welcomed all views, including those of separatists. They sought to build a coalition that could then engage in frank discussion with government leaders. CFU, acutely aware of the nation's angst, did not hide the issues from the rally's agenda.

The May Day effort included building a human ring around the Mall at precisely 9:00 am. The four mile ring demonstrated solidarity. The ring would spin around the Mall with attendees moving in and out of the rotation to allow full participation.

The idea for a human ring or chain had recent historical precedent. In 1989, the Baltic Way joined the people of Estonia, Latvia, and Lithuania in calling for their independence from the old Soviet Union. Chandler himself had some experience with human chains in the Catalonian region of Spain. *Via Catalana*, also known as the Catalan Way Towards Independence, had an estimated 1.6 million people forming a 300 mile chain on September 11, 2013. During Chandler's visit to Catalonia in 2019, he witnessed a repeat of the event.

While the Baltic and Catalonian chains were meant to spur

independence, the CFU rally emphasized a unification theme, something the nation sorely lacked.

Chandler correctly assessed the energy of the rally. He took a few pictures and video with his phone. He and Arianne mixed easily with the participants, some of whom recognized Chandler and encouraged him to keep working for the people. Patriotic music blared through loudspeakers placed all over the Mall. There were people holding signs supporting all political parties. The classic "Don't Tread On Me" rattlesnake flags also flew. Others took it further with "Don't Tread On Me" tattoos and Metallica's similarly named song coming from portable speakers.

There were also large banners of the president's "Plan for Prosperity" detailing each of the ten points and the requisite images of the "We Are the Future" slogan. The slogan's images had broadened since the beginning of the year to include more racial diversity, and the family image remained.

More important than the rally's energy, were the sparks exchanged between former lovers. The rally gave them a brief respite from the challenges of their relationship, even if Chandler was working during the event.

At 9:00 am, Chandler and Arianne joined the human ring, locking arms with other participants. They remained in the ring for ten minutes before dropping out. Neither could wipe the smile off their face. They made their way towards the Capitol steps where the invited speakers addressed the rally.

After the human ring had rotated for an hour, CFU lead organizer, Shelley Gray, spoke from the steps at a podium in front of the Capitol.

"Wow! Isn't this amazing? I'd like to thank all of you for making this day possible. This is how we do things in America. We may have our differences and we know how to resolve them, right?"

The crowd cheered. Miss Gray beamed at the adulation.

"A special thanks to my Citizens for Unity organizers who spent the last two months working with the local authorities to make this day possible. And how about a hand for the D.C. and Capitol police?"

The crowd responded with a mixture of polite applause and wild cheering.

Gray's image and voice projected all over the Mall on many video monitors and speakers. The crowd continued to give her strong ovations after her exhortations of unity. After addressing the rally for a few minutes, she introduced the keynote speaker from the CFU who also raised many patriotic themes centered on unity. Another speaker followed who espoused Libertarianism. The Honor Brigade and John King, the former Theocracy Party presidential candidate in 2020, followed with their own renditions of national unity.

Finally, Senator Matt Geringer thanked the crowd for coming and emphasized the importance of working through the constitutional process, highlighting the Supreme Court deliberations on the case of the election freeze.

Chandler and Arianne had positioned themselves within view of the Capitol steps. They had not spent this much time around each other for months. They held hands. Chandler wanted to freeze this moment in time.

Shelley Gray followed with closing comments. "I'd like to thank all of our speakers today and all of you who-"

The ensuing interruption would be one for the history books.

***

For those in the Mall, the ensuing events were surreal.

Before Shelley Gray finished her closing thoughts, the public

173

address system encountered static and the video boards flickered.

Shelley paused momentarily suspecting an audio glitch. She continued to speak for about thirty seconds until she realized people were pointing at the video boards.

The boards revealed the back of a bald, dark-skinned male head, peering over the top of an executive style chair. A small amount of light illuminated the seated figure.

Quinque said nothing at first, allowing the crowd's suspense to build. Chandler, ever the journalist, pulled out his phone and pointed at the nearby video board. The potential energy he expected at this rally would soon turn kinetic.

"Chandler, who is that?" Arianne tugged at his free arm.

"Me explaining that to you will be as difficult as putting socks on a rooster," Chandler said, shaking his head. "Basically, that person, is one of the people I interviewed but it's a lot more complicated than that, trust me."

Chandler panned with his phone camera to capture crowd reaction. It was as if they were in the middle of alien first contact.

The synthesized Stephen Hawking voice came alive.

"Greetings. It is refreshing to see such a fine crowd of citizens here today. Freedom of speech. Freedom of assembly. Isn't it wonderful? But you are no longer free. Every one of you is being watched by cameras and drones overhead. Microphones are all over this mall. Even your Internet is not about freedom. It's too centralized, not like what it was intended to be. My friends, you live in the deepest of Deep State. You can't escape it.

"For years you've been under the control of the Demopublican or Republicratic parties. You think these are two parties, yet really they're one in the same. Sure the third parties are also representing you, yet the Deep State will never allow them in or more likely, they'll

try to convert them.

"The message here today is about unity. The ancient human yearning is for community. We need to connect in smaller communities. The government will say we are secessionists. I ask you to look within and see if you reach the same conclusion. Do your own thinking. This is what we've evolved to become. It is in our genes. Now is the time.

"The corporations and government you know are no longer relevant. Ours is a better way. Peer-to-peer ecosystems will harness your wisdom and create value and govern better than anything you see today. The decentralization revolution is here.

"We, are the real future. We are the Five Tribes."

While Quinque spoke, D.C. and Capitol police chirped into their communication devices, figuring out how to shut down the interloper. Rally participants looked into the sky, searching for drones. Others looked for hidden listening devices. When Quinque finished his oratory, some in the crowd closest to the Capitol steps yelled at Shelley Gray.

Overhead drones dropped leaflets with Five Tribe icons, the Roman numeral "V" next to the Greek letter Tau. Some in the crowd, thinking the leaflets were manna from heaven, rushed to catch them before they hit the ground, knocking over other rally participants.

The crowd hurled objects at the large video screens. Quinque's image remained projected, the Hawking voice silent.

Capitol police grabbed Senator Geringer and other guests near the podium and escorted them away from the ensuing melee. Fights broke out. Police used non-lethal methods to disperse the crowd, including pepper spray and sound cannons. That only incited the crowd.

A large group near some trees by the Capitol steps formed a circle and began praying. Others on the opposite side of the steps sat, enjoying their marijuana joints. Attendees who were not sympathetic to President Jefferson tore down anything mentioning the Plan for Prosperity and its slogan, a slogan just appropriated by the Five Tribes.

Chandler, sensing further danger, grabbed Arianne and ran towards the Capitol South Metro station. Dodging other people, they knocked down a D.C. cop who promptly drew his weapon and ordered them to stop, informing them that they were being detained. He pulled out zip ties to restrain their arms and legs. Chandler played compliant and extended his arms, keeping his forearms together. After his arms and legs got zip tied, the cop restrained Arianne and pushed them both to the ground, telling them to stay put.

Arianne had a look of abject fear. Chandler knew they were in danger sitting there with hands tied. Being stationary in such a kinetic environment would prove hazardous to their health. He needed to quickly get off the "X" as his mentor Axel taught him.

He executed Axel's technique for escaping zip ties, first scanning the area to see if any cops were paying attention to them. He rocked forward to his knees and stood up. He raised his hands high above his head while maintaining forearm contact, his shoulders feeling the strain. Forcefully, he pulled his arms down past his hips and the tie lock came undone, albeit with contusions to his wrists. He reached into his wallet and pulled out a credit card knife, a gift from Axel, and cut his leg ties and then Arianne's. The melee continued around them.

Struggling to regain their breath, the two advanced their escape towards the Metro station, where they promptly discovered a disabled system. His cell phone had no service. He felt the percussion of his heart pounding in his ears. He needed another plan.

Now feeling safer, Arianne's mood flipped to anger. She grabbed the end of his shirtsleeve with both hands, yanking it violently, spinning him towards her. "Damn it, Chan! Here I am again in the middle of one of your fucking adventures. This is what I mean!" She flashed back to their escape from D.C. last Halloween after the release of his Global Financial Union video.

He grabbed her sweaty hand and guided them towards an alternate route. "Here, let's go north along 2nd Street."

She cursed under her breath, holding his hand, trying to match his pace.

Law enforcement had established a secure perimeter around the Capitol, Supreme Court, the Library of Congress and the Hart Senate Office Building. As they passed the latter building, they spied a vehicle headed towards them driven by Senator Geringer. They flagged the car, which slowed to a careful stop.

Chandler rushed towards the vehicle and tapped forcefully on the driver's window.

Geringer lowered it, peering guardedly over the edge. "Chandler, Arianne? What the hell are you two doing here?" The deep bass was absent.

"As usual, it's a long story, senator," Chandler answered. Arianne butted her hands on her hips, hurling considerable scorn his way.

"Do you guys need a ride? I think the Metro's shut down right now," Geringer said, the resonance of his voice more evident now.

"Yes. Please. Back to my condo! It's not safe here," Arianne announced, reaching for the rear door.

Arianne sat with Chandler in the back seat, looking out the

window the entire time, ignoring him and the senator. Chandler gave the senator a field level account of what he saw during the rally.

After the senator dropped them both off at her place, Chandler asked to come inside. She had no interest and spun away. He spied the "For Sale" sign in the window that he missed earlier in the morning. Standing alone and emotionally empty, he summoned a driver via the app on this phone, which had service.

***

He waited for over an hour outside of Arianne's condo, the skies progressively darkening with his mood. The disruption of the CFU rally delayed the appearance of drivers for hire who wanted to gauge the safety of the area before continuing towards Arianne's Georgetown neighborhood.

The driver tried to engage Chandler in conversation about the rally. Chandler gave pithy responses. The driver didn't realize Chandler had been at the epicenter of the rally's disruption.

Rattled by his attendance at the CFU event and despondent about his time with Arianne, Chandler called Axel after arriving at his apartment. He sprawled on the sofa, his feet propped high with the cushion and sofa pillows.

Not one to offer any words of advice regarding the ladies, Axel steered towards the melee at the CFU event. "When I received the news update and saw what was going on, at first I smiled, not because of the ruckus, but because of who appeared to disrupt the event. I had no idea you were there."

"I know you don't want to talk about Ari. That whole thing blew up on me in more ways than one. On the bright side, I got some film that will work well for the documentary. Oh, and believe it or not, Geringer was the one who gave us a ride back to

Arianne's."

"Really?"

"Yeah. That was weird. The other weird thing is that Arty didn't want to go. I can't figure out why either. He didn't have to travel far, and it seemed like a good idea. Arty could not have known about the rally blowing up though," Chandler commented, with hesitation in his voice.

"What are you suggesting?" Axel had told Chandler to stop obsessing about Arty's motives otherwise he'd drive himself crazy.

"It was an easy trip for him to just come from New York and film it rather than me with my cell phone. He wanted no part of it."

"We, or you need to settle this doubt about him once and for all," Axel commanded. "I'm not understanding what you're getting at, to be honest. If you have this problem with Arty, you just need to settle it." Axel had little tolerance for conflicts in professional relationships, such as what he witnessed between Arturo and Chandler.

"Your suggestion, maestro?" Chandler asked sarcastically, waving his hands as if conducting the orchestra.

As usual, Axel had a plan, requesting that he call Arty and demand a face-to-face meeting in D.C. If Arty had a hidden agenda for not wanting to attend the rally or if he knew something, Chandler needed to find out. Axel had been privy to interrogation techniques from a field guide someone passed to him a few years back. He suggested that with both of them at Chandler's place, they would attempt to find out a little more about Arturo Dutari.

Chandler sat up quickly in disbelief. "So your plan is to question a former intelligence agent? What are you thinking? And besides, I'm supposed to keep his past quiet, remember?"

179

"He may not break the way you're thinking Jack Bauer would break down a terrorist on that TV show. We should be able to assess his honesty, though. He may not tell us the whole story, but we might determine if he's being honest. Oh, and as far as me not knowing, I'll take care of that. You need to get past this issue because it's starting to tire me. Hang up and call him and then text me back and let me know when he's coming."

"OK. I'm not gonna ask you if you know what you're doing. I should know by now. Thanks Ax, once again for everything."

Chandler remained skeptical about the usefulness of the meeting. He trusted Axel more than just about anyone. He didn't call Arty right away, instead lying down to take a nap, not something he normally did especially this late in the day. His scrambled brain suggested a break. The cell phone got set with a one hour timer and he attempted to drift off without success. His thoughts filled with the angry look on Arianne's face when he dropped her off at her condo. Maybe she'd given up on them after today.

Frustrated by his inability to nap, he called Arty. "You're gonna say I told you so and I guess you were right all along."

"Chan, what do you mean?"

"The rally. At the Capitol earlier today. I was there and I brought Ari too."

"You did? Huh. I wasn't sure if you were going. I saw a news story come across the wire about it. I've been busy today so I didn't pay too much attention."

"I told you I thought it would be good for our piece. Besides, it was easy for me and I wanted to spend time with Ari since she's about to move soon."

"Oh yeah, how'd it go with *Ariana*?"

"Let's say it had its highs and lows. That's not why I called you. You and I need to talk. Man-to-man. Face-to-face. This time, I want you to come my way. When can you come to D.C.?" Chandler demanded.

"What's this all about? If this is about money, I can-"

"No, it's not. I can explain more when you get here. Not over the phone."

The men argued for a couple of minutes. Arty insisted that Chandler focus on the rest of their project, including a visit to the reorientation camp. Chandler remained convinced that the logistics of visiting that camp were overwhelming and beyond their capability.

With Chandler not budging, Arty relented and agreed to come to D.C. by mid-week to have their man-to-man talk.

CHAPTER THIRTEEN
CONFRONTATION

Chandler had no desire for another contentious, untrustworthy relationship with a colleague. Last year he discovered that his boss at the El Mundo network, Rafael "Rafa" Mendoza, was instrumental in a takeover in collaboration with the influential International Relations Council. He struggled to understand the nature of his dustups with Rafa until he figured out that El Mundo was destined to be the mouthpiece for a new international order.

When Arty arrived at Chandler's apartment they were friendly, yet both sensed that a difficult discussion lay ahead. The men made their way to the living room, sat on the fold-out sofa bed and chatted for a few minutes over cold beer. Sports were always a topic to break the ice with Chandler the Mets fan and Arty the Yankees fan.

A knock on the door took Arty by surprise. "You expecting someone?"

Chandler held up his index finger and walked to the door to greet his guest.

"Hello, Arturo. How are you?" Axel walked to the seated Arty and extended his hand. He then sat in the old, worn leather chair.

"Axel? What brings you here?" Arty asked, wrinkling his brow.

He had no reason to expect this guest. Chandler asked for a man-to-man conversation, not a three-way dialog.

"Oh, is this a bad time? Chan?" Axel coyly feigned sorrow. "My apologies, Arty, I told Chan I'd stop by. I was in town interviewing someone for my letter."

A still surprised Arty surmised there could be but one correct answer. "Sure, no problem. I guess I'll buy the next round."

Chandler took the bait and headed to his kitchen for another round of cold ones.

Axel's arrival was no coincidence. The plan had Axel dropping by unexpectedly and engaging in a regular conversation with them. Since he knew about financial markets, that's what they'd discuss first. They'd steer the conversation back to Arty's rehab project on his Yonkers home and discuss real estate trends. Chandler would return to a sports conversation about how the season progressed for his beloved Mets. During the sports conversation, Axel would feign boredom, appearing disinterested. He had little interest in sports anyway, giving him an opportunity to observe Arty.

Unbeknownst to Arty, they were trying to further establish his baseline of behavior. They wanted Arty engaged in relaxed conversation where he could avoid being evasive. Axel had a general idea of Arty's baseline. This exercise embellished it. He would look at cues like the position of his feet, his eye movement, and even how he sat. The baseline would help Axel determine when Arty became evasive or less than truthful.

After an hour of casual conversation, the conversation took a more intense turn.

Axel pivoted the flow, gaining a serious countenance. "Hey, why did you leave the intel agency? That line of work has to be fascinating. I've dealt with informal intelligence gathering for years. It's very stimulating."

Arty had no immediate response. He presumed Axel did not know about his past—Chandler promised. He also knew Axel possessed a formidable array of contacts. He couldn't reprimand Chandler without revealing his past. Likewise, he had to address

Axel's question.

"Kind of an abrupt subject change, I'd say," Arty replied. His pupils dilated. Axel's query activated his fight-or-flight response.

"I'm no intel agent, mind you. I do know how hard it is to establish contacts and the patience it requires. I never had formal training. Had to pick it up on my own," Axel commented, legs crossed, still as cool as a cucumber.

Arty shifted his position on the sofa and his feet started jiggling. "Chandler, you didn't tell me Axel was a comedian too." He hoped that comment would put this conversational thread to rest.

Axel, the pit bull, would not let the topic go. "Still though, you miss it?" He leaned back into the chair, hands clasped behind his neck. His icy stare chilled the room.

Arty crossed his arms and shot a baleful glance at Axel. His cinnamon skin gained a darker hue.

"Ax, I don't think he misses it that much. It was tough on the family, right Arty?" Chandler played along, taking the subtle cue. They hadn't rehearsed how they'd work on Arty. Chandler trusted his mentor. "I know I could have used his training a few days ago during that damn CFU rally, could've sniffed out the trouble beforehand, huh?"

Arty, unsure if Chandler had betrayed his trust or if he was merely egging on Axel, raised his voice. "What the hell are you guys talking about? Why are you firing all these stupid questions at me?" If his skin were pale, it would now be red, the most emotionally intense color, stimulating the heart and increasing the breathing rate.

Chandler and Axel looked at Arty as if he had accused them of murder. Arty realized the extent of his overreaction and went into a relaxation mode, uncrossing his arms, slowing down his breathing and making his breaths deeper. Chandler excused himself and headed to the bathroom, grabbing a sports magazine on the way.

An uncomfortable silence emerged after Chandler's exit. Axel maintained his stern gaze on Arty. Arty wanted to look for a place to hide.

"You might fool Chandler, but I can tell you're hiding something," Axel declared, now sitting up, hands steepled in front of his chest, rubbing his fingertips together.

"Hiding what? What the hell are you talking about?" Arty's defensiveness forced him to keep his arms at his sides to calm his emotions.

"I did some research and asked one of my contacts about you." This was a factual statement made by Axel, but he would fudge the truth as they continued.

"About me?" He bounced his index finger in his chest. "OK. Listen. I'm not sure where you're getting all this." He forced a smile, though his elevated blood pressure retracted it.

Omni assisted Axel's research and confirmed Arty's association with Panamanian intelligence. "I confirmed that you used to work for Panamanian intel. I find it interesting that they wouldn't still have some hook in you. With your background and experience, wouldn't it be nice for them to have an agent in country?"

"You're on a fishing expedition except you won't catch anything." Arty looked away from his interrogator.

"I'm sure the U.S. government would be happy to know that there's a foreign agent living in Yonkers that is investigating all this secession talk."

That comment caused Arty some discomfort, as evidenced by his foot rotation away from Axel.

"And what about the money you still owe Chandler? He told me you only wired part of what you owe him. I'm going to suggest Chandler file suit in civil court for breach of contract. I'm sure you won't want to be deposed especially if you're involved with an intel agency, right?"

A legal entanglement would be the last thing he needed. He had enough difficulty with his wife and their divorce, particularly when her attorney discovered payments he received from shell companies that were fronts for the intelligence agencies.

Arty needed to throw the pit bull a bone to unlock its jaws from his neck.

"I am making a documentary here. That is 100% legit. I had ties at one time to Panamanian intel. And yes, I worked in collaboration with U.S. intel. War on Drugs, that sort of thing. I already told Chandler all that. I don't want any trouble, man, please. I can't afford more legal trouble, OK?" Arty hoped the bone satisfied the attacking canine.

"Arturo, there's more here that you're not telling me." Axel could not be sure of that accusation yet he threw a line in the water hoping to snag something. "You need to come clean if you're going to put my friend in harm's way, or me. We almost got killed in that truck crash, you know. I think U.S. authorities knew something there. And who knows, maybe you did too."

"Honest. I didn't know anything. Believe me. I was mortified that something like that happened to you guys."

The normally clean-mouthed Axel Schultz fired another salvo. "That's fucking bullshit and you know it, Arturo! I'm going to tell Chandler to stop working with you and take you to court. I'm sure our friend Senator Geringer would be happy to know about your foreign agent status."

Axel yelled for Chandler to return. They heard a toilet flush and Chandler scurried out, wiping his hands with a small towel.

"What's up guys?" Chandler asked innocently, quickly sitting down next to Arty.

Axel tilted his head defiantly towards Arty, thinning his eyes. "Yes, Mr. Dutari. Tell us what's up."

Arty tightened his grip on the edge of the sofa, knowing he couldn't afford any undue attention. A burden he'd carried for many years finally wore him down.

He quickly released his death grip on the sofa, his torso heaving in reaction. "OK, guys wait!"

Arty admitted that Panamanian intel held something over his head from many years ago. While working in Panama City undercover for a news organization, he took money from a drug deal. The CIA, under a program known as Air Bridge Denial, worked with Colombian and Panamanian authorities to identify shipments of drugs coming into rural airports in both countries. The Colombian and Panamanian authorities used air force jets to shoot down the flights.

The CIA shot down a plane, full of cash, on the way back to Peru. It crashed in the jungle province of Darién, on the Panamanian side of the border with Colombia. Presumably the cash had gone up in smoke. Arty found out from one suspect that the cash never got loaded. Someone had tipped off the suspect that the CIA would shoot down the plane and reasoned he'd keep the loot for himself, hiding it in a storage locker in the Port of Balboa in Panama City. The suspect proposed a split of the loot with Arty. After a short stint in prison, the suspect would get his share.

Ordinarily, this would have been no temptation for Arty, but his mother had a life-threatening illness. An experimental procedure, only performed in Europe, could save her. Neither

Arty nor his mom had money for this surgery, so he opted to split the loot. Unfortunately, the surgery did not save his mother.

A short time later, Panamanian intel discovered the site of the wreckage and concluded there was no cash in transit. They questioned the suspect who gave up Arty in return for a reduced sentence and a small reward. The Panamanian government decided against prosecution, figuring Arty would be a valuable pawn.

When he moved to New York, the intel agencies of both countries agreed to use him cooperatively in the War on Drugs. They allowed him to work as an indie filmmaker in order for him to spend more time around his family. He agreed to pass information to U.S. intelligence during his documentary productions.

With broad drug legalization, he pivoted to domestic terror. If his cover got blown or he quit funneling intelligence, immigration authorities would deport him, since they never allowed him to acquire citizenship. Deportation would end any relationship with his kids.

"So I beg both of you not to do anything which brings any attention to my past. Keep this quiet. Please, no litigation," Arty supplicated, his hands clasped in front of his face.

"Wow, that story is uglier than a mud fence," Chandler said, his eyebrows stretched towards his hairline.

"Did you know anything about the CFU rally? About what might happen? That's why you didn't want to go?" Axel asked, maintaining the stern look of a principal dealing with a truant.

"My handler notified me to stay away from D.C. on May Day. He didn't mention why, so once Chan said he was going to the CFU rally, I put two and two together," Arty replied, looking down, rubbing his forehead.

"This documentary we're working on, is it legit?" Chandler asked.

"It is. I mean eventually I'll sell it to a broadcast network, but before I do, they'll screen it and let me know if I have to take something out."

"Has that happened on some of your other documentaries? The censorship?" Axel inquired.

"Yes. Of course. They'll let some stuff pass even if it is critical of the government; otherwise, I'd lose credibility. They get to pick and choose."

"This thing then about the whistleblower and the reorientation camps. I take it that won't make the final cut?" Chandler asked.

"They may let some stuff pass. If it's just some whistleblower, they'll quickly discredit that person. It's like Quinque of the Five Tribes suggested, they can rewrite digital history. Believe me, I've seen it happen. This is why you need to investigate the camps on your own. They won't let me do that. No way. As far as the whistleblower, they wanted me to find out who he was so they could put the clamps on him." Arty looked more relaxed now. The weight of the world had slowly come off Atlas' shoulders.

"I'm curious. What do you think of these separatist movements? Honestly?" Axel inquired, folding his arms. He remained unsure of the extent of Arty's veracity.

"I can't say I am 100% in agreement with them although I can see their point of view. For someone like me, if I could live in that panarchic style of government the Five Tribes talked about, it would be like gaining freedom from the shackles I have on my wrists. Guys, I just want to get back to a normal family life. Chandler, man, I'm sorry I got you involved in this. My handler thought you would be useful as a trusted journalist, and

I figured you wouldn't be working anywhere else for several months. I had to follow orders."

Chandler accepted his apology and the men shook hands. Axel insisted that Chandler continue business as usual in his interactions with Arty, lest arouse suspicion. They owed it to Arty and his family now that he'd come clean, at least for now.

Arty would never know that Chandler had betrayed his trust, even though Axel discovered it, regardless. This would be another instance of Chandler's mentors bailing him out of a delicate situation.

CHAPTER FOURTEEN
INTELLIGENCE

After an early breakfast, President Jefferson headed to the Situation Room, or Sit Room, where he would meet with his Chief of Staff Drake Hutchinson, Director of National Intelligence (DNI) Gerald Burkemper, National Security Advisor (NSA) Trent Carter, FSB Secretary Holloway, Under FSB Secretary Levi Saltzman, and the FBI Director, Ralph Elliott.

The Sit Room was a 5,500 square foot complex of rooms in the West Wing of the White House, containing a relatively small conference area and an intelligence management center. The Sit Room housed National Security Council Watch Officers who sat on curved, dual tiered rows of computer terminals where they received worldwide data. There were also five secure video rooms, a secure feed to Air Force One, and in a style befitting Get Smart, private phone booths resembling cones of silence.

The president normally sat at the end of a long, wooden conference table with six chairs on each side. On the wall opposite the president hung a large, ultrahigh definition video monitor, with similar monitors flanking the walls on both sides of the room. Staff placed pitchers of cold water at various points around the table. All attendees brought their own cups of coffee save for Under Secretary Saltzman, who poured himself water.

The meeting began with a review of the Morning Book which contained a copy of the National Intelligence Daily, the State Department's Morning Summary, diplomatic cables and intelligence reports. On a given day, more intelligence got presented than thoroughly reviewed. This day proved no different, except that the president's attention focused mostly on domestic concerns.

This day's Morning Book covered a heavy dose of secession activity and the recent incident at the National Mall during the CFU rally.

NSA Trent Carter opened the meeting. "Mr. President, we still are unclear how the Five Tribes managed to disrupt the CFU rally. We spoke to CFU organizers, D.C. police and others. That whole system, the video and the audio, was supposedly closed. More disturbingly, we think the Tribes's membership is growing. Their leadership's communication is encrypted and resides within the Dark Net, so there are challenges there, sir."

"What can you tell me about this spokesperson? What was the name again?" the president asked, as he thumbed through Morning Book.

"Quinque, sir." Carter extended his hand, showing five fingers. "The name is a play on the number five, in Latin."

"Clever. I'm hearing you say that intelligence collection is difficult with this group, particularly the leadership. So what are the next steps? How are we going to fix this, gentlemen?" the president asked, rotating his gaze about the room.

The rest of the staff stared at him.

After a brief silence, DNI Burkemper took the first shot. "Mr. President, allow me to sound like the grizzled veteran." Burkemper rubbed the non-existent facial hair on his chin. "When I began my intelligence career, we were looking for Soviet tank brigades, troop movements or ICBMs. We tracked all the Warsaw Pact forces. Those things stuck out like a sore thumb, easy to find but hard to kill. This modern sort of intelligence is the opposite. These guys are hard to find, but they'd be easy to get rid of once we found them. But even when we find one of them, sir, it would be like playing whack-a-mole. Another one would just pop up. There's no centralization with them."

NSA Carter amplified Burkemper's analysis. "Sir, this group presents challenges since they're hiding in plain sight. We can't target them geographically, so our GEOINT is of no use. Hell, one of them could live in my neighborhood. For the last few years, they've been a mostly peaceful organization with a smattering of cyber disruption. Our information suggests this will change. With all due respect, Mr. President, your executive order on the election freeze really set them off. Sources tell us they're awaiting the Supreme Court decision before they strike again."

"We've been told the Supreme Court decision is due soon," FSB Secretary Holloway interjected.

"There's no question about that, Mr. Secretary. They won't let this interrupt their summer break," the president added, eliciting laughter from everyone.

NSA Carter had more. "Mr. President, we know that the Tribes are not working alone. Some of their cyber activity is probably too sophisticated for-"

Jefferson interrupted Carter, slamming his hand on the table. "Probably? Come on, Trent! Aren't we beyond using a word like that yet? Probably?"

Carter amended his words. "Yes, sir. We feel that Omni has been and will continue to be a partner to the Tribes. That means that what lies ahead will be more severe. The Tribes have an ideology whereas Omni tends to be more random."

"It's too bad we just can't shut down their connections to the Internet. That would hit them where it hurts," Jefferson offered, with a wry smile.

"Sir, that would be difficult to do in practice. There is no law banning encrypted transmissions. We require businesses to transmit information in this manner with all the regulations imposed on them. We can't throw a blanket at the problem," Carter suggested, shaking his head.

"Mr. President, that would derail the entire economy in less than a day and our recovery is too fragile right now. It would be almost impossible to execute those disconnections in practice," Secretary Holloway advised.

"I can add that the project to completely isolate the federal government from the Internet is proceeding on schedule. That network will only be used for government communication with no connection to the outside world. Some people won't like it but we've identified the critical functions that need to be a part of it," Carter added, enthusiastically.

"Guys, thanks for the update though my comment about the Internet was tongue in cheek," Jefferson replied, generating forced smiles from everyone. "Anything to worry about with that Honor Brigade group?"

"Not that we can tell, sir, though they have a splinter group that will take up arms against government agents or the military. We hope they don't, sir, since it will be a violent conflict ending in the death of this group and some of ours too. We need to pay attention to them, but they are not an existential threat," Carter answered.

"Who can talk to me about the camps?" The president's question drew blank stares from everyone in the room, from those who did not know what he meant to those that needed to conceal the information.

Once again, another uncomfortable silence followed. FBI Director Elliott spoke this time. "Mr. President, it is my opinion that this topic not be discussed at all or instead with a smaller team. The nature of that project is such that plausible deniability is of utmost importance."

"I agree, sir. That discussion needs to be tabled," DNI Burkemper added.

"Oh, God. This isn't some project that's going to haunt me later is it, like that MKUltra thing is it?" Jefferson asked, mouth agape.

MKUltra was a CIA-sponsored program name given to a series of illegal experiments on humans focused on mind control, interrogation, and behavior modification that operated from the 1950s until halted during the Watergate crisis in 1973.

"Mr. President, I can brief you privately on that matter though I continue to stress plausible deniability," DNI Burkemper reiterated.

Burkemper convinced the president who moved on to another agenda item. "Very well, then. Mr. Holloway an update please on economic and financial matters."

Secretary Malcolm Holloway, handpicked by President Jefferson to lead the FSB, served as the architect of the economic recovery. Holloway had a distinguished career as Secretary of Treasury and a stint at the influential Global Settlement Bank. He possessed great intellectual capacity and would likely be the smartest person in any room.

"Just the usual complaints from businesses about all the reporting and data collection. All that data, however, has allowed us to develop algorithms that can immediately pinpoint where we need to fine tune the economy. We're telling banks where to lend and adjusting tax policies on the fly. It's working well. We're in control," Holloway concluded. He possessed an unwavering certainty that always put the president at ease.

The uber-entrenched FSB practically ran the economy. With all economic transactions now being tracked, they could levy taxes or provide credits on whatever they felt needed stimulation or cooling. A portion of the economy, however, fell under the radar.

"And how much of the economy goes through DigiNote these days?" the president asked.

DigiNote represented the preferred digital currency by those wanting to conceal their activity from the peering eyes of government and, these days, the FSB. Blockchain currencies like DigiNote were not yet illegal. The Jefferson administration reasoned that making them illegal would broaden their usage. They could do little to stop their use, regardless.

"A small percentage of the whole, sir. We have historical data. If we see a drop, we ask for reports explaining the deviation. Sometimes the reporting alone is enough to discourage this behavior. If they do fill out the exception report and we don't agree with the answers, we levy additional taxes on that company or individual. We've got that under control," Holloway replied. He sat erect in his chair, projecting supreme confidence.

"Brilliant, so-" A health emergency interrupted Jefferson.

Under Secretary Levi Saltzman wheezed uncontrollably, grabbing his chest and throat. He reached for the asthma inhaler in his suit pocket and took a couple of hits. Holloway, sitting next to him, came to his aid. The president called for one of the Watch Officers to take Saltzman to the White House Medical Unit. In short order, the officers helped Saltzman from the Sit Room, one officer under each arm, and quickly rushed him to medical care.

Secretary Holloway knew of his colleague's asthma, though he'd never seen it attack him like this. The rest of the room spoke in hushed tones, speculating about what had happened.

Immediately after Saltzman's evacuation, the president's chief of staff, Drake Hutchinson, who had stepped away during the meeting, rushed into the Sit Room with an urgent message. The District of Columbia Water and Sewer Authority reported a hack to their SCADA systems, disrupting their monitoring and control operations, and issued an urgent bulletin warning their customers to avoid drinking from the water supply. They determined that an improper mixture of chemicals got added to the water. Officials from the company suggested those with asthma would be the most at risk. The water company offered no timetable on the resolution.

A curtain of worry draped over the faces of everyone in the room. Burkemper and Carter reflexively placed their hands over their stomach. Everyone slowly pushed the liquids away. On cue, one of the Watch Officers came around the table with a large waste container, scooping up the poisoned drinks. The president ordered Hutchinson to notify everyone in the White House about the water situation.

Further discussion on the Morning Book ceased as speculation turned to who might have been responsible for the water company hack. There were many side conversations.

The president asked for quiet, tapping his hand forcefully on the conference table. "Gentlemen, let's bring this back, please! We're all concerned about Secretary Saltzman, but we have something bigger going on here."

"Sir, let me investigate this with my department," FBI Director Elliott suggested.

One of the Watch Officers came in and handed the president a printed bulletin. Everyone's gaze fixed on Jefferson, who wrinkled his nose and bit his lip.

"Let me have everyone's attention again, please. It appears that D.C. Metro has been paralyzed due to a system malfunction. We've got riders stuck in stations or in the middle of tracks.

Evacuations are underway. Damn it!" He pushed himself away from the conference table, the chair gliding smoothly over the floor.

Once again, the murmur of side conversations filled the room.

A statuesque, bald Secret Service agent popped into the room. He placed his hands on the back of the president's chair, tilting it back slightly, and requested his immediate evacuation in anticipation of further attacks. "Sir, you need to come with me right now!"

The president looked up at the agent in disbelief. "No! You guys are jumping the gun." He straightened his chair and used his heels to scoot back towards the table. "No! I'm not going to be scared out of my own house. The country can't see me bailing out during times like this. You guys figure out how to keep me safe right here!"

The Secret Service agent spoke into his microphone on his lapel, "Bear staying in Sit Room."

***

The last time Chandler met with Geringer, they watched the impeachment vote in the House, a vote that moved the action to a Senate trial where Geringer did not get his desired outcome. Chandler received his desired outcome after Geringer found someone from an intelligence agency to interview for the documentary. Geringer's success came with stipulations.

The recently retired government employee had a history with U.S. intelligence at a variety of levels with their final position being at Homeland Security. There would be no filming, and Chandler couldn't use the contact's name. Given the contact's familiarity with the senator, they agreed to conduct the interview in his office in the Hart Building.

Chandler arrived ahead of the intelligence contact to chat informally with the senator about the recent attacks. The men assumed their usual positions, Chandler in the leather club chair and the senator sprawled in his chair behind the massive desk.

"Did they ever determine exactly what happened with the water," Chandler asked, referring to the recent problem with the D.C. water supply.

"Just that the SCADA system was compromised. It's been two weeks and no one's claimed responsibility. I don't think we know who did it either. Everyone points to Omni, but I don't know. I guess I should ask your friend, Mr. Schultz, huh?" Geringer expressed mild annoyance. He always had reservations about Axel's relationship with the reviled hacker group, though they proved helpful last year prior to the election in revealing the Global Financial Union.

"If they were involved, they would never tell Ax and he would never ask them. That's not the relationship they have. Besides, that doesn't fit their MO. Not quite the Robin Hood approach, if you know what I mean?" Chandler respectfully defended his friend and mentor before pivoting to a related topic. "What about the Metro shut down? Three days, unbelievable."

"Same thing, no one claimed responsibility and no one seems to know," Geringer replied. "What's interesting here in the Beltway is that there's been more talk about the Senate trial and now the Supreme Court decision than these hacks. I guess we're becoming inured to all these attacks. I'll tell you that even though I didn't expect the Senate to find the president guilty, it was very important for the American people to see the process working."

"You've thrown so much effort at this, it's got to make you frustrated," Chandler suggested.

Geringer sat up in his chair and crumpled his brow. "I believe in doing things the way the Constitution says. One thing that does frustrate me is these damn secessionists or separatists or whatever you want to call them. That's not the way to do things. If everyone just does whatever the hell they want, we won't have much of a country any longer." The senator's voice trailed off into the low end of the audible spectrum.

"Weren't the Colonists dissatisfied with the British crown? What process did they have?" Chandler questioned the senator.

Before Geringer could answer, his chief of staff, Molly Sanders, knocked on the door and announced Susan Black, Chandler's interview subject.

Ms. Black spent her whole life in the service of government. Married at an early age to a member of the armed services, she later put herself through school, gaining a degree in Political Science from SUNY in Albany. Elected to the City Council of the New York State capital, she later served in the House of Representatives from District 20 where she was active in the House Permanent Select Committee on Intelligence. Dissatisfied with the partisanship and the broken legislative process, she returned to private life for a couple of years. During the Bush 43 administration, she received an appointment as Ambassador to Tunisia and later took a position in the CIA. She had the experience of seeing intelligence from both sides.

Susan Black's physical appearance belied her name, given the very blond hair and fair complexion. A tall woman approaching six feet in height, she carried herself with a grace and elegance normally reserved for royalty. A book would have balanced on her head with ease as she walked into the senator's office.

Chandler immediately stood and turned to Ms. Black. Geringer uncoiled his lanky frame from behind the massive desk and took long strides towards his just-arrived guest. "Susan, it's good to see you." Geringer shook her hand warmly. "I'd like to introduce you to Mr. Chandler Scott."

She gave him a polite handshake, "Nice to meet you, Mr. Scott. Your reputation precedes you." She glanced quickly at the senator. "Matt has said many good things about you."

"Nice to meet you too," Chandler said, smiling at the compliment. He'd always had a different vision of someone who worked for the CIA. If he didn't know better, he'd figure Susan to be a college professor. She had that learned sort of look about her.

The three sat down, Geringer back to his position with Chandler and Susan in the chairs in front of him. Susan covered the ground rules once again regarding the importance of concealing her name.

Chandler began the interview, notepad in his lap, with a broad point. "It's important for me, Ms. Black, to give viewers a look into the challenges of privacy versus security, which I'm sure you struggled with as you transitioned from elected official to the foreign service and then to intelligence."

She answered by relating similarities between intelligence roles and regular occupations. "I want to tell you that all intelligence services, or Homeland, or any other organization that's protecting our citizens, consists of ordinary Americans often asked to do extraordinary things. As an administrator in the CIA, I had an organization chart, budgets, and personnel issues like any other business. Trust me, we all had to watch our 'Ps' and 'Qs' when it came to budgets."

"That's a great point. It's important to know, as a taxpayer, that you have budgetary limits," Chandler smiled, not knowing if she appreciated the humor.

She folded the corners of her lips, acknowledging the attempt.

"Our biggest challenge is striking that balance between liberty and security." She rolled her eyes toward Geringer before continuing. "With all due respect to the senator, politicians and the media criticize us for not doing enough when they feel danger and then for doing too much when they feel safe. I should know since I went from being a critic while serving in the House to being a defender while working in the CIA. You know what they say about walking in someone else's shoes."

"How's the criticism tilting these days?" Chandler asked, balancing his palms in front of him.

"After what happened at the CFU rally, the Metro, and the water supply issue, I'm sure the intelligence agencies and DHS are feeling the heat for not doing enough. The public's demanded more from government, economically and with security. I know the senator and others are fighting the president on the election freeze and the creation of the FSB, but the reality is a large swath of the public is comfortable with Jefferson's approach and want more of it. 'We Are the Future,' you know." She looked up and to the right, imitating the characters in the slogan. "The public has grown accustomed to Washington doing something, anything. When governments create a vacuum, you open the door for the bad guys. You saw that example overseas when power vacuums occurred in places like Iraq and Libya. This is one reason many are critical now of the evolution of these secession groups like the Five Tribes or hacker groups like Omni, they're filling a vacuum, different from the Middle East, though the principle is the same."

A skeptical Chandler fired back. "Is it the same? In Iraq and Libya you had governments overthrown and then people with old axes to grind fought back."

Susan cleared her throat. "I should have been clearer. The

similarity is that tensions were brewing in those countries and then once authority went away, all hell broke loose. Here in this country, there have been tensions simmering for years now, and these groups fill the vacuum if government doesn't respond strongly enough. The public doesn't feel like government did enough to protect them when they had the chance, or even now."

"Part of the problem, though, is that the public really doesn't understand how the intelligence community (IC) operates. I'm sure there's so much more than meets the eye. Can you shed a little light on that?" Chandler continued, jotting down notes.

Susan became more animated with this question, eliciting passion. "The IC thrives when it's in the shadows. They view giving too much information as detrimental to their operation. So they are always going to err on the side of less. I used to argue within the IC that we needed to be more proactive in sharing before we got accused of some violation of civil liberties, especially now with so much domestic surveillance. When this information goes public through the wrong channel, also known as leaks, we get in a defensive position and that serves neither liberty nor security."

Chandler had never taken the time to consider the IC's position between the Scylla and Charybdis. "I suppose that's a strain not just for leaders like yourself but also for the men and women who do all the heavy lifting."

"I'm so glad you mentioned that," Susan beamed. "When you have analysts working on a particular case, they can get emotionally involved and even more so if they're surveilling or analyzing a domestic target. That domestic target probably has a family and responsibilities. We woke up to a different world after 9/11. I'm afraid we'll face another world now when the enemy lies within. You know, our Constitution tells us to plant the flag on the side of liberty, but don't kid yourself, once your children get threatened, it all changes and we think more about security than liberty."

"Since you're talking about 9/11 and domestic targets, is it fair to say that Stellar Wind opened the door for a surveillance state with no bounds? Can you see why that could cause discomfort, not just among civil libertarians, but anyone who uses a phone or computer?" Chandler referred to a massive data collection program authorized by the Bush 43 administration after 9/11. The Justice Department determined the president had legal authority to order these operations under a threat to national security. The Jefferson administration used that same line of thinking with the creation of the FSB and the election freeze, citing economic security and cyber threats—both considered precursors to national security.

Susan repositioned herself in the chair before answering this delicate question.

"Let me give you an example of this data collection regarding voice surveillance. The intelligence agencies, such as the National Security Agency, collected what we call metadata. Another way to say this, is that we collected details about data. This would have been detail like who called who, for how long, and what time of day. You'd be surprised how much you can do with just metadata." A smiling Susan left the audience wanting more with her last comment, though there'd be no encore.

Chandler attempted to extract more. "Does the collection stop with metadata or does it go further?" He tapped his pen on the notepad.

Susan didn't take the bait. "I can tell you that the CIA, NSA or any part of the IC tends to be conservative when it comes to the privacy of U.S. individuals. We briefed Congress on what we were doing with Stellar Wind though we had no legal obligation. That's part of what I meant when I said we should share information before something inaccurate gets out there. That's one of the reasons I agreed to this interview. We need to be, in a word, more translucent, telling you in general what we're doing and not delve into the tactical details. It's a better approach to give journalists more rather than less. If you tell them that there are certain things best left out of the story in the interest of national security, most of them will do the right thing. Chandler, you may face that choice at some point. But you won't today since there's nothing tactical that I'm revealing. My goal is to get you to understand daily challenges we face. Hopefully, you convey that in your production."

"I will," Chandler nodded. "Another important consideration for the IC are the policies set by the Jefferson administration or the legislators, wouldn't you say?" Chandler offered a quick glance in the senator's direction.

"People in IC are realists, whereas politicians are the opposite." She winked at the senator. "Although our friend, Senator Geringer, doesn't seem to exhibit that optimistic gene to the same degree. If Jefferson created the impression to the American public that we've figured out the Five Tribes or any other domestic group and then the Director of the ODNI tells him otherwise, we just ruined his day. His spokesperson will stand in front of the press, stumbling about why D.C. Metro was down or why the public's water supply got contaminated. While the IC doesn't set policy, if we're doing our jobs right, we can definitely set the proper boundaries for it. Then it's up to the policymakers to articulate them."

Chandler nodded his head slowly. "Uh huh."

Susan looked at her beckoning cell phone. "Excuse me for a

moment." After tapping a few keys, she signaled the end of the interview. "That's all I have for you, Mr. Scott. As agreed, you are not to quote me directly, understood?"

"Yes, ma'am," Chandler answered with a Texas twang, giving her a quick salute.

Geringer, who'd been silent throughout the interview, affirmed the stipulation in his low drawl. "You can bet he will, Susan."

***

He felt satisfied and grateful for the opportunity to interview Susan Black. He received exposure to both sides of the struggle, the Five Tribes and the intelligence/security apparatus keeping America safe. Though he understood both sides of this issue, many did not. The mysterious Habakk told him to keep doing the little things. Maybe he could build a bridge between competing political interests, or maybe he would just widen the chasm.

Starting his walk through the National Mall after the meeting in Geringer's office, he noticed the remnants of the May Day CFU rally. Torn banners and destroyed video boards remained despite the passage of three weeks.

Did the government want to send a message about the damage the Five Tribes caused? Would it have been better to erase the remnants of their actions?

Something the Jefferson administration had tidied up were the "We Are the Future" banners, seemingly in greater numbers than during the rally. There were new banners that had the family unit admiring the president's official photo. There were also new video boards outlining the president's 10-point Plan for Prosperity that included continuous audio. Jefferson wanted everyone in the Mall to see and hear his vision.

As he passed the Capitol, he recalled the rally and his time with Arianne. It went from being a hopeful moment for their relationship to one of pessimism within a few minutes. He called her at her new home in Winnetka, Illinois.

The conversation proved mechanical, like two friends getting caught up the happenings of their lives. He craved her verbal warmth and tenderness, chiding himself for these expectations. After a few minutes of impersonal chatter, she confessed that she remained shaken by the CFU event and even though she could not anticipate when she would see him, she still had feelings for him, despite the lack of expression in the conversation.

The conversation ended by the time he reached the World War II Memorial, where he took a seat on a bench. His cell phone indicated 1:00 pm. There were many people walking, jogging, cycling and otherwise enjoying themselves in the late May weather. Automated electric vehicles ferried government employees around buildings surrounding the Mall.

D.C. police were visible, cameras followed unusual activity, and drones buzzed overhead. A casual observer would deem nothing out of the ordinary, save for a few remnants of the CFU rally.

Looking forlorn after his conversation with Arianne, he felt a pat on the back of his shoulder from Habakk, dressed in his usual color scheme. "You look rather pensive, my friend." He took a seat next to him.

"Where in the hell did you-? Never mind." Chandler's encounters with Habakk had no predictability. "Yeah feeling low right now. I probably couldn't jump off a dime."

"Hmm. I guess you weren't a basketball player then?" Habakk said with a straight face.

"Mr. Habakk, honestly and with all due respect, you show

207

up, ask questions, sound like the wise owl, you disappear, and then we go through this again. I don't even really know who you are, and we've been doing this since when? When the market crashed in 2019?" Chandler's frustration emerged from his relationship trouble and his inability to understand this itinerant man.

Habakk placed his hand on Chandler's shoulder, rubbing it gently. "I believe I said the country would face major events in its history soon. Has that not been the case?" Habakk gave him a dulcet smile and floated his hand off his shoulder.

"OK, you're smart. I get it. But what's your end game?" Chandler had all the questions now.

Habakk, unperturbed, replied calmly. "Your questions will be answered in due time. Remember, I told you on New Year's Day about what statesman and philosopher Edmund Burke said about doing little things. It is more important than ever that you keep doing them. American democracy, or rather the republic, has been sliding into trouble for many years. Historians will debate the starting point. That does not matter. I related to you the crises that America had to pass through in her history. We have a different crisis now, one centered in rethinking what America means. There was so much debate on climate change, illegal immigration, law enforcement, race relations, foreign policy, and then came the avalanche of economic problems in 2008 and beyond. All of that turbulence created fertile ground for what you see today with the secession groups."

"You know something about the secession groups?" Chandler tilted his head defiantly and creased the corners of his eyes.

"Nations progress through crises when leaders make changes. It's the thunderstorm that washes away the pollen, leaving the air fresh and clean. The thunderstorm may knock trees down, yet everyone breathes better." Habakk took a deep breath, his diaphragm rising noticeably.

"And I thought I had metaphors," Chandler said.

A black Mini pulled up at the intersection of 17th Street and Constitution. Habakk waved at the car and asked Chandler if he needed a ride. A surprised Chandler accepted. Every other time, Habakk disappeared on foot or in a vehicle. As the two walked towards the vehicle, he did not recognize the license plate, speculating that it could be diplomatic. He did not ask Habakk either, figuring that he would not get a direct answer.

Before opening the door to the back seat, Chandler noticed the same driver who ferried him from Geringer's office to his apartment three months earlier. Habakk got in first, followed by Chandler.

"Chandler, you may recognize our driver. I believe he's given you a couple of rides from this area," Habakk said.

"Good, at least you weren't going to make some oblique reference to someone from history," Chandler replied, sarcastically.

"Hello, Mr. Scott, my name is Tomás," the driver said, turning towards the back seat, extending his hand.

Chandler extended his. "Nice to meet you, Tomás. I guess I still owe you for that ride?"

"As I said to you then, the ride was on the house," Tomás replied, smiling placidly.

"So who is the house?" Chandler asked, shifting his quizzical smile between Tomás and Habakk.

Habakk took this question, chuckling as he responded. "Why the house is the owner of the transportation company. In this case it is Tomás."

Tomás looked in the rearview mirror, making brief eye

209

contact with Chandler.

The three spoke little on the ride to Chandler's apartment. Habakk rode like a tourist on their first visit to the nation's capital. Chandler had difficulty assessing whether his wonderment was genuine or contrived.

Tomás drove the Mini as if in the middle of a DMV test. He maintained his speed within the limit; the stops were thorough, and the use of blinkers, impeccable. No doubt he'd get a perfect score for parallel parking.

After arriving at Chandler's apartment, the silent Habakk knocked Chandler over with a political question. "It will be interesting to see what the Supreme Court decides on their big case, don't you think?"

A stunned Chandler stammered to find an answer. "Well, ah, hmm, yeah. Sorry, you caught me by surprise with that one. I think the whole country will be watching that one."

Chandler remained still after answering, as if awaiting his driver's dismissal. "Oh, I guess I should get out now." He paused, flicking his eyes to one side. "There's probably no sense in asking when we'll meet again."

"We will meet again when the time is right. Have a nice day, Mr. Scott." Habakk's feathery touch on Chandler's shoulder calmed whatever latent tension he had about Arianne or the documentary.

He practically floated out of the car. Habakk and Tomás sped off, screeching the Mini's tires.

***

After another mysterious encounter with Habakk, and now Tomás, all he wanted to do was sit down with a cold beer in front of the TV. The day had its highs and lows. He felt good about the interview with Susan Black, then his emotions hit a nadir during his conversation with Arianne. Though his encounters with Habakk continued to invite questions that produced thought provoking answers, Habakk's feathery touch during the ride back with Tomás made him calm.

The old leather chair held him while he tuned his former employer's network, El Mundo. They interrupted their regularly scheduled programming with breaking news.

"We've just learned that the Supreme Court has reached their decision on the case before them, Geringer v. United States in the matter of determining the constitutionality of President Jefferson's actions freezing the results of the 2020 election. Let's go to our Justice correspondent, Peter Holt for more, Peter?

"Thank you. We've just received the press release from the SCOTUS. In a 5 to 4 decision, the Court ruled that due to the extraordinary circumstances facing the nation, furthered by difficult economic conditions and domestic terror concerns, presidential Executive Order 14666, temporarily suspending the election results of the 2020 campaign, is not unconstitutional since the country faces an existential threat. The Justices did advise the president to declare a date this calendar year when the 2020 election can be resolved in the House and Senate as constitutionally mandated. The dissenting opinion was written by Justice Rose who said, 'Today's decision marks a day when historians will say that the Court abdicated its responsibility as custodians of the Constitution.' Strong words by Justice Rose. I'd now like to turn it over to my colleague, Michelle Reyes, at the White House.

"Thanks, Peter. President Jefferson was alerted to the Court's decision moments ago, and plans to make a statement from the Oval Office later tonight. We will bring that to you live. Back to you in the studio."

Chandler had thought little about the Supreme Court outcome. Like much of the country, he conducted his life business as usual. Although Jefferson's executive order created initial turmoil, the business of the nation continued. There would be little question that many in the country, especially the secessionists, would be furious with the Court. Most of the public viewed it as another day in their difficult economic lives.

Voodoo Child alerted him of an incoming call from Axel. "Unbelievable, huh? Are you kidding me? I thought they'd declare the exec order unconstitutional and then throw it back at the president and Congress to get everything resolved."

Chandler reflected on his thoughts immediately after the announcement. "Honestly, Ax, I'm not sure if a lot of people are gonna care. It's sad to say. People are so caught up in what they're doing, there are so many distractions, the damn economy, and people afraid of cyber and kinetic terror in their backyard. They just want things fixed. Is this the end of this fight, then?"

"They could try to call an Article Five Convention of States," Axel explained.

During an Article Five convention, Congress can propose an amendment to the Constitution with a two-thirds vote in the House and Senate. The states can effect the same change via two-thirds of the state legislatures. Then, three-fourths of the states would have to ratify the amendment.

"They'll have an easier time calling a two-thirds convention in the states I would think, but the three-fourths for ratification will be very difficult," Axel opined. "I wonder if Geringer is planning something like that. I'll be curious to see what sort of amendment they would draft to get what they want."

"What a mess. I think-" Chandler got interrupted by an

incoming call from Arty. "Hey Ax. Arty's calling. Let me get this and call you back."

"OK, bye."

Chandler switched over to Arty. "Hey Arty. I guess I know why you're calling."

"I'm not going to say much about it over the phone. The shit is going to hit the fan soon. When can you come back to Yonkers? We've got some more work to do plus I need to know if you've thought more about that other thing we discussed." Arty referred to a clandestine visit to the reorientation camp.

"I guess I can be back there in a few days. I'm trying to get someone to sub-lease this place from me. You know Arianne's gone now, and not working for El Mundo, there's less reason for me to be here. Someone's supposed to come by in a couple of days. I'll text you, but it shouldn't be more than say, four days."

"OK. I'll await your message then. Stay safe, Chan. Bye."

Arty had never told him anything before about staying safe.

CHAPTER FIFTEEN
HACK ATTACK

Back in New York's borough of Manhattan after a successful apartment showing in D.C., Venus awakened him from his slumber with the sound of chirping birds. His beloved Mets had a game in Citi Field against the Cardinals, though he fell asleep when the game went into extra innings.

"The time is 7:00 am, Tuesday, June 8th. The outside temperature is 63 degrees," Venus announced.

"Venus, Mets score from last night?" Chandler said, in a raspy voice. The cotton mouth from the prior evening's beers asserted itself.

"The New York Mets defeated the St. Louis Cardinals 4-3 in 16 innings. Would you like a summary?"

"No. Start coffee."

"Would you like an important news update?" The last time Venus asked this question and he responded in the negative, he missed the start of the 2019 stock market crash. He'd learned his lesson.

"Yes, news update, please." He sat up to hear her.

Venus had much to say. Power failures at the New York Stock Exchange, the Chicago Board of Trade, and the New York Mercantile Exchange prevented overnight futures trading. The shutdown of these markets caused the London FTSE, German DAX, and France's CAC indices to plummet. The U.S. exchanges reported that their auxiliary power systems did not activate as programmed. Authorities were still investigating the outage, fearful the exchanges would not open on time, if at all.

In other news, protesters were blocking entrances to federal courts in various states along the East Coast, standing in defiance of the Supreme Court's decision judging the constitutionality of the president's executive order. One protester could be overheard, "If we can't get justice, no one else will!"

Honor Brigade splinter groups in Idaho declared parts of their state sovereign territory and mandated that the state's legislature conduct a vote on secession.

The news proved overwhelming before his trip to Arty's later in the morning. He wondered if there would be any disruptions in the Big Apple. There were always protests going on these days, though they often spared Manhattan. New York City's mayor, formerly the chief of police, had little tolerance for disorder.

After a shower and breakfast, he walked outside of his building to await his ride to Grand Central Station to catch the Hudson line that would take him to Yonkers.

He noticed nothing unusual on the streets of lower Manhattan, which looked nothing like the morning after the 2019 stock market crash. That morning he encountered a run on a local bank with the line wrapped around the block. A lone security guard stood by the front door while NYPD maintained order. He'd encountered the mysterious Habakk for the first time, though not through formal introduction. This morning looked ordinary until his phone made him realize that appearances were deceiving.

His cab pulled up to the curb. Distracted by his phone, he bumped his head on the door frame before falling into his seat.

"Mister, you're lucky you got me this morning. Our dispatcher is going nuts!" the cabbie yelled.

Chandler knew why he said that. "Oh, yeah, OK. I can see-"

"The subway's down!" the cabbie yelled, again. His animation pointed to the information screen embedded in the dash.

There were only so many cabs in lower Manhattan to cover the extra ridership. Some people probably stayed home while others fought to make it to work. Chandler looked for chaos on the streets and neglected to see the thinner crowds.

Grand Central Station, one of the largest railroad terminals in the entire world, was one of the most visited tourist attractions in the Big Apple. The cabbie dropped him off outside the 42nd Street entrance where a 13-foot clock surrounded by the Roman gods Hercules and Mercury, and the goddess Minerva greeted travelers. Hercules embodied strength and adventure. Chandler hoped he'd have the strength to embark on yet another, potentially dangerous adventure.

Entering the expansive Main Concourse revealed bustling, yet confused crowds. Chandler gazed up towards the astronomical ceiling, inaccurate in its depiction of the constellations, though no more so than his sunrise dream. The Station served as the nexus for commuter rail and subway lines, though not on this day as incoming passengers from commuter lines could not complete their journey via the disabled MTA subway trains.

The departure status board told him the Hudson line ran on time. He texted Arty to let him know. At this time of the day, most of the traffic would be inbound to Grand Central, so he secured a seat by himself in the front car. A video monitor in his compartment streamed an announcement by the Five Tribes, received by the NBC affiliate in New York City.

The Five Tribes would like to express their outrage at the Supreme Court's decision on the president's executive order. We'd hoped justice could be served. This is the ultimate corruption of the State when the judiciary is no longer independent. We will immediately begin plans for the establishment of our panarchic state.

At no time since the CFU rally did the Five Tribes or Omni claim responsibility for any disruption, whether that be with the D.C. water company or anything occurring today. During his hour-long ride, Chandler considered the possibility that other rogue groups were in operation, including some he'd never identified. Chandler also reflected on his interview with Quinque and the alternate form of governance he discussed, the panarchic state. That panarchic state would cut the government out of people's daily existence. His wondering almost made him miss his destination station.

Arty waited in his SUV outside of Glenwood station. He had more breaking news that eluded Chandler on the ride. Arty waved him in to the vehicle, his hands flapping with vigor. "Chan, you probably didn't hear this on your ride. Maybe you did!"

Chandler entered the vehicle, tossing his bag in the back seat. "Calm down, dude. You mean about the subway in the city?"

"No, man. There's this contractor, one of the largest, who works for the FSB that got attacked. Supposedly a Denial of Service attack where the hackers generated like 500 gigabytes per second of traffic. 500 gigs! Wow!" Arty said excitedly, not cognizant of the line of cars forming behind him. "*Coño*, let's get moving."

"That must have been some attack! Those servers must have been busier than a hound in flea season!" Chandler retorted, echoing his partner's excitement.

"Here's the thing, though. The hackers had help. They hijacked servers in the cloud, man! That's how they pumped out so much traffic to bog down that FSB contractor. No hacker has that many machines just sitting around for an attack, unless it was some foreign government." Arty's knowledge surprised Chandler. "Oh, and since this contractor does all this work for the FSB, it looks like the markets won't open. This is wild, man!" Arty banged the steering wheel in his excitement.

"This day just got more chaotic for everyone then," Chandler concluded. That would prove to be an understatement.

When they arrived at Arty's the two immediately went to the studio where large video monitors provided news feeds from different sources. One news feed reported that the nation's largest online retailer got hacked overnight. Omni revealed that the retailer passed customer browsing cookies to the National Security Agency, who were using data analytics to make determinations about the intent of private citizens. The government used the intelligence to thwart crime or domestic terror by predicting future hostility based on web browsing history. This predictive action harkened back to the movie, Minority Report.

Another news feed had unnamed FSB sources reporting that several top-level officials in the department including Secretary Holloway and Undersecretary Levi Saltzman were victims of spoofed emails appearing to originate from legitimate internal sources. The result of the action revealed passwords, throwing the FSB into chaos. No one claimed responsibility for the hack.

"Chan, all this stuff happening today, we gotta figure out how to work it in somehow. This is good stuff, man. I mean not good for the disruptions, but it's a good transition for us to put together the big conclusion here," Arty smiled, bearing all his teeth. He spun his chair a full revolution.

"So what exactly is the big conclusion? That the world is going to hell in a handbasket?"

"No man, no. We gotta wrap this thing up good. I know you can't reveal the source for the interview you had in Geringer's office, but did you ask them anything about the stuff the whistleblower talked about?" Arty's question centered on the reorientation camps.

"You're right. I can't say who I talked to and no, I didn't. I wanted to get their side of the story. If I had asked about those camps, Geringer would wonder where I heard that. I wasn't about to go down that path."

Arty still wanted his partner to consider the pièce de résistance, the reorientation camps. "OK. Listen. You know what would wrap this whole thing up, so I'm not gonna say it again."

"Yeah, I know," Chandler said reluctantly. He'd still not decided on that, given the voices in his head discouraging the Herculean effort.

***

The cyberattacks on the financial exchanges and the FSB contractor mobilized the president and his security team for a meeting in the Situation Room. Declarations of sovereign territory and secession votes in state legislatures were of great concern. Joining the president were his Chief of Staff Hutchinson, DNI Burkemper, NSA Carter, FSB Secretary Holloway and FBI Director Elliott. Levi Saltzman did not attend the meeting due to complications from his asthma attack last month.

Jefferson ordered bottled water for the refreshment this time. He sat in his usual position at the end of the long conference table. The large video monitor opposite Jefferson displayed a news feed of the events of the previous 24 hours.

After NSA Carter summarized the Morning Book, the

219

president began his agenda. "Secretary Holloway, can you give us an update on the status of your contractor?" The president referred to the action on the FSB contractor that had been a victim of a massive Denial of Service attack.

"Sir, they were completely overwhelmed. They claimed they'd never seen or read about anything like this, at least the scale of the attack. They had to go offline for several hours and as you know the exchanges did not open this morning. I'm of the opinion to just suspend any trading today, even if these systems get back online. I don't want to have to go through this again tomorrow without a guarantee of cyber protection," the composed Holloway answered. He'd already had conversations with the financial exchanges, warning them of this potential decision.

"That sounds fine, Mr. Secretary. What sort of economic impact do you foresee by closing trading and the FSB being down?" the president countered.

"I can't say with any certainty, sir." After pausing briefly to gather his thoughts, Holloway continued. "Well, let me clarify. Closing trading for one day will not cause too many problems. As far as my department being down, we know that we lose tax revenue. I have no doubt that businesses and individuals will take advantage of the down time to conduct transactions off the books. Then we have to go through the spin cycle with the business community about how we have to watch everything to fine tune the economy."

Before Jefferson could get to his next question, a Watch Officer scurried into the room and whispered something in the chief of staff's ear. The chief, sitting next to Jefferson, whispered in his ear. The rest of the meeting participants looked on as if to expect bad news after seeing his grimace.

"The Watch Officer has just informed us that we've grounded our federal drone fleet operating in the western states due to communication issues. It appears someone is jamming our signals. Several drones crashed in the Nevada desert when operators lost control of them. The field commander decided to ground the fleet."

The chief of staff, Drake Hutchinson, had grown frustrated with the incursions. "Mr. President, we've been dealing with these cyberattacks for some time and our response has been tepid militarily, sir. I know there's always hesitation about using our military against our own, but can't USCYBERCOM lend a more forceful hand?"

USCYBERCOM, aka United States Cyber Command, centralized command of cyberspace operations for the military. They were the soldiers on the front lines of the cyber wars. These soldiers looked more like the kids playing Call of Duty rather than the game's action figures. USCYBERCOM had the same challenges as the other intelligence organizations in balancing their duty and breaching personal privacy. They didn't seek to militarize cyberspace. They wanted to protect the military's assets—to be more defensive than offensive. There were many in the administration and the military who wanted the organization to assume a more offensive posture. The grounding of the military's drone fleet would hasten further discussion on the group's role.

The president pivoted stiffly to the DNI. "Mr. Burkemper, we've had that discussion for some time now. If we unleash the military in cyberspace against what we think are domestic threats, it's a slippery slope."

"Yes, sir. The problem we have is that these attacks are very distributed throughout a variety of networks. It's not as if we have a fixed target that we can attack with the Air Force or send ground troops to capture territory. Even the drone fleet, as you saw this morning, can be compromised. CYBERCOM's capabilities need to become more offensive." The DNI laid out the limitations of being the world's superpower against a distributed band of cyber bullies.

NSA Carter offered a temporary solution to the drone issue. "Mr. President, the Air Force recently engaged a DaaS contractor who could help fill the gap."

The president's eyes narrowed to thin slits as he stared at Carter. "Mr. Carter could you please tell us what the hell you mean by DaaS?"

Carter quickly responded. "My apologies, sir. Drones as a Service. There are enough drone pilots out there who have good aerial intel capability. They don't have our optics, though they can help us out in a pinch."

"Great! Now we have to outsource our intel capability." A disgusted Jefferson threw his hands up and looked towards the heavens. "Mr. Burkemper, what are U.S. allies able to tell us? Not all this hacking originates within our borders, I'm sure."

Burkemper, feeling Jefferson's gaze crawl across him, had to answer this question carefully. "Our overseas partners want to cooperate. My counterparts warn me that they have to be careful about angering their civilian population, who like ours, are struggling with the authority imposed on them by their own governments."

"So what you're telling me is, we're screwed for the moment?" Jefferson replied, shaking his head.

Silence fell on the room, cloaking these important men like mist.

The mist quickly cleared with an image displayed on one of

the side wall monitors. The chief of staff tapped Jefferson's shoulder, pointing to the monitor immediately behind Secretary Holloway. On the screen appeared a ceiling fan against a white background. The image proved unsteady, with mild shaking. After a few seconds, the monitor showed the face of a young lady who had just woken up. When the image became clear, Holloway realized that the video captured his teenage daughter in the bedroom of his Fairfax County, Virginia, home. The girl typed on her phone. Apparently the initial image used the outward-facing camera, and then his daughter switched to the user-facing one. She was sending a morning picture of herself to someone.

Holloway stood up as if coming to attention, yelling for the Watch Officers. "Turn off that fucking monitor! Now!" The tension in his jaw would have cracked a walnut. He feared what the audience might see next. In a matter of seconds, the monitor went dark.

Phone hacks of this nature were not uncommon. The popular phone operating system, Tobor, had known weaknesses and served as a frequent target for hackers. After Maxwell Technologies got hacked in 2020 with a variation of the Trident virus, CEO Larry Maxwell, Arianne's father, revealed that not only were they working on encryption software but also with Tobor's developer to make the operating system more secure. The government challenged the release of Maxwell's encryption software in federal court, citing national security concerns. The legal challenge delayed the operating system fixes, inviting more hacking. This would be another case of government intentions gone wrong.

Holloway scampered towards to the secure phone booth, the cone of silence, bumping into several chairs in his path. He hoped to end the peep show.

The meeting interruptions spawned a number of side conversations and chased the chief of staff, who wanted to access his phone, out of the Sit Room. The Sit Room did not allow for cell service.

Jefferson grabbed his half-empty water bottle and used it as a gavel on the conference table. The sloshing water muffled the thumping. "Everyone, please! Let's allow Mr. Holloway to take care of his family. Mr. Burkemper, I believed I asked a question."

"Mr. President, we're not screwed as you put it, but we've known for some time, years now, that our next battlefront would be in cyberspace. The Intelligence Community has been preparing for this. Candidly, sir, the enemy is just a little ahead of us."

No one said anything. The audience remained hypnotized by the monitors, waiting to see what might happen next.

Holloway, his spirit demolished, emerged from the secure phone booth. "Gentlemen." He gathered himself. His eyes watered. "My wife just informed me that I'd received a call from the hospital where Mr. Saltzman had been admitted yesterday for a respiratory infection. It is with a heavy heart that I tell you that Levi Saltzman died this morning due to cardiac arrest." He curled the fingers on one hand to wipe his eye.

The president jumped in. His eyes widened in the moment's shock. "Oh my God!" He brought his hands beside his head. "I thought he was just having problems with his asthma. How could? I mean. How?" He ran out of words.

Everyone one in the room swiveled their heads looking at each other, unsure of how to act or what to say.

"Sir, I have more. The reason he went into cardiac arrest was due to medicine being administered that he was allergic to. His doctor-" Holloway could not finish.

"Well, why the hell would they? How could that even happen?" the president interrupted, his nails dug into the table.

"Sir, they talked to the nurse that administered the medication and she verified the information on his chart. There were no medical records errors. When they informed Saltzman's wife, she claimed that the medicine they gave him was on the prohibited list. The Saltzman's kept a printed copy of his medical record and the hospital verified a discrepancy. The hospital concluded that someone hacked into Mr. Saltzman's medical records and deleted the culprit medicine from the prohibited list."

Holloway seethed with anger and clenched his fists. His arms shook uncontrollably. He burst into a tirade about his daughter's invasion of privacy and the murder of his colleague.

"These people are going to pay for this. Who the hell are they to invade the privacy of an innocent teenager? What does she have to do with any of it? And Levi, he was murdered in that hospital, murdered!" Holloway kicked the chair in front of him, sending it spinning on its axis. "Mr. President, tell me we're going to make these people pay?" He looked at the rest of the staff. "You better have a good plan! You better!"

President Jefferson, rubbing his face with both hands, offered no response.

Burkemper broke the uncomfortable silence that followed. "Mr. Secretary, Malcolm, we simply don't know who 'these people' are yet."

Holloway's meltdown continued. He directed most of his venom towards DNI Burkemper. The historically unflappable secretary, the master of control, the smartest guy in the room, could not come up with a rational explanation. He could apply no formula or policy to smooth things out or make them better. He sat in his chair, now tilting to one side after his violent kick, and covered his face with both hands, concealing his tears.

The architect of the president's economic plan, Malcolm Holloway, had just experienced a personal violation, the kind that would make any parent suffer. For the last 18 months, both men had worked on an economic plan that would reunite the nation. Jefferson realized that the FSB's logical approach and powerful slogans had instead further divided the country. He couldn't walk back the plan either.

There were people that didn't share his vision of the future, people that may not have understood the roots of their own frustration.

The president wondered if others in the room had the same sense of weltschmerz, that sense of weariness one felt when their ideal image of the world did not match its reality. He didn't ask.

***

Chandler and Arty had worked until midday when they broke for lunch. The two drove to Arty's favorite eatery in Yonkers called La Cubanita. There were no Panamanian restaurants near Arty's house, and he'd cultivated a preference for the Caribbean cuisine. The restaurant had a lively crowd, no doubt due to the favorable early June weather in New York State. The restaurant's interior featured unfinished walls with brick and horizontal wood paneling. The owner greeted Arty and the two began a conversation in Spanish that eluded Chandler.

The owner sat them in a corner booth, away from most of the patrons.

"They know you well here, dude," Chandler suggested, opening his menu.

A bashful Arty replied, "Yeah, me and the owner. It's weird, man, but he knows my ex. They grew up together. What's funny is, I used to bring Ynez here after I started dating her. I got to be good friends with the owner who's still friends with the ex. But no worries, man."

Arty suggested they order the *Caribe Pernilito*, a dish of slow-roasted pork accompanied by sweet plantains, fried onions and rice with pigeon peas. "This dish is more than enough for both of us. Trust me. You wanna get some sangria too?"

"No way. Not unless you want me to snooze the rest of the day," Chandler answered, still perusing the menu. "So what's so good about this *Pernilito*?"

"I like the pork for sure. The rice and pigeon peas, reminds me of home, a dish we call *arroz con guandú*," Arty explained. "And the plantains too, especially when they're sweet."

"I know I've heard you talk about plantains before."

"All I know is, I hope they have plantains in heaven, just like Panama's."

Chandler added, while folding the menu, "And I hope they have burnt ends there too. I'd probably have to ask St. Peter if my favorite Austin barbeque place could deliver."

The two men got a good laugh from that one. Arty ordered the *Caribe Pernilito* as he suggested with sodas instead of sangria.

"Ok. Listen. What about these reorientation camps? Come on Chandler, it will be a great way to finish this." Arty's focus did not change from earlier in the day.

"It might just finish me, dude. Remember, I don't have all the secret agent training that you have. I just wanna finish this thing now. We have some really good material, you have to admit. Plus, I need to figure out my life now with Arianne." Chandler felt her constant tug about changing his lifestyle.

"*Ariana, sí*. You finish this project with a bang, and she'll understand, right?"

The other tug on Chandler came from his internal "can do"

attitude and the exhortations from Habakk to continue doing the little things. There was a purpose greater than himself. "Seriously, Arty, no disrespect, but I don't want to lose her and I may have already."

The waiter served the formidable plate of *Caribe Pernilito*. Though he feared losing Arianne, Chandler had not lost his appetite, as evidenced by his quick ingestion of the Cuban fare. Arty's description of their lunch fit to the letter – tasty and very filling.

After lunch, the two resumed their work in Arty's second floor studio. Chandler still had great reservations about exploring the reorientation camp angle for the film. That assignment would be fraught with danger, not to mention Arty had provided no plan to make it work. Arty had a very different perception of danger, understandably, than Chandler.

Arty worked on film editing and Chandler on narration. Chandler received a text from Axel requesting a secure chat line. Chandler opened a special app that he got from Axel, which no doubt came from Omni. The app provided a secure chat session over the Internet via his phone.

REMOTE› TALKED TO GERINGER. IAP WILL WORK ON ARTICLE FIVE CONVENTION AND PUSH IT THROUGH STATE LEGISLATURES. HE'S PLANNING A PRESS CONFERENCE TO CALM UNREST.

LOCAL› OK. SWEET.

REMOTE› MY OMNI CONTACT SAID THEY ARE NOT RESPONSIBLE FOR THE ATTACKS. THEY'RE NOT SURE WHO IS. COULD BE FIVE TRIBES, HONOR BRIGADE OR

OTHER UNKNOWN PLAYERS OUT THERE JUST
CAUSING TROUBLE WITH ALL THE CHAOS SO THEY
CAN HIDE FROM THE BLAME.

LOCAL> OK. THIS IS GETTING TOTALLY OUT OF
CONTROL. IF OMNI DOESN'T KNOW. HEY, I NEED TO
TALK TO YOU ABOUT THE REORIENTATION CAMP
PIECE. MAYBE YOU KNOW SOMETHING ABOUT IT.
CAN'T TALK NOW. WORKING WITH ARTY ON EDITS.
TALK TO YOU LATER.

REMOTE> I'VE BEEN LOOKING INTO THAT. LET ME DO
MORE RESEARCH. BYE.

The two men continued to work on film editing and dialog until Arty received a text message that unnerved him. He fidgeted and walked around, going to the bathroom to wash his face. He exited with a small towel around his neck and announced, "I have to go, man." He gave Chandler a toothy grin, concealing his trepidation.

"Now? Why?" Chandler thought they were making great progress and did not want an interruption. He did not plan on spending the night.

"Ok. Listen. My handler just texted me and said I needed to take video to our drop area. I'd promised him something a couple of days ago and fell behind. My ex-wife's making my life miserable and we argued and-. Anyway, probably with all these attacks, they want to see if I have anything that might help. I'm sure they're scrambling, looking for any piece of intel. They may think they can figure out where that Five Tribes silo was located though none of your film with Quinque had geo tags.

229

"Yeah, who knows. So what do you want me to do in the meantime?"

"Just stay here and chill out, or work some more. I've got beer in the frig, plus there's plenty of food."

"Food? I'm stuffed from lunch! I'm still planning on going back to Manhattan tonight."

The tooth bearing Arty offered another suggestion. "Go to my patio and have a Cohiba. The humidor's in the family room next to the bookcase."

"Let's hallelujah the city. I can't believe you're offering me your Cubans. I must have done something right." Chandler, the non-smoker, appreciated the gesture.

Arty hurled the small towel towards his partner. He grabbed a memory stick and a waterproof envelope.

"I'll be back soon. I promise. Please don't follow me or track me or anything like that. It is for your own safety, OK?" Arty implored.

"Yeah, sure. I understand. See you in a little while. I'll be fine. What should I do if your ex comes calling?" Chandler teased.

"Tell her she'll be seeing a lot more of me in court if she keeps up with all her bullshit. She hasn't gotten rid of me yet!" Arty winked as he left the home studio.

CHAPTER SIXTEEN
THE DROP

Arty's eyes darted at his rearview mirror out of instinct — his situational awareness never lagged. He didn't think Chandler would follow him. Though he never bragged about his skills, Arty could escape from handcuffs, pick locks, hot wire a car, drive like James Bond, and be MacGyver when it came to improvising weaponry.

The drive took him to Croton Point Park, north of his home, also along the Hudson. He'd taken this route many times. His confession to Axel and Chandler proved to be cathartic, yet it could not assuage the tension of the covert interaction with his handler. The agency had assigned this handler since becoming an independent filmmaker.

Besides receiving payments from networks to whom he sold his work, he also received payments from what he presumed were front companies set up by U.S. and Panamanian authorities. The only thing he saw from them were bank wires that arrived periodically.

Croton Point Park encompassed 500 acres on a peninsula on the eastern shore of the Hudson. Archaeologists posited that Native Americans inhabited the area thousands of years ago. The name "Croton" came from an Indian sachem, or chief, which meant, "wild wind." Arty had never met his chief, his handler. More recently, the park served as the location of the oldest wine cellar in the state. The established drop area was an abandoned wine cellar with an entrance marked by a brick-lined arch.

He parked in the usual lot and walked to the drop area, practicing situational awareness by scanning his surroundings.

Park foliage prevented him from seeing everything, so he approached the drop more slowly, the previous season's leaves crunched under his feet. The weekday, overcast sky produced few day visitors, though overnight guests stayed in cabins and RV spots. He exercised caution and acted like he belonged.

Arriving at the abandoned cellar overgrown with brush with large mature trees providing a canopy, he removed one brick in the arch, nearest to the arch's crest. He slid his waterproof envelope into a carved out space, leveling an ant colony. He looked around once again, eyes bouncing from underneath his Yankees hat. Arty always wondered if his handler watched him with high-powered binoculars from another park location. For all he knew, the handler could pose as a park employee. There were matters of more immediate concern than his handler's identity. Chandler expected his return soon, and the two had work to complete. He replaced the brick in the arch, annihilating the rest of the ant colony.

His SUV sat three hundred and fifty feet from the drop area, or just about the distance that Derek Jeter's last home run traveled when he watched it in his beloved Yankee Stadium. It would take him a couple of minutes to reach it. A young couple emerged walking their Alaskan husky, no doubt leaving a trail of fur behind them. He smiled as he passed them, wondering how many more times he would have to visit this park.

He clicked his key chain to unlock the doors, looking over his shoulder before entering. The vehicle misfired during the ignition. He thought it strange since it never happened before to his late model SUV with all the bells and whistles. Given the vehicle's young age, he reasoned there had to be a problem with the vehicle's computer system rather than the plugs. He tried again. On the second attempt, the car started. He took no unusual action, waiting for the car to reach the normal, idling RPMs. The car remained in Park. The doors were not supposed to lock until he engaged the transmission. They did this time. He looked to the back seat out of confusion. The climate control came on as programmed, right at 71 degrees. The sound system remained quiet, as programmed. Scanning the vehicle's central console screen, he detected no warnings or system faults.

As he placed the car in Drive, music from all thirteen speakers attacked his auditory senses. The woofer in the back vibrated the car with heavy bass. His body felt its percussive effects from head to toe. He didn't recognize the song, so he lowered the volume. Once again, he looked towards the back seat. A healthy paranoia was an intelligence officer's best friend. Perusing the entertainment system in the central console gave him no insight about the malfunction. He placed the vehicle in Park and the audio system went silent. He made a mental note to make an appointment with his dealer. There were now three malfunctions: the ignition, the premature door lock, and the sound system.

Placing the car in Drive once again blasted music from all speakers. This time he left it on long enough to recognize it. He'd heard it many times in Yankee Stadium in the 9th inning when the closer, Mariano Rivera, trotted in from the bullpen. If successful, the closer had the last word, securing the victory for the home team. He beamed with pride when he saw his fellow countryman, Mr. Rivera, number 42, trot in from the outfield, his entry announced by Yankees PA man Bob Sheppard, nicknamed "The Voice of God." The lights would soon dim for the other team when Enter Sandman played during Rivera's warmup tosses. But he had no idea why it played now.

He placed the uncooperative car in Park again and tried to turn the volume down, this time with partial success. The words from Metallica's song reverberated in the car. Surely someone standing less than 100 feet away would've heard the music.

When he tried to unlock the doors, he couldn't. The switch clicked yet produced no action. The power windows would not work either. His heart pulsated quickly and firmly, the arteries in his neck pounded against his collar. There'd been tricky situations before. He got detained once at gunpoint by FARC, the Revolutionary Armed Forces of Colombia, in the jungle during a documentary on the drug trade. Only a substantial bribe got him out of that mess. He also had the incident as a youth in the Chorrillo neighborhood in Panama City, where he found himself surrounded by a gang armed with knives. He carried a scar on his back from that incident. These and other escapes led him to the mythical belief of his invincibility. He slowed his breathing to remain calm and reassessed the situation, a situation that suggested he move quickly—he needed to get off the "X." For the moment, he was alone and unafraid, just like his training had taught him.

A series of fast-moving images flashed across the digital touchscreen. Eventually they coalesced in the image of an American flag with a superimposed bald eagle. He stared at it, dabbing his fingers on the screen, attempting to clear the image. He tried again to unlock the car only to hear the useless clicking. The car's transmission would no longer engage, it remained in Park. He had but one option left. It might draw attention to himself, but he'd had enough.

He reached for his tactical pen in the console. He'd use the pen's pointed end to crack the corner of the driver's side window. The corner of automobile glass represented its weakest point. If the pen didn't work, he'd use the gun under his seat.

Before taking the drastic action, he'd call Chandler, the only person who knew of his whereabouts. Ordinarily he would not turn on his phone at this location for security reasons, though he'd never had this happen.

"Hey Chan, can you hear me?" Arty asked, calmly speaking into the mouthpiece.

"Arty?" Chandler yelled. "Can you turn that music down?" He could barely hear him over Metallica.

"Chandler, look I'm having some car trouble and it's weird, man."

"What did you say? Car trouble?"

"Yeah sorry, I can't turn down this fucking music either," Arty wailed. "*Coño*. At least it's a song that I like." Arty had the composure to find humor in the events. "Anyway, in case-"

Chandler heard a small explosion. "Arty? You there? Arty? Hey!"

The driver and passenger airbags exploded, as did the one on the driver side door. White powder filtered through the passenger cabin, like pollen coming off a flower. The driver side window cracked. The deflating airbags emitted a serpentine hiss. With Arty leaned forward slightly for his conversation with Chandler, the phone now rested on the floorboard. It had gotten blown back into his face, bloodying his nose. He experienced uncontrollable tremors and internal pain.

Chandler responded to the moaning, his voice projected from the floorboard. "Arty! Arty! What's going on there?"

Arty had no motor coordination and lost consciousness. The last thing Arty heard was Metallica, crooning about his beloved Mariano.

***

Chandler continued yelling into his phone, hearing only Metallica on the other end. At a minimum, he knew Arty's phone remained active, meaning the emergency medical services could locate him.

Chandler started another call.

"911, what is your emergency?"

A breathless Chandler replied to the operator. "My friend, I don't know where he is, but I think he passed out. His phone is still on so you should be able to find him."

"Sir, I hope this is not a prank call since we're flooded with emergency calls right now. Just understand that it will take some time for us to respond and we will prosecute you if this is a fake call. Can you give me his location?"

"I don't know honestly. I'm at his house in Yonkers, not too far from the Glenwood station. My guess is that he's no more than a one hour's drive from here."

"Sir, that is a large area to respond for an emergency. I want to warn you again that-"

"I'm being serious! I think something happened. Please!"

"Ok, please give me his number."

Chandler provided the number and the operator indicated they would dispatch someone to the scene.

Not knowing what to do next, he called his mentor. "Ax! Ax! Something happened to Arty!" Chandler fumbled his phone while almost falling out of the studio chair.

Axel, never one to sound alarmed, replied, "Chan, calm down please. Maybe we need to secure chat?"

"No! I know I'm as nervous as a fly in a glue pot. Hear me out!" Chandler caught his breath before continuing. "He left his house to take a little drive somewhere. Don't ask me where cuz I don't know."

Chandler detailed the rest of his interaction with Arty and what occurred in the vehicle, including the loud explosion.

"So what was he doing there?"

"Sorry, Ax. I'll tell you later. I called 911 and they're going to dispatch someone. I feel so helpless. I can't do anything. We had a great lunch and were working on the film and-"

"Was the car moving? Could something have hit him? Maybe he got in an accident."

"I don't know if he was moving. He just said he was having car trouble and it was tough to hear him with all the loud music."

"If you heard an explosion, it was a bomb, maybe a gunshot? If he was moving, then maybe you heard the airbags going off? I don't know."

"I hope the cops get there soon, wherever 'there' is."

"There is another possibility here, though it's way too premature to suggest this based on your information. Remember when we were riding with Blago in the truck?"

"Yeah. Oh shit! That's what you think happened?" Chandler relived the accident in Iowa where the truck tipped to one side, killing their driver.

"It's a possible explanation. Again, let's not jump to conclusions. The only reason I even brought that up is because one of my contacts just last week told me about a hacking attack in Romania where a crime boss got taken out by exploding an airbag, this time in a moving vehicle."

"OK, but that wouldn't kill someone," Chandler reasoned. "The whole point of the airbag is to save someone's life!"

"You're right. It wasn't the explosion that killed the crime boss. It was the gas mixture. Let me explain. The airbag explosion goes off with one gas, and then it's mixed with others to neutralize its toxicity. If the gas mixture doesn't occur properly, the passenger cabin gets flooded with sodium azide. So instead of producing a harmless gas mixture, the airbag delivers a

237

lethal blow."

"So what are you saying?"

"Jump on a secure chat please and we can finish."

Chandler complied, ending the conversation, and opening the secure app on his phone.

REMOTE› WHAT WAS ARTY DOING?

LOCAL› HE SAID HE WAS MEETING HANDLER. HE WASN'T GONNA BE GONE LONG. I HAVE NO IDEA WHERE HE WENT BUT IT COULDN'T BE TOO FAR.

REMOTE› I'M SORRY TO SUGGEST THIS WITHOUT MORE INFORMATION RIGHT NOW. YOU NEED TO ASSUME HE'S DEAD. WHO WOULD WANT HIM DEAD? AND WHERE WAS HE KILLED? WE DON'T KNOW THE ANSWER TO EITHER. ASSUME ALSO THAT YOU ARE NOT SAFE AT YOUR LOCATION. I COULD BE WRONG BUT LET'S PLAY IT SAFE. LEAVE ASAP.

He didn't want to believe Arty had died.

Axel could be wrong. He's never really liked Arty anyway. He's probably just thinking the worst.

Chandler also realized that Axel could be right and that it would be safer to heed his mentor's advice. He had nothing to lose by evacuating. Before leaving, he downloaded files from Arty's array of computers. Besides copying the fruits of their documentary labor, Chandler hoped there could be evidence in the copied files, leading to resolving Arty's mishap. Chandler also grabbed a couple of laptops and placed everything in a large computer bag. He also had to get off the "X."

He walked out of Arty's, surveilling the street, noticing a few kids on summer break playing Wiffle ball. There didn't seem to be anything else unusual, no persons in parked cars or people behaving oddly. No one appeared dressed out of season. He walked at a brisk pace to the Glenwood station, periodically looking over his shoulder. He had no idea when the next train to Grand Central Station would arrive.

How would Arty's family be notified? Arty never said where they lived other than close by.

At this time in the late afternoon, trains ran approximately every thirty minutes, so it wasn't long before a train arrived and he boarded safely. The trip back to Manhattan would be much earlier than he anticipated and full of worry.

He might have just lost a friend and colleague, now two of them within the last year, first Rafael, his boss at El Mundo, and now potentially Arturo. The responsibility for finishing this project might fall squarely on his shoulders. He also had to consider his own exposure to danger. *Think positive here, Chandler.*

By the time he arrived in Manhattan, he expected Arty, *Señor Suerte*, Mr. Luck, to call and let him know he was OK.

***

Back at Grand Central Station, the subway trains were running normally. Station authorities had cleared the morning's disruption. He noticed nothing else. His mind raced through a thick pea soup of confusion as he plodded through the station. He didn't notice protesters holding signs of President Jefferson surrounded by swastikas. There were sanitation workers cleaning a restroom whose toilets had overflowed, the smell of which made many passersby gag. Chandler had no such reaction, walking in a robotic manner towards the number 7 train that would take him to Times Square before jumping on the number 3 train to his final destination.

Venus greeted his arrival, coinciding with a late dinner. "Good evening, Chandler. Would you like to know what is available for dinner?"

Chandler walked straight to the couch, placing the computer bags on the coffee table, and laid down staring at the ceiling.

"Chandler? Are you preparing dinner or would you like to order out?" Venus persisted.

Chandler remained silent, anxiously waiting for his phone to ring, his colleague on the other end, laughing about his mishap.

Venus, sensing his presence in the living room, turned on the large video monitor. "Here is your last take out order. Would you like me to order the same?" On the screen Venus displayed an order from a nearby Thai restaurant. He'd overcome a temporary phobia with Thai food after his first date with Arianne went horribly wrong. He no longer asked for "Thai Hot", "American Hot" offered him plenty of heat now.

The screen did not get his attention, but Jimi Hendrix did. Voodoo Child played from his shirt pocket.

His first attempt to grab his cell phone resulted in a fumble. He picked it up quickly off the couch, not taking the time to identify the caller. "Arty? Where are you? That was a bullshit stunt you pulled!"

The response disappointed. New York State police wanted to speak to him. Under normal circumstances, Chandler would not have spoken to the authorities in the absence of his attorney. Axel had always cautioned him that police could misconstrue or misinterpret anything he said during otherwise routine questioning. The public often forgot that Miranda rights were not in effect during routine conversations. Within the last year,

240

with the rise in domestic terror events, law enforcement looked less favorably on people they perceived as uncooperative. There were even unconfirmed reports of FBI and Homeland Security arresting people for remaining silent and charging them with obstruction of justice.

"I'm sorry, can you tell me if you found my friend, Mr. Dutari?"

The state trooper had other things on his mind. "Mr. Scott, we need to ask you a few questions."

He didn't see himself as a suspect, though in the eyes of law enforcement, he very well could be. He thought it best to proceed with their questioning so that he could get his own question answered. Besides, he wanted the police to have as much as possible investigating the whereabouts of his colleague.

Chandler provided full detail about their collaboration on the documentary. The state trooper questioning him recognized Chandler as a former television personality from El Mundo, thus that part of his statement did not receive any scrutiny. There would be no mention of Arty's intelligence connection. Any such disclosure would be neither confirmed nor denied by the U.S. government.

When asked the key question about Arty's business at Croton Point Park, Chandler stated that Arty told him he was going to the store. Since Chandler had little familiarity with Yonkers, he couldn't provide any more detail. State police were already searching Arty's home for more clues. Fortunately, Chandler extracted needed files and equipment from the home before he left. No doubt they would have been confiscated as part of the investigation, thus paralyzing his film. He would omit this detail from the questioning.

"All right. I've answered all your questions, now can you just tell me where he is?"

"I'm sorry, sir, we're speaking to next of kin right now. We can't-"

"He's dead, isn't he? Oh my God!" Chandler whimpered. The tears flowed.

The public swamped New York State police with civil disturbance calls and additional protection for elected state officials added further burden. Chandler would only get a very terse response from the trooper on the other end of the line.

A phone call the next morning to state police headquarters confirmed the worst, Arty had died. Chandler did little the next couple of days, merely vegetating in his apartment. He called the Westchester County coroner, who suspected that Arty died as a result of exposure to sodium azide.

Police investigators suspected that when the airbags deployed in the stationary vehicle, an otherwise harmless gas instead became a fatal mixture of 100% sodium azide. The investigators said they'd never seen anything like it. The police were reluctant to call it a murder pending further investigation. For now, they attributed his death to a vehicular malfunction.

After doing some digging, he located Arty's ex, Ynez. He felt like he owed her something, though he didn't know what exactly. At least, he needed to introduce himself and reveal their project.

She related how she met Arty and all the good times they had together. Arty was a good father and husband, yet his work drove a wedge in his relationship with her. They enjoyed a happy family life when around, though his absence created friction. She didn't sign up for that kind of life when she met him and couldn't understand why he couldn't work as a journalist closer to home and not be on some adventure. That tension in their relationship resonated with Chandler.

Chandler could not tell her what her ex-husband did for a living. He doubted that Arty ever told her either. It would have placed her and the kids in danger.

Chandler worried that the remaining members of the Dutari family could still be in danger, especially since there were no suspects in what he perceived to be Arty's murder.

The video they compiled at this juncture required further editing, a skill he did not have. He hoped that whoever the buyer, that they could provide the final touches. Fortunately, Chandler located a couple of files on one of the laptops with a list of potential buyers. None were in the U.S.

Even though the whistleblower gave a compelling story, Chandler needed a firsthand account of the reorientation camps. This whistleblower had no face or name, and he couldn't assess the account's veracity.

He knew he had to finish this project to honor Arturo and his family. He hoped that Senator Geringer and Axel, his two most trusted advisors, could help him with the next steps.

Part III

The Camp

CHAPTER SEVENTEEN
AXEL'S PLAN

Chandler felt fortunate to have befriended Senator Matt Geringer. Their friendship took birth in 2019 when Chandler's father, Professor Gustavo Sáenz, gave testimony to the Senate Subcommittee on Economic Policy. Professor Sáenz impressed Geringer enough that the senator struck up a conversation with him at the conclusion of the testimony. Chandler, who was in the audience, got introduced by his father. Chandler's professional life had been punctuated by a series of mentor relationships with his deceased boss, Rafael Mendoza, Axel Schultz, and now Senator Geringer.

With everything on his plate, Geringer still granted Chandler an audience at his office in the Hart Building. Chandler asked his other mentor, Mr. Axel Schultz, to be present. Arty's death understandably shook him, and now he needed both answers and guidance. If he wanted answers, he knew he needed to come clean with Geringer about Arturo Dutari's true identity.

Chandler and Axel met at the security checkpoint in the Hart Building, and a security officer escorted them the rest of the way. The spate of attacks heightened the security level in all federal buildings. All guests now required armed security in transit to a senator's office. The security officer knocked forcefully on Geringer's door.

"Guys, come in, please," the lanky Geringer said, standing behind his desk, waving them in.

After a brief handshake, Chandler and Axel assumed their usual positions opposite the senator.

"Matt, thanks so much for meeting me. I need to talk to you about a few things, in person, and once you hear them, you'll realize why I couldn't say anything over the phone," Chandler explained. Though non-Catholic, he felt like a sinner before confession.

"Sounds serious, though I can't imagine it's anything that will knock me over these days," Geringer replied. The senator found himself knee deep in his usual legislative matters and efforts to constitutionally resolve the previous year's presidential election.

"I don't know if you heard in the news, I know I didn't mention it to you over the phone, but my colleague, the person I mentioned that I was working with on the documentary, Arturo Dutari, I always called him Arty, he died late last month." Chandler averted his eyes and turned his head, fearful he'd shed a tear.

"Oh my, God! I'm so sorry Chandler! What happened?" Geringer's formerly crossed arms fell to his lap.

"Matt, I think they murdered him," Chandler said, turning back to Geringer.

Chandler explained the details of his death, including the trip to Croton Point Park where authorities found his body in his SUV. Axel added his own speculation about the toxic gas that eventually killed him and the hacking exploit likely responsible for it.

"That's horrible! But why would anyone want to kill him? Did he have enemies? What did the police say?" Geringer fired in rapid succession.

"There's a little more to this story," Chandler paused, flicking his eyes to the side and biting his lip. He rummaged for how to complete his thought. "As you might imagine."

Chandler provided the details of Arty's involvement with

intelligence.

Geringer, equally surprised by Chandler's naiveté and Arty's undercover life, shook his head. "You had to figure you'd be exposed to danger, Chandler."

"I guess I didn't see it that way." Chandler's sense of adventure and his experiences as an international network correspondent and TV show host made him discount inherent dangers in most situations.

"You definitely get yourself in the middle of things. Like when I had to rescue you and Arianne from the CFU rally," Geringer offered with a wry smile.

"Oh, and Arianne. She's no longer in D.C. and our situation is complicated right now," Chandler lamented.

"Sorry to hear that. I hope you guys work it out. She's a keeper for sure," Geringer said.

"Senator, Matt, probably the biggest reason I'm here today is to ask you about something that came up during our film research. I won't get into all the details, but Arty got a video from a whistleblower who supposedly works for an intelligence agency, giving a tell-all about reorientation camps out in some western states. Have you heard of this?"

"Reorientation camps? Like what for high school dropouts?" Geringer seemed perplexed by the question, leaning in, placing his elbow on his desk, rubbing his considerable mustache.

"Not exactly."

Chandler explained how Homeland Security developed the camps to deal with the anticipated flood of refugees from Central American and Caribbean countries, and maybe others from the Middle East. Once the political situation in the U.S. grew more polarized, Homeland Security repurposed the camps for domestic use.

Geringer extended his hand towards Chandler, halting him. "Let me stop you for a second. Are you saying that we're rounding people up and detaining them in these camps, like they're criminals? What are they charged with?" Geringer leaned back in his chair, placing his hands on his lap, directing his steely gaze towards Chandler.

"I don't know that they're charged with anything. Maybe they are. I don't know, can't give you any more on that. Once they get there, they get assigned to some psych, ah, what was that again Ax?" Chandler asked, turning towards Axel.

"They get assigned a PSYOP officer or better said, a psychological operations officer," Axel replied.

Chandler continued after the clarification. "Yes, PSYOP. I couldn't remember the term. Anyway, that PSYOP officer works to reeducate them using virtual reality. They talk about supporting the country, patriotism and those kinds of themes."

Geringer narrowed his eyes and pursed his lips, his top one concealed by his thick mustache. Clearly, he had no idea. "I don't know what to say. Trust me guys, I had no clue any of this was going on. The only question I have is whether any of this is true. Who's the whistleblower and how credible are they?"

"They disguised themselves so I don't know. Arty got the video in St. Louis so he thought they worked in Geospatial Intelligence," Chandler replied.

"I can't just go knocking on Homeland Security's door and ask them about reorientation camps. As it is, they've gotten tight-lipped about anything they're doing citing national security. I was aware of Islamic detainees in camps after we started moving them from Guantanamo, but this PSYOP stuff, no, that I haven't heard."

"The video from that whistleblower raised many questions,

questions to which I need answers."

"Well, I don't know how you're going to get those answers, frankly." Geringer raised a skeptical eyebrow.

Axel, one of the most patient listeners anyone would ever meet, had some thoughts around getting those answers. First, he had his own agenda with the senator. "Hey, what's going on with the Article Five convention? Sorry for the abrupt subject change."

Chandler snapped his head towards Axel and gave him a disapproving look. Axel shrugged his shoulders and smirked.

Geringer hoped to convene the legislatures of two-thirds of the states for the purpose of amending the Constitution and overturning the president's executive action.

The senator paused for a moment to adjust to the new topic. "Ahh, I think there are enough IAP and TP members now in state legislatures and discontented GOP and Dem members who are tired of the president's actions. I started laying the groundwork for this a few months back, knowing that the Senate would be unlikely to find Jefferson guilty in the impeachment trial and just in case the Supreme Court went against us."

"Smart move on your part," Axel nodded.

"I am a firm believer that we have to follow the Constitution. What Jefferson did was flat wrong, illegal and unconstitutional. It's too bad the highest court in the land didn't see it that way. There is another path here. These secessionists and separatists think they're doing something noble, but all they've done is give the Jefferson administration more propaganda about safety, security, and the economy. It just feeds into the narrative about the need to expand executive power. Trust me guys, the president doesn't need any more help."

"The problem with the Article Five is how long it will take," Axel surmised.

"You're right. I think we can fast track this thing through the states just to know if we'll have the two-thirds. If we don't do something now, any future president could pull the same stunt and the Electoral College could have the same issue in 2024 especially with the growth of our party and the Theocracy Party," Geringer added.

"I think you've got the right approach too, Matt. I agree that these groups like the Five Tribes, while well-intentioned, are creating more chaos at a time when we need less. I'm a staunch Libertarian, though I also believe in the rule of law. If you don't like a law, then you change it and, well, that's all I have to say before I go on a rant," Axel concluded.

"Chandler, I want you to consider something for your documentary. I would like for you to listen to a panel of Congressional members from all four political parties and get their take on what's going on. Combine this with what you did with that person you met in my office a couple of months ago and I think you'll be able to present an even more balanced view and let people draw their own conclusions," Geringer suggested.

"Sounds good. Just let me know when you can arrange it and I'll be back here," Chandler answered.

Geringer concluded the meeting when his Chief, Molly Sanders, popped in and alerted him to his next appointment. "Sorry I can't have lunch with you guys today. I know I've mentioned our humble cafeteria to you before. You should check it out. Food's not bad."

Chandler and Axel took the senator's advice and walked to an eatery, called The Hungry Senator, on the floor connecting the corridor between the Hart and Dirksen office buildings.

***

Most Americans would probably conclude that the Hungry

Senator featured gourmet cuisine. In reality, the place had standard cafeteria fare, albeit with a broad selection, not unlike what you'd find on a college campus. Axel surveyed the menu and scoffed when they didn't have green tea, having to settle for an unknown brew. Chandler had no such issues with the beverages and poured himself a tall soft drink from the fountain. The men sat at an open table, intentionally separated from other patrons.

"I didn't want to say anything in front of Geringer after you started talking about the reorientation camps so-" Axel's conversational foray was interrupted.

"Huh? What were you gonna say?" Chandler asked, impatiently, taking his dishes off the tray.

"As I was saying, when we confronted Arty about who he was and you guys started talking about the whistleblower and the allegations, I got to thinking if there was any way to verify what that person alleged. If you guys placed that segment in your film without some verification, it could be easily discredited."

"I'm not sure I like where this is heading, Ax," Chandler said, biting into his ham sandwich.

"Please, let me continue. What if there was a way to verify all this? So, you know my contact at Omni, Phish." Axel referred to his primary contact within the hacker organization, responsible for revealing information about the financial maneuvers of the Global Settlement Bank and the Financial Stability Board prior to the 2020 presidential election. "I reached out to Phish and asked them to find out if there was any substance to this whistleblower."

"And?" Chandler inquired, while chewing.

Axel took a sip of his brew. "Oh, that's awful. They call that tea?"

Chandler, in between bites, did not appreciate the interruption. "Ax, come on!"

"And as many suspected, Omni has been providing limited support to the Five Tribes. Omni is sympathetic to their cause but has no interest in forming any sort of alliance with them or joining their movement."

"From what I've seen of Omni, they pretty much are lone wolves, so that's not surprising."

Axel dug through his salad, stabbing the seedless olives to eat individually. "Correct. Omni, as you know, hates big government and even though I think most of their membership is overseas, well frankly, I don't know where most of their operatives are, they're not happy about the election freeze so this has drawn them closer to the Tribes."

Chandler thought about this for a moment and recalled a conversation with his partner. "Arty thought the Tribes were getting help, makes sense."

"Phish told me there is someone sympathetic to the Tribes working for a contractor supporting one of the reorientation camps in Nevada. So apparently, the camps are real. Now what they do exactly in the camps, they don't know. From what Phish says, the sympathizer has their own agenda, they didn't say what. To be honest, Chan, it's not at all clear who this sympathizer is aligned with, Omni or the Tribes. The bottom line is that there is someone who is in one of the camps."

"So I'm waiting for the punchline here, Ax," Chandler said, slurping his soft drink, emitting a small burp following the hard swallow.

He looked upon his lunch partner with chagrin. "Manners, Chandler, manners. I asked Phish to find out if this sympathizer would be willing to work with a journalist to investigate this story further. I finally got my answer a couple of days ago."

Chandler dropped his sandwich on his plate. "Let me guess. I'm the journalist and the answer is 'yes'?"

"You are correct, grasshopper. I have taught you well," Axel smiled. "We're joking around right now but don't kid yourself, this is dangerous. Your life may not be threatened like it was in Afghanistan when you almost hit that IED. I have no idea what would happen if you were to get caught. At a minimum, you'd face some sort of federal trespassing charge, though I can't say with any certainty what else could happen legally or physically."

Chandler had to weigh this exposure risk against the voices in his head from Arianne and his mother. But with the memory of Arturo Dutari and the obligation to finish this project weighing on his shoulders, he asked, "How would this all go down? How's the contact gonna help me?"

"Some of those details need to be finalized. The general thought is the person would get you into the camp, you could wear a hidden camera and talk to some people there. Supposedly, this person knows someone in the camp that isn't too keen on what's going on there, whatever that is." Axel usually had details down to the 'nth degree so the words "general thought" and "supposedly" were disconcerting.

"I don't have anything like a hidden camera. I don't work for a large network, you know, so my equipment is pretty much non-existent."

"Don't worry about the camera. Phish said the Tribes would take care of that. I'm sure they have some pretty cool toys. One thing I did want to mention is that if for some reason you're caught, the person in the camp would disavow any knowledge of your identity and what you were doing. Don't count on the Tribes either. They're mostly cyber-jockeys. Infiltration is not

255

their thing. You're basically on your own."

"My own personal version of Mission Impossible, huh?" Chandler lamented.

"I figured after Arty's death and what you told me about this whistleblower, you were going to chase this lead. I know I'm not doing you any favors with Arianne, but at least this way, you can go there with a plan, a plan that has input from me and people I trust. I know you pretty well. You're still like a young buck, always ready to run."

"Can't argue with any of that. You probably think I carry my brains in my back pocket sometimes. It's who I am."

"Trust me, I know."

Chandler became somber while swirling his soft drink in the oversize glass. "We haven't talked about this. Assuming there was foul play, who do you think murdered Arturo?"

"You said the state police didn't provide any clues or suspects. We know what killed him and that image on his touchscreen." Axel referred to the image of the flag and the eagle left on the vehicle's digital touchscreen. "We know why he was there and what he was doing. It's hard to imagine his intelligence handler would want him dead. He was still a useful asset. We don't know if Arty had any enemies from his years working the War on Drugs and now the domestic terror threat. Let's be honest, even though he confessed his identity, there could still be much we didn't know. In his line of work, he may have told us just the minimum to keep himself out of trouble."

"The image on the dash screen. You think it was one of these secession groups? Though I don't get that since we were telling the secession story from their viewpoint."

"Chandler, let me suggest something. The thing about intelligence agencies is that they're experts at manipulation, deception, misinformation, and propaganda. You also have a state police force, with a million other things on their agenda, tasked with investigating the crime. They have no leads and few clues. The case may go cold on them quickly for lack of personnel. We will probably never know what happened. The only thing we can say is that he died at the hands of someone well-versed in the art of vehicle hacking. This was no simple vehicle malfunction. There were too many things going on there. After our experience with Blago, you should be very suspicious."

"What a world we live in. Sad, really." Chandler paused to reflect. He took a half-hearted bite out of his sandwich and spun the morsel in his mouth. His chewing labored. "I will go to the reorientation camp. Before I go, I'll take up Geringer's offer to listen in on this Congressional panel."

***

The senator's chief, Molly Sanders, made the meeting happen quickly. The members of Congress agreed to have Chandler present for a panel discussion led by Geringer. Chandler could listen and take notes, but he couldn't record audio or video. He could freely quote his sources.

The meeting convened in a conference room on the 9th floor of the Hart Building. He and Geringer were the first to arrive. They were followed by Texas IAP senator and former presidential contender, Alfonso Chancellor, Theocracy Party Representative, Milton Wise, Speaker of the House, Republican Janice Rossi, and Alicia Scarborough, the GOP nominee for president in 2020. Scarborough would be the only one not serving in Washington. No member of the Democratic party accepted the invitation out of deference to their leader, President Jefferson. All meeting participants, except for one, greeted Chandler warmly and thanked him for his work during the election cycle last year. Rossi gave him a curt acknowledgment.

Geringer opened the proceeding. "Thank you all for attending. I think everyone's familiar with the ground rules. I'll guide the discussion and Mr. Scott will take notes. I think it's important for us to be candid here and share our thoughts, especially during this difficult time in our nation's history. I regret that our Democratic colleagues chose not to attend, though I understand why. Let me start by asking each of you what your thoughts are about what's going on in our nation. Governor Scarborough, perhaps you'd like to begin?"

"Thanks. I feel honored to receive an invitation. I ran a hard-fought campaign last year and am in limbo now since the president didn't allow the election to proceed in Congress. I'd like to know if I'm going to serve the office. I tallied the second most Electoral College votes, so I think I have a fair chance of being declared the winner. The president has faced unprecedented challenges with cyber terror and the ongoing financial crisis; however he must respect the Constitution. I have no idea what the Supreme Court was thinking. Regardless, I am in full agreement with Senator Geringer, that we must follow a process and proceed with an Article Five convention. If we don't follow a process, we'll have a chaos worse than we have now."

While Chandler took notes, the rest waited for Geringer to speak.

Theocracy Party Representative Milton Wise filled the silence. "I guess I'll go next. My party's nominee last year, Mr. King, articulated the Deep State concern in an interview with Mr. Scott and in the final presidential debate. While I don't endorse his behavior during that debate, his words were prescient. In my darkest moments, I wonder if the secessionists are right. If I could play king for one day, I would abolish the Financial Stability

Board, the Federal Reserve, and cut the size of our military to get us out of our entanglements overseas. The government's got its tentacles in too many places and we're about as godless as a society can be. Senator Geringer, our politics are not in agreement, but I respect what you're doing with Article Five and your case at the Supreme Court. I just don't think anything will come of your efforts. Sorry for the pessimism. God will ultimately judge us, I'm afraid."

The potential wrath of God unsettled the group, creating another round of silence. The Speaker of the House, Janice Rossi, broke the uncomfortable pause. "I agreed to be here. I did. Senator Geringer, what you don't realize, or maybe you do, is that the one thing we didn't need in this country is more Congressional disruption. You put the country through an impeachment vote and a Senate trial. And what did it get us? Nothing, just more distraction. Instead of the Congress working on the people's business, we're fighting the president, who, by the way, is doing everything he can to save the country. I realize these comments seem strange coming from a Republican, but I feel strongly we need to support him now." Her gaze bore a hole in Chandler before she fired her next salvo. "Mr. Scott, you can quote me in your documentary that I was opposed to the impeachment, the Supreme Court challenge, and the Article Five."

Geringer knew the Speaker did not share his approach, always giving him a chilly reception when they met. As her party's leader, however, she felt an obligation to attend.

"Alfonso, I know you've got something to add." Geringer winked at the former IAP presidential nominee. He and Chancellor had worked the phones with Congressional representatives leading up to the impeachment vote.

"Without a doubt. I don't think I would be elected president even if the vote went to the House. Like Senator Geringer, I'd like to see the process play itself out. Why have a Constitution otherwise? That document exists for a reason. Yes, I want to see an Article Five convention. In fact, I'm sure the Texas legislature will have no problem with it. I won a state that had been a Republican stronghold. The IAP is making strides, although we realize the next president will be a Democrat or Republican. In 2024? Who knows, we may have a chance. Also, these secessionists, and believe me we have some in Texas, I don't agree with them. They aren't going to solve our problems, and they're very disruptive. Speaker Rossi, I know you think the IAP's responsible for derailing Congress with the impeachment process, but the president forced our hand. You were in the same meeting with me last year in the Oval Office." Chancellor referred to the historic meeting on November 30, 2020 where he told the President Jefferson he had no authority to issue his Executive Order 14666, freezing the election.

Chancellor continued. "I should have known from your silence in that meeting, Madam Speaker, what your intentions were."

The meeting continued for another thirty minutes, with each member expressing their concerns about the economy and domestic terror.

Geringer closed the meeting with his thoughts on the role of the press during times like these when intelligence agencies and federal authority appear to threaten the public. "The government has a responsibility to keep its secrets. Those secrets have kept this country safe from external threats. The threats are now within. The press no doubt feels like the government has the authority to keep these secrets until someone leaks them. That places the press in an unenviable position to decide what should be kept secret or revealed to the public. Journalists have to weigh the positives and negatives of revealing these secrets, yet I don't think the press is in the best position to make those judgments."

Geringer did not look at Chandler when making those comments, but he took them to heart. He would soon discover a government secret where he'd have to make this judgment.

CHAPTER EIGHTEEN
THE CAMP

Chandler returned to New York for a week to do more work on the documentary and get his things together before his trip to the reorientation camp. He had called New York State police to see if they had any leads regarding the untimely death of Arturo Dutari. The authorities continued to label his death an accident resulting from a system malfunction. Arty's ex-wife, Ynez, had retained the services of legal counsel who explored a wrongful death civil suit. If that case ever made it to trial, it would continue to expose the weak underbelly of vehicle control software, whether accidental as the authorities claimed or malicious as Chandler feared.

He spent a couple of days in Chicago, visiting Axel, rounding out his preparation. They were in secure communication with Omni regarding his contact in the reorientation camp. The Five Tribes allowed no communication with anyone outside their trust zone, thus Omni served as an intermediary. Since the Five Tribes and Quinque had already spoken with Chandler, albeit in a cloaked manner, they had some measure of comfort communicating through their temporary ally, Omni.

Chandler copied his video files and other data and brought them to Axel, who would distribute them to a worldwide, heavily encrypted peer-to-peer network. Axel had a great aversion to cloud storage, preferring the decentralized approach. If anything happened to Chandler, Axel would have the means to distribute the raw video to a network.

Satisfied with his preparation, Chandler took the Purple line train north to the Foster station in Evanston to meet Arianne at

Maxwell Technologies. She didn't have an official position at her father's company, though she provided an occasional helping hand on legal matters. It had been three months since he'd seen her, that fateful day at the Citizens for Unity rally. When he approached the Maxwell Tech building, he noticed how she cut the same striking figure she always had, her long auburn hair glistening in the July sun. He received a warm embrace and a kiss on the cheek, and a bright smile.

She hung on his arm as they took a leisurely walk to of all places a Thai restaurant where they relived their very first date in D.C. in the Spring of 2019. The embarrassment of their first date still lingered. He thought he could handle any spicy food being exposed to all kinds of hot chili from his younger days in the Lone Star State. Thai hot convinced him otherwise.

They enjoyed a nice lunch with mild spiciness and talked about their future. She still held firm that he needed to settle down. He assured her that his project would wind down soon. Still, she had no idea what he was doing, nor did she ask. If she knew details of this adventure, she'd surely protest. He dared not mention what happened to Arty. She never met him anyway, and it served no purpose to further alarm her. There would be plenty of time to discuss what happened later, after he finished the film.

The walk back to the Foster station took them on another journey down memory lane, in a different time and a different city, this time New York. For at least a couple of hours, Chandler could forget about what lay ahead for him professionally and personally. She gave him a brief but ardent kiss, this time on the lips. He didn't tell her when he'd see her again, only that he would soon.

The following day, Axel drove him to O'Hare where he would board American Airlines flight 17 with a destination of Las

Vegas. He'd visited Sin City in 2011 when one of his college friends got hitched. It proved to be a memorable bachelor party. His friend, a classmate from his time at the SAIS program at Johns Hopkins, came from a wealthy family. They spared no expense. He never told Arianne about that weekend, a memory that needed to stay in Vegas.

The slot machines in the arrival gate offered no temptation. He faced long enough odds with his pending investigation of the camp.

He rented a vehicle and drove 100 miles in the August heat of the Nevada desert towards the town of Rachel. His contact worked at Consolidated Food Services (CFS), which had built an enormous warehouse near the town from where they served a number of government facilities. The federal government owned most of the land in the state, estimated at some 80%, punctuated with facilities from the Department of Defense, the Department of Energy and the Department of Homeland Security.

Within the last year, CFS successfully bid on a large Request for Proposal (RFP) for Homeland Security to provide food services to an unspecified facility in Nevada. The RFP stated the facility could hold up to 500 government personnel and 500 people only identified as "camp occupants" with little other detail given. Executives for CFS presumed the occupants might be enemy combatants from overseas and former detainees of Guantanamo. Homeland personnel responsible for evaluating bid responses deftly evaded detailed RFP questions. The government could not afford to reveal too much ahead of an award.

CFS executives with knowledge of the RFP were later briefed on the camp's true occupants, domestic terrorists. The execs were told to sign a non-disclosure whose violation would subject them to lengthy prison terms and fines. Some at CFS regretted the contract award.

Homeland gave CFS specific guidelines regarding their movement in the camp, and their hours. Any employee working on site had to pass through a rigorous screening process equivalent to an enhanced security clearance with accompanying threats of prosecution.

Chandler had dinner in the town's only diner and then checked into the town's only hotel. He would not meet his contact until the next morning. Sometime around 2:00 am, he woke up in a cold sweat calling for Arianne. It was that dream again; the sun rising and setting in the eastern sky, followed by fireballs pelting the Earth. He grabbed his phone, thinking about sending her a text. Then he realized he couldn't send it since he was, as the Navy would say, in Emissions Control or EMCON status, prohibited from communication. His phone remained off, SIM removed.

***

The next morning, as instructed, he drove 30 miles out of town towards a small one story home in the desolate expanse of arid terrain. He spied the portable gas generator supplementing whatever electrical service the place had. A satellite dish mounted on the roof pointed towards the southern sky. A solar panel array littered the tiny backyard. The home had no landscaping. A dirt and gravel path off the state road steered vehicles to the front door.

A dog barked incessantly after he parked and approached the door. Chandler felt a wave of hostility in this harsh desert, glad the initial meeting occurred before the heat baked the area.

He took measured steps towards the front door, the crunching gravel audible above the din of the home's air

265

conditioning unit. After knocking, he heard the hum of a PTZ camera. He couldn't see it and figured it was in the light fixture to his right.

The loudspeaker by the door cracked with static. "You got some ID?" An annoying high frequency chirp followed.

Chandler carefully reached into the front pocket of his jeans, slowly pulling out his wallet, and retrieved his identification from the State of New York. He awaited his next instruction.

The speaker blurted out another crackle. He hoped the rest of the interaction would differ from a comedy skit of an old fast food drive-through.

"Put the ID in front of the light fixture to your right and hold it there until I say to move it."

He did as requested, listening to the hum of the camera lens focusing on his ID.

After a few seconds, he received his next command. "OK, you can move it. What do you want?"

In the drama of his identity verification, he forgot what he needed to say. The person on the other side of the door waited for the next stage of confirmation to ensure no compromise of Chandler's identity.

He slapped his forehead, recalling the word. "Rebellium."

A crack of static preceded the next instruction. "Repeat that word again."

"Rebellium."

Chandler hoped they wouldn't ask for a spelling. The word meant "insurgency" or "insurrection" in Latin.

The door opened slowly, clockwise. A stream of cool air bathed his face. He feared walking into the space in front of him.

"Come in." This time the sound didn't come from the loudspeaker. His fear did not allow him to lift his leg to walk. "I said, come in!"

He took the bait this time and took a couple of steps. When he cleared the edge of the opened door, a hard object rammed his temple, tilting his head slightly.

"Don't turn. Just keep walkin' towards that chair in the family room. When you get to it, sit down and face in the chair's direction. Don't turn around."

The object on the side of his head had to be a firearm, probably a shotgun, since he didn't feel the woman's presence that close to him. He did as ordered. He sat looking towards the yard and solar panel array.

"Tell me your name."

Chandler relaxed and rotated his body towards the woman, thinking it impolite to introduce himself by looking away from her.

The shotgun pushed back against his temple. "Mothafucka, I told you not to turn around. Don't make me use this."

He rotated back to the suggested position. "Easy. Easy. My name is Chandler Scott." His voice quivered. "I gave you the code word. What else can I do?"

His question went unanswered. The shotgun moved away from his temple, though he dared not try to find it. A telescoping rod extended beside him with a biometric scanner.

"Put your index finger on this."

He submitted to the scan and heard a single beep. Moments later, the dog, a sable and black German Shepherd, that barked incessantly before his entry, sniffed his legs.

"Ok. You can get up now and turn around."

In front of Chandler stood a tall black woman, fortyish, dressed in cargo pants and a tee shirt, her hair flattened by a ball cap. In her younger days, he imagined her as an athlete. She moved towards him and extended her hand. Her soft hand belied her initial hostility towards him. She smelled like a bouquet, undoubtedly from the body lotion necessary in the dry air.

"Hello, Chandler, my name is DeArthie Chapman. I apologize for all this. I hope you understand. I don't know if they told you much about me. I live out here in the desert by myself. There's too many crazies out there and I can't be too sure, you know. Now that I'm mixed up with these other people, I gotta watch out."

He assumed that the words "they" or "these other people" meant the Five Tribes, though he couldn't be certain. He'd carefully mention their name later. "That's fine, Mrs. Chapman," he said, noticing the wedding ring. "You can't be too careful these days."

She waved him towards the kitchen where they would sit across from each other at a small wooden table, replete with nicks and scuff marks on its legs and surface.

Since his arrival her mood went from hostile intent to gracious host, as she served him coffee and donuts. The food paled compared to what he could get in Manhattan, though beggars could not be choosers.

She joined the military after 9/11, serving two tours of duty in Iraq, where she met her husband. After their discharge, they settled in the D.C. area where she received an Associate's degree while her husband returned to college to get a degree in accounting. Freshly armed with their education and military experience, they went to work for the federal government. She worked at Walter Reed Medical Center as an assistant in physical therapy, and he for the U.S. Treasury.

After a few years of this routine, they grew tired of life in D.C. and wanted no association with the insular nature of the Beltway particularly after the federal government's continued expansion. They moved to Las Vegas where her husband had family and started a restaurant supply business.

She sipped her coffee, continuing her autobiography. "We was lucky, starting our business in 2012 after the market bottomed in Vegas, you know. Then the 2016 crash came and our business got bad. Whew, we got wiped out in the 2019 crash. People stopped coming to Vegas, the gambling business went to hell, hotels had a hard time. My husband, he got real bitter. He didn't think the 1% felt the pain of all the economic trouble. You know what I'm sayin'? He just saw the fat cats in D.C. That's why we left. We didn't want no part of it."

"You talk about your husband. Where is he?" Chandler surveyed the small home, expecting him to appear.

"Whew, that is a long story, child." DeArthie wiped her brow, removing imaginary sweat.

Mr. Chapman had become active on anti-government social forums on the Internet. She cautioned him about his activity since she knew authorities monitored those forums. Living in Vegas and in the depths of despair after losing their business, he gambled too much, frittering away the little savings they had. He didn't care, feeling his useful life had ended. She talked him out of a trip to Oregon, where he wanted to visit a "death clinic." Death clinics had grown in popularity in that state in the wake of the 2019 financial crisis. The clinics hooked people up with drugs designed by its "guests." The guest chose their mood or hallucination prior to the administration of terminal sedation. The clinics offered an alternative for economically desperate souls who preferred death to living in the country's present state.

DeArthie teared up describing what happened next. "One night, I was waiting for him to come home and when daylight came, he still hadn't come. I called Vegas police. They said the cameras caught him leaving the casino at 1:00 am and the street cameras followed him to our house where we lived in Henderson. They said that ALPR system, I think that's what they call it, showed him three miles away and then lost him." She used her napkin to wipe her eyes.

"I didn't think an ALPR system, if you mean the one that tracks license plates, could lose someone in a city like Vegas," Chandler speculated.

"The cops said there was records missing. Those missing records could have told them where my man might be," DeArthie explained.

"So he just disappeared?"

"He did. They told me the FBI got involved and started a bigger search. But nothing. Whatchu gonna do?" She shrugged her shoulders.

Times got more difficult, forcing her to sell the house in Henderson. She heard from a friend about a job with a company who claimed they had just won a government contract in a town about 100 miles north of Vegas. They were looking for people with food service experience. With a background in her restaurant supply business, she got a position with Consolidated Food Services (CFS). She bought her current home to be closer to her job.

"I got the job a month 'fore the election last year. Things was going fine other than my husband being gone. He is a good man. He never hit me. Just got real down on himself. I got real worried. Then he just disappeared. I cried almost every night, mm hmm"

"I can't imagine what you are going through, not knowing and with no leads or information concerning his whereabouts."

"Well, about three months ago I got called by someone who said they might know somethin' about my Juan. I didn't believe it since it wasn't like the police or nobody like that telling me."

"So who gave you this lead?"

"Child, I can't tell you that. They swore me to secrecy. This person said my husband could be in the facility where I was working and that it was some kinda camp. They took people there who, you know, people who were against the government. Then I thought about all the time my Juan was on those Internet forums, talkin' bad about the government."

Chandler persisted in knowing something about DeArthie's informant. "Can you tell me anything about the person who told you this?"

"No, I ain't telling you their name. They did say somethin' about some damn tribes, My Tribes or somethin' like that. I thought they was fooling me. Sounded like some hip hop group. You know what I'm sayin'? This person said that there were other people disappearing too."

The mention of disappearing people struck a chord with Chandler. His father, Gustavo, hailed from Argentina. After his senior year in high school, his mostly estranged father took him on a trip to his ancestral home where Chandler met the other side of his family. His grandfather, Armando, had a position as finance minister with the left wing Peronist party. The military coup of 1976 chased Gustavo out of the country. Armando, even with his left wing affiliation, survived the coup since he bought off prominent members of the military junta.

Other left wingers were not as fortunate. Many disappeared and were never heard from again. During Argentina's Dirty War, the military government operated a series of detention centers where they tortured and murdered detainees. The military

271

justified these centers in the name of national stability hoping to preserve the Western Christian life. Many records of these atrocities were destroyed after Argentina lost the Falklands War.

"I understand about disappearing people, believe me, but that is a story for another day," Chandler said, briefly reliving the Argentine memory.

DeArthie explained her work. She alternated between the giant distribution warehouse and working in the camp. CFS told their employees serving this camp that it operated as a detention center and did not specifically identify its occupants. The company prepared food and distributed other supplies to the camp. They had regular contact with the camp employees and scarcely any contact with camp occupants.

"So the person who told me about my Juan being in the camp came to me a couple of weeks ago and said someone was coming to meet me to show the world what was going on in here. I guess that's you, huh?"

DeArthie explained that she bore no allegiance to the secessionists and voted for IAP candidate Chancellor in 2020. She wanted her husband back. The Tribes were the only ones who provided any leads. The Tribes also saw her as an opportunity to have eyes inside the camp where some of their own might reside. Undercover work was not their forte. That risk fell on Chandler.

Chandler asked, "Have you found any evidence that your husband's actually there?"

"I saw a paper in the trash one day and took it home. 'J Chapman' was on a list. Next to his name there were some numbers and letters. I gave it to my contact, who said they'd study it. They thought it was some sort of treatment. Who knows, that may not have been my Juan."

DeArthie mentioned that she had met someone in the cafeteria. When she started asking questions about her husband and told this employee her plight, the person became sympathetic and agreed to do some digging.

"So this camp employee is my last hope. Mm hmm. Unless you do somethin' for me."

"No promises. I'm still surprised they linked me up with you. I should tell you that I interviewed one of their leaders for the documentary I'm working on. Ultimately, that's the reason I'm even here. Hopefully, we can find out something about Juan. I should also tell you, we had a government whistleblower who seemed to know something about these camps and the stuff they're doing here. It was creepy."

They spent the rest of the day talking about themselves, their lives, their hopes and aspirations. In another life, he may never have crossed paths with her.

"I prepared a room for you. You're supposed to stay here, they told me, right?" DeArthie asked.

"Yes, that was my understanding. My guess is, I would attract too much attention at that hotel in Rachel."

He hoped to escape the recurring dream about the sunrise and the fireballs.

***

When he woke up, he tried to remember his dreams. He couldn't. Perhaps out of sight was out of mind.

DeArthie already had breakfast ready for him when he shuffled back to the dining room, wiping the sleep from the corners of his eyes. The home had little delineation between dining room, living room, and kitchen. The German Shepherd lunged towards him, causing him to stagger as he got near the table.

DeArthie scolded the beast. "Get down, Diesel, before I smack you upside yo' head! He just likes you, child."

A rebalanced Chandler replied, "Good thing he likes me or I'd be flat on my back."

"I hope you like what I fixed. Sit down. I'm not real fancy plus I can get food at work too so I don't cook much." She pushed silverware and napkins in his direction.

"Thank you, DeArthie. Anything's good for me."

"Oh child, just call me Dee from now on. The only person who calls me that is my godmother. I'm named after her."

"Hmm. It's a name I'd never heard before and it's a very elegant name, if I may say."

"Thank you."

After his breakfast of sausage, biscuits and coffee, they discussed their action plan for the day.

The first order of business involved Chandler's facial alteration. He'd been told to let his facial hair grow. The considerable growth on his face acquired over the last two weeks gave him the suggested hirsute appearance.

The latex facial prosthetic was a new challenge. Prior to his arrival, a makeup artist visited Dee to give her rudimentary training in applying a facial disguise. A Tribes member had created the prosthetic on a 3D printer. Little did Chandler know that the Tribes already had a detailed facial map from his stay in the silo. Dee needed to make him appear like the picture on his falsified company badge. The disguise would be subtle, affecting nose curvature and width, adding a decade of age. They would have to apply the nose every morning. A little touch of gray to his dark mane rounded out the conversion.

Chandler proved a restless makeup recipient while sitting in the dining room chair where he'd eaten breakfast.

"Will you hold still, child? I'm not good at this and you're making this harder. You better get used to this. I'm gonna be in yo' face a lot from now on," Dee insisted, while she applied the water-based adhesive on his nose.

"Sorry, I'll work harder at playing a statue," he answered, stiffening his neck.

The Five Tribes facilitated his entry to the camp and conversion to CFS employee through a sophisticated hack into a government system. All employees in government facilities provided a two-factor authentication, something they carried and something unique to the individual. Factor one was an identification badge. A biometric characteristic, like a fingerprint, represented the second factor. The Tribes had already verified and stored his fingerprint when Blago picked him up. They substituted Chandler's biometric characteristic with that of a bogus contract employee for CFS. A separate hack took place in a CFS database to create the employee record and badge falsification.

While the Tribes were good at setting up the ruse, they wanted someone else to play undercover detective.

Dee had to pilfer a uniform from the linen supply at the warehouse. Chandler would wear khaki pants and a black polo style shirt with a white CFS logo on both sleeves. The shoes were white sneakers, and if he would be near food, he would wear the obligatory hair net; otherwise he'd don a black ball cap, also with the CFS logo.

Chandler emerged from his makeover looking like a CFS employee. One important detail remained.

"Now, remember your name on the badge. They told you about that, right?" Dee asked.

Chandler hesitated. "Ahh, yeah. No, that makes sense."

He'd forgotten that Axel covered that with him.

"Your name is Steve Rogers and you're supposed to be from Memphis. They said you already studied that before you got here," Dee asserted.

He did. Axel threw so much at him that it came to him slowly. "Yes, Steve Rogers from Memphis, I remember." He would need to develop a good mnemonic to remember that name. Chandler had never even been in a high school play, so impersonating someone would be a new frontier.

"But don't talk to anyone unless they talk to you. It's safer that way. If someone brings up the barbecue question, just say all those places are good, cuz you know someone's gonna ask. You feel me?"

Chandler had his own barbecue preferences, and they were in Austin. "OK, I'll try not to let anyone trip me up on that one."

Dee owned a large pickup. Chandler thought it odd that she owned a "big boy" vehicle, thinking it might have been her husband's. He didn't ask, preferring to avoid the mention of his name.

The drive to the camp covered 20 miles northwest in the Nevada desert. The temperature would reach 110 degrees. Providentially, their jobs were in the climate-controlled environment of the facility.

The facility sat near the Nevada Test Site, also known as the Nevada Proving Grounds, a 1,300 square mile area where the military conducted hundreds of aerial and underground nuclear explosions. After the Comprehensive Nuclear-Test-Ban Treaty in 1996, the United States no longer used the site for this purpose. In 2006, the government repurposed the land in the general area as western bases for the U.S. drone fleet and Homeland Security camps for detainees in the War on Terror and refugees. The remoteness of the area kept it away from prying eyes.

Axel had obtained an aerial map of the camp from someone who had leaked it to Omni. Chandler suspected the leak came from the whistleblower who reportedly worked for the National Geospatial-Intelligence Agency. Chandler and Axel used the map in the former's preparation for this infiltration.

There were two entrance gates to the facility. Gate 1 provided access for contractors, like CFS, while Gate 2 presumably served government personnel. Gate 1 had the usual "No Trespassing By Order of the U.S. Government" signs. Yet nothing obstructed passage through the dry land filled with cacti, wildflowers, and tumbleweed. After a mile of travel on an asphalt road, passage became obstructed.

High barbed wire fencing surrounded the facility with several elevated observation posts on the perimeter. The camp's front gate had security personnel and multiple cameras trained on the occupants of a vehicle. Alternating concrete barriers blocked the entrance, requiring a vehicle to take a serpentine path. This arrangement allowed security personnel to shoot and kill any intruder. Anyone foolish enough to attempt illegal entry would be as easy to target as a fish in a barrel.

Security amounted to private contractors like those seen in Iraq and Afghanistan. They were very much outfitted like U.S. military personnel, except their clothing bore no insignia, not even their company name. They wore ball caps and reflective sunglasses. Biceps and triceps bulged under the snug, tan colored tee shirts.

Dee formed a queue behind a couple of other vehicles entering the camp at the very popular 8:00 am start time. A security officer looked at Dee's badge and then walked around her truck to inspect that of Chandler's, aka Steve Rogers. A bomb sniffing canine followed with a perimeter search of her vehicle. Another officer came by with a portable fingerprint scanner to verify the second authentication factor. If the Tribe's hack failed, he would know shortly and be taken into custody. There were no biometric problems and security waved them through.

She parked her truck in a contractor parking lot next to a low rise building housing the cafeteria and other support offices. There would be another security checkpoint upon entering this building. Security personnel performed a full body scan to eliminate any objects from being introduced. That included cell phones or anything electronic.

Dee's work center comprised an office next to the kitchen. As a trainee, Chandler would do only as she said. One of her responsibilities involved the supervision of cafeteria workers. On this day she completed performance reviews on employees and a review of special diet menus. In another of her duties, she accompanied drivers responsible for delivering food and other supplies and sometimes drove the small delivery van herself. Her driving duties allowed her to introduce forbidden items into the camp.

Throughout the course of the last couple weeks, Dee introduced a couple of button cameras and listening devices in food containers she hauled into the camp. She scattered the surveillance electronics in her office and the bathroom to avoid detection. Chandler would gather and deploy them. One task on his first day called for him to relocate the electronics to the men's bathroom. He could operate freely there in the absence of monitoring cameras. CFS insisted on not having cameras in the bathrooms since they were recent defendants in a privacy lawsuit that they settled out of court. He hid the button camera inside of a toilet flush monitor and the listening device inside a soap dispenser. He spent the rest of the day with Dee, ostensibly receiving training in kitchen and cafeteria operation.

The mood in this camp was dour. The CFS employees did not mingle, and the camp employees spoke little among themselves while they ate. In this sort of environment, concealing his identity would prove less of a challenge than he anticipated. He used his internal voice throughout the day to remind him of his assumed name, Steve Rogers.

Towards the end of his first day, Dee pointed to the employee who sympathized with the disappearance of her husband, an Oriental man, who entered the cafeteria late in the afternoon for a snack.

The employee sympathizer did not make himself available the first two weeks, so they had to wait and be patient, not one of Chandler's virtues. For those two weeks, Chandler and Dee repeated the steps of breakfast, makeup, work, makeup removal, dinner at the house and sleep. Though he slept well, he never recalled his dreams, wondering if he had really experienced the disturbing sunrise and fireball event.

***

The third week of Chandler's life as Steve Rogers started like the other two. The monotony of his routine suffocated him. Though his cover remained intact, he'd made no real progress.

In the middle of week three, Chandler and Dee were eating after the lunch crowd thinned. A person appeared before them requesting assistance with the ice tea dispenser—the employee sympathizer.

The pale-skinned Oriental man looked to be in his mid-thirties, with thick black hair and longish sideburns. He fell on the side of being short in stature with a slim build.

"Excuse me. I think you guys are out of ice tea," the man

said, pointing at the cylindrical container.

"Yes sir, let me go fill it for you," Dee got up to tend to the man's request.

"May I sit while she takes care of it?" the man asked Chandler, aka Steve Rogers.

"Yes," Steve answered. The employee sat across from him.

An uncomfortable silence followed, with both men staring down at the table.

"Hello, my name is Steve Rogers." He extended his hand. It was his first introduction using the assumed name.

"Eugene Kim. Nice to meet you." The newly identified employee shook his hand. "I've seen you around for a couple of weeks now. You must be new, huh?"

"Trainee. Mrs. Chapman's showing me the ropes, you could say," Steve replied, snapping his head towards Dee.

"She seems like a nice lady. We talked once. I know one thing. This cafeteria runs pretty smoothly. My colleagues and I always comment on how well-mannered everyone is and the food is not too bad really," Eugene commented, with an asymmetrical smile. The right side of his mouth widened more than the left.

"I guess I'm learning from the right person then?" Steve suggested. "What sort of work do you do here, Eugene?"

"Information Technology. Pretty dry, boring stuff for most people. I work with databases and some applications they have here," Eugene replied, looking more seriously this time.

"I guess they must have a lot of folks here?" Steve asked. He had to make mental notes, since he didn't have the button camera mounted on his person.

"They do. They don't tell us much. Some of the stuff I see, kinda disturbing really," Eugene added, frowning.

"Disturbing? In what way?" Steve inquired. His hands,

formerly on his lap, would come to rest on the table, clasped lightly.

"You know, this isn't the stuff they want us talking about," Eugene said, giving a furtive look over his shoulder.

"I wondered what they did here. Everyone looks so…" Steve said. He darted his eyes upward, combing for the word.

"Depressed? Look, we're out here in the middle of the desert, it's hot as hell outside, in a sterile-looking facility with security guards that all look like they're on 'roids and with all these drab colors on the walls. There's nothing to look at outside in the few windows we do have. There's nowhere decent to live around here. We have people that drive from Vegas every day and the rest live on site in these pop-up containers. They've given us some exercise facilities, which is nice, I suppose. Oh, and they allow us to stream movies. It's not exactly a vacation here. They try." Eugene morosely described his plight.

"What about you? Do you commute?" Steve asked.

"I used to. Car pooled with a few guys from just north of Vegas. The problem is, there is so much land out here owned by the federal government; developers can't build anything. What's left are these real small towns, but no one is building there with the economy being what it is. Plus, you get a fair number of people that are transient."

"Eugene, given everything you say, how'd you end up here?"

Eugene Kim, a first generation American of Korean descent, hailed from northern California. Typical of many tech-savvy Millennials, he came out of college freshly armed with a computer science degree and plunged into the world of startup ventures. He bounced around hoping to score the big payoff when the company reached IPO status. Success never arrived. The stock crash of 2016 shuttered one of his employers, and the crash of

2019 took care of the next one. Out of work, with student loans, and an upside down condominium in Santa Clara, California, he secured this job at the camp. His unemployed wife remained in Santa Clara. His visits home were few, given the punishing 500 mile excursion. Many times he worked on Saturdays. Eugene's story would resonate with many.

Dee returned with a tall, cool glass of tea. "Here you go, sir. Sorry about that. I'll have someone look at it. It's good to see you again. Steve, you ready?" She looked at Steve, who initially did not acknowledge his name.

"Oh, yes! Mrs. Chapman, Eugene here is the first person who's taken any time to talk. It's nice." Steve hoped his words would provide a cue to Dee that the conversation could develop further. "Could we stay here for a bit longer, please? I'm caught up, ma'am."

Dee had spoken with Eugene once before, relating the story about her missing husband. She took a seat next to Steve and introduced herself. "Hi, I'm DeArthie Chapman. We talked once about my husband. Please call me Dee."

"Eugene Kim, nice to meet you. Yeah, I said I'd look around and see if I could find something. Sorry, I haven't gotten to that yet."

"Eugene tells me he's from Santa Clara, California, and that his wife still lives there," Steve said.

"At least you know where your wife is. My husband disappeared from Henderson awhile back. I'm still trying to find him. Mm hmm. There was a rumor that he was here. Nobody says nothin' about what's going on in this place. Then I'm thinking what he'd be doing here. The police in Henderson didn't help. How can someone just disappear?" Dee shook her head in despair, reliving the agony of her loss.

282

Eugene took note. "Again, I'm sorry, Dee. You did tell me some of the details before. I know it's not the same, but I miss my wife terribly. She's like 500 miles away. It's screwed up for us. At least I know where she is, though. Tell me again why your husband would be here?"

Dee looked towards the table, nervously folding a napkin. "He had went to those anti-government sites on the Internet. We lost our business, and he started gambling. It got rough for us. Then one night, he didn't come home. A friend of mine said that maybe cuz he was talking bad about the government, they took him to a special prison. Since when do they have special prisons in this country, child? Ain't this the United States?"

Eugene's life challenges paled compared to Dee's emotional loss. She connected with him in this brief exchange, which while hurtful for her to relive, may have proved beneficial for what she ultimately wanted. Chandler identified with both of them, separated from his love for reasons much more under his control. Listening to these tales made him question his undercover work.

Something in Eugene's shirt pocket startled him. "Sorry guys, I have to go. It was nice speaking with both of you, I hope we can chat again real soon. I think we have more to talk about." He finished one last sip of his tea, dribbling it on his chin. "Oops." He wiped his mouth and hurriedly walked out of the cafeteria.

His final words gave Dee and Chandler hope that the next step of their operation would be forthcoming.

***

It took several days for the next contact, further testing Chandler's patience. His stay in the middle of nowhere, USA grew tiresome. While he enjoyed DeArthie's company, he missed Arianne. He missed the life and energy of the Big Apple. He missed the discussions with his mentor, Axel. Making a phone call from DeArthie's home would blow his cover. He didn't even risk a secure chat with Axel from his laptop. The separation from his former life amplified his anxiety.

Eugene reappeared a few days later in the cafeteria, setting his tray on the same side as Dee, opposite Chandler, aka "Steve", who were eating lunch.

This time Steve had his button camera.

Eugene explained his hiatus. "Hey guys. Rough few days. I hate it when an application has a problem. Code has so many errors now since these companies throw untested apps to get them on the market quickly. Oh, and with government contracts, it's worse. They know once they win, they're on the gravy train for years. Those companies honestly don't care, and it's people like me that get stuck trying to fix their crap."

He ripped off a shred of his roast beef sandwich, scattering condiments over his plate.

"I'm lucky, I guess. I haven't had any big problems. My teacher's pretty good," Steve said, throwing a smile and a wink at Dee.

Eugene did not acknowledge Steve's comment before turning his attention to Dee. "I wanted to let you know that I had some down time during all the application testing and looked around the records. I looked for your last name, 'Chapman', and found something under a 'J Chapman.' The record looked old. Most of the fields associated with the record were blank. Strange really. I found some other records that looked like that too."

For the first time since they'd met, Steve saw a glimmer of hope in her eye. "Oh, Maa Gaa! What's that mean? Is he here?" Dee reached for Eugene's arm, squeezing it excitedly.

Eugene recoiled from Dee's clamping. "Hard to tell. I don't

know, really. I just saw that record. I don't want to give you any false hope."

Dee released his arm and leaned back in her chair. "Oh, OK." She looked like she'd taken a jab in the gut.

"I did want to tell you about something else, though. Maybe this will give you some hope, if your husband's in here. The people in this camp aren't called prisoners. They're patients," Eugene explained.

"Patients? Like sick? You mean we got a bunch of viruses around here?" a reanimated Dee asked.

"No. Consider them mental patients. Like a psych ward, but I don't think they're crazy,'" Eugene added.

"I'm confused. My husband had his problems, but he wasn't crazy like that. Let's be real, child," Dee asserted, crossing her arms.

Eugene realized he'd created some confusion. "I guess I shouldn't have used that word. Here's what I know. Each patient has a psych evaluation from someone called a PSYOP officer. The patient record has a field that gives a score. There's other fields though I don't know exactly what they mean. They've got these codes or acronyms. I've been working on the application and database for all this. That's one of the reasons I was hired. In my previous life, I dealt with software implementation and database maintenance."

Dee grew impatient. "I appreciate your experience, Mr. Kim. Now tell me more about the patients."

"Sorry, the patient gets the psych evaluation and then goes through some sort of mental training, they call it. I don't know what it is. Then they get evaluated again. Sometimes their score goes up and sometimes it goes down. The application gets the inputs and then comes up with the score. I should clarify. I didn't develop the algorithm, apparently the U.S. Army did or some company. I think the score has a predictive value for something, but again, I'm not sure. They didn't tell us."

What Steve heard agreed with the whistleblower's confession.

Eugene continued. "I started thinking about it and I believe the patients in this camp are here against their will. I mean it fits with what we've been seeing around the country. The secession groups, domestic terrorism and all that. You go online and you hear these rumors, like Dee's, about people disappearing. It's not powerful, important, elite people disappearing. These are just ordinary people. So I asked myself why? I can see the government has gotten far more authoritarian. I'll admit, I voted for Jefferson. After I lost my last job, he was the only one to step up and offer any sort of solution. And so what that he got accused of working with international organizations like the GSB. Somebody had to do something. Now, though, the more I look at it, I think Washington's doing more harm than good. If I'm part of something more sinister here, well I didn't sign up for that."

Steve got the break he hoped for. Eugene's suspicions supported the whistleblower, and now he needed more evidence. He needed to see it for himself. "Do you ever get to see these patients?"

"I don't. But looking at their records, some of them get special diets. You know the peanut allergies, gluten-free, kosher, those sort of things. Dee, I would think you'd know something about that?" Eugene asked.

"I thought those were special plates for the higher-ups. You think they're for patients? They never told us. We just made them up and gave them to people wearing those green smocks, like you see in hospitals," Dee answered.

Steve looked at Dee, hopeful that her answer would be in the affirmative. "Do your people ever get to take the meals to them?"

"Maybe somebody made a delivery back there. They never told me. The contractors don't care. They just do their job and go home," Dee replied.

"I heard there's a program starting soon where they want to expose patients to people other than their handlers. I guess the patients have been complaining about being confined here in Club Med," Eugene smiled, sardonically. "Anyway, they thought that having them interact with CFS employees to talk about the food quality or to custom tailor their meals, might improve their morale."

"You know, I'd heard about a survey but didn't think nothing about it. I thought it was for the bigwigs," Dee offered.

Eugene directed his attention to Steve. "If you have an interest in doing the food survey, you know, just to break up your monotony..." He looked sheepishly at Dee. "I'm sure Steve could use a little variety in his routine. I have access to security databases, so I could add him to the approved list for contractors with access to that part of the camp."

Steve wondered if Eugene offered to do this based on their recent conversations or if he knew his real identity. The question of how Eugene could know his identity would have no immediate answer in his mind. Nevertheless, Steve could not identify himself as Chandler Scott. There could be no guarantee of Eugene's ultimate allegiance to the Tribes or anyone else.

"Yeah, that sounds great. Anything to break things up a bit. Dee, I guess we'll have to review the survey," Steve said.

"That patient area, in case you didn't know, is on the other side of the medical building." Eugene pointed in a northerly direction.

Steve had an idea after reviewing the facility map with Axel.

"Oh, really? Well, I've never been over there."

"From the little I've walked around that medical building, I had to go there for an infection once, the security there is nothing like it is everywhere else." Eugene's disclosure of the security level revealed something Steve did not know.

In another week, Steve would get his opportunity to meet a patient.

***

Steve pushed a specially constructed food cart with separate refrigerated and heated compartments. A security officer escorted him outside past the medical building to the patient area. The midday desert sun made the cart's heated compartment redundant. The facility maps he'd reviewed with Axel were two-dimensional so this third dimension gave him more perspective. The security officer led him to a building that appeared like a college dormitory, though nicer than he remembered.

After entering the building, he walked on his own to room 1-B on the other end of the first floor. As he passed room 1-V, he slowed and noticed a cleaning crew at work. In the room he saw a bed, a bathroom, a dresser, a desk, two chairs, books on a shelf, and a video monitor. His visual foray caught the attention of a housekeeper, causing him to avert his eyes and quicken his pace.

He turned his body towards anything he wanted to record, given the button camera's 78 degree field of view.

When he arrived in room 1-B, he would engage the patient in discussion about the customized food menu and record scores on a worksheet. The government asked CFS to conduct the survey to placate the patient population's desire for more human contact.

Room 1-B looked exactly like the other he surveyed down the hall. The patient, who laid face up on the bed, appeared in good

288

physical health. Steve wondered if these patients always ate their meals in their rooms or if there could be a general area.

He pulled out the salad plate and soft drink from the refrigerated compartment and the pasta dish from the heated one, placing everything on the desk. This patient had a gluten intolerance and failed to inform the camp authorities about the adverse interaction. The CFS nutritionist devised a pasta substitute made of rice.

"Hello, sir, my name is Cha-," he caught himself before continuing. "My name is Steve and I'm here today to talk to you about your customized menu. I'll let you dig in and then we can talk." Steve sat on one chair while the patient moved to the other to begin his meal.

The patient pulled the plastic wrap off the pasta plate and grabbed the fork like a shovel, piercing the noodles. The napkin remained on the tray.

After a few bites, the patient introduced himself as Joe, a white middle-aged man with a large tattoo of a wolf on his right forearm. Joe seemed satisfied with everything, at least from the vigor with which he chewed and swallowed.

Steve grabbed his clipboard and pen. "Joe, tell me about the pasta."

"It's good, man. Real good. I guess it won't make me sick then?"

"Hopefully not, sir. On a scale from 1 to 10, how close does it taste to regular pasta?"

"Probably 8. It's good." Joe stabbed a grouping of pasta noodles and plunged it in his mouth. Red sauce seeped out of the corners of his mouth.

Steve went off script. "Joe, what are you in for? What illness do you have?"

Joe interrupted his chewing and put down his fork abruptly. "Illness? Shit. I ain't ill. I'm here cuz Uncle Sam thinks I'm bad. They don't like my politics, that's all."

"Just politics, huh? I guess you got a lot of action then in the last election. That was some election. Did your party do well?" Steve asked.

"Party?" Joe threw a scornful look towards Steve. "I ain't voted for no damn party in years. I can't stand any of them people. There's a lot of us out there too. It ain't just me. I hate 'em all. I lost all respect for 'em. They're all in cahoots. They do what they want." Joe expelled small pasta fragments during his mini tirade. "Sorry 'bout that." He wiped his mouth with the napkin.

"So are you what people call a secessionist?"

Joe took a swig of his soft drink and wiped his mouth with his free hand. "Hell no! They're dangerous people. They ain't gonna fix nothin'."

"What did you do wrong then?"

"I used to be on one of them blogs. A friend of mine did one, and then I ran it. Don't know much about computers but I figured out how to do it. I just told people on the blog to send a message to politicians about their rigged system. Send them hate mail and not to vote for any of the sons of bitches. I told people to stop filling out all those goddamn FSB forms. Stop using regular money and go underground with that other money, DigiNote."

"I'm sure they didn't like that. Did they catch you breaking any laws or just talking bad?"

"I don't know if I broke any damn laws. All I know is one day some agents from the FBI and DHS showed up at my house to ask me a bunch of questions. We must'a sat there for three or four hours. When I didn't answer the way they wanted me to, they charged me with some fucking crime, said I broke some stupid ass law. I'm single, so I didn't have to worry about nobody else. They arrested me and said I was going to some federal prison." He sent the next forkful of pasta like a projectile into his mouth.

"So what did your lawyer say?"

"She was some stupid ass public defender. Had no idea what they charged me with and said to take a plea deal. When I went in front of the judge, he said I'd been recommended for a rehab camp. I asked my attorney what the hell that was and she said if I didn't accept, I'd go to federal prison for 10 years. They said I violated a sedition law," Joe paused to expel a small burp after biting hard into his soft drink. "I damn well remembered that word since I had to ask my attorney what it meant. How you gonna send someone to prison for a law nobody knows nothin' about?"

President John Adams signed the Alien and Sedition Acts into law in 1798 and they remained on the books. The Acts were originally designed to imprison and deport non-citizens posing a threat or hostile intent to the country and to criminalize those making false statements critical of the government. The government invoked the laws during World War II and candidates referenced them during the presidential campaign of 2016.

President Jefferson issued a proclamation that granted the authority to apprehend and detain U.S. residents deemed to promote economic instability. Anyone decrying the FSB and promoting DigiNote usage fell into that category. Making unpatriotic statements about withholding election votes was also considered subversive.

"Did they tell you anything about the rehab camp?"

"Shit no! My dumb ass defender didn't know either. But I got here and they treated me real nice. I talked to a shrink and they gave me a PSYOP person. They're supposed to fix me of my evil ways." Joe laughed at that suggestion, making devilish horn signs with his fingers at the side of his head.

"How are they supposed to fix you? It's not like they can change your mind." Steve focused on keeping his torso still during the questioning to minimize video distortion.

"My PSYOP person said the rehab was for my own good and that they was gonna fix me of all these bad thoughts. They got me wearing this VR headset all day. You know what those are? I thought those were just for games." Joe swirled the drink in his mouth, hollowing out his cheeks.

Steve had some experience with them. "Yeah, I've seen them used for gaming and virtual travel." He recalled his visit to Yellowstone while staying in Quinque's silo.

"They got me watching people voting, political conventions, movies about World War I and II, anti-terror messages. Then they had me playing these games, and damn if I didn't win all the time. That was what I saw the first week, for hours and hours. Then they showed me lots of U.S. flags. Then we see all this shit about the Plan for Prosperity and how it's gonna be good for everyone. They even made this little movie with families talkin' all this stuff about 'We Are the Future.' After that was done, we took pills. I don't know what they was and they didn't tell us. It might have been to keep us from throwing up. You wear that headset for that long and you start feeling sick."

Steve reflexively lowered his eyes quickly towards his shirt button camera. "So did the pills help?"

"Yeah, especially with the next thing they did. I've only done it a couple of days. We put the headset on and some real fancy headphones and we see these weird images like we're flying through space or something. I can't describe it. At the same time, I hear this sound that starts out like a real deep, low sound and gets lower until I can't hear it but I can feel it in my ear. It's freakin' weird, man. After I get done, my head feels like it did one time after I got in a fight."

"You mean like a concussion?"

"I guess so. I know this. After the first time I did it, I had a real hard time remembering what happened that day. That's probably why I'm in here today with so much free time. I told them my head hurt." Joe demonstrated by rubbing his temples.

"Did they send you to a doctor?"

"Some guy in a lab coat checked me out and said something to my PSYOP. They were arguing about something. It's not the first time I've seen the PSYOP people and the doctors argue. Something's going on."

Steve knew that he didn't have much time before someone checked on him. He'd neglected to complete most of the survey. "Have you talked to any of the other patients?"

Joe set his glass down forcefully. "You keep thinking we're patients. I told you, we ain't ill like you think."

"Sorry."

"They try to keep us apart most days. When we're outside for exercise, though not too long in this godforsaken desert, I talked to this man named Duron. We're talking about the food here and he said something about being allergic to something, I can't remember, maybe it was MSG. I'm thinking he's a puss complaining about MSG. I told him this ain't no country club. Course I didn't say nothin' about my own problem." Joe offered a wry smile. "He talked about a program called Eliz something.

Duron said he talked to this other man that acted like a zombie, like his mind was blank, no emotion, and the man told him the next day he was going to that Eliz, or whatever, program. Duron then says he never saw him again."

The security officer appeared in Room 1-B and called for Steve, who quickly stowed Joe's dishes in the cart and tossed the clipboard on top.

"Thank you, sir, for your input. This will help us make our service to you better," Steve said, making sure the security officer heard.

His mind raced with thoughts on his way back to the cafeteria. He and Dee huddled in her office where he shared the few survey results and intimated that they had much more to talk about on the ride home. It would be quite a conversation, one which made Dee hopeful that she'd find out something about her Juan.

***

After meeting with Joe, Steve used the next encounter with Eugene to comment on how much he enjoyed seeing the other side of the camp. Ordinarily surveys weren't his thing, but it beat staying in the cafeteria all day. Steve mentioned that Joe befriended another patient by the name of Duron, who complained about something in his diet making him ill. Eugene investigated the patient record and confirmed the brief illness. He arranged for Steve to administer the next survey to Duron.

Steve loaded the food cart with fruit, sweet tea, and key lime pie in the cold compartment and fried fish with rice in the hot compartment. His security escort led him along the same path, this time to the second floor, requiring an elevator ride to room 2-K. Unlike the visit with Joe, the security escort walked him all the way to the room. Steve maintained his gaze straight ahead,

294

careful not to peek in other rooms. Duron's room had the same layout as Joe's.

"Good afternoon, sir. My name is Steve Rogers and I'll be conducting a food survey."

Duron, who laid on his bed, did not break his attention from the video monitor showing a dated college football game.

Steve placed the food on the desk. Duron waited until his server pulled away from the improvised dinner table. Unlike Joe, Duron held his fork between his thumb and index finger. He placed the napkin on his lap.

Steve took out his clipboard and sat, waiting a few minutes before beginning his questions. The wait proved uneasy since Duron eyed him in between bites, like a lion keeping an eye on its prey.

Hearing only Duron's mastication, and unnerved with the prolonged silence, Steve asked, "Sir, may I ask why you're a patient here?"

Duron continued to eat and drink, ignoring him. The only sounds in the room were the breathing, chewing, and slurping above the soft breeze of the air conditioning.

Steve tried another approach. "What are you watching? You looked like you were pretty focused on it."

Duron didn't flinch, continuing to eat as if alone.

Steve knew he couldn't continue to waste time, and this could be his only chance to find out something about the disappearing patient. He took more drastic action, slamming the clipboard on the chair's arm. The survey paper fell to the floor. "Listen, asshole, I'm trying to do my fucking job and you just want to be a prick. I get it. You don't want to be here and I don't want to look at your sorry ass."

Duron broke his chewing and took a drink of his sweet tea,

swirling it and puckering his lips before swallowing and exhaling in satisfaction. The laughter came as a surprise. "I know what you doin'. You tryin' to make me mad. This another damn test, ain't it? Y'all ain't bullshittin' me no mo." He took off the wrap covering the key lime pie and scooped a small amount of the whipped topping.

Steve retrieved the survey paper from the floor. "What test? I just asked you a simple question, trying to help your sorry ass with your damn diet."

"Look man, I don't want no trouble. Just let me eat in peace. You feelin' me? I know you one of those psych people testin' me and shit." Duron correctly assessed that he was being put to the test, though not the one he thought.

"Hey, I'm not a psych person. Do I look like one? I work for CFS. We do the food service here." Steve pointed at the logos on his shirt and hat, hoping that would start the conversation.

"Yeah, right. Prove it. I have a question for you then." Duron grew tired of the inquiry and would give Steve a test he'd surely fail. "Since none of these mother-, people here know anything about sports, tell me this shit then. That brother who ran for president last year, Alfonso. Where'd he go to school and what position did he play?"

Duron referred to the half black, half Hispanic IAP senator from Texas, Alfonso Chancellor.

Steve's sports passions centered on baseball, not college football. How fortunate that he knew this answer from his Texas childhood. "Hook 'em horns and he played QB." He made the characteristic Longhorn sign, extending his pinky and index finger.

"Damn, man! You do know yo' shit," Duron smiled, and nodded his head with approval.

296

Steve hoped that would break the ice. It did.

"I guess you ain't lyin' to me. I'll talk to yo' ass then. We ain't no patients here, dog. We inmates. Truth is, I served time back in 2006. I got caught with some weed, a lot of weed, in Illinois. My house got hit by Katrina, then we was sent to live in these FEMA trailers in Shreveport. I had no job, no money, a wife and kids. One of my boys came 'round saying he had something for me. I could make some money. You know what I'm sayin'? All I had to do was drive some weed to a town called Carbondale in Illinois. It was some bullshit luck though. I got pulled over cause the damn car my boy gave me had bad license plates. Trooper that pulled me over got suspicious, and busted my ass. Man, I ain't never been in no trouble and I gotta call my wife and tell her." Duron's voiced trailed off into a murmur, revealing his shame.

"So how long were you in prison?"

"I got out in 16, dog. I had so much weed on me. I just did my time. But when I got out, my wife gone and she took the damn kids. They went to stay with her mom in Texas."

"Did you move to Texas after that?"

"Yeah. Try gettin' a job after you been in jail. It's some bullshit, dog. This old white man gave me a break and hired me to work in his garage. I worked on cars before. We did everything but transmissions. The old man, Dalton, he started talking to me about government. He joined this group called Texas Nation and got me into it. Man, these people talkin' about breakin' up with the rest of the country. They told me that I should never have gone to prison cuz weed should have been legal already. I ain't never heard no shit like that befo', you know what I'm sayin'?"

"Texas Nation, huh? Never heard of it. Is it still around?"

"Yeah, dog. Dalton said the government had no right to ask

small businesses to fill out all them damn forms and they was stealin' money from him. He got on the Internet and they started holding these rallies. I went to them too. It was cool though, dog, cuz they didn't care who you was, White, Black, Latino, Chinese as long as you thought like they did. They wanted to be left the fuck alone. It was like a big brotherhood, and I didn't have to worry about someone saying I didn't have street cred cuz I was relatin' to all these other people, you know what I'm saying?"

"I do. It's good you didn't have to worry about race problems there. There's enough to worry about. Did you guys ever do anything with the Five Tribes?" Steve asked, hoping for a link.

"Naw man, naw. They sent messages to Dalton. He didn't want no part of that. These cats from Texas, man, them some independent mofos. They wanted to do their own thing and they weren't into all the tech shit either. Dalton told me he respected them Tribes . They could do what they wanted, but no he didn't join up with them."

"How did you end up here?"

"Some men from FBI and DHS came by the garage one day and accused Dalton of breakin' all these laws, some FSB bullshit and working folks up to be violent and shit. I think they called it 'sawdishin.' He started cussin' at 'em and they cuffed him right there, threw his ass down after he spit on them. They saw me working on a car with my Texas Nation shirt and hat and asked me questions. I wasn't gonna bullshit them. I told them what I thought about the election freeze and all the bullshit Dalton had to do just to stay in business. Them bitches cuffed me too. I never saw Dalton after that."

"You got arrested, so how come you didn't go back into the slammer? You were an ex-con."

Duron became very animated in his response, tilting his head and putting his arms on his hips. "That's the funny thing, dog. The judge told me that they had this special rehab camp. It wasn't no prison and my sentence would be shorter. I had to take that mothafucka, you know what I'm sayin'? I spent ten years locked up and the hell if I was goin' back."

"Ahh. Interesting."

Duron's days were very much like Joe's. There were endless hours on the VR headsets with patriotic themes and games that made the patient feel successful and independent. There were headphones with sounds felt more than heard, and probes on different parts of his body, plus all the pills.

The time had come for Steve to broach the subject of the "Eliz" since time grew short. "I talked to this patient the other day and he said he saw this zombie person, showed no emotion, and the patient said the next day they were doing the "Eliz" program, or something that sounded like that. Then he never saw the patient again."

Duron nodded his head in agreement. "Oh, you talkin' 'bout the Illijum. Yeah, my PSYOP said that if they don't fix you, you can go to that special program."

"What's so special about it?"

"They said it was a special place for our souls to find peace. Sounded like them preachers in the old time gospel hour." Duron's face temporarily had a placid appearance, reliving a Baptist church from his youth. "They bullshittin' us with that. They just sending them mothafuckas back to the pen. Some of them cats rather be in prison than sit here and go through all this mind control bullshit."

Steve thought it strange that going back to a penitentiary would be described as "Illijum" since that word had no meaning

299

for him. Maybe it was a new slang term for the penitentiary? After his security escort arrived, he retrieved the plates and glass and stowed them in the cart, tossing the survey clipboard on top. He thanked Duron for the survey, even though he'd done none of it.

***

He spent the night after meeting with Duron, talking to Dee about the special program, Illijum. For a moment, it gave her hope that the program could be a lead to locating her Juan.

Duron could have been confused about either the name or the program's nature. Internet searches were risky from Dee's place, he dared not attract any unnecessary attention. He could do a Dark Net search though he had little experience with it and feared he'd mess something up. He'd have to go on memory. Presuming the accuracy of Duron's assertions, he'd need to find out more about this program.

The next day he met with Eugene in the cafeteria after lunch and they discussed Illijum. Eugene felt more comfortable with Steve and Dee. For him, just having someone to talk to in the desolation of his existence in the camp proved cathartic. Steve dared not ask him about his political sympathies with the Tribes, if he even had any. His cover remained intact and he couldn't risk compromise at this stage. He would probe Eugene, who'd been cooperative, carefully.

"So have you ever heard about that special program, Illijum?" Steve asked.

"Illijum? No can't say that I have," Eugene replied.

"One of the patients said he'd met someone that got sent to a special program, in case the current one didn't work."

"I've seen something on patient records that suggested an alternate program. It had the abbreviation 'EP", maybe that's what you mean?" Eugene speculated.

"Hmm. Well 'EP' doesn't sound like Illijum. I mean it's possible that the guy I was talking to had it wrong."

Eugene chuckled. "He might've been drugged up, you never know. You seem very interested in this."

Steve hesitated in revealing too much. Despite Eugene's cooperation, the next step in the undercover work would be the most dangerous. He appealed to Eugene's sense of empathy. "You know I'm bored. Dee's very good with me. I'm like you. I have bills to pay and my job prospects weren't good. I had to jump on this. Not much going on in Memphis these days and it's gotten more violent. Can you blame a guy for trying to make his job more interesting? Besides, you said yourself that there may be some things going on in this camp that you don't support."

"I hear you. And yeah, I don't want to be part of something I wouldn't be proud to tell my kids about some day. I do know what you mean about trying to make things more interesting. I was doing some leading edge stuff in Silicon Valley and now this. I'm way overqualified for this job." Eugene looked down and rubbed his forehead with the tips of his fingers before popping his head back up. "You know, speaking of overqualified, what about you? Did you go to college?"

Steve had to think quickly, recalling the background history concocted for his cover. "Yes, I attended Southeast Missouri State and got a degree in Political Science with a History minor. The degree didn't do me much good after the economy tanked. Things are tough all over as you know. I saw this ad posted on a job board, applied and got it."

"Interesting. I wondered about you. So why are you so interested in that special program?"

"I wouldn't be, except what the patient said. He said he was told it was a place where souls go to find peace, yet he thinks it's just a federal penitentiary. How can a soul find peace in a federal pen?"

"You got me. I mean we really don't know everything that's going on here, do we? I told you that I always thought these patients aren't here of their free will. You have to conclude that with the security and being out here in the middle of nowhere." Eugene sketched a perimeter of the camp with his index fingers. "You've got the high barbed wire around the place and guard towers. There's all these private security people that look like they just came out of a video game. Part of me thinks all the security is to keep people out rather than the patients escaping. Hell, where would they go out in this desert. If they got too far off track, they'd run into a military base or giant craters where they used to test nukes back in the day."

"Yeah, I never really thought about it that way. Then again, it's not as if someone driving through Nevada would ever come by here." *Other than an investigative journalist looking for a big story.*

"Listen, Steve. I'm not supposed to ask questions, but I'm curious like anyone else. I'm not comfortable with where this country's headed. I think there are a lot of people that think the way I do and don't know how to express it without landing on some bad boy list." This had been the first time that Eugene expressed any political opinion.

Steve seized the moment. He would see where Eugene landed with a bold proposition. "What if there was a way to learn more about this Illijum? The reeducation stuff these patients talk about is creepy. I could go find some journalist or get on the Dark side of the Internet and tell my story. Maybe that's the way to express it. I gotta do something more meaningful than this dead end job."

A concerned Eugene responded quickly. "I don't know, Steve, that sounds dangerous."

"Eugene, man. Grow a pair! We've both been saying how bad our job prospects are and come on, man. I read things that are going on with these groups like the Five Tribes and Honor Brigade, and honestly some of the stuff they say makes sense. I'm not saying I want to join them. Things are pretty messed up in D.C. Look at what happened with Congress. They impeached the president and he almost got kicked out of office. Look at all the stuff that happened after the Supreme Court made their decision. It's not just me thinking this way. I remember someone telling me that freedom doesn't come without cost and responsibility. I'm stepping up to the responsibility. If something bad is going on here, don't you think people should know about it?" Steve wondered if he'd revealed too much of himself.

Eugene extended his hand in a halting motion towards Steve, attempting to douse the enthusiasm. "Whoa, Steve, that's a lot of stuff you're spewing there. I get what you're saying. But I have more to think about than myself. I have my wife. I need this job. Nobody's paying my bills. I don't think it's my place to make moral or political judgments here."

Steve continued his plea. "I'm not asking you to take any big chance. I'll do that. Just see if you can find out more about Illijum, that's all."

Eugene's emotional and rational mind were in conflict. Despite the objectivity of assessing his financial condition, Steve appealed to his emotion. "Ok. I'll research this a bit and let you know. Give me a day. I need to get back to work now. Until tomorrow." He got up quickly, leaving behind his tray. For Steve, taking care of the tray for information about Illijum was a great trade.

***

He returned as promised the next day with information. The two men met in the cafeteria's corner after most of the lunch crowd dissipated.

Eugene couldn't tell Steve exactly what the program entailed though he suspected the program's administration occurred in a lab in the hospital's basement and evidently at night. Concocting a story about a network problem, Eugene went to the hospital and to the equipment closet located in the basement. There he discovered that two of the rooms were cabled differently than the others. They were connected to a separate network to which he did not have direct access. He noted the cable labeling and proceeded to those rooms for a closer look. They were locked. Looking inside, they were devoid of the same equipment that he saw in the others. Not wanting to attract more attention, he retreated to his office after the brief inspection, knowing there were cameras trained on him.

Steve's mind hatched a plan. "How could I get access to that room?"

"There's no way, Steve. You can't just walk around there. What are you thinking?" The suggestion exasperated Eugene.

Steve could not be dissuaded that easily. "If you're a patient in the hospital, that would get you one step closer."

"Are you planning on getting sick? You must be bored," Eugene replied with a harsh, derisive laugh.

"That can't be too hard to do. I could get sick."

"That hospital is for patients and employees. They probably wouldn't take a contractor there."

"Maybe not, but we're out in the middle of nowhere. They'd have to take care of you somehow."

Eugene understood he had a battle on his hands. "Yeah, it's called the clinic. I'm sure Dee talked to you about that. Besides, even if you made it to the hospital, there are cameras on the floors and rooms. You'd never make it."

Working with Axel for several years made Steve's, aka Chandler's, mind very flexible. Its pliability would be put to the test. "You work in IT. I'm sure you're pretty skilled. What if you disabled the cameras or did something to allow me to walk around? You seem to know your way around things. Show me some of that Silicon Valley ingenuity, Eugene."

Eugene reflected before responding. He flipped his eyes upward. "I don't know. What you're asking is-"

His sober response would be unwelcome.

"You saying you can't do it? Like you don't have the skills?"

A Silicon Valley techie would be undaunted by this challenge. Eugene had tackled complex problems before. This one would be no more so. His boredom, the separation from his wife, and his reservations about an authoritarian government coalesced into a firm response that lifted his chin swiftly into the air. "Ok, I'll help you. No guarantees though."

Steve extended his hand for a "high-five" which Eugene reciprocated.

"Don't get too excited yet. I've got to figure out a few things to make this work. I'll be in touch." Eugene left with his tray this time.

Steve returned to Dee's office to finish out the day. On their ride home, he informed her about Eugene's cooperation.

She listened intently before throwing cold water on his plan. "You have one big problem, child. Mm hmm. How are you going to get admitted to the hospital?"

In his haste with Eugene, he neglected to develop that part of it. "Honestly, I have to think about that."

Dee continued dousing him with cold water. "They also want CFS employees out of the camp by 8:00 pm and don't forget they have that clinic too. They'd send you to that clinic and then probably send you home so you could get your own doctor."

The frigid water momentarily arrested his plan. A few minutes of staring into the vast desert expanse from the passenger's seat of Dee's truck revived it. He reasoned that if someone got sick at the end of the day, they'd be admitted to the clinic. If the illness proved significant enough, they might transfer the patient to the hospital since the clinic closed at 6:00 pm. The hospital would monitor his condition overnight and then either release him or transport him to the nearest facility. Dee thought the plan could work, though it might not materialize as he suggested.

The illness presented the next challenge. He couldn't feign being sick. It had to be the Real McCoy. Years ago, while working on an assignment for El Mundo, he contracted a bacterial infection in Southeast Asia. When the hospital administered sulfonamides to combat the infection, he experienced an adverse reaction.

Steve thought he could recreate that suffering. "If I give myself a dose of sulfonamides, I can induce the allergic reaction and get admitted at least to the clinic. And I'll do it at the end of the day."

Dee released the steering wheel with her right hand and gently slapped his head. "You are crazy, child. You might really hurt yourself. Why would you do this?" Dee shook her head in disbelief, alternating looks between him and the road.

"Dee, we're this close." He showed her his thumb and forefinger an inch apart. "We could find out something about your husband."

Locating her husband motivated Dee more than anything else. "Where are we gonna get the medication?"

Steve grabbed Dee's phone and did a quick search. He queried the Reperio search engine very generically with a single term, "sulfonamide" and got clues. "I'm sure there are no drug stores anywhere around here close. There are some medications that have sulfonamides in them, like diuretics, diabetes medicine, and a bunch of sulfa drugs. You have anything like that?"

"Yeah, now that you mention it, when I got sick a few months back, the doctor gave me something with sulfa. I forgot about that. Gave me a whole lot more than I needed. I guess he figured living out here, it was a hassle to travel so far for medicine. I still think this is a dangerous plan. You don't even know how much to take." Dee wanted to learn about her husband, Juan, though not at the expense of someone else's health.

Steve understood the risk. He also understood the importance of finishing the project to honor Arturo. The plan would take shape over the next week through several encounters with Eugene.

CHAPTER NINETEEN
ELYSIUM

Chandler set the plan for discovering the true nature of Illijum. Late in the afternoon of his shift, while in the men's room, he moved the button camera, taping it into the pocket of his pants. Keeping it as a shirt button would be perilous given his expected encounter with the medical team. He inserted a small listening device into the heel of his shoe. He also inserted a Short Range Device (SRD) into a pen also taped in his pocket. He'd use the SRD to communicate with Eugene during his hospital stay.

Dee again questioned him about the decision. She didn't want the guilt if something went awry. He remained firm and swallowed her pills while in the men's room and walked back to Dee's office. The two waited for the medication's reaction, passing the time as if engaged in work.

It came swiftly and violently in less than an hour. The impending feeling of doom descended upon him first. Then came the flashback to his recurring dream, the sun rising and falling in the eastern sky with fireballs bombing the Earth. He broke out into rash and hives. His eyes swelled and he struggled to breathe. He looked as if he'd been in a boxing match and then taken a swim in a poison ivy bath. The Thai hot spiciness that burned his mouth on his first date with Arianne paled compared to the discomfort he felt after taking the pills. He questioned the sanity of this experiment. He longed for a simple evening at home with Arianne.

A panicked Dee called the camp clinic. She had not prepared for the emotion of watching Steve suffer the reaction.

In less than three minutes, a nurse rushed to the cafeteria. By this time, Steve had titled back in his office chair. Tears streamed out of his eyes.

The nurse took his pulse and noted the swelling and pale skin. "What happened to this man?"

"He's got a bad knee and took some medication. He said he ran out, so he borrowed some from someone else," Dee said, excitedly, as she stood over him. She didn't want to confess that she had provided the drug. The knots twisted in her belly.

The nurse reacted with stern displeasure. "Why do people do that? He must be allergic to something in it. Do you know if he has allergies?"

"I don't know. We usually don't ask our contract workers that. Can you just help him, please?" Dee felt the stunt had gone too far. The whole thing might backfire.

Steve wheezed and struggled to breathe. "Ohh. I'm having a hard…" He pulled harder on his lungs.

The nurse made sure his airway remained unblocked. She called the clinic. "I need a gurney here now! In the cafeteria."

The swollen-faced Steve managed a few words while attempting to sit up. "My stomach. It hurrrtss. I feel dizzy."

"Everyone's supposed to have online medical records. What's his name?" the nurse said. "I don't want to give him something that might hurt him worse."

Dee considered the possibility that there were no online records for this fictional employee. "Steve Rogers." She hoped that the Five Tribes took care of this by copying Chandler's information to the fictional record.

Two orderlies appeared with a gurney. The nurse got on her phone once again, her diagnosis complete. "I'm bringing in a Steve Rogers, CFS contractor, possible anaphylaxis, get the epinephrine ready." The nurse turned toward the orderlies. "Put this man on the gurney and move him as quickly as possible to the infirmary."

The orderlies hoisted Steve on the gurney and slowly jogged out of the cafeteria. The nurse followed at a similar pace. Dee looked on with growing concern. If something grave happened to Steve, he'd be on his own. She wouldn't know who to contact. If the medical team found out Steve's true identity, he'd really be on his own, per the agreement.

After arrival at the infirmary, the orderlies rushed him to an examination table. Steve's medical records appeared on a screen. The Five Tribes or Omni perhaps, had created a medical record after all with accurate allergy information for the patient. One of the infirmary nurses stripped off his pants and plunged the epinephrine shot into his leg. Steve arched his body in silent pain.

His breathing improved. His blood pressure rose as a result of the shot, though not approaching levels of concern. They placed him on oxygen and hooked him up to a Ringer's Lactate IV.

In an hour, he regained his senses. A nurse came to his side, patting his arm. "You're lucky, Mr. Rogers, damn lucky."

He looked up at the nurse, confused. "Huh, what?" *Who's Mr. Rogers? Oh, wait, that's me!* The medication made him forget his impersonation.

The nurse wagged her finger at him. "That medicine you took for your knee, it made you go into shock. That's why you don't take other people's medicine! And what's wrong with your knee, anyway? Your medical record doesn't show any knee problem."

The medical record manipulation would not reveal a non-existent injury. A still groggy Steve Rogers came up with something. "Oh, yeah, I slipped the other day in the kitchen and I twisted it. It was a little sore."

The nurse admonished him. "Next time something's 'a little' sore, take ibuprofen. Please! You're lucky you didn't stop breathing."

He knew he had to play the role of a reluctant patient, especially this late in the day. Looking up at the clock, he said, "I see it's 6:00 pm. When can I leave?"

The false request proved wholly necessary. "Leave?" The nurse shook her head while patting his. "Mr. Rogers, we're going to have to move you to the hospital to watch you until the morning."

His reluctance persisted. "Why? I want to go home." He attempted to sit up.

The nurse responded by placing her hand on his shoulder. "No you don't. Now Mr. Rogers. Please. Relax. You can't stay here since we go home at 6:00 pm. We're moving you to the hospital. They can take better care of you there."

The nurse stepped out of the examination room and called the orderlies. "He's ready." Turning back to him she said, "Please try and relax. You should be better by the morning."

A couple of minutes later, the orderlies returned. This time they would move him to a hospital bed, lifting him from the exam table.

He had enough coherence to trace his journey from the infirmary to the hospital. The orderlies took him down one level through an underground corridor connecting the two locations. They emerged from the elevator back on ground level. From what he remembered studying the camp layout with Axel and visual observation, this hospital had a single floor with the additional area in the basement, as confirmed by Eugene.

There were few rooms occupied. One appeared to have military personnel. Several had MPs standing guard. Another room had a civilian. The orderlies moved him into his private room and secured the bed. The Ringer's Lactate bag remained hanging from the IV stand.

A comely nurse entered, speaking to him in a dulcet tone. "Mr. Rogers. I heard you took some medicine you shouldn't have?" She caressed his arm.

He sheepishly replied, "That's what I heard. I'm feeling much better though." He hadn't seen a woman this attractive since the last time he'd seen Arianne.

"That's what they all say." She hooked up his finger to monitor pulse and oxygen saturation. "The doctor will be in shortly."

Shortly ended up being thirty seconds. "Hello, Mr. Rogers. I'm Dr. DeCastro. You had a pretty decent case of anaphylaxis. It looks like the shot helped, so that's encouraging. Given that you had this happen to you before, we're keeping you overnight."

The medical record accurately reflected his episode in Southeast Asia.

"Our medical training tells us that 20% of people experience biphasic anaphylaxis, which is just another way of saying you could have another bout within 12 hours. We'll put a little something in your IV to help with that. Please don't hesitate to call the nurse's station if you need something. I hope you'll have a restful night, Mr. Rogers." The doctor exited.

The nurse glanced at his vitals. "Please try to relax. You're stable now. We'll bring a little something for you to eat. Not too much, though," the nurse said as she exited.

Steve noticed the molding of her scrubs around her derriere.

The characterization of "a little something" to eat proved

accurate. He received a slice of toast and some fruit with a glass of milk. He took small samples of each.

The video monitor showed a Colorado Rockies baseball game to which he paid little attention.

They had dressed him in a hospital gown. His clothes hung in the closet. He wandered to the closet, dragging his IV stand to check on his micro equipment. He'd taped the camera and the SRD, concealed in a pen, to the inside of his pants' front pockets, mitigating the risk of them falling out during his medical episode. He pulled the listening device from the heel of his shoe and wrapped it in his hands.

The next steps were out towards the nurse's station. His leg remained sore from epinephrine shot. Feigning temporary confusion, he placed the listening device under the lip of the counter at their station. The nurses descended upon him quickly, scolding him for leaving the room.

"Mr. Rogers! Now what did the doctor tell you? Let's get you back to your room," the comely nurse said, grabbing his arm carefully. He enjoyed her escort back to the room.

She scolded herself for not noticing that he'd unhooked from the finger monitor. Apparently, her cackling with another nurse impeded responsiveness this time, thankfully for him.

After getting him back in bed, she informed him another nurse would come by to check on him at shift change time around midnight.

He hoped she would be as easy on his eyes. When satisfied that he would be uninterrupted, he attached the other end of the listening device to his ear, hoping to pick up information from the nurses. For the next hour he listened to the nurses talk about their lives. He fought the urge to doze, still recovering from his allergic reaction.

When the graveyard crew arrived, he stowed his earpiece behind his back. A nurse, not as easy on the eyes, came to check on him at 12:05 am. After a check of her patient, she returned to the nurse's station.

Steve reinserted his earpiece and listened.

"This is like what, your third day here."

"Yeah."

"You'll get used to it. The overnight hours. It's not like a regular hospital where you might have worked before, you know. We'll have a few patients, but they usually don't stay here long. If the patient's case is that severe, they'll send them to another facility, military or civilian. We're not equipped for that much here."

"True. It's been pretty quiet my first two nights."

"The only time we might get something more complicated is if there's a problem with the Elysium Protocol."

The word "Elysium" piqued Steve's attention. He readjusted his earpiece.

"Elysium? What's that?"

"They're supposed to give you that in the training manual. Have you read it?"

"Not all the way. I figured I could read at night, while I'm here. I live in Vegas. When I'm there, I want to pay attention to my kids. I'm gonna be on for 10 days and off for 10. I can read it here."

"Girl, I'll save you some reading time."

The revelation would overwhelm Steve.

***

The camp administered the Elysium Protocol as a final option for patients whose return to civilian life would pose a threat to themselves or others. Some patients exposed to VR reeducation

314

and drug ingestion responded adversely to the protocol and experienced severe side-effects. The behavior modification came with side-effects including paranoia, suicidal thoughts, brain damage and hypervigilance. U.S. Army doctors had warned of the potential for devastating side effects, to the consternation of domestic counterterror and security organizations like DHS and the FBI.

Nevertheless, the government security apparatus wanted to test the new frontier of prisoner rehabilitation. In time, it would be an easier sell to politicians. The country had adopted a kinder, gentler approach that focused on rehabilitation instead of punishment.

The medical teams in the camp realized they had damaged patients beyond repair. At the very core, these patients had no meaning left in their lives. The program robbed them of their motivation to pursue life's challenges, challenges essential to human existence.

They offered the affected patients an opportunity to experience the Elysium Protocol (EP) instead of confinement to an insane asylum. Asylums had made a comeback of sorts in America over the course of the last decade with a dramatic rise in emotionally disturbed people. Doctors researching the phenomenon suggested the stress of modern living in the information age was closely correlated to increases in depression, chronic stress, and a variety of mood disorders.

Researchers linked these disorders to increases in domestic abuse and other violent crime. With mass murders on the increase, the Department of Health and Human Services made it a national policy to have psychiatric physicians commit more people to asylums, reviving a practice that faded in the twentieth century.

Camp officials presented the EP in a much more favorable light. The reputation of chronically underfunded asylums in the U.S. made other alternatives significantly more appealing, especially when Elysium participants could pick from a variety of programs that calmed their troubled souls and took them to paradise.

The nurses continued their chatter.

"Wow. Glad you told me about all that. That's a lot to digest. I'll have to read more. So they run the EP in this camp?"

"For sure. They do it on the lower level. The doctors running the program said they needed more privacy, for some reason."

"When do they run the program?"

"Usually at night. I think there's one tonight at 2:30 am. We're supposed to be on standby if the patient experiences a medical problem."

"Huh, I wonder why they run the program in the middle of the night? What sort of problems do they have?"

"I'm not for sure. The whole time I've been here, I haven't had anyone brought to me."

It finally became clear to Steve. What Duron heard as "Illijum" was really Elysium. The "EP" that Eugene noted on a patient record stood for Elysium Protocol. The PSYOP officer described Elysium as a special place for souls to find peace during a conversation with Duron.

Elysium or the Elysian Fields represented the afterlife in Greek mythology. Homer described it as paradise, a place to live a blessed and happy life where people would indulge in whatever they pursued during their mortal life. For the patients in this camp, the Elysium Protocol represented the vehicle that would take them away from the VR behavior modification.

Steve needed to witness EP for himself. Everything he heard

from these nurses, combined with information from the whistleblower, plus what Eugene saw in the basement confirmed his next action. He'd worked out a plan where Eugene would hack into the vital sign feed from his patient room to pass normal data. Eugene would also have to modify the surveillance camera feeds in the hallway and basement level so Steve could be free to film whatever occurred in those lab rooms, which he now discovered could very well be the EP.

At 2:15 am he signaled Eugene with the SRD, notifying him of his impending departure from his room. Eugene had assigned himself to perform system maintenance overnight. Steve received an acknowledgment from Eugene.

He disconnected the IV bag from the port on his cannula, placing tape around the device. He then unplugged from his finger monitor, hoping his vitals would transmit normally.

Eugene, on top of his game, faked the vital signs as if Steve remained connected.

After changing into his regular clothing, he walked out of his room, peeking towards the nurse's station to see if anyone glanced in his direction. They remained engaged in chatter, oblivious to the surroundings.

Steve scurried down the hall towards the fire exit, desperately hoping Eugene commandeered the security camera feed. The feed on this floor projected to the nurse's station. The basement feed, as Eugene suspected, went somewhere else. There were no other patients interred on his wing, making the walk down the hall less perilous.

After tiptoeing down the stairs and arriving on the lower level, he came to a door with a small center pane of glass, at eye level, where he saw a hallway with dull lighting. A door sat on the opposite end. He opened the door and took half-moon strides down the hall, the SRD in his pants pocket in the event he needed to signal Eugene. There was little comfort with this part of the plan, given that Eugene could provide no assistance at this juncture. The camera operated from the top button on his shirt. Steve flew solo at this point.

The first room on the floor had a solid metallic door and an adjacent observation pane. There were no occupants inside. Same for the second room, offset slightly on the other side of the hallway. When he reached the third room, configured identically to the first two, he observed a white man lying naked on a hospital bed. The upper half of the man's body lay elevated at a sixty-degree angle, his head attached to a VR headset. There were other probes on his head, chest and genital area. An IV came out of his right arm, dripping something from a bag. He also had a probe attached to his index finger that fed a vital sign monitor. The room had an otherwise sterile appearance, painted satin white from floor to ceiling.

Steve positioned his camera next to the glass to eliminate reflection. The naked man appeared to be in the throes of ecstasy. He smiled at first and subsequently moaned, not painfully but pleasurably. The final evidence of his ecstasy was obvious. After a couple of minutes, it became apparent the man no longer breathed, his body limp. The vital sign monitor showed no life, a red light followed.

What the hell killed this man? His instinct made him want to jump into the room and save the man. What could he do beyond CPR? But he knew he could do nothing. There were cameras trained inside the room. Eugene hadn't done anything about them. He'd blow his cover. *I should run upstairs and grab a nurse.* That would blow his cover as well. *Why aren't there any doctors here in the first place?* He broke out in a cold sweat, his heart palpitated. The cannula bounced on his arm from the increased blood pressure. He was experiencing the allergic reaction all over again. He needed to look away from this man. The horror of his death was overwhelming.

He staggered to the room across the hall where there was another patient, this time clothed. Steve pressed his shirt against the observation panel. Another white man, his torso propped up at a sixty-degree angle, had a VR headset attached. There were probes, all concentrated in the cranial region. An IV came out of his right arm, as the other man had. This man also smiled, although in a different way, as if looking at something beautiful. Maybe he admired the Mona Lisa at the Louvre or Mount Denali in Alaska. Steve imagined himself with the same look the first time he visited Iguazú Falls in Argentina. It didn't matter. This patient met the same fate. The vital sign monitor showed no life and the red light came on.

"Why are these people dying?" He went through the same progression of emotions again. A wave of guilt overwhelmed him. To save these men, he'd have to blow his cover. He feared the fate that might fall upon him—it wouldn't be a simple trespassing charge. He might end up here as well. *What would be my VR simulation?*

He heard an elevator descending and scampered down the hall, taking refuge behind the closed door from which he entered. Two orderlies, dressed in white smocks, entered the hallway and walked towards the room with the ecstasy patient. *Why orderlies? Where are the doctors? The nurses?* Steve placed his ear against the door to glean something. The orderlies commented that they hoped they could leave this miserable world the same way these guys chose to.

Chose to? They wanted to die? How can that be?

He watched the orderlies enter the room and remove the body, covered in a white sheet. Still no medical personnel were on hand.

"Man, you know this dude did the sex program. I wish they'd tell us ahead so we could at least wipe the body down. Give the man some dignity," one orderly said as he rearranged the white sheet.

"I know, but at least he went out with a smile on his face. You know the woman in his VR program probably looked like a porn star. I hope I can go out this way," said the other orderly as he fist-bumped his partner. He was envious of the dead man before him.

Steve retraced his steps back up the fire exit and into his room. He changed back into his gown, secured the camera and SRD in his pocket and reconnected the vital sign monitor on his finger. He struggled to reconnect the Ringer's Lactate IV into the cannula port. He sent Eugene a signal via the SRD, indicating he had returned to his room.

The realization of the Elysium Protocol's intent had descended on him like an avalanche. The Elysium Protocol was nothing more than a place to discard the victims of a mind control experiment gone wrong. Already damaged mentally, the patients were told they were going to a better place. Perhaps some knew what fate awaited them, a fate better than spending the rest of their years in an asylum with no hope of release. How many of these patients would have chosen death over trying to eke out an existence in a financially punishing world where government authority encroached on every aspect of their lives? How many people, like the orderlies, envied the way these patients left the realm of the living?

What would the families of these patients be told? Would they just "disappear" like Dee's husband, Juan?

There would be no sleep for Steve Rogers the rest of the night.

***

The duty nurse after the 8:00 am shift change told him he looked tired, like he hadn't slept a wink. Little did she know how true her words were. She said nothing about the IV, perhaps due to his impending departure. She could only offer a shrug.

Breakfast arrived shortly thereafter. Like dinner, he had little appetite for this meal. The nurse informed him there'd be an orderly to walk him back to the cafeteria. He would need no wheelchair, just rest and relaxation. He dressed with alacrity, wanting to make sure he secured the video recording device, SRD, and the listening device.

The orderly barely acknowledged him. He looked miserable being there. Steve wondered if this orderly also hauled away the expired bodies from the Elysium Protocol like the day's rubbish. He didn't want to ask.

People, like these orderlies, were willing to trade a few minutes of ultimate pleasure, bodily or psychic, for death. Presumably, the patients had no idea what awaited them. He witnessed a new depth of despair for humanity.

He speculated that the deceased probably ended up as subjects for the continuation of the mind control experiment. Whoever administered this program no doubt dissected the bodies to find out what went wrong. And then what became of the bodies? Did they have a proper burial? Did their families know? Or were they incinerated with the rest of the lab waste?

The events witnessed evoked haunting memories of human experimentation from Nazi concentration camps.

They walked outside to a blinding sun that rose patiently in the eastern sky. The orderly escorted him all the way to Dee's office, which sat empty. He said nothing as he left.

It didn't take long for the orderly to lose his lifeless appearance. A security officer approached the orderly in the cafeteria, within view of Dee's office, and engaged him in discussion. The orderly pointed towards the office while the security officer glared at Steve. Steve occupied himself shuffling papers when the security officer, accompanied by the orderly, returned to grab his attention.

"Mr. Rogers?" the burly officer asked.

"Yes." He lifted his attention from the paper shuffle, paranoia gripped him.

"Mr. Rogers, I know the nursing staff recommended you go home to rest, but I'm going to have to ask you to wait here," the security officer demanded, pointing his hairy arm towards the floor.

"Wait? What? Why?" He sounded desperate. He fidgeted and broke eye contact with the officer. Desperate men were guilty by their behavior. "I'm exhausted. I won't be any good here today. I'm just straightening some things out before my boss, Mrs. Chapman, gets here. I'm surprised she's not here yet." He continued moving the paper mound.

The officer raised his voice. "Mr. Rogers, I need you to stay here, please. I don't want to argue about it." The guard walked away, destination unknown.

The orderly, previously mute, addressed him with sardonic contempt. "You must be in trouble. He was asking me about you. I guess they wanted to escort you from the hospital. They don't like people just walking around." With those brief comments, the orderly walked away, stealing glances at Steve.

He picked up the phone in Dee's office and rang Eugene.

"Eugene, good morning. Still there I see. I bet you must be

tired from last night and all the work you did. I had a rough night myself in the hospital. Next time you're down here I can tell you all about it." Steve had no intention of communicating anything vital during this conversation. The call served as a signal to Eugene that he had returned to the office.

Eugene said nothing about his overnight work. "Really? I feel bad for *you*. You *should* really go home and *get* some rest. Hopefully, Dee won't miss you while you're *out* of the office." He emphasized the words "you", "should", "get", and "out" to an inordinate degree. "Don't let me keep you from getting the rest you deserve. Talk to you later, Steve."

The emphasized words suggested that something had gone amiss in their plan. He got the drift. "Thanks. I will. Talk to you later."

Unsure of what to do next, he walked down the hall leading to the parking area. Dee, who normally would have been at her post by now, headed towards him at a brisk pace, taking short, rapid steps.

Steve smiled and greeted her. "I'm glad to see you. I need to get-"

She hooked him by the arm, spun him around, pulled him close, and whispered breathlessly in his ear. "This man, he showed up at my house this morning. He was waiting outside. Lucky, I didn't shoot him. My dog was going crazy, child. The man said he knew you. He knows your real name. He wore a black, short-sleeve shirt, tan slacks and tennis shoes. Said his name was Thomas and that you was in danger. Did you tell anyone else what you was doing?"

Steve whispered back, spying the hall behind her, looking for the security officer who wanted to detain him. "You mean Tomás, probably. He sort of knows me. It doesn't matter. I don't have time to explain. What else did he say?"

"He told me to get all your things and give them to him. I don't know how, but he knew what you was doing here. I was real nervous, child. You never told me this was your plan. But he insisted. I was afraid he'd do something to blow your cover. Oh, and he's here," she said, her eyes circled over his shoulder.

"Here?" Steve pointed to the ground and craned his neck towards the other end of the hall.

She squeezed his arm a little tighter. "Don't look down there. He'll be coming any second now. I hope I didn't do nothing wrong."

Steve twisted his arm away from her, hoping to restore the blood flow through his brachial artery.

Tomás walked down the hallway towards them, dressed in army attire, an MP sleeve on his arm. Steve turned to face him, unsure of what would transpire. Making no eye contact with Steve, Tomás cuffed him, hands in front, said nothing and grabbed him by his right arm, tingly from Dee's earlier death grip.

Steve turned towards Dee, not understanding what would happen next. "Bye Dee."

"Good bye, child," she said, misty-eyed. "You take care of yourself." Dee offered a melancholic wave. It was his last image of the woman who'd made his investigation possible.

As they walked down the hall towards the parking lot, they were approached by a security officer who said Steve needed to be detained for questioning. Tomás pulled a badge out of his front shirt pocket and flashed it at the officer. He did not speak. After a brief inspection, the security officer waved them on.

The morning sun blinded Steve again. He'd been in a dark environment the last twelve hours on top of working in a facility with few windows to boot.

Tomás placed him in the rear seat of an official looking vehicle with military plates. He flashed the badge once again at the entry checkpoint and drove onto the road connecting the camp to the highway.

Steve would now revert to Chandler, who waited until they were out of view of the camp before beginning his questions. "Can you tell me what's going on? Your timing was perfect. And who are you supposed to be?" He raised his hands up above seat level. "Oh, and what's up with these handcuffs?"

Tomás glanced at the rearview mirror. "You always have so many questions, Chandler."

"Well, excuse me for wanting to understand my life!" Chandler banged his cuffed hands on his lap.

Tomás glanced at the mirror again. "Habakk sent me. He thought you might be in danger."

"How could he have possibly known that? Did he talk to Axel?" Chandler asked, grateful yet dumbfounded about being in the vehicle.

No answer came, just glances in the mirror.

"Is Habakk working with the Tribes or something? Come on, dammit!" Chandler's emotions gave way to his growing frustration.

"I'm sorry. I have your belongings in the trunk. I surprised DeArthie, I'm certain. I apologized to her, that is all I could do." Tomás said, alternating his glances between the mirror and the road, hoping to calm his passenger.

"Where are we going?"

"We need to evacuate you. It will be too risky for you to fly out of Las Vegas. Your adventure almost made you a patient in that camp. You should understand that. Please be comfortable. The ride will be long."

"Sorry to be redundant. Where are we going?"

"Chicago."

"Chicago? That's a lot farther than two hoots and a holler away. Why are we going there? Oh, and these cuffs?" He raised his arms above his head.

Tomás grinned. "Yes, the handcuffs will come off if you hold your hands like you have them now and pull them apart forcefully. They're not real."

Chandler removed the cuffs as instructed. "That was real slick. You'll have to tell me where you got these. They'd be great at a party."

"Mr. Scott, please drink the cold herbal tea from the thermos next to you. It will help you rest. You look very tired."

He poured himself tea from an insulated container. A plastic glass sat in the cup holder on the back side of the center console. He had no idea what he drank, though it pleased his palate.

What he discovered in the camp proved to be more disturbing than anything he expected. The government had established a detention camp for those who were not on board with the political and economic order. Rather than punishing them, the authorities administered a far-reaching mind control experiment in a comfortable environment using a combination of virtual reality and drugs, with the goal of producing docile citizens.

The experiment was both brilliant and sinister. The experimental failures were given a chance at their own version of paradise or a sentence to the funny farm. Little did the failed patients know that their paradise, the Elysium Protocol, was a death sentence. The Elysium Protocol was the final solution for an experiment gone wrong.

He wondered if DeArthie's husband, Juan, had met this fate. She would probably never know. She'd be the unsung heroine whose identity he'd have to ultimately conceal. He also left, not knowing what would become of Eugene. Both he and Dee would become anonymous actors in the final chapter of his documentary.

He faced a big decision. Would he reveal all details of the reorientation camp? Was he qualified to make the decision regarding the information's release? The country was still reeling from the president's 2020 election decision. How could they possibly accept this?

He'd soon drift off to sleep.

CHAPTER TWENTY
DOCUMENTARY

After crossing into Utah, Tomás pulled over into a rest area and changed his clothing out of the military garb. Their travels took them through Denver, Omaha, and Des Moines. Chandler had no idea how Tomás continued to drive without a full night's sleep. They pulled over for gas, coffee and food, eating in the car. Fast food served as their dietary staple. Twice, the seemingly indefatigable Tomás had to pull into a rest area to catch a few winks. Chandler remained in the back seat the entire time, at Tomás' insistence, so that he could rest as much as possible. Thirty hours later they arrived at Great Lakes Tower, Axel's home in the Windy City of Chicago.

Around 4:00 pm, Tomás pulled into the circle drive in front of the building and buzzed Axel's condo. He grabbed Chandler's gear from the trunk and bid him farewell in Spanish while acknowledging Axel with a nod of the head. Chandler was inured by now to the Habakk and Tomás operation. His attempts to extract information from Tomás during the cross country trek were met with dulcet smiles and pleasantries that had nothing to do with the queries.

Tomás sped away to a destination unknown.

"Chan, you look like crap." Axel mussed the top of Chandler's hair. "I think it's time for you to shave and get rid of your prosthetic nose."

In the hasty escape from the Nevada camp, Chandler never removed it. He always had DeArthie do it for him. He reached for it now, wiggling it from side-to-side.

"Good to see you too, Ax. You have no idea. The last day has been a blur. I don't even know how I ended up here."

"Let me help you with some of this, and you can tell me upstairs." Axel grabbed his gear and put his arm around him, drawing him in closer. The elevator led them to the 55th floor condo overlooking Lake Michigan. Though Chandler wasn't home in the conventional sense, he felt Axel's fatherly presence. Chandler would be the closest thing the never-married Axel would have to a son.

When they entered the condominium, Axel demanded an immediate shower for his guest. His nose couldn't be fooled. "I've got some electric clippers in there too, so you can shave. I also have something you might be able to use to get rid of that latex snout of yours. The bathroom is yours, sir."

He had not been this hirsute since college. He pruned his beard and followed it with a close blade shave. Next he took off the nose, wiggling it gingerly. For the first time in six weeks, he saw the real Chandler Scott staring back at him in the mirror, albeit with a longer mane. The tepid shower revived him. Wearing his regular attire also helped him regain a sense of normalcy.

"Chan, come on to the kitchen when you're done, I fixed something for you."

He gladly accepted the sandwiches and green tea waiting on the kitchen counter.

Axel watched him devour the food and slurp the drink. "I guess someone's hungry."

"Forget my eating. Tell me how you know Tomás," Chandler said, mashing the ham and cheese.

"About 7:00 am today, I get an unsecured call from someone identifying himself as Tomás who said he was bringing you here.

I told him I had no intention of continuing the conversation since I had no idea who he was. Plus, I suspected it might be a set up. I couldn't take the chance and just about hung up. He insisted he was legit, even mentioned Arianne by name, and he seemed to know things about you that only a close friend might. That made me even more suspicious. I began to wonder if he was affiliated with the Tribes. I didn't want to ask in case it was a trap. He said he was getting you out of trouble, which was entirely plausible given what you were doing. I kept my mouth shut and just listened. The man told me he thought he'd be here by 3:00 pm or 4:00 pm. I didn't even ask if he knew where I lived, though I guess he could have found out if he really tried. So I figured I'd wait and see if he showed. He didn't miss that time by much. So who is this guy?"

Chandler took a swig of tea and wiped his mouth with a napkin. "Ax, truthfully, it's such a long story and I don't know if you'd believe me, anyway."

Knowing there were other more germane items for discussion, Axel took the conversation in another direction. "I can wait on that explanation, although it better be good. Look, there's something you should know. Phish sent me a message telling me to go to a Dark Net site and look at a file from a reorientation camp out west. They didn't know where it was located. The file, or I should say files, were supplied by someone working inside one of the camps. We can look at it later. I just wonder if it will be in accord with what you saw."

Chandler had seen much in his journalistic career, though nothing could have prepared him for what he discovered in Nevada. "When I tell you what I witnessed there, it will shake you to your core."

"Very well, then. Before we do anything, please call Arianne

330

and let her know you're safe."

Axel left for his office and gave them privacy.

Chandler longed for her while in Nevada. His anticipation grew during the cross-country ride back to Chicago. With no contact for weeks, he wondered how she'd react.

Relieved when she answered, the sound of her voice brought him great comfort. It warmed her heart too.

"Chan, it's so good to hear your voice. I've missed you." Her voice conveyed a warmth he'd not heard in some time. Maybe his absence made her heart grow fonder.

"I've missed you too, honey. I feel like I'm back on terra firma."

She understood his immediate priorities and set a compromising tone. "I know you probably have a lot to take care of, and you know I'm not gonna ask you about what you were doing, so just let me know when we can see each other, all right?"

"I will. I just need some time with Ax, OK? I promise we'll see each other real soon." Her eagerness to see him made the time he needed to complete his work more painful.

"Love you, Chan."

"Love you back, bye."

He took a triumphant spin on Axel's kitchen counter chair and hopped off for the short walk to Axel's office. There he settled into the office chair opposite Axel's desk.

"Your smile tells me things went well with Ari. I'm glad. So tell me, did you find what you were looking for?" Axel leaned back in his chair with his hands clasped behind his neck.

"I found it and much more. It's worse than I thought, to be honest," Chandler rubbed his eyes in recollection.

He'd executed the undercover work to the best of his ability, yet nothing he'd ever done professionally or working with Axel could have prepared him for the Elysium Protocol.

"Bottom line, Ax, the government is involved in a non-lethal scheme to reorient opposing views. They control people's thoughts through the use of virtual reality and drugs. I met a couple of, they call them 'patients', who by any traditional standard, were not criminals. They got charged with violating federal laws anywhere from an FSB regulation to sedition."

Axel leaned towards Chandler, his right eyebrow rose. "Fascinating and sinister. It's a quiet way to deal with dissent. You change their thinking. There must be some powerful technologies involved. The government just looked at this as a mind control exercise where no one gets hurt."

Axel's conclusion encountered an immediate refutation. The student challenged the mentor.

Chandler's expression sobered. "That's the problem though, Ax. People *are* getting hurt. More than hurt."

"You mean like physically hurt?"

"Not everyone reacts well to the treatment protocol. The side effects are far-reaching. My God, they suck the life out of them, literally. Releasing someone like that into society is a recipe for disaster so they give them a choice."

"A choice? This can't be good." Axel clamped his jaw with his hand and gapped his mouth.

"These patients know they're mentally shot so they're given the choice of going to an asylum or the Elysium Protocol."

Axel, upon hearing the word 'Elysium', leaned back in his chair and placed both hands on his bald scalp. An ashen hue covered his face. He recalled the word from his studies of Greek mythology.

According to this mythology, the word referred to the afterlife as contrasted with Hades, which referred to the underworld.

Elysium represented the place where the chosen would remain after death, living in a paradise.

Chandler waved his arms at his host. "Ax, you still with me? You looked like you were off somewhere."

"Sorry, yes, I was reflecting on something. Continue."

"When they were given those two choices, they all took Elysium. Who'd want to go to an asylum? Anyway, in the Elysium Protocol they allow the patient to select a VR simulation."

"Do you know what choices they had?"

"What I recorded and saw with my own two eyes gave me an idea. One man opted for a sexual experience while another had a look as if he viewed something aesthetically pleasing."

"I presume their arrival in the Elysian Fields followed shortly thereafter?"

"Yeah, they were hooked up to IV bags. At the end of the VR session, they, they, well they died." Chandler took a deep breath to recompose himself. "There was a vital sign monitor."

Neither man spoke for an extended time, both reflecting on what happened to these helpless patients. Chandler stared towards the lights of the Chicago skyline. Axel stared at Chandler, cognizant of the shock he must have felt witnessing this. He could see the pain on Chandler's face and wished there was something he could do to wipe it away.

"So what are you going to do, Chandler?"

When Chandler finished his interview with retired intelligence employee, Susan Black, she mentioned that he might encounter something that could affect national security and have to decide if it served the public's interest to reveal it. Senator Geringer also told him that the press could face unenviable positions where they needed to make decisions about preserving government secrets, secrets that were important to maintaining national security.

He'd have to decide if revealing the camps and the Elysium Protocol served the public interest and weigh that against national security concerns. If he revealed what he learned, he might set off a series of events that would further threaten the integrity of the nation. If he said nothing, he'd compromise his integrity as a journalist. Journalists served an important role in checking government power. It would be a difficult decision.

"I think back to what Susan Black and Geringer said. What would happen if the American public learned about these reorientation camps? You yourself have said that Americans don't seem to care much beyond what is happening to them economically. The president still enjoys a lot of support and the secessionists have pissed off quite a few people. I'm sure everyone's tired of all the hack attacks." Chandler's sober assessment brought him no comfort.

"Don't take this the wrong way. You really have gained a new level of intellectual maturity in the last couple of years. I don't know how the majority would react if they learned about these camps and what's going on inside. Some people honestly won't care. They're more worried about themselves than the freedoms guaranteed by the Constitution. A secession group would use the revelation as further evidence of a government gone mad. The hackers would have a field day with this. Some in government would suggest you were being subversive and irresponsible and charge you with some violation of an FSB reg and throw your ass in jail. They would try to discredit what you did. They'd say the film was doctored or tell everyone that they're concerned about what you found and put together some sort of panel to look into it. Then they'd let the investigation perish in the dustbin of history."

"I never worried about ending up in jail, to be honest. I think journalists realize that could happen. We're always looking for a career-defining story, but this is so much more than I bargained for. Honestly, I wish now that I'd never taken on this project. I've put our lives in danger, a truck driver got killed, Arty died, and I may lose Arianne. What I saw in that camp will haunt me forever. And now I will feel responsible for what happens after I make this decision."

"Don't be so hard on yourself. I agreed to help you. I feel bad enough about putting you in that camp. I'm glad you got out of there safely. And we don't know what happened to Arty. If this was my story, yeah, I would have no hesitation about telling my readers. But I'm in a different place than you. I'm an old man and while my readers would appreciate it, it would never go mainstream. I also know that I'm not one to express my feelings. You and Arianne, I'd hate to see something like this drive a bigger wedge between you two. I don't have any children of my own. You guys are the closest thing. I don't want to see anything happen to you."

Chandler felt touched by the sentiment. "Believe me, you don't know how lucky I am to have you in my life." He tried to inject levity. "I guess if they don't like what I have to say, I can go to another country, maybe Argentina."

"You mean live in exile like Snowden or Assange? I'm sure Arianne would love that. You have a big decision about what you're going to include in the film. You're tired now. Get some rest. You may think about it differently in the morning."

Axel had already prepared his guest's bedroom, aka the office where they were conversing. The sofa bed had served him well a couple of years earlier during a long weekend upon his escape from D.C. after releasing the GFU video.

"Yeah, I feel like I've been chewed up, spat out and stepped on. Let's call it a night."

Tonight the dream had other players. Eugene and DeArthie joined him in the sunrise observation. Neither spoke. After the sun rose and fell in the eastern sky, the three of them dodged fireballs. The fireballs rimmed the pallid faces of the men whose death he witnessed during the Elysium Protocol. There were also fireballs with the faces of Joe and Duron, the two patients to whom he spoke. Illuminated by the fireballs were the sculpted faces of Washington, Jefferson, Roosevelt, and Lincoln, floating high above, granite tears streaming down their faces. President Jefferson ran towards him waving a "We Are the Future" banner and yelled something which he could understand only as he got closer. Jefferson yelled, "Keep the mouth shut, shut, shut!" and lunged at his throat with the pole holding the banner.

The shock awakened him. The clock on his phone read 3:14 am.

***

Unlike the time he'd spent in this makeshift bedroom a couple of summers ago, the morning sun bouncing off Lake Michigan did not bore into Axel's office to wake him up too early. The Autumnal Equinox a couple of weeks earlier and his nightmare ensured a later wake up time.

Chandler walked out of the makeshift bedroom, rubbing his non-existent beard, and ambled toward the noise in the kitchen. Axel, always the early riser, had a breakfast of eggs and toast ready for him on the counter. Axel satisfied himself with a protein shake chock full of fruit.

In between bites of his eggs, Chandler asked, "What are you taking now?"

He observed his host popping several pills, chasing them with his elixir.

"You know I'm always testing new formulations. I'm not a young buck like you."

"These eggs, oh man, I forgot what fresh eggs tasted like. My contact in Nevada, DeArthie, she didn't cook much so we ate a bunch of microwaved food." Chandler savored the meal.

"That's why you don't see a microwave in this kitchen," Axel responded. He had an aversion to the appliance. "You haven't said too much about your contact, DeArthie. How did things go with her?"

He licked his lips after sipping coffee. "She scared me at first." Chandler recalled the shotgun encounter. "But once we started talking, everything was good. You know the whole reason she even helped had to do with the disappearance of her husband. Somebody made contact with her, suggesting they might know of his whereabouts. She never divulged the contact, although she intimated it was someone from the Tribes."

"Yes, I would agree. That was the understanding I had from Omni. I felt bad sending you out there without everything having been nailed down."

"Don't worry about it. I knew what I was getting myself into. DeArthie and her husband lost their business after the 2019 crash. He got really bitter and became vocal on anti-government sites on the Internet. He railed on the 1% and the Elite. I think that's why he got nabbed and ultimately, he disappeared."

"There's more of that going on now. Local police departments are at a loss, and the FBI doesn't help. Disappearances are nothing new. It's happened elsewhere." Axel explained a dark chapter from another South American country.

Political oppression and state sponsored terrorism occurred in

Chile under the leadership of General Augusto Pinochet from 1973 until 1990. The regime created an intelligence agency staffed with thousands for the purpose of ensuring national security. That intelligence apparatus established interrogation and detention camps where prisoners were tortured by waterboarding and a gruesome technique they called "*La Parilla*", Spanish for grill, where they fed electricity through the body.

The psychological torture broke down the prisoner by destroying their will and dignity. Many political detainees disappeared. The repressive policies of Pinochet gave rise to silent protest by Chilean women during a dance called the "*cueca sola.*" The *cueca* was a dance performed by a man and woman, each with a handkerchief. During the *cueca sola*, the women would dance alone, their invisible partner representing someone who had disappeared.

"The two guys I talked to that were patients didn't disappear, in that sense. I got the impression their extended families knew they were in some sort of prison. They simply got offered a different kind of sentence. Both had public defenders. Since a camp sounded better than a federal penitentiary, they took it."

"What we have now is a State that is trying to exert more control, more authority, although implementing it in a far more benign way, at least from their perspective. It would be barbaric, not to mention political suicide to attempt what Chile and Argentina did. They came up with another way, and you had a firsthand look at it."

"This attempt at control is a modern version of techniques from the past. Like you said, we'd like to think that our country would never resort to the types of barbarism of those regimes in Chile and Argentina. Virtual reality is simply the modern way for implementing this sort of thing."

"Let me tell you about a program the CIA implemented years ago. Let's move to the living room. Just put your dishes in the sink. I'll deal with them later." Axel grabbed his own glass and placed it in the sink. "You may see how history tends to repeat itself, just not in the same manner."

After moving to the living room, Axel told Chandler about a dark chapter from the country's past.

MKUltra was a CIA mind control program performed on human subjects for interrogation and torture using drugs. Unsuspecting U.S. and Canadian citizens were subjected to techniques manipulating their mental states and brain functions. The program engaged universities and research institutions in the testing. Some testing was consensual, as subjects were given LSD and heroin. Much of the detail surrounding the program went up in smoke when the CIA ordered thousands of pages of files destroyed in the wake of the Watergate investigation.

"So I guess it's possible that these patients were being administered drugs as part of their treatment. One patient mentioned that," Chandler commented.

"Possibly. Who knows? Which brings me to what I wanted to tell you that I didn't yesterday," Axel previewed.

Chandler's pupils widened in anticipation. "What?"

"Yesterday, I told you that Phish gave me files from someone who claimed to work in a reorientation camp. I looked at them. One had a roster of names from a database with several fields, including codes I couldn't decipher. Another file had commentary from U.S. Army doctors. Many 'test subjects', as they called them, experienced paranoia, schizophrenia, and suicidal tendencies. A small group of doctors wanted to resign. There was intense pressure from above, it didn't say from whom, to continue. A group of doctors recommended a cessation until they could identify why subjects were becoming mentally ill."

"The part about patients getting mentally ill is consistent with what I heard."

"Another file said that there had been an alternative therapy developed with computer scientists working for the government. The therapy tried to help those failing the program. The treatment still involved the use of VR, but with an administration of secobarbital and pentobarbital. That's where the file ended. It may be that what you saw, the Elysium Protocol, involved this approach. It gave those patients a ticket to the afterlife—they didn't know that's where they were going."

"It makes me think that's what happened DeArthie's husband. She'll probably never know." Chandler had hoped that his undercover work could bring her peace. "I pray that I didn't expose her to any danger."

"According to Omni, the way they set up your fake identity, she should be able to disavow knowledge of who you were. The authorities will probably be angry with CFS for not doing their due diligence in hiring a contractor."

"I sure hope so. DeArthie really is an unsung heroine." He stared off into the waters of Lake Michigan, wondering how she was getting along in the aftermath of his camp incursion.

***

They had yet to discuss Chandler's decision about what to include in the final product. After being awakened by his nightmare, his mind raced with thoughts, images flashing as if PhotoReading® a lengthy novel. He thought less about the charges he could face than the fallout from his revelation. How would a country react that still had, in the eyes of many, an illegitimate president holding office? He considered the possibility that the president didn't know.

It wouldn't be the first time that subordinates kept nefarious actions from the nation's leader. Would Arianne give him an ultimatum once the project ended? He considered calling Senator Geringer for advice, though he feared the reaction. The mysterious Habakk, who always appeared at the right time and had the right thing to say, told him how important it was for him to do the little things; otherwise he'd be doing nothing. He also owed it to Arty, who insisted that he get a firsthand look at the camp. He'd never know if Arty just wanted him to go there to finger someone like Eugene or if there were more noble intentions. Axel would support him no matter the decision.

"Ax, you're probably wondering what I've decided. We've been avoiding the subject so far this morning."

"I didn't want to push it. You'd bring it up when the time was right. Is this the time?"

Chandler would not reveal the details of his dream. "I had a revelation of sorts last night. Considering everything and my training as a journalist, I don't think I could forgive myself for keeping what I saw from the public. I realize some people will turn a blind eye and others who will agree in the necessity of the camp in the name of domestic security. It's not who I am and not how I was raised." Chandler would also not reveal his encounters with Habakk. He still didn't know what to make of the mysterious man who deftly probed his mind and offered sage advice.

"I think I know where this is headed. After Arty died, I wondered how you'd market the documentary. So I did some investigating."

There would be no chance to sell this to a US-based network who might fear an advertising backlash or a suspension of their FCC license. El Mundo, the Argentinian-based network that

341

formerly employed Chandler, wouldn't touch it either now that it served as a mouthpiece for the Global Financial Union. During Chandler's time in the camp, Axel contacted an old friend who ran an up and coming financial news network out of Singapore. They agreed to look at it.

"I've got someone coming over a little later this morning who's going to bring some voice recording equipment, a better microphone, and a better computer for video processing, in order for you to finish," Axel said.

"Oh, that's great. I'm not the best editor so hopefully your Singaporean friends don't expect a finished product. They'll get the content, good content, and that's all I can promise." Chandler hone his experiences in front of the camera.

Axel's friend arrived later in the morning with the microphone and other equipment. The rest of the day, and well into the night, Chandler and his mentor worked on integrating the camp video and detail into the portion already completed by Arturo. Although not a finished product by network TV standards, it served its purpose.

They delivered a portion of the video through a secure channel to a server in Singapore, after deciding to call it a day around 1:00 am Central. In Singapore, the clock read 2:00 pm, just enough time in the business day for Axel's contact to evaluate the documentary submission.

***

There would be no need for Axel to make breakfast since Arianne would arrive around 9:00 am to meet Chandler in the cafe on the ground floor of Great Lakes Tower. It had been so long since he'd seen her that he forgot how stunning she looked. The sight of her made him recall the first time, at the White House Correspondents' Association dinner in the spring of '19.

In an event littered with starlets, she stood alone. Her auburn colored hair, long and flowing, the eyes a deep blue, the broad shoulders and taut waist mesmerized him. The only difference this morning was the absence of the black sequin gown, replaced by tight-fitting jeans, a light sweater, and a Cubs ball cap.

He saw her first and called out to her as she stood outside the cafe. She ran, arms extended, and embraced him for what seemed like a minute, her chin firmly planted on the back of his shoulder, the gentle feel of her breasts against his chest. They pulled their faces away from each other and kissed; he had not felt her lips like this in months. Neither spoke. Hand in hand, they walked into the cafe and sat themselves in a booth, side by side.

"Oh my gosh, I can't believe I'm here with you," she said, gazing intently into his eyes, quivering with excitement. "I'm glad you're back safely."

"I know, it's been too long," he said, stroking her hand with his left and holding it with his right.

The waitress approached. "Can I get you coffee, tea?" They both ordered coffee. "I'll be back shortly and you can order then."

"I know you haven't asked me about what I was doing. Let me just say that this story is more explosive than what I released last year about the election."

"I'm sure whatever you work on, Chandler Scott, is always explosive. How could it be any other way?" She smiled and fondled his pinkie.

"The story had a personal cost." He told her about Arty's mysterious death.

She placed her palms on her cheeks in disbelief. "Oh my God, Chan. I'm so sorry!" She wrapped her arms around his right arm, placing her head on his shoulder.

"I know. I can't believe Arty is gone, especially how the whole thing went down. I don't think the police have any more leads today than when it happened." He shook his head again in disbelief.

She mourned the deaths of those directly involved with him. "This is why I want you to really think about what you're doing. All these people dying. Rafael last year. Then the accident you were in that killed the truck driver and now Arturo, and my gosh, Chan, he left behind a family."

She also remained troubled by the death last year of one of her father's employees, Tyler Sawyer. He saved an important software project at Maxwell Tech after Arianne accidentally infected the company network with the Trident virus. And that whole incident occurred when she tried to help Chandler.

The waitress returned with the coffee. "What can I get you two?"

Arianne ordered a cheese pastry while Chandler got a sesame seed bagel with cream cheese.

He held her hand in between his. "I know what you're saying, Ari. I'm sorry."

"Don't be sorry. You expect me to just wait around until you've conquered the next big story. I know this is important to you, that's why I've given you the latitude. And I know it's important for the country. Even though my dad was pissed at you last year for us having to leave D.C. like fugitives, he admired what you did. He thinks journalists, especially independent ones, are essential. That's one reason he thinks that Jefferson has gotten away with so much, because the press is silent. But you have to understand he isn't happy about his daughter being in the middle of all of it, given that she has a choice."

"I know we have deep feelings for each other and I know we'll make it through this rough patch." He remembered Habakk's words last New Year's Day at The Battery. "There is so much going on in this country now. We're truly at a crossroads and I thank God we have someone like Matt Geringer in the Senate willing to challenge what he sees and challenge it in the right way. I'm also thankful that I can play some part in all of it. It's my responsibility to give the public a view and let them interpret it."

"He's just one guy, Chan," Arianne said, with heavy skepticism in her voice. "Look what happened with the election last year, and we still don't have an official president."

"It's more than just him. There are others who are doing it a different way. They're just fighting in the only way they know how. I'm doing my little part." Habakk emphasized how important it was for him to do the little things, yet his project was far from little. "When our documentary gets released, Jefferson and the rest of the government will have to answer tough questions."

The waitress returned with their order. "Let me know if I can get you anything else."

Arianne broke off a small part of her pastry. "Will you be in trouble after you release the video?"

She caught him chewing on his bagel. "Hang on." He chewed a little more. "If something were to happen to me, it would just bring more suspicion. I can't believe the Jefferson administration would want that. They'll say they're trying to be stewards for the nation's security. Well, I'm doing my job too, even though I could get charged with something. And if you believe your dad, that's what I'm supposed to be doing."

"Yeah."

Chandler spread more cream cheese on his bagel. "So, what have you been working on since I've been gone?"

"Dad really wants me to work at Maxwell Tech. You know I

tried that once and didn't like it. I'm not sure what I'd do there. There are plenty of law firms in Chicago. I could probably land something in corporate law. I just don't know."

During the rest of the breakfast, they reminisced about the wonderful time they spent in New York and D.C. They caught up on family matters and enjoyed their company. After breakfast they took the elevator to Axel's condo, where she spent a few minutes catching up with Chandler's mentor. She could tell the fidgety Axel had something important he wanted to share with Chandler.

"OK, I can see you two have to get back to work. Bye Ax, good to see you again." She gave him a hug before pointing at Chandler. "You. Come here." She planted a long, passionate, full of desire kiss and sauntered out the door.

Her back side hypnotized Chandler. Even Axel stole a look.

"Earth to Chandler. Come in, please." Axel mocked his mesmerized guest. "That was some kiss. I can only imagine what it must be like when I'm not around."

Chandler laughed. "Yeah, except there haven't been any of those lately."

"Maybe we can change that," Axel said, optimistically. "I received an email this morning from Singapore. They want to move forward."

Chandler closed his eyes in contentment. The realization of months of work, losing a colleague, and the horror of the camp, took a weight off his mind.

"Just a little wrinkle, though. They are worried that your bank account may be under surveillance right now and would rather transfer the funds elsewhere."

"It's not as if I have some offshore account set up under a shell corporation. Hell, it's too hard to do that now with all the FSB regulations anyway," Chandler said, derisively.

"I told them, with your approval, that they could wire funds to my private account. Don't worry it will be in US Dollars." Axel reminded him that implementing the world currency, the Mundi, would not come into effect until the beginning of next year. This sort of transaction would be more difficult in the future.

"How much am I getting for the film?"

"Remember the figures we discussed before you left for Nevada?"

Chandler wanted to make sure that if something happened to him, the film would be released as is.

"Cool. We just need to make sure Arty's family gets their share."

They executed a blockchain-based smart contract, and the Singaporean network wired an initial deposit to Axel's private account. Axel securely transferred the remaining portion of the documentary using distributed servers in different countries hours later. The rest of the funds arrived later that day.

Chandler would have to wait a couple of days to preview the finished product, which he viewed on a secure, encrypted channel courtesy of Axel. It could not have gone better. He hoped Arty would have been proud of the effort.

The Singaporean Financial News Network (SFNN) would broadcast the documentary the following day at 7:00 am EST/ 12 noon GMT/ 7:00 pm Singapore time.

CHAPTER TWENTY-ONE
PRESIDENT RESPONDS

The president's day started in the Oval Office with a morning briefing with his chief of staff, Hutchinson and NSA Carter. The Morning Book had no mention of the documentary since this briefing would roughly coincide with its release in Singapore. Most of the discussion centered on separatist activity and declarations of martial law in some large U.S. cities.

It took little time for the documentary to impact the news cycle. After its broadcast on the Singaporean network, other networks around the world asked for rebroadcast rights. U.S. networks were slow to pick up the story, with some attempting to verify the documentary's authenticity before giving it any credence. Once they did, they interrupted their morning programming with "Breaking News" updates. El Mundo, Chandler's former employer based out of Argentina, barely mentioned it.

The White House received a barrage of calls from U.S. residents. Congressional representatives fielded thousands of calls from alarmed constituencies. Foreign leaders called the White House to verify the story. Some were aghast while others wanted access to the technology. The Internet went wild with speculation.

The president, who by then was meeting with a delegation from the Global Settlement Bank and the International Relations Council, made a hasty exit to confer with his team in the Situation Room. His chief of staff, DNI Burkemper, NSA Carter, the Secretary of DHS, Victor Haydon, as well as the head of the FBI, Ralph Elliott met him in the conference room.

Everyone assumed their seats, Jefferson on the end of the long conference table. Since the meeting was not on the schedule, there were no refreshments on the table, perhaps a good thing.

Jefferson wasted no time with greetings or pleasantries. "Can someone please tell me, what in God's name is going on here with this documentary?" His seething anger made his blood boil.

The silence proved deafening. The entire team sat erect in their chairs and gave him blank stares. If this were high school, no one wanted to rat out the guilty.

Jefferson asked again, squeezing the life out of the pen in his hand. "Is anyone going to answer? I presume everyone knows what I'm talking about?"

DHS Secretary Haydon took the first shot. "Mr. President, sir, with all due respect, in the interest of national security and invoking the doctrine of plausible deniability, I suggest a limited exchange on this matter." His colorless voice conveyed little emotion.

"Mr. Secretary, the phones have been ringing off the hook. Congressional leaders are up my ass. Foreign leaders have been calling. Oh and need I remind you that I escaped an impeachment vote earlier this year and now Senator Geringer is trying to convene an Article Five. With all due respect to you, *sir*, I need an answer now." Jefferson had little patience for the Secretary's approach. His irritation with the encounter grew.

"Sir, I'm going to have to agree with the Secretary on this," FBI Director Elliott added, trying to maintain calm in what was quickly becoming a cauldron of anger.

The public expected the President of the United States to be omniscient. Jefferson had to know the entire functioning of government, a wholly impossible task given the complexities of modern governance. Those with less knowledge of the political process and those outside of the Elite in business and government were most likely to vent their anger at the most obvious political actor, the president. The term "plausible deniability" emerged in the 1960s, a creation of the CIA, to shield senior officials from the potential repercussions of illegal or politically damaging activities prior to them becoming public.

"You might agree with him Mr. Elliott, but to quote a famous movie line, I'm the H M F I C!" Jefferson immediately clarified who was in charge, banging his fist on the table. "I need answers, now!"

Secretary Haydon stumbled to explain as he wiggled in his chair. "Mr. President, we've had these problems going back a few years, sir. After your election in 2016, the domestic situation deteriorated, and I'm not suggesting it had anything to do with you. The internal discontent had been growing for some time. The natives got very restless and the domestic security apparatus needed other options. We had to do something, sir."

A frustrated President Jefferson wanted more. "Well, that's a great history lesson that I think we all knew, keep going!" His steely gaze burned a whole in Secretary Haydon's eyes.

The FBI Director, Elliott, took his turn. "Sir, I want you to also think about the domestic situation starting in 2014. In particular, I want you to recall the specific increase in law enforcement officer involved shootings of civilians. Then we had the rash of police ambushes. Wearing body cameras bothered many of our officers, who felt like their every move was being scrutinized. The level of trust deteriorated badly."

DNI Burkemper chimed in. "Let me also add, sir, that we inadvertently created a terrorist diaspora with all of our military activity in the Middle East. Sure we killed thousands of them on the battlefield and yet, at the same time, many escaped to Europe,

Asia, and America. Those terrorists set up shop within our borders and executed jihad against our citizens."

NSA Carter followed. "Mr. President, we also had to worry about home grown terror cells. The economic situation deteriorated in such a way that people started taking the law into their own hands. We should not forget the barrage of attacks against IRS offices, Federal Reserve banks, and now FSB buildings. There are separatist organizations sprouting like splinter groups from the Honor Brigade. Those are dangerous cells since many of their members are former military. And you know how much time we spend combating cyber terror with Omni, never knowing their next target. Now we have a real stealth organization with these Five Tribes. There are also a bunch of small-time operators who are causing all sorts of cyber disruptions, so it's not just the groups we often discuss."

"Thank you very much for summarizing what we all should know gentlemen, but what does this have to do with anything?" Jefferson asked, throwing his palms in the air.

Everyone looked down at the table, appearing to occupy themselves with paper shuffling. They all waited for the one person who could deliver the unwanted news.

That person would be Chief of Staff, Drake Hutchinson. Hutchinson had a long history with the president going back to their time in California. Hutchinson, a former venture capitalist, served as an instrumental figure in Jefferson's 2016 campaign, a campaign that featured a bruising general election against his Republican opponent. While both campaigns took a hard line against terror, Jefferson's Republican opponent emphasized a continuation of the enhanced interrogation techniques leaked by CIA operatives and later investigated by Congress.

These techniques included aggressive grasping and slapping,

diet and sleep manipulation, waterboarding, and the humiliation associated with nudity. These controversial techniques were used to induce a feeling of helplessness to make the rest of the interrogation resemble an interview. The intelligence agencies stressed that the interrogation techniques were but one tool in their arsenal that emphasized knowledge of the terrorists and what motivated them.

Domestic human rights observers suspected the government would eventually use these techniques on U.S. citizens either supporting jihadist terror cells or on separatists and secessionists. Jefferson's Republican opponent strongly advocated these interrogation techniques on U.S. citizens while Jefferson did not. Nevertheless, the nation's internal security needed attention.

Hutchinson pivoted his chair towards Jefferson. "Mr. President, during my time as your campaign manager for the '16 election, I became aware of scientific breakthroughs in virtual reality."

"You want to talk about game consoles now, Drake?" Jefferson asked, thinning his lips and shaking his head.

"Sir, as far back as 2011, there was discussion that psychedelic drugs would be the next frontier in mental health treatment. These drugs proved helpful in treating autism, PTSD, OCD and other illnesses. However, the word 'psychedelic' had strong connotations to a 1960s drug culture that many were not comfortable with. Before your '16 campaign, a partner in my venture capital firm made an investment in a VR company that developed software targeting mental health and behavior modification. I read the firm's research documents, and it very much seemed like they were having success on par or better than the psychedelics. I met with the company's chief scientist and asked if she thought the technology could be applied to interrogation or other behavior modification targeting social and political malcontents. I hoped it could be applied to the self-radicalization problem with Muslim terrorists and secessionists." Hutchinson paused, hoping Jefferson would cease his own line of questioning and catch his drift.

"I'm probably not going to like what you're going to say next, am I?" Jefferson ran his fingers through his hair.

Hutchinson continued the explanation. "Perhaps not, sir. The country was fragmenting badly. With VR usage becoming so popular, this company suggested placing subliminal messages within VR gaming and educational software to mold the younger generation. They also created these games where success was all but guaranteed, making people feel good about themselves, you know, successful and independent. Psychologists have told us making people feel this way is the number one way we can stop these Muslim terror cells and secessionists."

"Great. So now these companies are putting subliminal messages in games. What does any of this have to do with this documentary from Singapore?" Jefferson asked, tapping his fingers in metronomic fashion. His patience had worn thin.

Hutchinson cleared his throat and grabbed a drink from the bottled water he brought. "I kept that research to myself, obviously to protect my VC firm's investment and also to keep it from the Republicans. This is why I wanted you to advocate kinder, gentler means of interrogation because I knew this company could develop a product for use by our intelligence and security agencies." Once again, he paused, as if looking for support from the others. No one spoke. He had the floor.

"Very well. Continue. I'm sure you're not done." Jefferson's voice tightened. He folded his arms and leaned back in his chair.

"This company, Cerebrum Technologies, worked with U.S.

Army scientists and CIA interrogators, tailoring the VR software for application towards interrogation and behavior modification. By the time of the '16 election, I knew the software had been used by our intelligence operatives overseas with some success. If you recall, sir, the intelligence community repudiated your GOP challenger on the whole interrogation issue. Your GOP challenger didn't know what I knew about the software. That success led the company to extend their efforts towards domestic counterterrorism, including these separatists and secessionists."

"Oh, my God. So you're saying, and the documentary suggested, that we're engaged in a broad mind control effort, or as you called it 'behavior modification', in the name of counterterrorism?" Jefferson leaned forward, his fists clenched against each other.

"Yes, sir. There have been some unforeseen problems. A number of patients reacted poorly to the treatment protocol. What they found were some patients who couldn't be converted; they became more radicalized than they were before they started. Others experienced neurological problems. The Army doctors and scientists as well as professionals from Cerebrum developed a humane approach to dealing with these patients—the Elysium Protocol. They knew these patients could never be released back to civilian life. They could never be reformed. Think about all the problems we've had with mass shootings and the calls for more spending on mental health. The only alternative would be confinement to an asylum where they'd live in a sedated state for the rest of their lives. The Elysium Protocol gave them a choice of dying comfortably within their own selected fantasy."

A pool of sweat had erupted on Hutchinson's forehead. He looked drained from the explanation, gulping his water bottle for comfort.

The rest of the staff were thankful they didn't have to deliver this bombshell.

"How the hell am I gonna explain this?" His face reddened. His eyes watered. The muscles in his neck stiffened. He took a deep breath to control his emerging rage. He was the President of the United States. Rage would not befit the office.

DNI Burkemper responded with a cool, level tone. "Mr. President, you should exercise caution. The intel community is careful about revealing too much of what we do to the public and by extension those we track. We have to keep the enemy uncertain about the limits of what we might do. The enemy would better be able to resist."

Jefferson became agitated with Burkemper's recommendation. "Enemies? These are civilians, for God's sake! Could anyone construe what's going on in these camps as torture?"

"Sir, we need to be very careful about the use of the word 'torture', which in legal terms constitutes a felony. That's not a rat hole we want to go down," DHS Secretary Haydon added, cerebrally.

No one followed up, waiting for Jefferson to speak. He didn't and instead got up and walked around the room, coming to a stop behind Chief of Staff Hutchinson.

Hutchinson couldn't bear the silence or the presence hovering behind him. "Sir?"

Jefferson spun Hutchinson's chair so that the latter faced him.

He bent down, craned his neck towards Hutchinson and growled, "Drake, you knew about this all along." He spun Hutchinson back towards the table.

He walked behind DHS Secretary Haydon, venting his ire at the top of his bald head. "Rat hole? Where do you think this is

355

now?" A fine mist of spittle landed on the shiny scalp.

The secretary trembled, unwilling to turn his chair and face his president.

The president marched back to a position behind his own chair. He motioned with his index finger around the table. "And the rest of you! No one considered what plausible deniability would mean. None of you will have to face the American people. I know we all have a job to do, but my God, what have we become? We have to manipulate the very essence of a human being to make them social and political conformists? A venture capital firm gets wealthy from this cozy partnership with a company who has a back door relationship with our government. No wonder Americans are tired of the Elite in business and those in the Beltway."

Jefferson shook his head in disgust, realizing that he was part of the problem.

***

This would be the most difficult speech of Jefferson's career. He needed to look the American public in the eye. The fallout from Chandler and Arty's documentary gave more ammunition to those groups of people wanting to separate from the United States of America. Jefferson had a solemn duty to hold the nation together. He would attempt to do that from the place America identified as the seat of executive power, the Oval Office.

New versions of "We Are the Future" posters on wooden easels next to the presidential desk greeted Oval Office visitors. The desk sat at the end of the oval with the U.S. and presidential flags flanking it and the presidential coat of arms on the carpet immediately in front.

The camera's red light came on. The shot narrowed, first showing the flags and the posters, and then focused on the president's head and shoulders.

"My fellow Americans. I want to first thank you for your patience during these difficult times. Our economic plans are in full swing and we're seeing the benefits of increased international cooperation as sponsored by the Global Settlement Bank. The economy has stabilized and we anticipate better times ahead. The intelligence community is working hard on your behalf to keep you safe, both in the real world and the virtual world. We continue to be challenged by domestic organizations and individuals who would rather see the end of the Republic as an organized ruling body. Some are advocating a complete separation from our Union. I know most Americans are on the side of peace, justice, and our way of life. The United States is unique in the world, and we are the example for freedom-loving people. There must be structure within that freedom; otherwise, we devolve into chaos.

"Yesterday, the Singapore Financial News Network released a video documentary made by two U.S. journalists. The documentary's last segment included secret video recordings and audio from what was reported to be a detention camp in the State of Nevada. The activities conducted in the camp were described as behavior modification using mind control techniques with virtual reality. The documentary also suggested that patients not responding to the treatment experienced the onset of mental illnesses and were given an alternative to a psychiatric asylum. Unbeknownst to those patients, that alternative involved their deaths. The documentary also featured an undercover government whistleblower currently employed by an intelligence agency that corroborated allegations concerning the detention camp.

"I convened my national security team and asked them about the allegations and was shocked to learn that they were mostly substantiated. While I was aware that Homeland Security operated detention camps, I understood their use to be for enemy combatants associated with the War on Terror or immigrant refugees. My personal attention has been diverted towards resolving our economic crisis. In addition, the Executive Branch's attention has also been occupied with the impeachment vote, the trial and the Supreme Court decision associated with my Executive Order 14666. Now the country faces another distraction with an Article Five convention being proposed by members of the opposing parties.

"My fellow Americans, consider the great country in which you live where your leader can take swift action to prevent financial calamity and yet be challenged through a constitutional process. The process has worked and will continue to work. I only regret that my challengers are placing their own political aspirations ahead of the economic safety and security of the American public. I'm confident our country will work through the challenges placed before it.

"I wanted to address you, the American public, to be as transparent as possible. I respect the fabric of our nation too much to make excuses. In the minds of some of you watching, there is little I can say or do to rectify the situation. That's fine. Ours is a nation of intellectual diversity. We need that for a healthy Republic. My lack of knowledge of what occurred in these camps was a failure of people more than process. Processes are only as good as the people who execute them, and yet we will always be subject to hopes and weaknesses.

"I would like to suggest a broader question. If we treat intelligence gathering and domestic counterterrorism with the same models you're accustomed to seeing from local law enforcement, we will be less safe. Benjamin Franklin said, 'It is better a hundred guilty persons should escape than one innocent person should suffer.' This is true after the commission of a crime and during the evaluation of guilt during a trial. Counterterrorism can't wait until the crime's commission, and we must avail ourselves of the latest technology to keep you safe. He who has the most knowledge wins.

"Beginning tomorrow, I will appoint a panel of experts to study our interrogation techniques and reorientation efforts used in domestic counterterror operations. This panel will include people from outside of government as well as prominent members of our intelligence and federal law enforcement organizations. The panel will make recommendations on these topics, which I will then bring to Congressional leaders for more consideration. The Jefferson administration will keep your best interests in mind when implementing the conclusions of the appointed panel.

"I remain as confident now about the future of this nation as I did when I first sat in this chair in January 2017. Remember, we are the future. May God bless you and may God Bless the United States of America."

The camera stopped recording. No one entered the Oval Office. Jefferson stowed papers inside his desk, then turned to look with satisfaction at pictures of his family. He left and walked with his head down to meet his wife for dinner in the White House.

***

A year ago on Halloween Day, Axel ferried Chandler and Arianne in his SUV out of D.C. to evade the press, eager to interview Chandler about Omni's release of his video, ostensibly hacked from the El Mundo archives. On this early Sunday morning, Chandler could walk leisurely, without a costume, from his apartment to The Battery. It was a cool, crisp fall day. A fleece jacket sufficed. He'd been back in the Big Apple for a few days. No one on his early morning jaunt appeared to recognize him, his pulled down Mets hat no doubt concealing part of his face, the sunglasses taking care of the rest.

There were a few decisions in front of him—his career, where he might live, and Arianne. He didn't know if he'd face charges for his undercover work at the Nevada reorientation camp. There was also the matter of the country's direction. President Jefferson's Executive Order 14666 had survived an impeachment, a trial, and a Supreme Court decision. The Supreme Court cautioned Jefferson that while they understood the need for a temporary suspension of the results, the election needed a decision in the House and Senate before the end of the year. That meant a precious two months remained. No one knew what would happen if Jefferson ignored the recommendation of the Court. Would Congress act on their own?

He sat on a bench looking towards Lady Liberty, her torch glinted in the sharp morning sun. Thankfully, the sun ascended naturally. A familiar face sat next to him.

"Chandler, it's a beautiful morning, isn't it?" Habakk appeared in his usual attire, dark sweater, khaki pants, and tennis shoes. He wore no sunglasses.

Chandler attempted to inject Halloween humor, turning towards his guest. "So is it really you Mr. Habakk or is it Tomás in disguise?"

Habakk appreciated the attempt, uttering a polite laugh. "I'm glad you are in good spirits. You've had a difficult few months and now your project is complete. What lies ahead?"

Chandler looked towards Lady Liberty in contemplation. "I don't know. You notice that I'm not surprised by your sudden appearances any longer. Tomás' appearance at the camp was a welcome sight, though!"

"I'm glad you're getting more comfortable with my presence. My aim is not to scare or startle." Habakk rubbed his shoulder with an imaginary balm of reassurance. "How is your love? You are still with her?"

"It's complicated. We were together last week and it seemed like old times. You gave me confidence when you told me love can conquer the challenges we face." Chandler recalled the conversation from the previous year.

"I believe that. That future is in front of you. Let's talk about what you accomplished and what may come next." Habakk turned towards him. "Your film project laid bare your country's counterterror apparatus. It remains to be seen if the public will demand a curtailment of the authority by the Praetorians."

"Strong term there, Praetorian," he bristled.

The term "Praetorian" referred to the bodyguards used by Roman Emperors, though their role proved to be much broader than its modern analog, the Secret Service.

Habakk clarified what he meant by the term. "It's part of the protective structure that guards the Elite. It's the Elite that understand the consequences of government action first. Truly, they may instigate it like they did last year with the Global Settlement Bank and the International Relations Council. They were the ones ultimately responsible for the new economic order, the Global Financial Union, and understand the consequences of their policies. The rest of the public is unprepared and may suffer since their knowledge comes later."

"That separation between Elite and the rest is responsible for much of the country's division," Chandler opined, looking for approval. "I honestly think the Elite, whether intentional or not, divides the rest of us." He drew an imaginary vertical line with his index finger.

"I mentioned to you last New Year's Day that society is responsible for its own intellectual laziness. When we lose our vigilance and lose our desire to learn and ignore the future, we open the door for the sort of political mischief you see today. The gift provided by nature is the ability to counter the mischief. Those separatists and secessionists you interviewed are part of the counterweight," Habakk continued.

"You support those groups then?" Chandler narrowing his eyes.

Habakk smiled gently. "I neither support nor reject them. I'm merely suggesting that they're the outgrowth of that intellectual laziness about which I warned. That idea of separation is nothing new. In 19th century America, there were non-conformist communities where people learned to think and act independently. That didn't mean they were necessarily secessionists. Some famous abolitionists spent time in these communities. Think about how their defiance of authority affected the trajectory of the country's history."

"I had no idea."

"These groups you interviewed, they are definitely thinking and acting independently. They will use technology to make their separation easier."

"Oh, you mean with hacking and communications security?"

"They want to get out from under the control of the most profitable business on earth, government. Government only has its power from the public that grants it to them. These groups are reducing government's power by dropping out. Those that remain are also reducing government's power by using that digital currency, DigiNote. Let's not focus strictly on government. Governments come and go, right?" Habakk looked for an immediate response.

"Sure, we elect House members every two years, Senate members every six years, presidents every four years and there are plenty of political appointees spinning on the carousel between business and government," Chandler answered, tracing circles with his index finger.

"Precisely. The Elite recognize this and support governments accordingly. I heard someone from the Elite class once say, 'It's time for the Elites to tell the ignorant masses…' The Elite won the most recent financial war. They have their new world currency, the Mundi, and the FSB made using cash a hostile act." Habakk paused for effect.

"I guess the war is over since they won, right?"

"Wrong!" Habakk wagged his index finger. "The Elites created a system where they can track every minute detail and they may have what they consider valid reasons for doing so, economic stability, national security, etc. What they can't always predict is how the public will react. I can assure you they did not expect terrorists landing on American shores. I'm sure they did not expect the Five Tribes. The laws of physics and the inability of governments to control an economy cause these unplanned events."

"The president is the one with the guns though, Mr. Habakk."

"That just means people get hurt either directly with bullets or indirectly with what you witnessed in that reorientation camp." Habakk rebutted his assertion with a pronounced frown. "From a moral point of view, there are two types of people, those believing in coercion and those believing in voluntary interaction. When a society has too much of the former and not enough of the latter, you get sharp division."

Chandler reflected on Habakk's last statement. A curious wash blanketed his face. "Is this the point when you'll ask me to consider doing something?"

"There was a famous Russian philosopher who felt that in any given moment, a person and by extension a society, may have a limited set of choices. The freedom comes from the ability to be able to choose. He suggested that freedom preceded existence. That's powerful." Habakk flexed his biceps for emphasis. "The separatist groups are expressing their freedom by choosing a different path in a country of fewer choices."

"So you don't want me to do anything this time?"

Habakk smiled, squeezing his shoulder. "I think you've done what you can to shed light on the struggle. The advantage of this time in history is technology allowing everyone to see what is going on. Western civilization gave three very important contributions to humanity: free markets, the rule of law, and representative government. Society's challenge now will be to hold on to all those contributions. We must not be strangers to history."

"So if you had to lay odds, what would they be? You know, society holding it together, so to speak? The United States of America still being the United States of America?"

He'd never heard Habakk laugh with any intensity, until now. "Oh my. I'm no odds maker, Chandler. That chapter in history has yet to be written, though I suspect it will be an exciting one."

Habakk got up and stood in front of a still seated Chandler. He leaned in and shook his right hand, placing his left over both.

"Take care, Chandler." Habakk walked away along the promenade with his characteristic half-moon glide.

Chandler always dreamed of pursuing the big story. Maybe this dream had him. Habakk made sure he stayed in a dream that would not let him wake up. Habakk gave him the courage to stay in the dream that selected him. Chandler hoped his dream could awaken the nation to the predatory nature of the Elite, so that they could avoid being swept up in yet another manipulation.

A peregrine falcon tried to sweep up an unsuspecting dove, diverting Chandler's attention from the departing Habakk. The dove escaped harm after taking a short flight away from an unleashed cockapoo an instant earlier. Chandler shook his head and smiled, thinking that it must have been the dove's lucky day. He took a leisurely stroll back to his apartment hoping the nation would have the dove's good fortune.

The story continues. What lies ahead for Chandler and the United States? Follow Chandler Scott in the next book in the series, Division. Updates posted on author web site (www.JimMosquera.com). Read the novel, 2020, where it all got started.

Jim Mosquera

ABOUT THE AUTHOR

Jim Mosquera has an academic background in Industrial Engineering and held management positions in the telecommunications industry. Developing expertise in financial markets and economics through his own study, he produced a column in a national publication and edited a financial newsletter.

That work led to a series of books on the economy and financial crises known as the **Escaping Oz** series (Protecting your wealth during the financial crisis, Navigating the crisis, An Observer's Reflections). He is also the author of the **Chandler Scott** series.

Sentinel Consulting, a firm he founded in 2014, assists businesses with financing and debt restructuring. Mr. Mosquera is a frequent contributor to numerous financial news outlets.

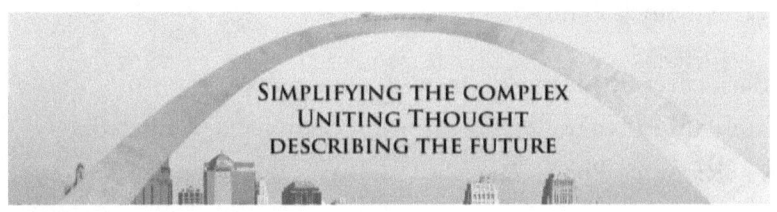

SIMPLIFYING THE COMPLEX
UNITING THOUGHT
DESCRIBING THE FUTURE

His non-fiction work will make you question proposed solutions to financial and economic problems. His novels are so realistic, the stories will hit close to home.

Follow the author at https://JimMosquera.com

CREDITS

Book cover design by Jim Mosquera using art that was altered from the following sources:

Front cover background - Copyright: <a href='http://www.123rf.com/profile_ssilver'>ssilver / 123RF Stock Photo</a>

Back cover background - Copyright: <a href='http://www.123rf.com/profile_andreykuzmin'>andreykuzmin / 123RF Stock Photo</a>

Front cover block letterpress - Copyright: <a href='http://www.123rf.com/profile_alicephoto'>alicephoto / 123RF Stock Photo</a>

Back cover male head - Copyright: <a href='http://www.123rf.com/profile_decade3d'>decade3d / 123RF Stock Photo</a>

Back cover fist through screen - Copyright: <a href='http://www.123rf.com/profile_grandeduc'>grandeduc / 123RF Stock Photo</a>

Special thanks to Kate for reviewing the final draft.

www.ingramcontent.com/pod-product-compliance
Lightning Source LLC
Chambersburg PA
CBHW031314280626
47169CB00019B/1607